# SAVING GERALDINE CORCORAN

HAZEL WARD

Hope St Press

Copyright © 2022 by Hazel Ward

All rights reserved.

This is a work of fiction. Names, characters, places, and incidents either are the product of the author's imagination or are used fictitiously. Any resemblance to actual persons, living or dead, events, or locales is entirely coincidental.

No part of this book may be reproduced or used in any manner without written permission of the copyright owner except for the use of quotations in a book review.

www.hazelwardauthor.com

# 1

## TAINTED

GERALDINE – 2019

'Let me in. Let me in, little pig,' said the voice behind the door.

The knob turned this way and that. The door rattled. Softly at first, then harder. Louder. Angrier.

'Let me in, Geraldine.'

Geraldine opened her mouth wide but nothing came out. She wanted to scream. She wanted to call out for Ada, but Ada wasn't here anymore. There was no one left to call out to. The wolf was at the door, and no one could help her now. She pulled the blanket up to her eyes.

'I said let me in.'

The door shook violently. It burst open. Suddenly, the room was filled with the wolf's disgusting odour. She reeked of it too. It was all over her, winding its way up her nostrils and down her throat, to her very insides. She was tainted now. She'd never be rid of it. Never.

A dark shadow drew closer. She opened her mouth again. This time, she found a scream.

. . .

In her head, she was still screaming but the room was quiet.

Geraldine opened her eyes. Naturally, she was in her usual bed, not the one of her nightmares. Although why she had the duvet stuffed in her mouth, she had no idea. Perhaps she'd done it to make sure she didn't wake Arthur. Silly really: she could have choked to death and, even in her sleep, she should have known that she never really screamed out loud. In all the years, the scream had only ever been silent.

Arthur, of course, was sleeping like a baby, blissfully unaware that his wife was dripping in sweat and in a state of high anxiety. She checked her face. Yes, it was wet. She'd been sobbing into her pillow again. Honestly, that man could sleep through an earthquake.

Minnie, on the other hand, was all too aware of Geraldine's distress. In the half-light of the darkened room, Geraldine could see that she was sitting upright a few feet away, her head cocked to one side. The next minute, she was at the side of the bed, sliding her wiry muzzle under Geraldine's hand. Geraldine stroked the dog's head. Minnie always had a calming effect on her. Sometimes, it was all she needed. Sometimes, it wasn't.

She slipped out of the bed and tiptoed barefoot onto the landing with Minnie padding along beside her. In the bathroom, she washed her face in cold water and patted the back of her neck with her damp hands. Despite Minnie's efforts, she could still feel her heart pounding. Geraldine closed her eyes and tapped out a rhythm on the sink edge. When she opened them again, Minnie was looking at her accusingly.

'You did your best, Min, but it's the big day tomorrow,' she whispered.

Minnie let out a little whimper. She understood.

Geraldine caught sight of herself in the mirror. What an ugly old thing she was. A hideous, dirty, filthy, revolting creature. She wiped fresh tears from her eyes and blew her nose on some toilet paper.

'Tainted,' she muttered quietly to herself.

She heard Arthur stirring in the bedroom, switched off the light and crept back to bed.

## 2

## THE BIG DAY

GERALDINE – 2019

Geraldine hated this day. She hated it so much that it was hard for her to put a finger on just how deep the hatred went. Pretty deep. She knew that much at least.

'Nearly ready, Gee?'

Arthur shouted up to her from the bottom of the stairs. If you could call it a shout. Arthur didn't really raise his voice. It wasn't his style. Especially today of all days.

She summoned up her cheeriest voice: 'Won't be long,' realising, as soon as she said it, just how fake it sounded.

She didn't know why she bothered with all that pretence. They'd been married for fifty-five years and he knew her inside out. Almost.

She practised a casual smile in the mirror knowing full well that even if she rehearsed for a hundred years, she would never be able to pull one off. The words, rabbit and headlights sprung to mind. Geraldine focused and had another go, this time a little less casual. Still awful. An exasperated gasp slipped out from somewhere deep within the workings of her body. Smiling was yet another thing she probably shouldn't bother with today. Even if they didn't know why, they'd all know as soon as they saw her that she was on edge. It was the same every year. In fact, they'd probably be amazed if she wasn't.

Arthur appeared in the doorway. She wondered how long he'd been there and if he'd been watching her.

'All set?'

'I said I won't be long. Didn't I say?'

'Yes love, you did but we'll be late if we don't get a move on.'

'Well, it's not like she's got anywhere to go, is it?'

'Very true.'

He grinned at her and all at once the wary old man was gone, and standing before her was the dreamy boy she fell in love with all those years ago. Her smile came then, until he spoiled it by adding: 'But the others have, and we've got that table booked for lunch.'

Ah yes, the others. The Corcorans. Her delightful sister and brothers, and their husband and wives. Yes, she knew her sister, Janet, hadn't been a Corcoran since she married Trevor, eons ago, but that didn't matter. They would always be the Corcorans to Geraldine. She herself had been Geraldine Wilde since 1964, and she'd been happy to lose that dreadful surname. But this day had a habit of reminding her that deep down, she would always be Geraldine Corcoran. She couldn't escape it.

'Just wait downstairs, will you? I'm nearly ready,' she snapped.

'Right you are. See you down there.'

He gave her a peck on the cheek and went back down. She noticed he'd left the door ajar. In readiness for more spying, no doubt.

Geraldine yawned. God, she was tired. It was the lack of

sleep, of course. Partly the nightmare and partly the sheer dread. It was the same every year. If she had any sense she'd just stop going to this bloody thing. But then she'd have to face the wrath of Janet. Her big sister would not be best pleased and, even though they were all old enough not to care, none of them wanted to upset Janet.

She took a deep breath in and held it while she did the little thing she always did to relax. It had helped last night and it helped now. Feeling slightly better, she let herself breathe again and went down to join Arthur who was waiting in the hall, her coat in his hand.

He held the coat open for her. For a reason she couldn't quite put her finger on, the gesture irritated the hell out of Geraldine. She made a point of ignoring it, snatching it off him and throwing it on. Arthur said nothing. He was treading on eggshells, as he always did on this day, and as he so often did on countless other days. This is what she'd reduced that beautiful boy to – an old man who tiptoed around his wife. Poor Arthur. It was at times like this when she despised herself the most.

Minnie trotted in from the kitchen, an expectant look on her face. The sight of her helped to ease Geraldine's nerves. Despite never having had a dog before, she'd fallen in love with Minnie the moment she set eyes on her. She'd been the runt of the litter, a tiny little thing, hardly bigger than a mouse, with strangely oversized ears which is why Geraldine had called her Minnie. That tiny pup was quite a size now, and her ears were more in proportion to the rest of her. She probably had a little more growth in her too, but it didn't matter to Geraldine how big she was. Minnie was still her baby.

She laid her hand on Minnie's back which was actually

the colour of a fieldmouse so, in an odd way, the name did still fit.

'Sorry, sweetheart, you can't come with us today.'

'I'll take her for another walk when we get back,' said Arthur. 'Ready?'

She nodded. He opened the front door and, with one last look at Minnie, Geraldine stepped outside. She got into the car and gripped the handbag that was on her lap.

Arthur slid a CD into the slot. It was Dusty Springfield, 'I Only Want To Be With You'. He'd bought that record for her on her eighteenth birthday. They'd listened to it so many times back then, it was a wonder they hadn't worn it out. He squeezed her hand. She looked over at him, and there he was again – that young lad. Her dreamboat. Her knight in shining armour.

Geraldine's brothers, Phil, Tony and Ralph, were waiting for them just outside the graveyard. Tony waved. In one hand he was holding a plastic carrier bag with the heads of some nondescript flowers poking out. They were the sort you bought in garage forecourts, or supermarkets. Arthur would probably know the names. He was very knowledgeable on that sort of thing.

Janet got out of her car, leaving husband, Trevor, sitting sheepishly in the driver's seat. She gave them a withering look – most likely unhappy about the wait. 'We were beginning to think we might have to send out a search party.'

'Sorry. Had to sort the dog out before we left. She doesn't like being left behind,' said Arthur.

'Don't worry about it,' said Tony. 'It's a nice day to be out in the fresh air.'

Phil laughed. 'Easy for you to say, Tone, you look like

you're dressed for an Arctic winter. Come one, let's get this over with and get in the bloody warm.'

Janet tutted. 'That's not very respectful, is it? No one forces you to come, Philip.'

Phil smirked. 'Wouldn't miss it for the world.'

'I'll wait with Trevor, shall I?' said Arthur.

Geraldine nodded. She would have liked him to come with her but this family tradition did not allow for partners. It was a private, family moment, according to Janet. Clearly, she didn't see husbands and wives as family. They were only invited to the lunch and booze-up afterwards.

Those that were allowed, trudged along the leaf-sodden path until they assembled in front of Mavis Corcoran's grave.

'Hello Mum. Here we are again,' said Janet. 'How have you been keeping?'

'She's dead, Jan. How do you think she's been keeping?' said Phil, and everyone except Janet and Geraldine laughed.

Janet ignored them. 'We still miss you, Mum.'

They went quiet. Ralph, the youngest of them all, cleared his throat and someone gulped very loudly. Geraldine wasn't sure who it was and she had no inclination to find out. If she did that she'd have to look around, and that was something she had even less inclination to do.

Apart from those few interruptions, the silence seemed to go on and on, until even Janet tired of it. She emptied some dead flowers from the grave's memorial vase, whipped out a bottle of water from her bag and poured some into the vase. Tony handed her a fresh bouquet, and she dropped them in and arranged them. It wasn't exactly artful but Janet seemed satisfied with her attempt.

Geraldine could see now that there were four pink roses in the bouquet. Their mother's favourite, not that she got them very often. She'd probably had more pink roses since she'd been dead than when she was alive.

Geraldine fixed her gaze on the flowers but she was aware that her sister was moving leftwards to carry out the same procedure to the neighbouring grave. She was aware too of a faint and unpleasant smell in the air.

'Wish I'd brought a trowel. Needs a tidy up,' said Janet.

'I'll come over next week and do it,' said Tony.

'Thanks Tone.'

Janet finished primping the flowers and scooped up some rubbish. Her eyes shot past the men and settled on Geraldine.

'That's a bit better. What do you think, Gez?'

Geraldine's attention was still firmly on their mother's grave. Despite that, she could feel everyone watching her; waiting for her to survey Janet's handiwork and approve. All she had to do was turn her head to the left and nod. That was all that was needed for this charade to be over, but Geraldine couldn't do it. She just couldn't. The heat rose from her chest to her throat, to the back of her neck and then to her face. The faint smell was growing stronger now, almost overpowering. It was the familiar smell of the wolf. She felt sick and dizzy. She needed to do the thing. She put her hand in her pocket and moved it very slightly up and down.

Janet threw the empty water bottle into her bag and snapped it shut. 'Well?'

'Very nice,' Geraldine said at last.

Phil turned away first.

'Well done, Jan. Now let's go to the pub.'

# 3

## DELAYED BY AN EMERGENCY DASH

NETTA – 2019

Netta surveyed the little business kitchen that she and her two business partners rented. It wasn't much but it suited them perfectly. Just like the business itself. All three of them mucked in and did whatever was needed to keep moving it forward.

Neil was the driving force really. He was the one with the cooking skills. Even if it was only jams and pickles they were making, he had the gift to elevate them to something special.

Netta brought her own skills to the venture too. A long corporate career in her previous life had given her the background needed to make the business work. Although it wasn't as sexy as being a talented cook, it was still as necessary.

Her eyes fell on Kelly who was wiping down the surfaces. A cold-hearted analyst might suggest that Kelly brought very little to the partnership, but they'd be wrong. It was true, her cooking and business skills were limited but she was a hard worker, and tough with it. That toughness was an asset when decisions needed to be made. Sometimes,

Kelly had the oldest head, despite being not much more than a kid.

Neil counted the jars of jams and pickles on the worktop for the final time.

'All there. I think we're done. You two go home, I'll lock up. See you tomorrow.'

Netta let her eyes sweep around the room again. Everything looked clean and clear, and the stock was ready to be taken to the market in the morning.

'I'm not going straight home. I promised Mum and Dad I'd look in on them first. It's the anniversary of my nan's death. My mum's mum. The family go every year to visit the grave together, then they go to a pub for a meal and a piss-up. I said I'd pop my head around the door and say hello.'

'That's nice,' said Neil. 'Give my love to Geraldine.'

'Oh that'll make her day. You know she's got a mum-crush on you, don't you?'

Neil laughed. 'It's a two-way thing. She's my perfect mother-figure.'

'You wouldn't say that if you'd had to live with her.'

'Of course I would.'

'Trust me, you wouldn't,' said Netta. 'See you here in the morning.'

'Yep. Seven o'clock. Did you hear that, Kelly? Seven o'clock tomorrow morning.'

Kelly might have been hardworking but early mornings were not her strong suit. She rolled her eyes at Neil.

'When have I ever let you down?'

'Well, there was that time—'

Kelly threw the wet cloth at him, shutting him up before he could give any examples.

'I'll be here earlier than that, naturally.' Neil grinned as Kelly gave him the finger before leaving.

Netta followed Kelly outside.

'I can give you a lift as far as Kings Heath, Kel, if you're all right to take the bus the rest of the way.'

'Cool. Okay if I charge my phone up? It's dead.'

Kelly jumped into the car and plugged the charger into the socket without waiting for an answer.

'Hey, do you think we could get here for half-six tomorrow? That'd wipe the smile off his face.'

Kelly getting up in time for six-thirty? That would be something akin to a miracle.

'We could certainly try,' said Netta.

Kelly slunk down into the seat and closed her eyes. 'Piece of cake.'


They were almost at the bus stop in Kings Heath when Kelly's phone started beeping.

Netta pulled the car over near the stop. 'What is it?'

Kelly was already scrolling through the messages. 'It's my nan. She's in hospital. They think she's had a stroke.'

'Which hospital?'

'Queen Elizabeth.'

'I'll drop you off.'


The traffic was horrendous. Before they'd set off again, Netta had messaged her dad to let him know she was going to be a bit late, but she hadn't banked on the combined efforts of roadworks and rush hour to delay her even further. They were crawling along at a snail's pace.

'Are you okay?' she asked an anxious looking Kelly.

'Dunno. Fucking traffic.'

'We're not too far away now. Shouldn't be long.'

'Yeah, but what if we're too late? What if she's dead?'

Kelly let out a little gasp, as if the thought had just occurred to her and was too shocking to imagine.

'Did your dad say anything about her condition?'

'He said she's comfortable, whatever the fuck that means.'

'That sounds promising.'

'D'you think so?'

'Yes. She's in the best hands.' Netta bit her lip. She'd been trying not to say that awful, meaningless cliché but it had slipped out.

'Thing is Net, my mum was in that hospital. The last time I was in there was the day she died.'

Netta reached her hand over to Kelly's.

'You'll be all right. I'll come in with you and stay as long as you need me.'

'I'll probably be fine once I get inside and see Nan. It's just … you know.'

'Yes, I do,' said Netta. 'Oh, I think I can see the traffic moving up ahead.'

Suddenly the line in front of them jolted into action and they were off. Halfway up the road, they saw two crumpled cars had been pushed to the side.

'Looks like they've had a prang. Drivers look okay though,' said Kelly, sounding a bit brighter.


They just about managed to find a parking space. It seemed like everyone in south Birmingham had a need to visit the hospital at exactly the same time as them. Kelly's phone beeped through another message as they walked towards the entrance.

'It's from my dad. They've moved her to a ward.'

Inside the hospital, Netta found someone who could help with directions while Kelly hung back, looking apprehensive.

She took Kelly's arm. 'Shall we?'

She was trying to sound positive, even though she wasn't feeling particularly positive herself. She wouldn't have said this out loud, but she too linked this hospital with death. Most recently, Edie, the previous owner of Netta's house, had died here.

But there were two more losses in this place that had come before that. Losses that had had a profound effect on Netta. One was the death of her grandmother, Ada Wilde. The other was the loss of her baby after a miscarriage. So yes, she understood exactly how Kelly was feeling at this moment, and she would do her best to help her young friend through it.

They arrived at the ward. Kelly waved to an old woman in one of the beds. The old woman tried to smile but it was obvious she couldn't manage it. That said, she didn't seem as bad as they'd feared.

A man sat at the side of the bed holding the old woman's hand. As they got closer, he smiled wearily. 'All right, Kel?'

'Yeah,' said Kelly. She leaned over and kissed her nan on the cheek. 'You all right, Nan?'

Kelly's nan mumbled something incomprehensible.

'She can't speak properly yet. Make the most of it, eh Mum? It won't be long before you're telling us all off again.' The man's voice caught on his words.

Kelly attempted a laugh. 'Yeah, too true. Net, this is my dad and my nan.'

'Hello,' said Netta.

She'd hadn't met Kelly's dad or nan until now but she could see the family resemblance in all three generations.

'Pleased to meet you, Netta,' said Kelly's dad. 'Sorry it's not in better circumstances.'

He smiled but his red, swollen eyes betrayed his feelings.

'You on your own?' said Kelly.

He nodded. 'Your aunties and uncles are on their way.'

'Well, I'm here now.' Kelly sat down facing her dad and took her nan's free hand. She was back to her normal self again.

Kelly's dad smiled again. 'That's all she needs.'

Kelly smiled back. Her relationship with her dad was what you might call a bit seesaw, but today they seemed to be united by their concern. Netta suddenly felt like an intruder.

'I'll head off then, shall I? Leave you to it.'

Kelly looked as if she'd forgotten Netta was there. 'Oh! Yeah, okay. I'll be back in a minute, Nan.'

She followed Netta out of the ward.

Netta waited until they were in the corridor. 'Will you be all right?'

'Yeah. I'm okay now I've seen her. You go.'

'Anything you need, just message me,' said Netta.

'I will. What about tomorrow though? I don't think I'm going to be able to do the market.'

'Don't worry about that. We'll manage.'

Kelly nodded but it was obvious her mind was already elsewhere. 'She don't look too bad does she, considering?'

'No, she looks pretty good.'

'Yeah. Listen, thanks. I owe you big time.'

. . .

When Netta got to the car, she took out her phone and noticed a message from her own dad asking how long she was going to be. She sent him one back saying she was just leaving the hospital and asking if it was still worth her going to the pub.

A reply came back straight away:

*'Yes please. Quick as you can. I'll be a while yet.'*

'Bit of an odd message,' she muttered to herself.

# 4

# ABANDONED WITH A STRAWBERRY SPRITZ

GERALDINE – 2019

Well, if she thought the day couldn't get any worse, Geraldine was wrong. Bad enough that she'd had to go along, yet again, with that ridiculous memorial trip but now she'd been abandoned by both her husband and her daughter. Her endurance was pushed to its absolute limit. She was teetering on the brink of a nervous breakdown. She really was.

She'd been frozen stiff by the time Janet finally let them leave the graves. She'd been in a bad enough mood already, but what really took the biscuit had been seeing Arthur and Trevor, all pink-cheeked and cosy in Trevor's car. They'd obviously kept the heating on. Didn't they know there was a climate crisis? If Liza knew, she'd have been outraged. Her granddaughter was very much the climate activist these days.

As soon as he saw them, Trevor had been at Janet's heels like a big doting puppy. 'Everything go all right?'

Janet had given her husband the same withering look she'd given Geraldine and Arthur earlier. 'Of course. Why wouldn't it?'

Tony, Phil and Ralph had already been making for Tony's car when Janet had turned the look on them.

'Are you boys travelling together? Phil, I thought you could come with us.'

But Phil had already sought refuge in Tony's car and looked quite settled.

'Right, we'll see you at the pub then,' Janet said, with an exasperated huff.

Arthur had waited for the others to drive off before switching on the engine. In the passenger seat, Geraldine had gone back to clutching her handbag, still feeling sick, and more than a bit cross. How could Janet have singled her out like that? And why did she insist on treating them as if they were small children?

'Boys?' she'd exclaimed. 'I mean, for goodness sake. Phil's older than me and the other two aren't that much younger.'

Arthur had chuckled. 'It is a bit silly, isn't it? How did it go?'

'Bloody awful as usual. Can we take the long route? I need time to regather.'

'Your wish is my command.'

He changed the CD and the Beatles played 'Michelle'. By the time it had finished and Arthur had done a few detours, Geraldine had relaxed and had forgotten to berate him about the climate.

Naturally, it hadn't lasted long. As soon as they'd got to the pub and she saw them sat around the table she'd felt her stomach twisting. Her brothers' wives were there – Ralph's mousey Sheila, who got quieter with every passing year; Tony's snidey Eileen, and Phil's Fenella. Confident, stylish Fenella.

Two empty seats had been left for them. On one side of them was Sheila and on the other, Fenella. Geraldine had been trying to decide which of the two would be the least annoying to sit next to when Sheila decided it for her.

'Get lost, did you?'

She'd sniffed and laughed at the same time, making a quite unpleasant sound. After that, Geraldine had plumped for the chair next to Fenella.

A small glass of wine had helped to make the gathering fairly passable. The meal hadn't been too bad and, while not exactly good company, Fenella was loud enough to drown out both Janet and Eileen.

When they moved into the lounge, Phil had sat between her and Fenella and she'd had a chance to talk properly to her favourite brother. All in all, Geraldine had been considering the afternoon a success. One quick drink with Netta, when she arrived, and they'd be able to go. And then Arthur had shown her the message. Kelly Payne's grandmother had been taken to hospital and Netta was giving her a lift there.

'She sent it over an hour ago but I didn't hear the ping,' he said. 'I'll drop her a line to see how long she's likely to be.'

Another hour had passed and there had been no word from Netta.

'I won't bother her, in case it's bad,' said Arthur, 'but there's a chance she might still turn up so we'd better hang around.'

Geraldine's thoughts had immediately turned to their dog.

'What about Minnie? She needs her dinner and a walk.'

'I could pop home and sort her out. I'll be back in an hour and a half. No more than two.'

Stuck in a pub with this bunch for an hour and a half, without Arthur? It didn't bear thinking about, but they couldn't leave Netta to face them on her own, and neither could they neglect poor Minnie.

'All right. Try not to be too long.'

'I'll be as quick as I can. I'll message Nettie to let her know what's happening.'

'No, you get going. I'll do it. It'll give me something to do.'


So here Geraldine was. Abandoned. Phil had disappeared. Gone to the bar again, no doubt. Fenella was staring into space with a stupid grin on her face, and Janet was rabbiting on about Mum – same old drivel she came out with, every year.

Time seemed to be dragging on but it had only been fifteen minutes since Arthur had left, although it felt much, much longer. Geraldine was breaking out into a cold sweat just thinking about it. How could she have been stupid enough to agree to this? She should have left with Arthur and sent Netta a message to tell her not to bother, and then this dreadful day would have been over for another year.

Where was Netta? Surely she should be here by now? She suddenly remembered she was supposed to be sending Netta an update and began to tap out a few words on her phone.

'Here you go, bab. Get that down yer.'

Geraldine looked up from her typing and Phil shoved a large glass of something pink and fizzy into her free hand.

'What is it?'

Fenella leaned over him. 'It's a Strawberry and Lime Spritz, Gez. It'll help take the edge off things. Try it. It's delicious.'

Geraldine took a cautious sip.

'Nice, isn't it?' Fenella's eyes were like saucers. She was clearly well on her way to inebriation.

'Yes, it's very refreshing,' said Geraldine.

Fenella gave her what was probably intended to be a sympathetic smile but, actually, looked more like a drunken leer. It was all a bit off-putting. She rested her hand on Geraldine's knee.

'I expect it's all been a bit much for you today, hasn't it?'

Geraldine moved her legs discreetly away from her sister-in-law's reach. 'Well … it's always a difficult time.'

She was humouring her, of course. Fenella had no idea just how difficult it was. None of them did.

Fenella moved her hand seamlessly to her husband's knee. 'Phil hates it. Don't you, Phil?'

Phil opened his mouth to speak, but Fenella's question appeared to have been a rhetorical one because she wasn't stopping for breath.

'He only comes to shut Janet up.'

Luckily, the pub was noisy but Geraldine glanced over at Janet, all the same. She was chatting quite happily to Eileen, oblivious to Fenella's disclosure. She wouldn't be quite so happy if she knew what Fenella had been saying. Even though Geraldine knew she was being childish, the thought of it made her snigger.

Fenella raised her glass. 'Drink up. There's plenty more where that came from.'

Geraldine put her phone on the table. She'd message Netta in a minute. She swallowed down a mouthful of the

Strawberry Spritz, or whatever it was called, and then another.

'You know, this really is quite lovely.'

## 5

# GERALDINE GETS TIPSY

NETTA – 2019

Netta pulled up in the pub car park, sank back in the seat and closed her eyes. It had been a long day. She'd gone from the foodbank where she, Neil and Kelly volunteered, straight to the office to get everything ready for tomorrow's market.

It wasn't an office really, although it did have a little room next to the main kitchen unit that they used as an office, rest room and everything else room. They still called it the office though.

The day had been busy enough and, before Kelly's bad news, she'd been quite looking forward to a quick drink in the pub with her mum and dad, and the rest of the Corcoran clan. Well, not looking forward to it exactly. It wasn't the kind of do that you looked forward to. The Corcorans were nothing like her dad's extended family. He'd been an only child, but his cousins were more like brothers and sisters. They were an easy going bunch, the Wildes, and their get-togethers were fairly good fun. Her mum's family, on the other hand, were more like hard work than fun. Right now, the idea of spending an hour or more trying to entertain them was suddenly looking less appealing. But a promise was a promise.

Aside from the one from her dad, there had been no other messages. Netta hoped everything was all right with Kelly. She worried about her as much as she did her own kids. Possibly more sometimes.

She switched on the overhead light to check her appearance in the rear-view mirror and was appalled by the state she found herself in. After a rummage in her bag, she found her make-up and gave her face some attention, then looked in the mirror again. The face was marginally better, but the hair was a mess. She wasn't a woman who carried a brush about her person, or in the car for that matter, so she did the best she could, using her fingers as a comb. Another quick glance made her give up. The aunts and uncles would just have to take her for what she was. She was already very late and her mother was bound to be getting jittery.

The Corcorans were in the lounge, circled around two tables. The oldest, Janet, was holding court with her husband, Trevor, at her side. He was a sweet man, Uncle Trev. Technically, he wasn't a Corcoran, so that was probably why.

Her mum's younger brothers sat on Janet's side – Ralph with his wife, the mostly silent Sheila, and Tony with Eileen who sniffed as soon as she spotted Netta. The woman seemed to have a permanent cold.

Her mum's older brother, Phil, and his wife, Fenella, were on Trevor's side. Fenella was fifteen years younger than Phil and a bit upmarket for a Corcoran man, but Uncle Phil was pretty astute when it came to marriage. So far, he'd had four attempts at it and all his wives had provided him with a social and financial leg-up. When he outgrew one, he already had the next one lined up. But Netta reckoned Fenella was going to be a keeper, because Phil was creeping towards his late-seventies now, and unlikely to find such a good catch again. Also, Fenella was a successful and twice-divorced businesswoman with a big house on the Suffolk coast. She knew her way around a prenup contract. If Phil ever left her, you could be sure he'd regret it long before the decree absolute hit the mat.

Sandwiched between her younger and older siblings was her mum, Geraldine Wilde, nee Corcoran. She had her back to Netta and was talking to Phil and Fenella. There was no sign of Netta's dad, although there was an empty seat next to her mum.

Phil asked Netta what she wanted to drink and announced that it was his round. He and Tony went off to the bar. So her dad wasn't at the bar then? Toilet maybe?

Sweet Uncle Trev told her to sit in the empty seat next to her mum, who was still deep in conversation with Fenella and hadn't noticed Netta's arrival. The two of them were leaning so far forward they were practically lying face down on the chair between them. If Phil hadn't vacated it a few minutes earlier, it might have bordered on indecency. It was certainly strange. Especially since her mum and Fenella weren't actually that friendly.

'How are you, Netta? How are the kids?' said Janet. 'Your mum said Will's at university now.'

'Yes, York. He was going to go last year, but he deferred it for a year so he's only just started.'

'A gap year they call it, don't they?' Janet tutted. 'I suppose he's had a year of swanning around the world at your expense.'

'Not at all. He's been helping out at the foodbank where

I volunteer, and at a centre for people whose first language isn't English. He's been quite marvellous actually.'

'Oh.' Janet looked slightly put out and, with the wind taken out of her sails, seemed to have no retort. Netta took that as a sign their chat was at an end.

Uncle Ralph and Silent Sheila acknowledged her but didn't speak. Although, on closer inspection, they appeared to be communicating with each other telepathically using the occasional bob of the head, or tiny twitch of the lips for emphasis. Netta wondered how they usually conversed at home. She didn't remember their kids being particularly quiet but maybe that was just the excitement of being in the company of people who spoke at normal levels. Maybe when they got home, the whole family reverted to the telepathic bobbing, twitching thing.

Eileen looked as if she was eyeing her up for another sniff, and possibly a word or two. The prospect sent Netta into mild alarm. She quickly turned away from Eileen's glare and scoured the pub for her dad. He couldn't still be in the toilet. It wasn't like him to go AWOL. By now, her mum and Fenella were almost intimately intertwined. It felt rude to interrupt them but it was either that or subject herself to Sniffing Eileen. She tapped her mum on the shoulder.

'Hello Mum.'

Without looking backwards her mum brushed her shoulder as if swatting a fly and carried on talking. A hasty glance in Sniffing Eileen's direction told Netta that she was moving in for the kill. Netta braced herself.

Thankfully, Phil and Tony returned with the drinks. Only then, did her mum push herself upright and notice her.

'Oh hello love, didn't see you there. Been here long?'

'Only about ten minutes.'

'Oops. Sorry.'

'That's all right. Where's Dad?'

'Didn't you get my message?'

'Er, no, I don't think so.'

'Funny. Hang on.'

Her mum picked up her phone, slapped her hand on her mouth and started giggling in a most un-Mum way.

'I forgot to send it. Shall I send it now? No, I might as well tell you, seeing as you're here. He went home to check on Minnie after your message about being late. We thought I'd better wait here for you.'

She edged over and whispered loudly into Netta's ear. 'Couldn't leave you stranded with this lot, could we?'

A little burp escaped from her mouth. Netta caught a waft of strawberry and, possibly, gin.

'Have you been all right on your own, Mum?'

Her mum waved her hand. 'Yes, no problem. F'nella's been looking after me.'

She picked up a drink from the table – a pink fizzy concoction – and took a mouthful. 'Lovely stuff this. Ooh the bubbles make you want to sneeze, don't they? Eh, F'nell, I said the bubbles make you want to sneeze, don't they?'

'What's that you're drinking?' said Netta.

Her mum shrugged. 'Dunno. Strawberry Splits, I think it was called. I say, F'nell, what's this called again? Strawberry Splits, was it?'

'It's a Strawberry and Lime Spritz,' shouted Fenella, more loudly than she needed to.

Netta's mum did another Strawberry burp.

Fenella tottered over and crouched between them.

'Geraldine needed something to steady her nerves, bless her. She doesn't cope well when Arthur's not with her. Do you, love?'

To Netta's surprise, her mum shook her head slowly.

Fenella shook her head too, even more slowly.

'No. Can't say I blame you with this bunch, darlin'. I had to have a stiff one before I left the hotel today, and Phil was very nearly half-cut by the time his taxi turned up. Anyway, I'm off for a wee, before I burst.'

And with that she left.

'Never realised how lovely that woman was before now,' said her mum.

Netta scanned the drinks menu for a Strawberry and Lime Spritz. It turned out to be flavoured gin mixed with Prosecco and soda.

'Have you had many of those, Mum?'

'Only a couple to help with the nerves. It's done the trick. Oh look, here's Arthur.'

Netta's dad found a stool and perched next to them.

'Hello, my lovelies. How's Kelly's nan, Nettie?'

'She's okay, I think. It's early days yet. She's had a stroke.'

'Who's Kelly?' sniffed Eileen.

'She's Netta's lodger,' said her mum.

'Friend,' said Netta. 'She's my friend and business partner, who also happens to live in my house.'

Eileen sniffed in reply.

'Poor Kelly. I suppose she'll be at the hospital for a while then,' said Netta's dad. 'That'll leave you a bit short for the market tomorrow, won't it? I would offer to help but I've already said I'd give Clyde a hand on his allotment.'

'Clyde? Who's that then?' Eileen butted in again.

'He's a friend, Eileen,' said Netta's dad. 'He lives near Netta. We both like a bit of gardening. He's got an allotment, and sometimes he lets me help him out.'

He turned away from Eileen before she had a chance to ask another question.

'I'm sure Neil and I will be able to manage,' said Netta.

'I'll do it,' declared her mum. 'I'll come and help you and Neil. Lovely Neil.'

Netta's eyes fleetingly met her dad's, then his shifted to the glass of pink fizz in her mum's hand.

'Gee, I think you might be a little bit tipsy. Best not to make offers you might regret in the morning.'

Her mum let out a loud harumph.

'Oh sod off, Arthur. You can be such a spoilsport sometimes.' She looked over at Fenella who had now resumed her seat. 'F'nella thinks I should do it, don't you F'nell?'

'Do it, Gez,' said Fenella, with a wink. 'Whatever it is.'

So that was it then. Her mum was coming to help them on their stall tomorrow. Netta had better alert Neil.

## 6

# HANGOVERS AND OLD HAUNTS

GERALDINE – 2019

To Geraldine's surprise, and slight disgust, there was a bacon sandwich on the kitchen table in front of her. Arthur must have put it there, so softly that she hadn't even noticed, until she uncradled her head and opened her eyes. Thinking about it, she had picked up on the smell when she lumbered into the kitchen and dropped down onto the chair, but she'd had her mind on other things at the time. Things like getting rid of this horrendous headache.

Arthur had clearly foreseen her dilemma and had two paracetamols and a glass of water ready for her. It would seem he'd also decided that what she most needed now was a couple of thick pork rashers, encased in fluffy white bread. Apparently, a bacon sandwich was one of the best things you could have for a hangover. Although, how Arthur knew that was beyond her, since she'd never, in all their years together, seen him hungover. Or drunk, for that matter.

'I've grilled it so it's not greasy,' he said, with what looked suspiciously like an amused twinkle in his eye.

She lifted the top slice to inspect the contents more closely. He'd even cut the fatty rind off but, oh dear, Arthur cooking breakfast? Whatever next? Normally she did all the cooking. It wasn't that Arthur couldn't cook. He could make a perfectly passable meal when she let him. But he had his jobs, and she had hers. She preferred it that way. She knew where she stood. There was a sense of order to it. A sense of control. But today was not a normal day. Last night she'd had, what Arthur had laughingly called 'a skinful' and this morning, she was feeling a little bit delicate. As a result, she'd have to let this transgression of his slide, and accept his breakfast gracefully.

'Best to eat it while it's still hot,' he said.

Geraldine took a tiny bite and chewed it until she could face swallowing it. The next mouthful went down quicker, so she had a third. It was actually quite tasty. She polished off the rest of the sandwich and washed it down with some tea.

'Better?' he said.

'Yes. Thanks, love. Sorry about last night. I don't know what came over me.'

'Four glasses of Strawberry Splits, I should think,' said Arthur. The corners of his mouth turned upwards and they both began to laugh.

'Was I embarrassing?'

'Of course you weren't, you daft beggar. You were lovely. Very funny. You'll have to drink cocktails more often.'

'No thank you. Bloody Fenella.'

'Do you remember offering to help Netta and Neil on their stall today?'

'Yes I do. That's another reason not to drink cocktails again.'

'I'm sure they won't mind if you tell them you're not up to it.'

'I suppose not.'

That was an option. Geraldine considered telling Netta

that she'd changed her mind. There was no harm in that, surely? After seeing her in that state last night, Netta probably wasn't really expecting her to turn up anyway. She'd understand. Perhaps she'd send Netta a message. That way she could spend the day trying to put yesterday's whole shoddy business behind her.

Unfortunately, Geraldine knew it wasn't going to be that simple. It would be some time before she'd be able to blot out every awful minute of her family get-together. From meeting them at the church, to waving them a cheery 'ta-ra' as she exited the pub while being held up by Arthur and Netta. Legless. Her of all people.

She put her head back in her hands. Had she really told Arthur to sod off? Yes, she had. And did she really just sit there, like a demented old dear, while Fenella – in her most patronising voice – told Netta that she couldn't cope without Arthur? Yes, she did. She even agreed, in a fashion. To make matters worse, she had a sneaking suspicion that, in a way, Fenella was quite accurate in her assessment, but she resented her pity. She didn't want anyone feeling sorry for her, thank you very much. And another thing. While it might be true, she didn't need it to bandied about willy-nilly by her sister-in-law, and she certainly hadn't needed to admit to it.

'Do you want me to phone Netta?' said Arthur.

She lifted her head away from her hands, for the second time that morning, and tutted. 'I haven't made up my mind yet.'

'Okay, love. I'll leave it with you then. I've going to have to go now. Will you be all right?'

Geraldine tutted again. Another one who thought she couldn't cope without him. 'Yes, yes. Just go. I'll be fine.'

'If you're sure?'

'Stop fussing around me, Arthur.'

'All right, Gee. Let me know what you decide. I'll take Minnie with me. She'll enjoy it.'

Arthur smiled and kissed the top of her head, but she saw the crestfallen look his smile had quickly replaced. Eggshells. She'd done it again. Perhaps he deserved it this time though. If he hadn't left her yesterday to listen to them all going on about what a saint Mum had been, Fenella wouldn't have been able to get to her. But then, he had to go home to see to Minnie after Netta's message. They couldn't have left her alone for that long. Netta then. It was her fault for being late. No, that was no good. She couldn't help Kelly's nan taking ill like that. Kelly? No. Fenella. Bloody Fenella with her fancy clothes, her fancy ways and her fancy pink, flipping cocktails. She was to blame.

Arthur drove off just as the phone rang. Since there was no one else to answer it, she had to do it herself.

'All right, Gez? It's me, Jan. Enjoy yourself last night, did yer?'

There was a hint of sarcasm in Janet's voice that made Geraldine's jaw clench. It had started then, had it? No doubt they were all laughing at her. Making jokes about snotty Geraldine getting her come-uppance.

'Well, you have to let your hair down now and then, don't you?' she replied.

'Most of us do, Gez.'

Geraldine waited for her to finish the sentence, but Janet obviously didn't think there was any need to elaborate. The implication was clear enough. She was not like most of them.

She felt rather aggrieved by Janet's unspoken assumption that she wasn't capable of enjoying herself. Mainly because it was untrue. She had no problem having a good time with her family, and even with some of Netta's friends. What she had a problem with, was drinking yourself stupid. Or worse. And, being out of control. She couldn't abide that. Geraldine could have told Janet that. She could have expressed surprise that none of her siblings agreed with the sentiment. But if their shared history had taught her anything, it was that the best course of action was to button your lip and say nothing. So she did just that, and waited for Janet to pick the thread of conversation back up.

'Anyway, me and Trev are having a bit of a wander round some of the old haunts this morning. We'll probably get a pub lunch before we go back to Ludlow. Tony and Ralph are meeting us.'

The old haunts. Jan's favourite pastime every time she came back to visit. If she loved them so much, you had to wonder why she'd left Birmingham in the first place.

'Do you want to come?'

Geraldine sighed a silently inward sigh. Please God, save her from the old haunts.

'Sorry Jan, I'm helping Netta and her friend on their market stall today. You know they've got that jam and pickles business? They sell it at the farmers' market in Moseley. You might not have heard last night, but I said I'd give them a hand.'

'Oh, okay. Never mind. Maybe we'll bump into you later then.'

'Yes, maybe.'


Geraldine stepped out onto the street. It was sunny but there was a nip in the air and she was glad she'd put on extra layers. That was October for you. You could never trust it to be quite warm enough, especially if you were going to be standing outside all morning.

After the phone call from Janet, she'd messaged Netta to say she'd see her at the stall. She'd all but made up her mind not to go but she'd been caught between the worse of two evils and, with the prospect of Janet seeking her out, she'd had no choice but to choose the least perilous.

It wasn't that she didn't like spending time with Netta. Or with Neil for that matter. In fact, if push came to shove, she'd have to admit that she often preferred Neil's company to Netta's. Sometimes, even to Arthur's. He was just so easy to get along with. The perfect son. Except that he wasn't her son, obviously. No, it wasn't that. It was the prospect of having to talk to all those people she didn't know – strangers. She knew it was stupid. Especially since she used to work in a shop. But that had been different. She'd known most of the customers then, and Ada was there. She stroked her arm absent-mindedly and told herself it would be all right. She'd be able to pull it off. Nothing to worry about really.

On the way there, she thought about her sister, brothers and Trev roaming around the old streets and reliving the memories of their youth. Geraldine couldn't understand the fascination herself. She'd never been one for looking back at the past. Or forward to the future, come to think of it. The present was her domain. Her happy place. Most of the time, anyway.

She would have cheerfully skipped yesterday, fast forwarded to today. All that nonsense about tidying up the graves. Who cared really? Tony only offered to get into Jan's good books. At least Phil made it plain that he'd rather be somewhere else. What was it Fenella had said last night about him needing a drink first? Typical Corcoran. Always got to be boozing. She frowned. That wasn't a very nice thing to say about him. Particularly given that he was anything but a typical Corcoran. Truth be told, none of them were that bad. She could tolerate them all separately. It was just when they all got together that it became a bit too much. Too much talk of the past. Too many memories. Suffocating. That's what it was.

The bus trundled along the High Street, past where Ada's shop used to be. It was a café bar now. Arthur had tried to get her in there a few times but she couldn't bring herself. It felt like sacrilege somehow. Geraldine wondered what Ada would have made of it. She probably would have approved. In fact, knowing Ada, she probably would have had a chain of café bars herself. She was always one for looking forward.

Neil and Netta were already set up when Geraldine arrived. Neil gave her a hug and a kiss. Not Netta though: it wasn't her style. It wasn't Geraldine's style either. Not that they didn't love each other. They just weren't huggers.

Thankfully, Netta didn't mention last night. Her daughter wasn't always the most tactful of people but today, she seemed to have made an effort. She went off to get Geraldine a warm drink while Neil explained what to say if anyone asked about the different products.

'Here's a list of what's in each product. It's on the jars but we still get asked, so we keep it all here, in one place, for easy reference. Netta said you used to work in a shop?'

'I used to work for Arthur's mum, but that was years ago.'

'That's all right. It's a bit like an old-style shop experience here. You'll be fine.'

Geraldine raised her eyebrows. 'I'm glad you think so, Neil.'

Neil took her hand and smiled. 'I know so. I'll be here right next to you, if you need me.'

She felt his warmth transferring over to her cold hand. She wanted to say thank you, but the words wouldn't form in her mouth. Instead, she smiled back at him. There was something about Neil that reminded her of Ada. Suddenly everything felt a little better.

# 7
## SHOWDOWN AT THE MARKET STALL

NETTA – 2019

Netta refilled the empty spaces on the stall. It was turning out to be a good day today. Their business was relatively new but things were going okay. When they'd first started making jams in her kitchen at home, it had been an enjoyable way for her and her friends to spend time together. The recipes were Edie's, the elderly lady who'd lived in the house before her.

In the beginning, they sold the jams at church fairs. When they ran out of those, they graduated onto local markets. By the time they'd begun to make a small profit, Neil and Kelly had been keen to take things further and turn it into a business. Netta hadn't been convinced it was enough to pay them a living wage but, after being made redundant, she was in no rush to look for a real job so she agreed. Then, last year, they bagged a contract with a small chain of delis. It provided the first step to expansion. Now, they had contracts with other delis and farm shops; stalls in local producers' markets; more products, and a proper commercial kitchen.

They were busy but not so much that they couldn't carry on volunteering at the foodbank. To her delight, the hobby had turned into a proper job that still allowed her to do the things she valued.

Today was their fourth stint at the Moseley market and it was looking like their best one yet. It went like that sometimes. People had to see you there a few times before they trusted you enough to buy. But Netta suspected there was another reason for today's success. Quite an unexpected one, as it turned out. Her mum was here instead of Kelly.

It was true that Kelly could be a bit off-putting for some people, but she'd mellowed quite a lot this year and had been working hard at not frightening the customers away. Also, Kelly drew in the younger people, so there were normally some benefits to her being here. But her mum? Shock news! Her mum could sell better than any of them.

The fact that she'd turned up in the first place had been a complete surprise to Netta. Even when her mum messaged that morning to say she'd see them at the stall, Netta hadn't really expected her to come. Netta's dad had called her from his friend Clyde's allotment and warned her that her mum was feeling a bit under the weather. That usually meant she was having one of her black moods.

Over the years, there were a number of phrases that passed between Netta and her dad to hint at the state of her mother's mind. It was a code that both of them knew was there, but neither of them acknowledged. 'Under the weather' was one of the most often used. Along with 'feeling a bit tired', and anything with the word nerves in it. So, when her mother had actually turned up, looking a bit off-colour, Netta had to assume that this time, her mum was feeling genuinely ropey which shouldn't really have come as a surprise. In spite of developing a recent liking for Prosecco, her mum generally didn't drink much more than a small sherry or a glass of wine with a meal. Last night had been the exception, which was a pity because she had looked like she was having a lot of fun.

Netta had thought about mentioning that this morning but one look at her mum's tense, forbidding expression told her to keep it to herself. In fact, it was better not to mention last night at all. Instead, she'd taken the coward's way out and offered to get the tea, leaving Neil to put her mum at ease, as only he could. The move had paid off because when she got back, her mum had seemed a little less on edge and was busy familiarising herself with the products.

'I can't promise I'm going to be any good at this,' she'd said, 'but at least you've got an extra hand if you need to take a break.'

Netta hadn't expected her to be any good at it either but to her amazement, her mum turned out to be a bloody brilliant saleswoman. She watched in awe as her mum sweet-talked a couple of hipsters who'd only asked for a jar of marmalade.

'Good choice. Have you tried the lemon and lime flavour as well? It's delicious on toast, a nice mix of sweet and tangy. I like to have a slice with that and a slice with the orange marmalade. Now, while you're here, you look like you might enjoy a bit of avocado or a good cheese. Yes? I thought so. Have you tried this pickle? It's a special Caribbean recipe, with just a hint of spice that complements both of them really well.'

The hipsters succumbed and she packed them off with all three items and a cheery wave.

'Make sure you come back and let us know what you

think of them. We're here every month. Don't forget to tell your friends. Bye both. Lovely speaking to you.'

It was not like her mum at all but then, neither was getting pissed as a fart. Two surprise revelations in twenty-four hours. Netta would need a sit down if any more came out.

'Geraldine, you're a natural. Isn't she, Net?' said Neil.

It seemed Netta wasn't the only one to be astounded by this hitherto unknown sales expertise.

'You are. I had no idea,' said Netta.

Her mum looked a bit embarrassed. 'I suppose all those years of working in your gran's shop haven't been entirely forgotten.'

'What did you sell in the shop?' asked Neil.

'All sorts of things. Whatever Ada could get at a good price and whatever there was a call for. Lots of spam and tinned corned beef when I first started working there, but it changed as time went on. Ada was very adaptable. She could sell anything, to anyone.'

Netta smiled. As a child, she had often been allowed to sit behind the counter while her mum helped out during the busy periods. She even had her own little toy shop at home and Granny Wilde would teach her the sales patter. It was a shame she'd forgotten it all.

'You learned from one of the best, Mum.'

'I did. I'm channelling my inner Ada, as Liza would say.'

Netta could imagine Liza saying those very words. Her daughter and her mum had a nice thing going on between them. Very like her relationship had been with Granny Wilde. Granny had been dead four years now and Netta still missed her.

Netta's phone rang, interrupting her thoughts. It was

Kelly. She moved away from the noise of the market and the traffic to answer it.

'Hi, how's it going? You still at the hospital?'

'Yeah. It's going all right. Nan's sitting up now. She can't move her left side but she's already told me off for having a go at my dad, so she's definitely still got all her marbles. At least I think that's what she was doing. It's a bit hard to understand everything she says,' said Kelly.

'That sounds positive. I suppose if you can keep your temper with your dad it would be better for your nan.'

'Yeah, I know. But he's so fucking useless, Net, it's hard. I'm trying though, for her sake. They told us the first three days are the danger zone so I am actually doing my best not to upset her. How's it going there? Are you managing okay without me?'

'Don't worry about us, we're doing fine. My mum came to help.'

'Yeah? She okay with it, is she? She coping?'

Netta thought carefully before answering. She didn't want Kelly thinking she'd left them in the lurch. Or that she'd forced her mum into doing something she didn't want to do. Neither did she want Kelly to think they were doing better without her.

'She seems to be enjoying herself.'

'Yeah? That's a relief. The doctor's come to see Nan. I'd better go. I'll see you tonight sometime.'


Netta could see her mum talking to three men as she got closer to the stall. Or rather, they appeared to be talking to her. She couldn't tell for certain because they had their backs to her, but her mum seemed to be listening to them and, judging by her face, it was making her uncomfortable.

Not unusual for her mum except that she'd been quite happy when Netta left her. What's more, those three men looked very familiar.

When Netta reached them, she saw that they were Trevor, Tony and Ralph. Trevor saw her.

'Here she is. Hello Netta. I was just saying to Geraldine, we've lost Jan. She bumped into someone she used to know and we left them to have a chat,' he said.

'Hang on, I can see them.' Tony lifted his hands in the air. 'They're on their way over.'

Janet was with them almost straight away. Although not that tall, she was thick-set and sturdy-looking, and always managed to appear larger than she actually was. She made the woman at her side look small and insignificant in comparison.

The woman was beaming at Netta's mum. 'You've hardly changed, Geraldine. I would have known you, even if your Janet hadn't pointed you out.'

Netta's mum stood open-mouthed.

Janet rolled her eyes. 'You remember Rita, don't you?'

Her mum clamped her mouth shut and shook her head.

'Rita Sweeney, as was,' said the woman. 'Bree's big sister. Don't tell me you've forgotten Bree? Breda Sweeney. You two were thick as thieves.'

At last, her mum found some words: 'Breda? Oh yes, I think I do remember a Breda from school. We lost touch after I left though, I'm afraid.'

'She still talks about you,' said Rita, her expression suggesting she was hoping for a better response.

'Does she? She must have a better memory than me then.'

'She lives in London now. Did very well for herself. Went to university and everything.'

The three women fell silent. Janet seemed a bit agitated, Rita a bit disappointed and her mum, just a tiny bit miffed. Netta decided it was time to step in and save the day.

'Uncle Phil not with you?'

'He went back to Southwold this morning,' said Ralph. 'Saturday is Fenella's busiest day.'

'At least that's his excuse,' cut in Janet.

'I'll have to go. I've got frozen peas in my shopping and I can't have them defrosting. You've got my number, Janet. Give me a call. Next time you're back in Birmingham, we can have a proper chat. Bye Geraldine. I'll tell our Bree I saw you. She will be pleased.' Rita took two steps then turned around to deliver the killer blow: 'Even if you don't remember her.'

Janet watched Rita hurrying through the crowd, no doubt in a rush to get those peas into the freezer.

'That was a bit rude, our Geraldine.'

Her mum huffed. 'What was I supposed to say? If you don't remember someone, you don't remember them. No point in pretending you do.'

Janet turned and narrowed her eyes. Her nostrils inflated like a bull about to stampede. Netta's mum shuffled her hands around in her coat pockets, and her neck moved up and down as she gulped fiercely, but she seemed determined to stare Janet out.

Trev clapped his hands making everyone blink.

'Right then, let's have a look at these jams, shall we?'

After a strained discussion about the places they'd been to visit, Auntie Janet left with the men in tow. They'd purchased an array of products. That was mostly Trev's doing. He probably felt the need to make up for the stand-off that had just taken place

. . .

The market was winding down. They made a few more sales, then packed up their remaining stock and found a café to get something to eat.

Neil pulled out a chair for Netta's mum.

'You were a real asset today, Geraldine. Don't tell Kelly, but we've had one of our best performing days, thanks to you.'

Her mum's features morphed into a tight little grimace. Something had changed in her since the Corcorans' visit. She'd been having a good time until then and now she was keyed-up. Janet did have that effect on people sometimes: she could be a bit overwhelming. Or perhaps it was that woman, Rita.

'Everything all right, Mum?' said Netta.

Her question was met with a blank stare. 'Yes, of course. I'm just a bit tired.'

'Okay. That was funny, Auntie Janet bumping into her old friend like that.'

'Yes, I suppose it was. Don't know why she brought her to see me though. It's not like she was my friend. Honestly, Janet does go overboard sometimes.'

'You don't remember Rita's sister then? Bree, I think she said her name was.'

'Hardly. I mean, I was friends with a girl called Bree for a while, but I had lots of friends at school. If she meant anything to me I'd have stayed friends, wouldn't I? Clearly she couldn't have, because I didn't. Case closed.'

She snatched up a menu and buried her head in it.

Netta glanced over at Neil. Was it just her, or did he think something was a bit off too? She tried to communicate this to him by way of an inquiring look. He shrugged. Maybe he thought so too then? Unless he was just shrugging because he hadn't got a clue what she was giving him strange looks for.

Her mum threw the menu down on the table. 'I can't eat anything. I'll just have a cup of tea.'

Yes, something was definitely a bit off.

# 8

## FLIES IN THE OINTMENT

### GERALDINE – 2019

When Arthur came home, the first thing he asked was how she got on at the market. Geraldine fobbed him off with a bit of flannel about it being like riding a bike and it all coming back to her quite quickly. She chose to say nothing about Janet turning up with Rita Sweeney. Luckily, she was able to steer him clear of any further talk by asking about Clyde and the allotment. That kept the conversation going all through dinner and, afterwards, Arthur was so tired that he fell asleep in front of the TV.

Some wives might have been a bit peeved about their husband spending the day out, digging up someone else's dirt and then dozing off as soon as his bottom hit a comfy seat, but not Geraldine. For a start off, it meant there was less chance of him asking again about her day, and she didn't really want to talk about it. But the main reason was that she liked to see his face light up when he talked about the allotment. All of Arthur's working years had been in an office. He'd always been clever, but he loved doing things with his hands – fixing, making and growing things. He was one of life's natural nurturers, and he'd found a kindred spirit in Clyde.

They hadn't been friends for long. Not much more than a year. Arthur had been tidying up Netta's front garden one day when Clyde passed by and stopped for a chat. What neither of them realised at the time was that Clyde was going to play a big part in the Wilde family's future life. It was Clyde who arranged for the allotment holders to sell their spare fruit to Netta and her friends, to make the jams. More importantly, Clyde had a big dog called Colonel who was rather fond of Netta's dog, Maud. A little too fond, you might say, since the result of his passion was four puppies, one of which was Minnie, who had definitely changed Geraldine and Arthur's lives for the better.

Arthur was such a quiet sleeper that even his snores were barely audible. Just little puffs of air and the slightest of whistles. It was comforting to watch him. Geraldine switched off the TV and slowed her breathing down to match his. It felt quite peaceful. As if she and Arthur were one. She marvelled at his ability to relax her, even when he wasn't conscious. She reached out to touch him, then stopped herself. It might wake him and then the pleasure of just sitting there, observing him would be lost.

There were so many things about Arthur Wilde that made her full with love for him, she couldn't even begin to list them. When they first started courting, she couldn't believe her luck and it was still a constant surprise to her that this sweet, gentle man was hers, in spite of everything she threw at him.

Arthur stirred and opened his eyes. He gave her a quizzical look. 'What are you doing?'

She smiled. 'Nothing. Just looking for that dashing young man who swept me off my feet.'

'Did you find him?'

'Of course. He's still in there.'

He chuckled. 'You old romantic, you.'

She got up and kissed the top of his head.

'I thought that was you. I'll make us a hot chocolate. You look done in, my love. Early night tonight, I think.'


As soon as they got close to Netta's house, Minnie began to whine. She was usually very good in her travel pen in the back of the car but when she realised where she was going, you could sense the excitement building in her. It was the same every week and always at this point in the journey.

'Here we go again,' said Arthur. 'She's a smart girl, our Minnie.'

He was concentrating on the road but there was obvious pride in his voice. Minnie was his baby too.

'Nearly there, Min.' Geraldine put on her most comforting voice, which was not as easy as you might think, given the last forty-eight hours. Still, it was all over now. Everything was back to normal.

They pulled up outside Netta's house. By now, Minnie was frantic with excitement. As soon as they let her out of the car, she bounded up the drive and scratched at the back gate. Arthur opened it and she tore off to join in the pandemonium that was being wreaked on Netta's back garden. It was Sunday morning, a special time for Maud and Colonel's puppies, when they all got together for a walk in the park. First though, they liked to tear around the garden creating general chaos.

Frank walked through the gate that connected his garden with Netta's. He said something to greet them but she couldn't hear it over the racket. Frank was a nice man.

Big and broad, with a Northern Ireland accent that Geraldine rather liked. In some ways, he reminded her of Arthur, but quite a bit rougher around the edges.

She was never sure how to describe Frank to people. He was much too old to be called Netta's boyfriend, and manfriend sounded a bit peculiar. Was he Netta's partner? She always thought you had to live together to be that, but Netta and Frank lived next door to each other. Geraldine decided it probably didn't matter how she described him. Her daughter had spent too many years married to that despicable worm, Colin Grey. Too many years being made miserable. Frank made her happy, and that was all that counted.

Frank's dog, Fred, was chasing around with Minnie and Betty, the only one of the puppies that had stayed with Netta. Just one pup missing. Five minutes later, Neil and his husband, Chris, arrived with Buster and they were all set to go.

It was a lovely crisp morning and nice to be outside. Once inside the park, they spread out, breaking off into smaller groups. The space allowed Geraldine to move away if a conversation got tricky, but most of the time that wasn't needed because she and Neil were talking about cooking. It was something they both enjoyed.

By the time they got back to Netta's house, the younger generation were up, and hungry for the bacon and sausage sandwiches that she and Neil usually rustled up between them. Will was home for the weekend and his girlfriend, Belle, had stayed over. Such a pretty, pleasant girl. Lovely manners. They were so well suited.

Liza was being her usual funny self. She was quite hilarious sometimes. Geraldine couldn't think where she got it from. Not from her mum: Netta had a very odd sense of humour. Certainly not from her father either. Colin Grey didn't have one ounce of humour in his body, as far as she could see.

The only fly in the ointment was Kelly Payne, Netta's lodger. Or 'friend', as Netta liked to call her. It irritated Geraldine that her daughter put Kelly on the same level as Liza and Will. She knew that Kelly had had a hard life, in spite of being only a year older than Will but family was family, and Kelly Payne was not family.

Of course, it wouldn't have been so hard to stomach if Kelly had been more agreeable; if she wasn't quite so foul-mouthed or even if she was a bit less intrusive and didn't tease Liza quite so much. But Kelly had a mouth like a sewer; she was – what Geraldine believed young people called – 'in your face' all the time, and she ridiculed Liza at every opportunity. The surprising thing was that no one else seemed to mind. Not even Liza and Will. It was all very perplexing.

'How's your nan, Kel?' asked Neil.

Kelly stopped eating her sandwich. 'Not really sure. The doctors think she's doing all right but I dunno. Carol, the woman who lives with my dad, she's talking about finding a care home for her.'

'That's quite quick, isn't it?' said Will. 'She's only been in hospital a few days.'

'That's what I said but she seems to think she's a fucking expert, and my dad just agrees with everything she says.'

'What does your nan say, have they asked her?' said Arthur.

'Have they fuck.'

Liza put her hand on Kelly's shoulder. 'I'd want to be asked.'

Kelly nodded. 'Yeah, me too.' She seemed to be miles

away but then she grinned at Geraldine. 'You had a good day yesterday then?'

'Well, you know … I was just trying to help out.'

'I heard you was the star saleswoman.'

'Were you, love?' said Arthur.

She told herself not to be irritated by his astonished expression. She'd played it down so much last night, how could he be anything other than astonished?

'She was great,' said Neil.

Liza punched the air. 'Go Nan. Hey, Mum said you bumped into someone from your past as well.'

'Really? Who was that then?' said Arthur.

So, Kelly Payne was not the only fly in the ointment today. Geraldine glanced at Netta who was looking more than a little shifty. Quite right too. It wasn't her news to share.

'Oh no one you'd know. She was Janet's friend really. I just knew her younger sister in school. Honestly, I hardly remember her.'

She gave a little laugh to qualify the ridiculousness of it all.

Arthur nodded. He seemed to have believed her. He turned to Netta.

'Frank says you're making a start on decorating the study. Need some help?'

It was almost midnight. Geraldine was staring at the thin ray of light peeping through the crack in the curtains They'd been in bed for well over an hour and Arthur was doing his usual nearly noiseless sleeping. She wondered if she was the reason he did everything so quietly. If he'd married someone else, someone normal, would he have been louder? Would he have woken the neighbourhood with violent snores that shook the house? She couldn't imagine Arthur ever being like that, but who's to say? If Len Corcoran hadn't insisted on her leaving school; if her mum hadn't found her a job in Ada Wilde's shop, things could have been very different.

## 9

## MEETING THE DREAMBOAT

GERALDINE - 1961

It was warm for April and Geraldine left her coat at home that morning. Mainly because she only had the choice of her duffle coat or mac, both of which were school regulation bottle green and tatty. They'd come from a jumble sale when she was in the first year. They'd been massive on her then but she grew into them and, eventually, out of them. Since there was no younger sister to pass them down to, she'd been forced to wear them anyway, even though the sleeves were more like three-quarter length and the buttons didn't do up across the chest anymore. She looked stupid in them, and her mum had said it was important to make a good impression. So the coats stayed at home and she wore her best dress. Janet had given her one of her cast-off handbags and she used it to carry the jam sandwiches that her mum had made her.

She had a long walk so she soon warmed up and everything was fine, until it rained. Now she was standing outside Mrs Wilde's shop, looking like she'd been for a swim without taking her clothes off first. The rain had stopped and the sun came back out about fifteen minutes ago. For the first ten of those minutes, Geraldine had been hoping the sun would dry her off. For the last five, she'd been trying to pluck up the courage to knock on the door.

Without notice, the door blind rolled up and her courage was no longer needed. The woman on the other side of the glass stared at Geraldine, open-mouthed.

Geraldine gulped. She wasn't sure what to do next.

The woman's mouth closed, but she carried on staring at Geraldine, as if she couldn't quite work out what she was looking at.

Geraldine had never met Mrs Wilde but she'd seen a photograph of her with her mum and her auntie Fran, from when they were teenagers. This woman was a lot older but she was tall and slim like the girl in the picture, and had the same features. Geraldine was certain it was the same person but the photo, being black and white, hadn't prepared her for the full colour effect of seeing Mrs Wilde in the flesh. She was quite striking with her pale skin, sandy hair fixed up in a bun, and icy blue eyes. Her mum had said Mrs Wilde was a handsome woman. At the time Geraldine had thought it was a funny way to describe a woman, but she could see now what she meant.

Embarrassed by the state of herself, Geraldine pushed her hair behind her ears and tried to straighten out the dress that had wrinkled up with the dampness.

After a few more excruciating minutes of assessment, Mrs Wilde unlocked the door.

'Geraldine Corcoran?'

'Yes, miss.'

'Come in, Geraldine. You look soaked to the skin. Don't you have a coat or a brolly?'

'No, miss. Sorry.'

'You don't have to call me miss, love. I'm not your

teacher. My name's Ada. Let's see if we can sort out those wet clothes.'

She took Geraldine through the shop, to a kitchen at the back. Geraldine's clothes were clinging to her and she was glad of the warmth from the gas fire. Mrs Wilde told her to sit by the fire.

'Warm yourself up. I'll see what I've got upstairs for you to wear until your things have dried out.'

Geraldine sat in the quiet kitchen, shivering, even though she was only a little bit cold. She could hear faint voices coming from upstairs and then Mrs Wilde calling her to come up.

She was waiting for Geraldine at the top of the stairs.

'I've laid out some clothes on the bed, in there, and a towel to dry off. You can use the hairbrush on the dressing table and there are some bands to tie your hair back into a ponytail. It's smarter and more hygienic. The clothes are a bit old fashioned but no one will see them under your overall. Have you had some breakfast?'

Geraldine nodded.

'Well I was about to have some toast. You might as well have some too. It'll be a while before we get the chance to eat again. I'll be in the kitchen, just down the hall there.'

Mrs Wilde closed the bedroom door behind her, leaving Geraldine alone to take in the room properly. It was very glamorous with its fancy wallpaper and curtains, big fluffy pillows, and a silk eiderdown. Nothing like any of the bedrooms in their house. The bed was a double, although Geraldine knew for a fact, there was no Mr Wilde. Her mum had said he'd come back from the war and didn't stay long enough to change out of his demob suit. She remembered it because it was one of the few things that made her dad laugh.

She gave her hair a good towel dry and put on the fresh clothes. They felt expensive and weren't that old fashioned. She'd worn a lot worse. Perching nervously on the chair in front of the smart dressing table, she brushed and tied her hair. Everything on the table was neat and tidy, including the make-up and perfume bottles. Geraldine would have liked to have taken the top off the perfume bottles and sniffed them, but she didn't dare.

She put the chair back in its place, folded her wet dress and was about to leave when she heard the voices again. One of them was Mrs Wilde, the other sounded like a man. She waited for a couple of minutes, until the voices stopped, then opened the door and followed the polished parquet hallway, past a second set of stairs that led up to another floor, towards the kitchen.

The kitchen was big and bright with red cupboards and all the mod cons. Her mum would be so jealous. Mrs Wilde was sitting at a table in the middle, buttering toast. She pointed to a chair opposite her.

'Sit down and help yourself.'

The butter had been spread so thick over the hot toast that it slid around as it melted. Geraldine picked up a slice carefully, so's not to spill it onto her borrowed clothes, and ate it in small bites, out of politeness.

Mrs Wilde poured some tea into a proper china cup, with a saucer, and pushed it over to her.

'Your mum tells me you're a quick learner. Just what I need. The girl you replaced was rather slow, unfortunately. We tried but it was never going to work. We had to part ways. Still, she's got a decent factory job now, so she's happy. You were at the grammar school, your mum said. Swanshurst, was it?'

'Yes, mi … Yes.'

'My son's at King Edward's. He loves it there. Did you like school, Geraldine?'

'Yes, I did.'

Mrs Wilde sighed and looked straight into Geraldine's eyes as if she was weighing her up. Geraldine didn't like it. It made her blush. She looked down into her lap.

The sound of a door opening and closing above them broke the silence. Footsteps tripped down the stairs, along the hall and towards them. Then, in the doorway were a pair of feet, legs and … not a man. A boy, in school uniform.

He was tall and lean, like Mrs Wilde and had the same sandy hair and pale blue eyes that crinkled up as he grinned at her and said: 'Hello, you must be Geraldine. I'm Arthur.'

## 10

## JOINING THE MERRY BAND

GERALDINE – 1961

Arthur Wilde was still standing in the doorway, grinning from ear to ear. The blush that had started with Mrs Wilde's examination of her, had now taken over the whole of her body, and the heat of it was oozing from every pore. Geraldine was beginning to sweat. She wanted to say something bright and breezy and confident, but in the end she could only mutter: 'Hello.'

Mrs Wilde tutted. 'Get a move on, Arthur, or you'll be late.'

He walked over to the table and snatched up a piece of toast. 'I've got plenty of time.'

'Well don't come running to me if you get into trouble. You know very well you've missed the bus.'

He gave his mother a cheeky wink. 'You know me, Mum, I'm a rebel.'

Mrs Wilde's seriousness crumbled. 'Without a cause. Stop messing about and go.'

'See you later.' He kissed his mother's cheek, then glanced at Geraldine. 'Bye.'

Geraldine gave him a shy smile but he was gone before

she was able to say anything, which was probably just as well because she was dumbstruck.

Mrs Wilde sighed and said to herself: 'He'll be late.' She gave the dirty crockery a rinse and set them down on top of one of the cupboards. 'Right. Let me show you around downstairs before we open up.'

When she'd first walked through the shop, Geraldine had been too self-conscious to notice anything about it but now she could see it was bigger than it seemed. It was probably twice the size of the shop next door, but you wouldn't have known it because it was so full.

The middle section of the shop was like a general grocery store, with tins and dried goods piled high on shelves that ran all along the back wall. The long counter that kept the shelves of stock and customers apart held a few bits of fresh food, like bread and cakes, and a selection of tins with the price knocked down – mostly spam, corned beef, and pilchards.

To the left was a smaller counter that seemed to be solely for the purpose of selling make-up, other toiletries, and stockings. Another counter to the right was the central point for general knick-knacks, household goods and bits of everyday hardware. The shop seemed to cover everything.

Mrs Wilde pointed to the knock-down tins on the back counter. 'I buy whatever's going cheap for that section. We get a lot of customers who come in specially for the week's bargains. I don't sell fresh meat or dairy. It goes off too quickly.'

At nine o'clock, Mrs Wilde unlocked the door and flipped

the 'Closed' sign over to 'Open'. She positioned herself and Geraldine behind the back counter.

'You can watch for the first couple of hours, unless it gets too busy. But we should be all right, and Ruby will be in at ten. Just try to remember to smile, Geraldine. Customers like a friendly face.'

The first hour went by so fast, Geraldine hardly had a chance to breathe. Although she wasn't serving the customers, Mrs Wilde soon had her running around after a tin of this or a packet of that. She only realised it was ten o'clock when a big woman, with an enormous bust, came in and walked behind the counter.

The woman's hair was permed and bleached, like Diana Dors, and she wore lots of make-up. Geraldine's mum would have said she looked like a tart, but Geraldine thought she was beautiful. When she saw Geraldine her bright red lips parted into a smile.

'Hello, bab. I'm Ruby, the part-timer. Geraldine, isn't it?'

She went straight through into the back kitchen without waiting for a reply.

'Tea's ready, Ada,' she called out five minutes later. 'You two have a cuppa and I'll stay out front. I'll call you if it gets busy.'

'Fifteen minutes then, Geraldine,' said Mrs Wilde. 'While we're having a break, let's see how good you are at sums. Here's a pad in case you need it.'

Mrs Wilde began to call out numbers to be added or subtracted. Geraldine was pleased to find that she could do most of them in her head, without needing to write them down. By the end of the break, she'd only had a couple of sips of the tea but Mrs Wilde looked pleased. She must have done all right.

'Finish your tea and then come back out the front. We'll

do a few more tests over the next few days, just so I know what you're good at.'

'Yes, Mrs Wilde.'

'Ada, love. Just Ada will do.'


At one o'clock precisely, Mrs Wilde locked the door and turned the notice back over to 'Closed'.

'Half an hour for lunch and then we'll do some stock taking before we open up for the afternoon,' she said.

'Upstairs or down?' asked Ruby.

'I thought we'd go up today, Rube. I've got some leftover cottage pie in the oven that should stretch to three, if you're interested? Cottage pie all right with you, Geraldine?'

'Yes. Thank you. That would be very nice.' She didn't like to say anything about the sandwiches hidden in her handbag.

She could smell the cottage pie as they walked up the stairs. It reminded her of school dinners. She wondered what her friends were doing now; wondered if they were missing her as much as she was missing them. She wondered if Bree was missing her. It was Monday. Double history after dinner, followed by maths. Bree always hated maths. She'd probably say Geraldine was the lucky one, not having to do it. If she was thinking of her at all.

Geraldine followed Ruby along the hall to the kitchen. This time her eyes roamed through an open door to the living room. Like the hallway, the floor was polished wood, covered mostly by big tapestry mats. It was so posh. There were pictures, in frames, on the walls. If you could call them pictures. She guessed they were proper art. They didn't have art in her house, just one picture of a horse and cart her mum had got with her Green Shield stamps.

She sat at the kitchen table, eating the cottage pie, which was nearly as nice as her mum's, while Ruby and Ada talked, mostly about Ruby's kids and her mother. From what Geraldine could gather, Ruby and her kids lived with her mother. There was no talk of a husband. Maybe Ruby didn't have one either.

'You're a quiet one,' said Ruby. 'Like a little mouse.'

Mrs Wilde turned her attention to Geraldine.

'She's just shy. Nothing wrong with that. It's all a bit new to her. A few weeks ago, she was in school uniform. All this, it's a different world. I expect you'd rather be back at school wouldn't you, love? You should be, by rights, a clever girl like you.'

Geraldine couldn't look at them. Her throat felt hard and raw. *Just keep swallowing*, she told herself. *Just keep swallowing*.

Ruby squeezed her arm.

'You'll be all right, bab. We'll look after you. Proper little team, we are. Aren't we, Ada?'

'Yes, we are. I'll tell you what, Rube, go down and get one of those Victoria sponges off the counter. We'll have a slice to celebrate Geraldine joining our merry little band.'


Geraldine ate the jam sandwiches on the way home: she didn't want her mum to be upset. She'd give it a few days before she told Mum she didn't need any, just in case today was a one-off.

She was taking the long way home so she didn't have to go past Bree's house. Bree would probably be looking out for her, and Geraldine just couldn't face her. It hurt too much right now. Maybe in a few weeks, when she'd got school out of her system and got used to working.

Earning her keep, that's what her dad called it: 'It's about time you earned your keep. No point in school when there's good money to be picked up.'

That was it. There was nothing left to say about it. No arguments. No pleading. Geraldine did as she was told.

At least she didn't have to work in a factory, like Janet who'd gone straight there from school, until she got married. At least her mum had managed to persuade her dad that she was better suited to shop work. And working in a shop didn't seem so bad. Mrs Wilde and Ruby were quite nice really. At least, they probably would be, once she got used to them.

She was lucky that her mum knew Mrs Wilde. She'd been Auntie Fran's friend really, but Auntie Fran was killed, along with her mum's parents, when the house was bombed in the Blitz. Her mum talked about Auntie Fran all the time. She had two brothers and they'd survived the war, but Fran was the only sister. Her mum didn't really keep up with her brothers. She always said they didn't get on, but Geraldine had the feeling that if Fran were still alive, they'd be close.


The minute Geraldine got to her street, her mood dropped and, as soon as she opened the front door, it plummeted further.

Her mum was waiting, her face a mix of forced pleasure and anxiety.

'Here she is. We were beginning to get worried, weren't we, Len?'

Her dad barely looked up from his paper. 'Five more minutes and that would've been your tea in the bin.'

'Sorry,' said Geraldine, without looking at him. It was

never a good idea to look at him. Especially when you were in trouble.

'Make sure that woman knows what time you need to be home by in future.'

Her mum cast her eyes over her. 'What on earth are you wearing?'

'Mrs Wilde lent them to me. I got soaked in the rain this morning.'

'Why didn't you take your mac? I'll have to wash and iron them before you give them back to her.'

'She said not to worry. She said to take them back as they are and she'd do it.'

'You'll do no such thing. I'm not having Ada Wilde thinking we're dirty.'

## 11

## THE DISAPPOINTING RESPONSE

GERALDINE – 1961

It was Saturday morning. Geraldine's first at the shop. The week hadn't gone too badly. She'd only made a few silly mistakes and Ada hadn't minded. Most of the customers had been nice, although there were a couple of exceptions. One old lady was particularly rude and lost her temper when Geraldine got flustered. Ada had been out the back at the time which made it even harder.

Luckily Ruby took pity on her. She came over from her usual place behind the cosmetics counter and started talking to the woman, giving Geraldine time to find the box of starch she was after.

'How's your Iris, Mrs Price? I expect her youngest is at school now.'

'Would be, if she hadn't gone and had another one,' said Mrs Price.

'And Reg, how's he?'

'All right, I suppose. His lungs are playing up again. You should hear him in the mornings. Can't stop coughing until he's had his first fag. Helps to clear them out, you see. The doctor told him to cut 'em down, but what does he know?

He's not much older than that one.' She pointed to Geraldine. 'Bit of a dolly daydream. She won't last long.'

'Oh I don't know, Mrs Price. She's only been here since Monday. She's doing all right.'

'Hmm.'

Mrs Price pinched her lips together and looked Geraldine up and down with a face so sour, Geraldine had to stop herself from shuddering. The old woman snatched her shopping away and counted out her change, very precisely, then turned on her heels.

'Bye, love,' said Ruby with a fixed grin on her face. Through the corner of her mouth, she said: 'Miserable old trout. She's the same every time she comes in. I don't think she's smiled since 1945.'

She winked at Geraldine and they both started sniggering. Mrs Price had given Geraldine the jitters but Ruby had sweetened everything, and Geraldine finally began to feel like one of the team. It had started off being one of the worst moments of the week but had ended by being one of the best.

Not quite *the* best though. That had to be seeing Arthur Wilde when he came home after school. After her first morning, Ada told her to come in half an hour later which meant she missed him leaving but he stopped in at the shop most days when he got back. Generally, he only stayed for five or ten minutes before going upstairs but it was enough to perk up Geraldine's day. He was such a dreamboat.

Perhaps she'd see more of Arthur today. She walked along the High Street wondering what he did with his Saturdays. She used to spend hers helping her mum in the morning and seeing Bree in the afternoon. Not anymore.

. . .

Geraldine knocked on the shop door. The blinds were up but it was still locked. Ada popped her head out of one of the windows above and a few minutes later, she opened a wooden door to the side of the shop. Behind it was a staircase that went directly up to the flat and a narrow hallway that led to the back of the shop.

'Morning, Geraldine.' Ada's voice tinkled, as if she'd just broken off from a laugh. 'There's some tea in the pot upstairs. Go and help yourself. There might be some toast left as well. Karen's up there – my niece. You remember I told you she works here on Saturdays?'

Geraldine heard Arthur before she got to the kitchen. By the time she reached it, there were butterflies in her stomach.

Arthur was dressed in drainpipe jeans and a plain white T-shirt. He looked like a pop singer. He was with a girl who Geraldine recognised from school. Although she didn't really know her, she knew the girl was in the fifth year. The girl was wearing a pair of slacks with a neat top.

They were larking about so much that Geraldine didn't think they'd noticed her, but then Arthur said: 'Geraldine will back me up. Geraldine, don't you think 'Poetry in Motion' is a great song? Karen thinks it's soppy.'

They both looked at her and she immediately coloured up. 'I … er … I like it.'

Arthur leaned back in his chair. 'See! It's just you, Karen. You've got no taste.'

Karen ignored him and turned to Geraldine.

'I know you. I've seen you around school. Weren't you in the fourth year?'

'Yes. I left at Easter.'

'Why didn't you stay on until the end of summer term?'

Geraldine felt another flush of heat on her cheeks.

'I was fifteen in December, so I was allowed to leave at Easter.'

Karen screwed up her eyes. 'Yes, but…' Then, the penny seemed to drop. 'Lucky you. My dad's making me stay on until I'm eighteen. Same with Arthur. Auntie Ada wouldn't let him leave, even if he wanted to. Mind you, he's such a swot he doesn't care.'

Arthur turned his eyes on Geraldine. 'Take no notice of Karen. She doesn't know when to shut up. There's tea and toast if you want it.'

He pulled out the chair next to him.

She sat down, her heart thumping. 'Just a cup of tea will be fine, thank you.'

'I'd have a piece of toast, if I were you. It gets pretty busy on Saturday mornings. You might need the extra energy,' said Karen.

Ada appeared in the doorway.

'Ten minutes, ladies and then we're open. Arthur, homework.'

He smirked and shot his hand in the air. 'Ja wohl, mein Führer.'

Karen giggled but Ada didn't look so amused. Arthur poured a cup of tea for Geraldine and one for himself.

'See you later girls, I've got swotting to do.'

As Karen had predicted, it was very busy. Ruby came in at ten as usual. During the week, she'd moved around between the different counters to wherever she was needed, but Saturday seemed to be the day that most women bought make-up and stockings so Ruby spent all morning glued to that counter.

A lot of Ruby's customers were girls, a bit older than Geraldine. They were probably spending their wages on make-up. That's what Janet used to do when she lived at home. On a Friday night, she'd hand her wage packet over to their dad and he'd give her some back for herself. On Saturday mornings, she'd be straight out to the shops to buy something new. Maybe Geraldine would do the same with her money, when she got some time off. Not yet though: she was working a week in hand, so she wouldn't get paid until next week.

At one o'clock they all went upstairs for dinner. Except for her first day, they'd taken their dinner break in the downstairs kitchen but it wasn't big enough to fit them all in. Arthur had finished his homework a while ago and had been out on his bike doing deliveries, just getting back in time to eat.

Ada had laid out a spread of cheese, pork pie and ham, with fresh crusty bread and pickles. It was like a fancy Christmas spread.

'We always have a cold lunch on Saturday. It's easier,' said Ada. She never called it dinner. Always lunch.

Arthur and Karen joked about all the way through the meal. They got on so well they were more like best friends than cousins. Geraldine thought the way Arthur treated Karen was like how Phil was with her. Although, they would never have joked around at the table like Arthur and Karen. Phil always said it was just him and Geraldine against the rest of them. Sometimes it did feel like that, but now he'd left home as well as Janet and she hardly saw him. Now it was just her, Tony and Ralph, and it wasn't the same.

'Do you need me this afternoon, Mum?' said Arthur.

'I've got a couple of jobs for you to do then you're free. Are you going out?'

'There's a new coffee bar in town I was going to try with my mates.'

'Okay, love. Will you be back for dinner?' said Ada.

'We'll probably go to the Wimpy, so don't worry about me. If you girls want to come later, there'll be plenty of us there.'

'Like who?' said Karen.

'The usual crowd. Den, Rod, John.'

He winked as he said the last name and Geraldine guessed he was teasing Karen. She must have been sweet on John.

'Hmm, I'll think about it,' she said. 'Do you fancy it, Geraldine?'

'I can't. Sorry. I'm already doing something tonight.'

Geraldine didn't want to tell them that she wasn't lucky enough to be able to pick and choose how she spent her spare time. She didn't want to say she was too afraid to ask if she could spend it with them.

Arthur cut himself another slice of cheese. 'Okay. Might see you later then, K.'


Geraldine walked home that evening thinking about her day. Ada had given her some of the bread and cakes that hadn't sold to take home. Her mum would moan about taking charity from Ada, but she would appreciate them really. Ada had also pushed a ten bob note into Geraldine's hand, even though she wasn't due to be paid yet.

'This is just a little bonus for doing so well on your first week. It's not proper wages so you don't need to give it to anyone else. Put it away and spend it on yourself, love.'

Geraldine opened her purse and looked at the note folded inside. A whole ten bob. She'd never had that much to spend on herself before, assuming she did spend it on herself and didn't tell her mum and dad. She hadn't made her mind up about that yet. She was too busy being disappointed about Arthur's response when she said she couldn't go to the coffee bar. She didn't know why she'd hoped he would take it harder. It wasn't as if he'd have any interest in her, a boy like him. He'd be much more likely to be interested in someone like Karen.

'Gez! Gez, wait!'

Geraldine stopped dead. She knew that voice. She turned around to see Bree running towards her. She'd been so engrossed that she'd walked past Bree's house without realising.

Bree slowed down and came to a stop in front of her.

'I've been looking out for you all week. How are you?'

'I'm okay.'

'Did your mum tell you I've called round a few times?'

'Yes, she mentioned it.'

'I thought you might have come round to mine.'

Geraldine snorted. 'I can't, can I? I'm at work all the time.'

'Not all the time.'

'Most of the time.'

'How about tomorrow? Do you fancy going out tomorrow afternoon? We could go to the park–'

'No. Sorry, I'm busy.'

'Wednesday afternoon then? It's half-day closing isn't it? I could meet you after school.'

'I have to work. We do stock-taking.'

'Oh, okay. When's the best time for you, then?'

'I don't know. I've got to go or I'll get in trouble for being late. I'll come round when I can. See you.'

Bree looked completely dejected. It wrenched at Geraldine's guts. They'd been best friends since before senior school and had always been inseparable. They'd spent hours in Bree and her sister's bedroom talking about boys, clothes, and pop stars. They'd even planned their futures, after they'd taken their A-levels. She was closer to Bree than anyone. Even Phil. She hated lying and hurting her like this but being with Bree, knowing that she was doing all the things they'd talked about doing together, was too much to bear. Geraldine would never take her A-levels now. She'd never go to college, or university, and get a good job. She was a shop girl and that was all she was ever going to be.

## 12

# AN UNWELCOME VISITOR

GERALDINE – 2019

When Geraldine woke up, she was alone in bed. The chink of light was still shining through the curtains only this time it was daylight. She couldn't remember how long she'd been looking at that gap last night, but she was sure she'd heard the first birdsong of the day before she finally dropped off. And even then, she was dreaming about Bree. Bloody Janet. Bloody Rita Sweeney.

Going to university had been Bree's dream. She was the one with the big ideas. So it came as no surprise when Rita said she'd done well. Geraldine could imagine Bree getting to the top of whatever profession she chose. Not just because she was clever and determined, but also because she was outgoing and popular. Unlike her.

Geraldine had been the quiet, studious type that normally got overlooked. It suited her to be that way at home, but she would have preferred to be more like Bree at school. That was the problem with spending your childhood trying to disappear into the shadows. Before you know where you are, it becomes your default mode and you really do start to disappear. Whether you want to or not. Being

Bree's best friend was the only thing that made her worth knowing, as far as the other girls were concerned. There was no doubt in Geraldine's mind that there'd have been a string of contenders queuing up to be the new best friend, once she'd created the vacancy.

Not that Bree had been easy to shake off. She'd made plenty of attempts to save their friendship and even came into the shop a couple of times, which only made things worse. Geraldine really didn't want to be seen in her shop girl's overall. She couldn't bear the thought of Bree seeing her like that; of Bree pitying her. It must have been about a year before Bree finally gave up and left Geraldine alone. It took a lot longer for Geraldine to stop missing her.

Arthur was listening to Radio 2. She could hear the overly cheerful sounds of the DJ's chatter floating up the stairs. She checked the time and was horrified to see that it was midmorning. She shot out of bed, pulled on her dressing gown and hurried downstairs.

He was in the kitchen, doing her jobs – again! He switched the kettle on and dropped two teabags into the pot.

'Morning, sleepyhead.'

She scowled at him. 'How could you let me sleep in so late?'

'I did speak to you but you were dead to the world. I thought you must be tired. Are you feeling okay?'

'No I'm not. I couldn't sleep last night. I've had too much sleep this morning, and now I've got a headache.'

Arthur frowned. She was well aware that her outburst didn't make sense, but she was irritated by the whole situation and she had to blame someone. He should have woken her.

'I mean, in all our years together how many times have you known me to have a lie-in? How many?'

He looked as though he was trying to count up the number of times in his head.

'Never mind,' she snapped. 'It was a rhetorical question.'

'Right you are, love.'

He smirked at her and she melted. She could never be angry with him for long. Besides, it wasn't really his fault. It was Janet's. She was the one who turned up with Rita bloody Sweeney, spoiling her day.

'Oh Arthur, I'm sorry. I didn't mean it. I'm so horrible.'

'No you're not. You're just tired. Go and have a sit down in the living room and I'll bring your tea in.'

She did as she was told and a few minutes later he brought in the tea. Minnie was at his side. She put her head in Geraldine's lap and nuzzled into the folds of her dressing gown. It was enough to bring a tear to her eye.

Arthur gave her his clean, fresh hankie.

'My poor darling. What's brought this on?'

She blew her nose. 'I don't know. I suppose I've just been a bit tense over the last few days. I'll be all right once I get back into my stride. I'm just being silly.'

He kissed her cheek. 'I'll give Clyde a ring and let him know I'm not coming today. We'll have a quiet day together, just you, me and Minnie. That might help.'

She'd forgotten he was going back to finish off with Clyde today. Immediately, she felt guilty. He had enough on his plate, having to live with her. She wasn't going to deny him one of the things he enjoyed most.

'You will not. Go. Take Minnie with you. A quiet day on my own will do me good.'

. . .

Arthur had been gone a couple of hours and, after showering and getting dressed, Geraldine felt a bit better. She finished off her lunch and told herself that she needed to get a grip. If Ada was still here, she'd say it was time to shake off the past and be bold. Oh Ada. Geraldine heaved a great sigh. If she wasn't careful she'd be in tears again.

The doorbell rang. It was probably somebody selling something – energy, double glazing, or God. It didn't matter which one, they all made a beeline for their street. She checked who it was from behind the nets in the bay window and was surprised to see Kelly Payne – the last person she either expected, or wanted, to see today. She was about to sneak back behind the curtains, but Kelly's head twisted in her direction and the game was up. She had no choice but to let her in.

Geraldine half-opened the door. She didn't want to appear too welcoming.

'Shouldn't you be working?'

'Nice to see you too. I've been at work this morning. I've got to meet my dad about something, then I'm going to the hospital.'

'What are you doing here then?'

'I'm early, so I thought I'd kill some time with you and Art.'

'Arthur's not here.'

'Oh. With you then. Is that all right?'

No, it was not all right, but Geraldine was not about to say that.

'You'd better come in. Do you want a drink?'

'Nah, I'm good, ta. Don't wanna put you to any bother.'

'It's no bother, I've just made a pot of tea.'

Geraldine knew that she'd made it sound like it was a

huge bother but that wasn't her fault. Kelly shouldn't be here, invading her privacy.

Kelly took off her coat, or rather Netta's coat. Geraldine recognised it as one Netta had worn back when she had a high-flying job in business. She wondered if Kelly had asked permission before taking it. Unlikely. She had a pretty peasant-style top on. It reminded Geraldine of one she'd had in the seventies.

'Huh, my nan makes tea in a pot as well. She says it tastes better,' said Kelly. Her eyes began to well up.

Geraldine had never noticed before how green they were. Poor kid. She was worried about her nan.

'She's right, it does,' she said, her voice softer. 'Have you eaten? Do you want a sandwich?'

'Nah, you're all right. Neil's been force-feeding me his homemade shit all morning. You know what he's like.'

'Just tea then.'

They sat in the living room, neither seeming to know what to say in the absence of Arthur, so their conversation came out in short bursts.

'How's your nan?'

'She can speak a bit better but not much change otherwise.'

Geraldine nodded, then as an afterthought she added: 'My mum had three strokes.'

'Oh, right. Didn't kill her then?'

'Well, the last one did but…'

'Okay.'

'But she recovered after the first and the one that did for her was a couple of years later. I mean she'd had a hard life, so she did well. Considering.'

'Nan might be all right then, for a bit.'

'You never know. Don't lose hope.'

'I won't.' Kelly stood up. 'I'd better go. Thanks for the tea. Sorry I just turned up unannounced.'

'That's all right. You're welcome to come whenever you like.'

Geraldine could have slapped herself. Had she really just said that? How stupid of her. All she could hope for was that Kelly Payne was as clever as everyone said she was. If that was the case then she'd realise, she really wasn't welcome at all.

## 13

# WHAT WAS IT ABOUT OLD PEOPLE?

KELLY – 2019

Well, that was a barrel of laughs! If Kelly had known Arthur wasn't going to be there, she wouldn't have bothered. Geraldine was always such hard work, and she was obviously stressed out because she was doing that thing again. Stroking the arm of the chair.

Geraldine had this habit of tapping her index finger like she was counting, in between the strokes. One, two, three, four. Another stroke. One, two, three, four, and again. Four strokes in all. Twelve taps. She always did it when she was stressed.

Kelly couldn't believe that she was the only one to notice Geraldine had problems dealing with stuff sometimes. It was obvious but no one ever mentioned it, except Netta and Arthur. And even then it was only stuff like: 'Oh she's a bit under the weather.' It seemed to pass Liza and Will by. Maybe it was because they'd grown up with it. That could make you miss what should have been slapping you in the face.

Kelly noticed it. She could see these things because she really looked at people. That's what comes of watching your mum slowly die; every day looking for signs of deterioration. Yeah, thanks Mum. The experience had left her with a unique perspective. Like a special gift. For instance, it hadn't taken her long to spot that thing that Geraldine did with her hand.

And all that shit about come whenever you like. What was that all about?


Kelly went into the café and looked around for her dad. He was with Carol. The two of them were facing the window and she was talking to him. No. She was talking at him. Giving it the old blah, blah, blah. His head was bobbing up and down like it was on a spring. It reminded her of one of those joke nodding dogs that people used to put in their cars in olden times. Liza bought one for Arthur last Christmas.

'All right?' Kelly flopped into a chair opposite them.

Her dad looked up. His eyes were bloodshot, like they hadn't seen any sleep in weeks. Typical.

'All right, Kel? Wanna drink?'

She shrugged. Why was everyone always forcing drinks on her? It was like they couldn't speak without having a cup in their hand.

'Yeah, okay. I'll have a latte.'

Carol got up. 'I'll get it. I need the loo anyway. You two have a chat. Do you want a cake or something, Kelly?'

Kelly sighed. It was bad enough with the drinks but they've gotta keep pushing food on you as well? Fuck's sake. 'Yeah, whatever.'

Carol smiled with that patronising step-mum smile of hers, ignoring the atmosphere Kelly was quite clearly trying to create. Or was she just doing it to wind her up? Kelly couldn't make up her mind.

Her dad waited until Carol closed the toilet door behind her.

'Do you have to do that?'

'Do what?'

'Treat her like shit. She's doing her best.'

'Good for her.'

'It's not her fault, you know.'

'Which bit's not her fault? The bit about Mum dying, or the bit about you falling apart. Or is it the bit when she moved in, before Mum wasn't even cold in her grave?'

'None of it. What is your problem with Carol? The boys get on just fine with her.'

'Only because they're too young to remember the facts.'

'And so are you. Fact one. Carol and me got together two years after your mum died. Fact two. The one thing your mum said to me, over and over again, in her last months was, find someone else. The kids need a mum, and I don't want you to be lonely.'

'Fuck off. Next you'll be telling me she'd be happy about this.'

Her dad jabbed the table with his finger. If he could, he'd have probably preferred to poke it in Kelly's chest, but a table in a crowded café was all he had.

'You need to grow up, girl. You're twenty now. It's about time you got rid of that massive chip on your shoulder.'

He glanced up at the counter. Carol's concerned face must have reminded him what he was there for. 'Look, let's not get into a slanging match. It's not why we're here.'

Kelly leaned back and folded her arms. 'No? Why are we here then?'

'We found somewhere that'll take your nan. A nice care home. Before you get all arsey again, we've spoken to Nan and she's happy to go there.'

Kelly sat up. 'We? You mean you and Carol?'

'Yeah. She's my mum, Kel.'

'Yeah, and she's my fucking nan.'

Carol came back with a tray of drinks and chocolate brownies. She looked kind of embarrassed. Kelly guessed that was because the people in the tables nearby were looking over to see what the fuss was. She would have happily told them all to fuck off and mind their own business, but she was trying to exercise a bit of decorum. Besides, she sometimes came in here with Neil and Netta, after the Kings Heath market. She didn't want to be barred.

'I was just telling Kelly about the place we've found for Mum.'

Her dad's eyebrows were moving up and down, like the biggest hint ever for Carol to jump in and say something. What a cock.

Carol took the hint: 'It's a nice place, Kelly. Really nice. We're very lucky to get the offer so soon. Some people have to wait ages.'

Kelly sent a dirty look Carol's way but she ignored it and carried on talking.

'The thing is, the doctor said your nan's gonna need help for a long time and, we really wanted to move her in with us but …'

'But she won't have it,' said her dad. 'She said she doesn't want to be a burden to any of us.'

'We can take you there to have a look if you like. It's only up the road,' said Carol.

Kelly bit a corner off her brownie. They were like a proper double act now, her dad and Carol. Backing each other up. Completing each other's sentences. Just like he used to be with her mum. Except her mum was funny with it. You could never describe Carol as funny.

'No thanks. I'm going to see Nan.'

'Talk to her about it. She'll tell you,' said her dad.

'Yeah, right. See ya.' She took a gulp of her latte and snatched up the rest of the brownie.

As she walked past the café, Kelly glanced back through the window. Her dad's head was in his hands. Weak bastard. Carol had her hand on his shoulder, then she looked up and for a moment her eyes fastened on Kelly. Kelly stared her out, even though she had to crane her neck to do it as she got closer to the end of the window. It pissed her off that Carol kept on staring back with a stupid smile on her lips, like she was mocking her.

Kelly moved on to the window of the shop next door, caught sight of herself, and wished, not for the first time, that she looked more like her mum than her dad. Her mum had been pretty and everything about her was soft and round. Her curves, her face, her lovely wavy hair. She'd been upset about losing that with the chemo. Most of the time, she put on a brave face about the whole cancer thing but the hair falling out, that really got to her.

One time, Kelly walked in on her crying over it. She'd hugged her mum and told her it didn't matter how much hair she lost, she was still beautiful and anyway, she'd rather have a bald mum than a dead one. Not the best choice of words but she was only eleven at the time. It made her mum laugh though. Then she said: 'Don't tell your dad about this, it'll only upset him.'

Jesus Christ. Her mum was dying and that was all she was bothered about. What was it that was so special about that dickhead? Why was everyone always so worried about him? And why did she have to look like a carbon fucking copy of him? Every time Kelly looked in the mirror, all she could see was him gawking back at her.

She stopped and examined herself in the window of a fried chicken shop. She was all bones and sharp edges. Wiry, her nan called it. What was the word Netta used? Gamine, that was it. Kelly had looked it up in one of the dictionaries in the study. Useful things dictionaries. It meant attractively boyish, or some such shit. Trust Netta to always find something good to say. You could have a face like a pig's arse and she'd say you had a lovely complexion.

She bloody loved Netta. She was like her mum and her best mate ever, rolled into one. Kelly didn't want to think about where she'd be now if it hadn't been for her. Probably still having to suck up Craig's shit. What an excuse for a boyfriend he'd been. Actually, what an excuse for a man he'd been. Although, she didn't realise that until she met some who were proper nice. Like Neil, Chris, Frank and Arthur. Not that they counted really because Neil and Chris were gay, and Frank and Arthur were old. They counted as men, obviously, but not boyfriend material. There was only one man like that and he was off limits, no matter how sweet and nice, and totally hot he was. And anyway, she wasn't his type. He liked pretty girls with soft, round curves and long blonde hair. Pretty girls like her mum, and Belle.

The guy behind the counter in the chicken shop was giving her a funny look. He was probably thinking she was taking too long to decide what she wanted, and maybe she was up to something else. She puffed herself up to look more threatening and gave him a look back that said: 'Fuck you mate. It's a free country. If I want to stand here and glare at myself in the window, I fucking well will.' It would have probably worked better if she hadn't softened her style lately. Being aggressive was harder to carry off wearing a flowery vintage top and this smart coat that Netta had given her.

The chicken shop guy must have thought so too because he just shrugged and went to serve a customer. Maybe she should go back to wearing hoodies and skinny jeans. No, that was not gonna happen. She was finding a new style now, thanks to her new mate, Robyn. Who'd have thought Frank's glamorous daughter would turn out to be bestie number three? Well, her only other bestie besides Netta and Will. All right, maybe Neil as well.

The first time she'd seen Robyn, Kelly thought she was going to be a proper stuck-up posho, what with her looking so amazing and being really brainy. How wrong was she? Rob had turned out to be the nicest, most brilliant person. Not in the least bit stuck-up. It was just a shame she lived so far away in Edinburgh.

Chicken shop guy was grinning at her now. He must have thought she was giving him the come-on. Shit. He probably thought she fancied him. Time to move on. She gave him a sideways look just before she walked away.

He waved and blew her a kiss. The cheek of him.

She opened the shop door and shouted above the customers' heads: 'Just so's you know mate, that is highly fucking inappropriate. Check yourself.'

She walked down the High Street towards the bus stop, feeling mighty pleased with herself. Who needed a hoodie anyway?


'I don't want you making a fuss,' said her nan.

The words were still coming out a bit funny, what with her mouth not working properly yet, but Kelly was getting used to it. She could understand her nan pretty well now.

She sat at the side of her nan's hospital bed, picking at the top blanket. She was still angry and the blanket was the nearest thing she could take it out on without upsetting anyone.

'But it's not right, Nan. Your kids should be looking after you. Or, if not them, me.'

'Don't be stupid, Kelly. You're too young. You should be out with your friends instead of worrying about me. And your dad, and your aunties and uncles are all at work. They don't have the time to look after me properly.'

'They would if they weren't so fucking useless.'

Her nan slapped her arm with her good hand.

'Stop swearing. You know I don't like it. Anyway, lovely as my children and grandchildren are, I don't want to live with any of you, thank you. You'd all drive me up the wall. I already know someone in that home so it won't be all strangers, and I'll be with people my own age. They do all sorts of activities as well. I'm looking forward to it. And it means I can get out of this place. So, my mind's made up. I'm going.'

She gave Kelly a hard stare that told her not to bother trying to change it.

Kelly sighed. What was it about old people? Sometimes they just didn't want help. What with Geraldine and her nan, she'd had her fill of them today.

## 14

## GERALDINE GETS RILED UP OVER NOTHING

NETTA – 2019

It was Sunday morning. Earlier, on their usual walk, they'd all been wrapped up against the cold November weather. Now, they were back enjoying the relative warmth of Netta's creaky old heating system. Most of them were piled into the study, admiring its make-over.

At the beginning of the year, the room had been choc-a-bloc with the papers, books and memorabilia that once belonged to the late Edith Pinsent. But they were all gone now, passed on to Edie's son.

Once she'd cleared the room of Edie's paraphernalia, Netta had decided to put her own stamp on it. First to go was Edie's father's oak desk. It had been a wrench to part with it but it wasn't needed, and took up too much space. By and large, she'd kept the books that had been crammed into the floor to ceiling shelving that ran along two walls, only losing some old business and accounting manuals. The desk and manuals turned out to be antiques, and the money she got for them paid for the redecoration and a smaller, more practical desk for Liza to do her homework on, when she was staying over.

Today, with the floor freshly sanded and varnished and the paint dry, they'd moved the furniture in there – the new desk; a sofa that had come with Netta from the flat she'd lived in before moving here; an old armchair that had always been in there, and a bright, modern rug for the floor.

'It looks really nice. Much better,' said her mum.

Her mum been quite chirpy these last two weeks which was a relief. For a while, after the market, it looked like they were heading for another of her 'under the weather' periods but she seemed to have pulled herself out of it.

'I'm going to use it as a sitting room and a proper study and office. Frank's bought me a record player so I can play my old records,' said Netta.

'It's a kind of room-warming gift. Plus, it means I get to listen to my music over here too,' said Frank.

'Great idea. I'll have to bring some of mine over,' said her dad.

Her mum tutted. 'You've certainly got enough, Arthur. I don't think we'd notice a gap in the shelves.'

She was always pretending to be exasperated by his love of music but she was just teasing him. Netta knew her mum enjoyed his record collection as much as he did.


After they'd all eaten their fill of bacon and sausage sandwiches, people started to trail off home or, in Kelly's case, to see her nan. Eventually there was only Netta and Frank left and they were putting the finishing touches to the new-look study.

Netta had some boxes of her own things that had been stashed away in her bedroom for a while now. One box had been with her since she'd moved out of the house she'd shared with Colin and the children, four years ago. Two more had been brought over last year by Colin. It was a gesture that had probably been more for Liza's benefit than anything. Liza had told him he'd been a crap dad and husband and needed to up his game. Netta suspected the boxes had been Colin's way of proving to Liza that he was trying to do just that.

From Colin's boxes, Netta took out her old records and put them with her new stereo. There were photos from her university days in there too and she picked out one that was special to her. It was one of her with her uni friends, including her old boyfriend, Doogie, and her best friend, Claire.

It had been painful to look at that picture during that awful period when she'd been very much under Colin's thumb. Her wilderness years, as she often thought of it now. Her split with both Doogie and Claire – the two people who were the centre of her world back then – had left Netta anchorless and empty. Easy prey for Colin. Earlier this year, she'd reunited with them both and now, she felt complete. These days, it was nice to see the photo and be reminded of what was an exceptionally good time. She put it aside, ready to be framed.

The other box contained the usual family mementoes – photos, cards, and childhood awards. Netta remembered how she'd hastily stuffed them into that box the day she'd been forced out of the family home, her heart heavy and her eyes full. It had been no wrench at all leaving Colin behind but the children, that had been quite a different thing. But that was all behind her now. Liza and Will had forgiven her and their relationship had never been stronger. She picked out some photos of the kids when they were small and put them on the pile for framing.

Last of all, she picked up an assortment of items that

had been rolled up into a plastic bag. They were the things she'd kept from when she and her parents had cleared out Granny Wilde's home after her death. Netta had never been particularly close to her maternal grandmother, Mavis Corcoran, but Ada Wilde had been a constant in her life. When she was little, they always seemed to be at Granny Wilde's and, even when she was older, she often found herself there.

Her mum made no secret of the fact that she loved Ada dearly and the feeling was obviously mutual. In truth, she was far closer to Ada than to her own mother. Nanny Corcoran was always a distant figure who they hardly ever visited and when she died, it didn't seem to make a scrap of difference to Netta's mum. You would have thought they were acquaintances instead of mother and daughter. Contrast that to the effect Ada's death had on her and the difference made it all the more shocking.

As far as Netta was aware, Nanny Corcoran hadn't done anything to warrant such apathy, but it was difficult to know for sure because her mum rarely talked about her childhood. All Netta really knew was that her grandfather, Len Corcoran, had been unpleasant and no one mourned his passing. And she'd only found that out from her dad quite recently. The only other thing Netta knew was that her mum idolised Ada and, knowing Ada as she did, she could understand why.

Considering Ada was brought up in the poverty of the inner-city slums of Birmingham, she was considerably well read and cultured. She'd once told Netta that she'd only married Arthur's dad, Alf, because she was sick of sharing a bed with her sisters, and when she was married she found that sharing with just one man wasn't all it was cracked up to be either. So the war came as a bit of a blessing in that respect. At least she got to sleep on her own for once. There was no need to make any adjustment after the war either, because Alf left her within a week of coming home. Another blessing, as far as Ada was concerned. She maintained that being a single parent had given her the impetus to make something of herself, so that she could provide for her son. It was the gateway for her to be herself, without having to ask anyone's permission.

When Ada died, it shook the Wilde household to the very core. She was ninety-two and yet no one expected her to go so soon. It felt as if Ada had been snatched away from them, too early, and it took a long time for them to get over losing her. To be honest, Netta wasn't sure if her mum had actually got over it yet.

Rummaging through the bundle of cards and photographs, Netta found what she was looking for. It was a folding picture frame that opened out like a triptych. It held three photos. In the middle was a young Ada holding a baby. Netta's dad. To one side was her dad as a small boy. To the other, her mum and dad on their wedding day looking like a couple of trendy mods.

The frame was coming apart and the glass in one of them had cracked. It had been that way since she moved into this house but she hadn't got round to reframing it. She carefully edged the photos out to keep them from tearing. She took the one of Ada and her dad out first. Next, she took out the picture of her dad.

Frank came in from the kitchen with two mugs of steaming coffee.

'What's that you've got?'

'It's my dad.' She handed it to him.

He examined the sturdy, sunny little boy beaming back at him. 'He hasn't changed much.'

Netta held up the frame. 'Look at this one. Mum and Dad on their wedding day.'

'Wow. I should have guessed they'd be mods. Your mum was pretty hot. I can see where you get it from.'

She poked him in the side. 'That's my mum you're talking about, you pervert.'

She tried to take the last photo out but it was wedged in and so was the glass. Frank went back to the kitchen and found a flat knife to prise it out with. With great care, she slid the knife in behind the photo and managed to lift it slightly from the backing, then she inched it out slowly until there was enough for her to hold onto, with pinched fingers.

When the photo was halfway out, they could see the problem. There was something behind it. A piece of yellowing paper, folded into the shape of the frame. She carried on edging the picture out from behind the glass, until it was free and the glass itself was loose enough to slide out without ripping the paper.

Opening it as delicately as she could, she spread the paper out on her new desk. It was a letter. More of a note really. Unsigned, but it could only have been from one person. He'd died when she was a baby, but from what her dad had said about him, it had to have been from Len Corcoran. She read it again, and again, because she couldn't quite believe what she was reading:

*'I know what you're up to, you filthy bitch. Don't think I'm going to let you sully my daughter with your dirty ways. You and that queer you call a son.*

*You send our Geraldine home, or I'll have the police on you.*

*Send her home tomorrow and don't expect her back.'*

'Shit. What the fuck is this?' said Frank from over her shoulder.

'I think it's from my mum's dad, to Ada. It's vile. He sounds horrible.'

'Yes, he does. He obviously wasn't too keen on your dad. I'm assuming that's who he's referring to – probably just because your dad liked to dress in the trendy fashions. That was all very new in those days. I expect the older men found it a bit threatening.'

Netta shook her head. 'No, there's more to it than that. All that stuff about sending mum home. And anyway, he wasn't just insulting Dad. Look what he said about Ada. How could anyone say such things?'

'What will you do with it?'

'I don't know. I feel I should show it to Mum and Dad. Ada must have kept it for a reason. Perhaps they'll know what it was.'

'Net, are you sure that's wise? Your mum and dad seem perfectly happy as they are. They may not welcome being reminded that her old man was a nasty old shite.'

'I know, but…'

She didn't know what to say. Her instincts told her that they should see this, but she knew he didn't necessarily see it the same way.

She waited until Tuesday, after her shift at the foodbank, to go to her parents' house. Frank had cautioned against rushing straight over there without thinking through the consequences, but it had been two days and it was eating away at her.

Her mum answered the door.

'Hello love, this is a nice surprise. Your dad's taken Minnie up to the allotments to help Clyde out again, so it's just me. Just come from the foodbank, have you? I'll make some tea. I expect you could do with a cup.'

Netta followed her into the kitchen and watched her mother make the drinks. She was dithering. She'd hoped her dad would be here to help things along. She'd been planning all day, unable to concentrate on anything solid. But now she was here, she didn't know what to do. Perhaps she should wait for him. Perhaps she was wrong and Frank was right, and the last thing her mother wanted, was to be reminded that her father was a vicious-tongued arsehole. But it was the words he'd used to describe Ada that drove her on. The kind of words that no one should ever use to describe Ada. They'd compelled her to come here and find out why he would say such things.

'When do you think Dad'll be back?'

'A couple of hours yet. He loses all track of time when he's down there. I reckon he'll get one himself soon. Don't know what I'll do then. Have to get myself a pair of wellies and join him I suppose. Or else I shall never see him. Or Minnie.'

She looked quite pleased about it. Time was, she'd have been quite tetchy about that sort of thing but these days she was a lot better about embracing change. Perhaps that was a good sign.

'Was there something you wanted to see him about?' said her mum.

'Both of you really. I was going through Granny's things the other day and I found a letter tucked away behind one of her old photos. I thought you might have seen it before. I … I … think it might be from your dad.'

But for a slight twitch of the mouth and the inklings of a grimace, the change in her mum's countenance was almost imperceptible, but Netta could see her stiffening.

'What on earth makes you think your gran would have a letter from my dad? They only lived a few miles apart. If he had anything to say to her, I'm sure he'd have come to see her.'

Netta took the letter from her bag and handed it to her mother.

Her mum held it between her fingers and stared at it, like it was something alien to her. After what seemed like an age, she sighed and unfolded it. She scanned it quickly. Had she had time to read it? Netta couldn't be sure. She refolded the letter then handed it back to her.

'Tucked behind a photo, you said? Very strange.'

'Have you seen it before?'

'No, never.'

'Do you recognise the handwriting?'

'Yes, of course. It's Len Corcoran's.'

'Mum, the things he's written. They're so…'

'Malicious? Yes, well that was him all over. He was a nasty man.'

'I know. Dad told me.'

'Did he? What did he say?'

'He just said he was a horrible man and nobody grieved for him when he died.'

She snorted. 'He was right there. That man was a mean and vile brute who drank himself stupid every night, and made our lives a misery. He never had a decent word to say about anyone, and we all despised him. That's all this is, Netta. It was typical of him. He was jealous, that's all. Ada had made something of herself. She was a wonderful, gracious woman who was admired and loved by everyone and he hated that, because he was nothing. And he didn't like the idea of her improving me, either. Thought I was getting above myself just because Ada used to take me to the museum, or gave me a book to read. And as for that rubbish about your dad, that's all it is. Not that there's anything wrong with being gay, but your dad was very much a full-blooded male and still is. I can assure you of that.'

Netta shuddered. 'Mum! I didn't need to know that.'

'Well if you don't like what you hear, maybe it'll teach you not to poke your nose in other people's business.'

Netta bristled. This was not going the way she'd hoped. She could have kicked herself for not waiting for her dad. He'd have taken it a lot better. He'd have made it a lot easier too.

'I'm sorry, Mum. I just thought—'

'Just thought what? Just thought you'd get me all riled up over nothing? Just thought you'd upset me with this, this filth from a man who hated everyone, and everyone hated back?'

'No, I didn't mean to upset you. I didn't think—'

'Yes, well, that's the problem with you, Netta. You just don't think.'

Her mum tapped the table with her right hand then suddenly stopped and clasped her hands together.

Netta took a deep breath to calm herself down. She had to try to rescue this.

'I really am sorry, Mum. I can see now, I was wrong but I just thought you might want to see it, as it was from your dad.'

'Well you're wrong, on all counts. I didn't want to see it, and he wasn't my dad.'

## 15

# BACK TO THE BEGINNING
### GERALDINE – 2019

Geraldine flushed the toilet for the third time, but the bathroom still smelled of sick. She sprayed some cleaner all around the bowl. After a good scrub of that, she did the same to the sink. Then she washed her face, brushed her teeth, and cleaned the sink again. The smell seemed to have gone but she cleaned the floor, just in case she'd splashed it.

Satisfied that she'd managed to destroy all traces of her undoing, she went into the bedroom and lay sideways on the bed, curled up like an unborn baby. How could Netta have done that to her? She began to whimper. The whimper turned into a howl. Her own daughter. How could she have been so cruel?

Netta wasn't to know, of course, but if only she'd stopped to think. She should have known better than to bring that disgusting letter here. Especially since Arthur had told her what a vile man Len Corcoran was. But then, Arthur didn't really know just how vile that was. She'd never actually told him.

She began to wonder what exactly Arthur had said to Netta, given the limits of his knowledge about her family.

She'd always done her best to shield him from her early life. It wasn't something she ever wanted to think about herself, let alone talk about. Talking about it made it all the more real, and reality had its own special way of sullying the most precious things in life.

She wiped her eyes. Arthur telling Netta about her unhappy childhood? That was funny – the blind leading the hare-brained. If she wasn't so upset, she'd be laughing. She tried to imagine how the conversation had gone, and when they'd had it. Neither of them had mentioned it before, but that was nothing new. They often talked about her behind her back. They had their own secret code, specifically about her. She'd worked that one out years ago, but she didn't let on. They liked to think she was stupid. Someone to feel sorry for. Well, let them think it. Let them fool themselves.

She'd almost set fire to that letter, there and then, but she was worried Netta would have read something into her reaction. Something Geraldine preferred to remain buried. Not wanting to draw attention to herself, she'd stupidly given the letter back to Netta, and offhandedly suggested she should bin it. It was only now that Geraldine realised, she should have kept it and put a match to it herself. Netta had a habit of doing things her own way, regardless of the chaos she caused, and the prospect of her not destroying it was a strong possibility. More than that, there was every chance she would mention it to Arthur in one of their secret chats, in spite of Geraldine's implicit instructions not to bother him with it. It may not be next week, or even next month, but sooner or later, Netta would show Arthur that letter. And then, there'd be no turning back. He'd see Geraldine for what she really was, and she'd lose him.

The trepidation began to rise in her. Her insides were like hot liquid bubbling, swaying, and sloshing around. She pulled her knees up tighter. So tight, she began to feel sick again. It was no good. If she didn't get moving she'd be back in the bathroom with her head in the bowl. She got up and ran to the dressing table. She needed to do the thing, quickly. She stroked the top of the table, then tapped – one, two, three, four – stroke; one, two, three, four – stroke; one, two, three, four – stroke. Twelve taps and four strokes altogether.

Geraldine waited for the pains in her stomach and chest to go away, but they were still there. Her breathing was so tight and that liquid was threatening to come up and out. She tried the thing again. Still no better. If anything, it was getting worse. She could hardly stand now. It was no good, she was going to have to go back the beginning. She lurched for the nearest wall and flattened herself against it. It was cool against her sweat-filled brow and felt good. But there was only one thing that would make her truly better, something she hadn't done in years.

Placing her right palm flat against the wall she followed its surface along to the corner, then did the same on the next one. Without removing her hand, she stepped around or over obstacles, and didn't stop until she reached her starting point. In total, she went round four times; always the same direction; never removing the hand, until the very end.

Her back against the wall, she slid down to the floor. She felt calmer – no more sickness or tightness. The light outside was nearly gone and the room was only half-lit. Arthur would be on his way home. He'd come in and find her here in the dark. A useless blob, and no dinner in the oven either. Normally that would have bothered her, but it didn't seem to matter anymore. All she could think about was poor, sad Geraldine Corcoran and the year her life changed forever.

## 16

## PHIL'S THEORY

GERALDINE – 1961

Geraldine pulled the blanket up over her ears, but it was no good. She could still hear the row downstairs. She shuffled further down the bed and put the pillow over her head. Even that couldn't drown out the noise.

She sometimes wondered if it was all in her mind and not really happening at all, if her dad wasn't really battering her mum in the room beneath her. She'd have liked to believe that, but she'd seen too many morning-after bruises for it to be true. She knew that when she got up tomorrow, some part of her mum would be black and blue and no one would say a word about it. No one in the family, and no one in the neighbourhood. Her mum would do her best to hide the bruises and make out everything was normal. She'd stop and talk to the neighbours over the garden fence, or on the way to the shops, and not one of them would mention tonight's racket, or the mess she was in. As far as they were concerned, it wasn't their business. Even if her mum ended up dead one night.

Geraldine hoped Tony and Ralph were sleeping through

it, which was hardly likely. It was a rare Saturday night when they weren't woken up by the sound of their dad shouting his mouth off, or their mum crying. Often both. Poor Ralph was so scared, he still wet the bed sometimes.

With nothing to muffle them, her dad's sharp, spiteful words penetrated her bedroom's bare floorboards: 'I should have thrown you out with those two bastards years ago, you filthy whore.'

It wasn't the first time she'd heard him say that, but it never failed to terrify Geraldine. Probably because of Phil's theory. Before he'd left home, Phil had told her that they were the two bastards in question. He was certain their dad had been in a Japanese POW camp from at least a year before he was born, until after she came along. Geraldine wasn't sure if she believed that, but it certainly explained why their dad picked on Phil more than any of them. With Geraldine, he didn't so much pick on her as ignore her, most of the time. But it was still enough to fill her with dread, whenever he was in the house.

When she was in the infant school, one of the teachers would gather them round on Friday afternoons and tell them stories. Usually, it was Geraldine's favourite part of the week, but one day she told them the story of the three little pigs. It made Geraldine cry. Some of the boys teased her about it. They chased her around the playground afterwards, shouting: 'I'm gonna huff and puff and blow your house down.' They didn't understand. How could they? She wasn't crying because she was scared that the wolf was at their door. She was crying because, even at that young age, she knew it was already too late. The wolf wasn't trying to blow their house down. He was already living inside and, sooner or later, he was going to gobble them all up.

The sound of her mum begging for forgiveness was enough to make Geraldine's insides tighten into a hard knot. She pulled her knees up closer to ease the pain but the tightness moved its way up to her lungs. She could hardly breathe. She had to get some air. She crept quietly over to the window and opened it enough for the autumn night to give her some relief.

When breathing became easier she placed her hand on the wall and traced it from one corner to the next, until she'd gone all the way round and come back to the window. Still jittery, she went round again, a little more slowly this time. By the time she'd returned to the window, she was calmer.

It was a new thing this walk. Something she'd started after Phil left. She didn't know why, but touching the walls like this, feeling the room around her, it helped to block everything else out. She closed the window and noticed that the noise downstairs had stopped. Perhaps they could all sleep now.


The next morning she got up as normal and helped her mum in the kitchen. There were no bruises on her mum's face but, when her mum rolled up her sleeves, Geraldine spotted some new ones that hadn't been there before.

Her dad got up late and sat in his armchair, brooding over the paper. Ralph and Tony stayed out, only coming in for Sunday dinner.

After dinner, her dad went straight out to the pub. He had a set pattern on Sundays. He went to the pub until they threw him out for afternoon closing. Instead of coming home, he visited his mother, Ma Corcoran, and stayed for his tea. Then he went back to the pub, until they threw him out again.

The relief was visible as soon as he was out of sight. Her mum and brothers settled down to watch the afternoon film. Normally Geraldine did the same, but today she was meeting Phil in town.

Before going out, she changed into the new dress and cardigan she'd bought with the money she was allowed to keep from her wages. While she was on the bus, she put on some lipstick that Ruby had given her from the old stock. Ada normally let Ruby have them but she said it was the wrong colour for her. Geraldine eyed herself in the little compact mirror Ruby had also given her. She was looking quite sophisticated. She wondered what Bree would make of her now.

She got off the bus by the Bull Ring and strolled along the quiet streets towards the cathedral. It was a nice day and, even though everywhere was closed, it was great to be away from home. Geraldine hadn't seen Phil in ages and was really looking forward to spending some time with him.

When she reached the cathedral she scanned the grounds that surrounded it. There were a lot of kids her age, and a bit older, hanging around in groups on the grass. Some of them sat around two boys playing guitars, doing their best to sound like the Everly Brothers. It was all quite exciting. She wandered across the grass, checking for familiar faces. She wasn't just looking for Phil; she knew Arthur and Karen sometimes came here. It was Karen who'd told her it was a great place to hang out on Sunday afternoons, which was why she'd suggested it to Phil. Although she did have an ulterior motive. She was hoping she might bump into Arthur. Not that she'd told Phil. She hadn't told anyone she fancied Arthur. Not even Karen. Karen had probably guessed though.

To Geraldine's disappointment, Arthur was nowhere to be seen. She spotted Phil on one of the benches. He was smartly dressed in a sharp-looking suit. He'd been a teddy boy for a while but that didn't last too long, although he still wore his hair in a quiff. He looked her up and down as she got closer.

'All right, bab. You're looking proper grown-up.'

'Thanks,' she said, feeling pleased with herself. She pointed to the group around the boy singers. 'Do you wanna go and sit over there?'

'Nah, you're all right. I might mess up the threads. What do you think of them?'

'Very smart. I'm honoured.'

She stopped herself from saying 'but a bit over the top for a Sunday afternoon.' She couldn't help wishing he'd dressed down more so that they could sit with the other kids. She would have liked to have been part of that crowd, maybe with Arthur sitting on the grass next to her.

Phil grinned. 'It's not for you. I'm going to tea at my girl's parents' house after. Her name's Cissy. She lives in Solihull.'

'They must be posh.'

'Yeah, they are. They've got a big house with two toilets. Both inside.'

Geraldine's eyes widened. Phil was going up in the world.

'Serious, is it?'

'I think so. We'll see. Anyway, how's things at home? Old Grunt being his usual self, I suppose?'

The boys were singing 'Cathy's Clown'. Some of the kids were dancing along to it and Geraldine wished again that she was part of that crowd. She wanted to be dancing on the grass with Phil, and with nothing on her mind but music and having fun. She didn't want to be sitting on a bench, with him in his best suit, being forced to recall last night. But Phil was waiting for an answer.

'He was at it again last night. Talking about the bastards.'

'Us, you mean.'

'You don't know that for sure, Phil.'

'Yes I do. I saw Uncle Paddy in the pub a couple of weeks ago. You know what he's like after a few drinks. Can't keep his mouth shut. So, I asked him when the old man was in that POW camp. He said he went missing just before Christmas 1942, and they didn't know he was alive until after the war. He reckoned Grunt didn't come straight back either. It was just after you were born, according to Paddy. Now do you believe me?'

'Maybe.'

If it had been someone other than one of her dad's brothers she might have been more likely to, but the Corcorans were all as bad as each other. She didn't trust any of them to know the truth, let alone speak it. In some ways, she wanted to believe it as much as Phil. He hated Grunt so much that he would rather face the consequences of being an actual bastard than be his son. Geraldine was more reticent in that regard but then, it was easier for boys. No one was going to point the finger at him and say he was probably as loose as his mother. And, if they did, he could easily punch their lights out. Girls weren't quite so able to get away with it. Despite that, the idea of not being related to Len Corcoran and his repulsive family had its appeal, but she needed to hear it from someone more reliable than Uncle Paddy.

Of course, Phil was so desperate to distance himself from their dad, that he'd ignored one obvious question. Unless he didn't care, as long as he could prove he wasn't Len Corcoran's son.

'But if he's not our dad? Then, who is?'

Phil shrugged. 'No idea.'

**17**

## WHAT HAVE YOU DONE?

NETTA – 2019

Netta's mum didn't come for the walk that Sunday. She never missed the Sunday walks but Netta's dad said she was feeling a bit under the weather. As usual, they both understood what that meant, so neither of them passed any further comment on it but, in her heart, Netta knew it was the letter. The look on her mum's face had been enough to make her realise that she'd made a terrible mistake. She really should have listened to Frank and kept it to herself.

It wasn't the first time she'd rushed in and done something that she thought was right without fully considering the ramifications. If it had been the first, then she may have been able to cut herself some slack but, the truth was, she had form for being this stupid. She had to stop doing it, and she had to make things right. So she said nothing to her dad about the letter. She was following her mum's wishes. One of them anyway. She couldn't bring herself to throw it away yet.

'Do you think your mum's all right?' said Frank.

They were standing, side by side, on the front path, waving everyone off.

'I don't know.'

'You showed her the letter?'

She hadn't yet confessed to him that she'd screwed up but he'd guessed.

'Yes. Before you ask, it didn't go down well.'

He nodded slowly. 'Does your dad know about it?'

She shook her head.

'Are you going to tell him?'

'I don't know. She asked me not to. I've fucked up, haven't I?'

He put his arm around her and pulled her closer, without answering. He didn't need to. She already knew what he was too kind to confirm.

He said again: 'Are you going to tell him?'

'Probably. When the time's right. I'll go and see her at the end of the week. Give her time to work it through. I'll think about showing him after that.'


As it turned out, there was no need to wait until the end of the week. When she and Kelly got home from work on Wednesday evening, her dad's car was outside and he was in the kitchen with Frank.

'All right, Art? What are you doing here?' Kelly was obviously doing her best to make the situation seem normal, but they could tell by her dad's agitation that it was anything but.

Ignoring Kelly, he turned to Netta and said: 'It's your mum. She's really not well.'

'Do you mean not well, as in hospital not well, or as in Mum not well?' said Netta.

'Not hospital, but I've never seen her this bad. I'm not

quite sure what to do. She won't tell me what's wrong, and she won't see a doctor. I'm all out of ideas.'

Frank raised his eyebrows at Netta and gave a slight nod of the head.

'Kelly, I think we need to give Netta and Arthur a few minutes alone.'

He ushered Kelly outside and, for once, Kelly did as she was told without comment.

Her dad waited for them to close the back door.

'Netta, is something going on that I don't know about? Frank's being very mysterious, you're being cagey and your mum's taken to her bed and won't tell me why. If something's happened, you need to tell me. I mean it, Netta. I really do. Tell me. Now.'

She cleared her throat. 'I found a letter, in Granny Wilde's things. I showed it to her.'

'What letter?'

'It was from her dad. I found it hidden in a broken picture frame.'

'From her dad?' For a moment he looked as if he couldn't quite take in what she was saying. 'Where is it now?'

'In my desk. Mum told me to bin it but I–'

'Show me.'

Netta went in to the study, her dad following behind her. She'd never in her entire life seen him so angry. She took the letter out of the desk drawer and handed it to him.

He read it quickly, then again more slowly. He shoved the letter into his trouser pocket and shook his head.

'Oh Netta. What have you done?'


Netta was still reeling with the guilt of what Liza and Kelly were calling, Lettergate. Neither she nor Frank had told them what the letter actually said, but that didn't stop the girls speculating. Her dad had taken it with him on Wednesday, and told her to stay away for a while. But it was Saturday afternoon, Kings Heath Market was closing up, and they'd just packed away their remaining stock. They were only up the road from her parents' house and she could wait no longer.

Kelly's nan's care home wasn't too far from Netta's mum and dad, so she dropped her off on the way. Kelly was chattering on about all the things her nan was doing at this new place and how it had given her a new lease of life, but Netta was only half-listening. She had other things on her mind, like the way her dad had said to her: 'What have you done?' She had a feeling she was about to find out.

At first, Netta thought her dad wasn't going to let her in. It seemed to take a long time before he decided to let her cross the front door threshold.

'Your mum's upstairs. I'll see if she'll see you.'

Again, it seemed like she'd been standing in the hall for ages before he came back down.

'She'll see you. Don't tire her out. She's been up all night.'

The bedroom was in semi-darkness. The blackout style curtains her parents favoured were closed, even though the winter sun was shining outside. There was an unpleasant smell in the air. Vomit and sweat. Her mum was in the middle of the bed, propped up by several pillows, and partially hidden by the quilt pulled up high. She looked small. A tiny grey dot in a mound of duck down. Just one frail hand protruded from her protective bed linen. It was placed on Minnie, who was lying next to her. Her mum was staring at one of the walls and made no attempt to acknowledge Netta's presence.

One of the dining room chairs was next to the bed. Netta sat down on it.

'Hello, Mum. I thought I'd stop by to see how you are. We've been doing the market today. We did okay, but we missed your sales patter. Neil sends his love.'

The sound of Neil's name brought a flicker of recognition across her mum's face.

'He said to get well soon. We need you on the stall.'

Netta's mum turned her head slowly and gave her a cold, hard stare, as if she despised her. The shock of it made Netta sit back and ask herself the same question that had fallen from her dad's lips earlier that week, what the fuck had she done?

Her dad came in with some drinks. He gave one to her mum and sat on the other side of the bed, next to Minnie.

'Try and drink it, sweetheart. It's quite weak, so you might be able to keep it down.'

Her mum gave it back to him. 'In a minute, I promise. Arthur, will you take Minnie for a walk? She needs some exercise.'

'If that's what you want, Gee. Netta, will you keep Mum company until I get back?'

'Yes, of course.'

If that look of revulsion was anything to go by, she wasn't sure that her mum really wanted her there, but she knew what her dad was hinting at. He was afraid to leave her mum alone.

They sat in silence until the front door shut. Her mum edged herself up slightly and looked towards the window. 'Has he gone?'

Netta went over to the window and opened the curtains slightly to watch her dad and Minnie walking down the street. 'Yes.'

'Did you bring the letter?'

She returned to the chair. 'Dad has it.'

'So you've shown it to him, even though I told you not to?'

'I had no choice, Mum. He's so worried about you, and so am I.'

Her mouth contorted into a hideous sneer.

'Come off it. You never worry about anyone but yourself.'

## 18

## DISHWATER, GNAT'S WEE AND A LATE REGRET

GERALDINE – 2019

Netta looked stunned. Stunned and appalled. As if she was trying to work out just who this person was that was lying in her mother's bed, looking like her mother, but acting like a madwoman. A nasty, spiteful one at that.

Geraldine could tell her accusation had stung her. It was the eyes that gave it away. Windows to the soul they called them, didn't they? That was certainly true in Netta's case. From a little girl you only had to look at those eyes and you could tell exactly what she was thinking – good, bad, sad, or downright distasteful. She always had the most dazzling eyes – dark blue windows to the soul. No wonder men fell for her the way they did. Arthur reckoned she got them from her. Geraldine couldn't say. Aside from making sure she looked neat and tidy, she wasn't one for staring at herself in the mirror. Pointless, when all you saw was ugliness. So, she had no idea if he was right or wrong, but he would know. It was the first thing he'd noticed about her, apparently. The first thing he'd loved about her.

She looked into her daughter's eyes now. Her precious

only child. She hated hurting her like this, but it was for her own good.

'You should have ripped it up when you found it. We'd have been none the wiser if you had. Ada should have destroyed it. I don't know why she kept it.'

'But why did she have it in the first place? Why was he telling Ada to send you back home? I don't understand.'

'You're not supposed to understand. I don't want you to understand. It's my business, not yours. And not your father's either. At least it was, until you stuck your size nines in it.'

'But if we don't know, how can we do anything about it? Please Mum, let us help. Let me help.'

'You can't help. No one can. You've just made it worse.'

Netta's eyes were wet. Geraldine swallowed down her own tears. She'd been sick so many times that her throat was raw. She took a sip of the insipid tea that Arthur had brought up for her. It was quite revolting. Why he thought drip feeding her this gnat's wee would make her feel better, she had no idea.

Netta was giving her one of her earnest looks, and those bloody eyes were pleading for absolution. This is what she'd done to her family. Her husband was on eggshells again and her daughter, a blubbing wreck. Geraldine wanted to hold Netta tight and say she understood. She wanted to tell her not to worry, that everything would be all right, but she couldn't. She had to push her way. She had to push them all away – Netta, Arthur, Liza and Will. It was the only way to save them from her.

'If you really want to help, you'll go away and stay away.'

Netta gasped. 'Do you hate me that much?'

'Don't be silly. Of course not, but I'm no good for you.

I'm not a nice person, Netta. Surely, even you've worked that one out yourself. And when all this comes out…'

'All what comes out?'

The front door opened and closed. Arthur was back. He came straight up and stuck his head around the door. Minnie slipped around his legs, jumped up onto the bed and put her head on Geraldine's lap. Geraldine played with the dog's soft ears. Minnie was such a comfort.

Arthur picked up the cold tea.

'Shall I make you another one, sweetheart? You must be parched.'

She nodded. 'Maybe a bit stronger, love?'

'That's the spirit. What about you, Netta?'

'Netta was just leaving,' said Geraldine.

Arthur and Netta exchanged looks. They were doing that secret code again. She'd put money on them talking about her as soon as they got downstairs.

'I'll come back tomorrow,' said Netta.

She hovered over the bed for a minute, presumably waiting for a reply, or maybe a kiss. Geraldine hoped her silence conveyed the message that she couldn't quite bring herself to speak – 'Don't come'.

Netta and Arthur went downstairs, leaving the bedroom door ajar for Minnie to come and go. Geraldine strained her ears to hear what they were whispering, but they were too good at it and she could hear nothing. She sank back down into the bed. It was beginning to smell. By rights, she should have changed the bed linen by now and, what with all this vomiting and lack of showering … well. Ada would be appalled. Normally that would trouble her, but Ada had let her down. Ada had let their secret out.

She heard Arthur on the stairs and closed her eyes. He

tiptoed in, placed the tea quietly next to the bed, and tiptoed back out again. Eggshells.

When she was sure he was gone, she sat up and took a sip of the tea. Dishwater. A step up from gnat's wee but dishwater, none the less. Nearly sixty years she'd known him and he still hadn't learned to make a decent cuppa.

Sixty years. That was a lifetime for some people. Funny really. If she had been allowed to stay on at school and make something of herself, she might have been able to keep her head down, until she was able to get a good job and earn enough money to rent a flat with Bree. She might have been a great success. Just like Bree. She might even have found the courage to stand up to Len Corcoran. She might not be the hideous, wretched person she was now. How wonderful to be someone else. Someone who was strong and confident.

A tear rolled down Geraldine's cheek. For the first time in her life, she regretted ever meeting Ada and Arthur Wilde.

## 19

## SIR ART, THE KNIGHT IN SHINING ARMOUR

GERALDINE – 1961

'Mrs Wilde's asked me to do a few extra hours in the build up to Christmas. Just Thursday, Friday and Saturdays.' Geraldine held her breath and waited for her dad to say something.

'Oh ar, and what did you tell her?' He didn't look at her. He hardly ever looked at anyone. He just carried on shovelling his tea into his mouth.

'I said I'd have to ask if it was all right.'

'She paying you, is she?'

'Yes.'

'Double time?'

'Time and a half.'

'That would come in handy, Len. For Christmas, I mean,' said Geraldine's mum.

'My money not good enough for yer, then?' he snarled.

Geraldine flinched. For a second, she thought she was going to be sick. She was trying to work out if her dad was going to erupt and if he was, who was going to get it. It would have been easier to do if she was brave enough to watch him but if he caught her, she'd probably be the one he chose.

On the other side of the table, Tony and Ralph kept their eyes on their plates and were trying to eat without making any noise.

'Of course it is love, but I just meant it would be a bit extra. Give you a bit of a break so's you could have that Christmas drink you missed out on last year. What with our Phil moving out, and now Janet's expecting … well.'

Even their mum was scared he was going to blow. You could tell by the way she was fidgeting with the tablecloth and trying to make everything sound perfectly normal.

'Well what?'

'Well … she'll be so close to her time, she won't want to be cooking. I thought it might be nice to have her and Trev here for their dinner.'

'Did yer now? And when were you going to mention it to me?'

'I only thought of it today, love. You know I wouldn't say anything before asking you.'

Her dad threw his plate into the middle of the table and sat back. Geraldine, her brothers and her mum all held their breaths. Len Corcoran had only two moods. Dark and darker. They were all waiting to see which one he would grace them with today. All hoping it would be simply dark. Dark, they could just about cope with.

'Tell her you can do it,' he said at last, 'but don't expect any tea when you get back. If you're not here when it's put on the table, you don't get none.'

The chair scraped on the lino as he got up.

'And the money comes straight in here. No dipping into it. We'll need it if we've got two extra mouths to feed over Christmas.'

He walked away and everyone else sank down into their seats, like four balloons deflating. Tony's eyes widened and he did a silent tut. One of these days he was going to get caught and then there'd be trouble. Ralph looked as if he was about to burst into tears. Later, when Grunt was at the pub, she'd give them both the sweets Ada let her have. That would cheer him up.

Geraldine helped her mum clear the table. The boys sneaked out of the back door. Ralph was going to his friend's, a few doors down. Tony would hang around on the street corner with his mates. They'd both come back when their dad went out.

Her mum started the washing up and Geraldine stood by with the tea towel, ready to dry. The telly was on in the living room. Grunt was watching the news.

'Don't worry love, I'll put something by for you to eat. You can have it when he's gone out,' whispered her mum.

'It's all right Mum, Ada said I can eat with them. It'll be easier if I do that, won't it? He'll be none the wiser, so he can't go off on one.'


She couldn't sleep that night for the excitement, daft as it was getting excited about working extra hours. She loved being at the shop. Ruby was so funny. Always telling silly stories about her kids and her men friends. When she was in, the time just flew by, and even more so on Saturdays when Karen was there. At first, she'd missed school and Bree, but having a new friend in Karen made it easier to bear. But she also treasured the time she spent alone with Ada.

Ada Wilde was the nicest, cleverest woman she'd ever met. Even cleverer than her teachers, as far as Geraldine could see. Not only had she started a business on her own, from a market stall, but she'd also gone on to educate herself at night school.

Ada was always giving her little presents too – books to read and a couple of really nice dresses that Ada said she didn't wear anymore, but they were in perfectly good nick. She sent sweets for Geraldine's brothers, and the ends of stock for her mum. She didn't make a fuss about it either, like she was being charitable or anything. She'd just say something like: 'Oh by the way love, are these any good to you? They'll only go to waste if not.' As if you were doing her a favour by taking them. Strange to think Ada and her mum came from the same street and were nearly the same age. You'd never have guessed it to look at them.

The other reason she liked being at the shop, was Arthur. With the build up to Christmas, he'd been spending more time behind the counter and they'd become friends. She still fancied him madly but he was spoken for. Karen told her he had a girlfriend called Tina who went to the girls' grammar school, next door to his school. Arthur never mentioned Tina and Geraldine was convinced Karen was wrong, until this week when Tina turned up at the shop, all moon eyes and giggly. It was obvious then that they were courting and Arthur didn't think of Geraldine as anything more than a friend.

Geraldine's consolation prize was that she got to hear all the latest pop singles, because Arthur was mad for them. He loved pop music, rock and roll and the American blues music. She'd never heard of half of them before. Ada liked it all too and she let him play them as often as he liked, on the radiogram, while they were eating. This was Geraldine's favourite time, when she could pretend that this was her family and that she wasn't part of that other family, a few miles up the road.


'When does Ada want you to start?' asked her mum the next morning.

Geraldine added some sugar to her Weetabix and mashed it up in the milk.

'This week. It's already getting busy. Even Arthur's had to help out.'

Her mum sat down at the table.

'Arthur? That's Ada's boy isn't it? He's about the same age as you, isn't he?'

'Six months older, I think.'

'See a lot of him in the shop, do you?'

'No, not really,' she said, trying to sound vague and disinterested. She didn't want her mum knowing she was sweet on Arthur. She might tell Grunt. 'He's still at school. He's just been helping out after, now it's getting busy, with it being Christmas.'

'I've seen him about. Seems like a nice enough lad, if you like that sort of thing. Quite a sharp dresser. Takes after his mum that way. She always did like her clothes, did Ada. Knew how to dress to look better than she was. I reckon that's why Alf fancied her, seeing as he fancied himself so much. He was another one for the clothes, and showing off. Probably thought she'd look good on his arm. Didn't last long though, did it? For all her airs and graces, he still buggered off, first chance he got.'

'She seems to be doing all right on her own,' said Geraldine. She didn't like the way her mum spoke about Ada, especially considering Ada was always giving them food and stuff. She'd never noticed it before, but her mum could be quite two-faced sometimes.

'Ada will always fall on her feet. She's made that way. If she wants something, she'll get it. And good for her, I say. I don't judge her for it. If I was like her, I'd have been long gone and taken you lot with me. But I'm not, and that's my look out. And as for that boy of hers, if your dad's right about him, you're wasting your time my love.'

'What do you mean?'

'He's a pansy. According to your dad, anyway. Mind you, he thinks any bloke who doesn't wear a flat cap's a pansy, so I wouldn't set too much store by his words. Just you be careful my girl. If he's anything like Alf, he'll get you into trouble and won't stick around long enough to wet the baby's head.'

'He's not my boyfriend, Mum. I hardly know him. Anyway, he's already got a girlfriend.'

Her mum smiled. 'Is that so?'

On Thursday, they put up some Christmas decorations in the shop. Ada had bought some extra Christmas stock, and the shop was full to brimming. Somehow, they managed to find space for a tinsel Christmas tree that they took their time in decorating.

'We've got some of these in stock. If customers see one up, looking nice, they'll be more inclined to buy them,' said Ada. She was canny like that, always thinking of ways to get people to part with their money.

One of those ways was the Christmas Club. Customers paid in as much as they could throughout the year, to help pay for some extras. They were already coming in with their club cards to redeem the money they'd put by. Most popular were the family-sized tins of biscuits, Quality Street and Roses. Dates and jellied fruits were going quickly too, along with tins of salmon and ham.

Except for sour-faced old Mrs Price, everyone was in a good mood and it was so lovely in the shop that Geraldine didn't want the day to end. She took as long as she could to eat her dinner in the flat upstairs but eventually she had to go home. She thanked Ada for the meal and got up to go.

'Arthur will walk you home,' said Ada. 'There are too many idiots drinking too much at this time of year. He'll make sure you get home without being accosted.'

Geraldine was about to say she'd be all right, but Arthur went to fetch his coat. It appeared to already have been settled. It was an unexpected bonus and she accepted the offer, even though she was sure that none of the drunks would notice her. She doubted that Arthur would really be able to look after her, if it came to it. She knew he definitely wasn't a pansy, but he was very gentle and sweet. Most likely, she'd have to look after him.


'You don't really have to walk me home, if you don't want to,' she said as they made their way along the High Street.

'Who says I don't want to? It gets me out of homework, and I like talking to you. You're the only person who doesn't get bored within two minutes when I talk about music,' he said.

'I bet Tina doesn't get bored.'

Arthur looked amused. 'Don't be so sure. Talking of which, I've just bought that Ray Charles single, 'Hit the Road Jack'. Do you like it?'

'Oh yes, I love it.'

'I'll play it for you tomorrow, if you like?'

'Yes please.'

Two lads, a few years older than them, came tumbling out of a pub as they passed it. They looked like teddy boys. Arthur put up his arms to stop them falling into them.

'Whoa, watch it, fellas.'

One of them gave him a funny look and Geraldine froze. They were going to beat him up, surely?

'All right, Art,' said the other one. 'This your girl, is it?'

Arthur shook his head. 'Friend.'

The boy looked her up and down. 'Right. If you're looking for a fella, darlin, I'm available.'

Arthur laughed. 'She's not, mate. See you Sunday?'

'Yup. Sorry, love. We've had a bit to drink, but if you do change your mind, just tell Art to let me know.'

Arthur led her away.

'Sorry about that. They didn't mean any harm. But Mum was right. It's probably best if I walk you home.'

'Those boys don't go to your school do they?'

'No. They both work, in a factory somewhere. BSA I think. I see them around. We like a lot of the same music.'

'I thought for a minute they were going to hurt you.'

'That pair? I think I could do more damage to them than they could to me.'

Geraldine threw him a sceptical look.

Arthur shook his head. 'You don't believe me, do you? You think I'm a sop, just because I'm a grammar school kid.'

'No, no, I didn't mean…'

His cheeky grin cut her short.

'I'm only kidding. But in case you were worried, my uncles taught me how to box. My grandad was an amateur boxer and he taught all of his kids how to take care of themselves. Even my mum. She's got a great right hook, you know. You wouldn't want to get on the wrong side of her, believe me.'

Geraldine giggled. 'You're quite funny sometimes.'

'Only sometimes? I'm insulted. Crikey, it's cold. Are you warm enough?'

She was freezing. Her hands and toes were numb and there was every chance her nose was going to drop off with the cold. but it didn't matter: Arthur was walking her home.

'I'm all right, Art.'

He smirked. 'You've discovered my nickname, Miss Marple. Give me your hand.'

She looked at him, confused. Did he want to hold her hand?

He held his out. 'Give it to me.'

She pulled her hand out of her pocket. He removed his gloves and wrapped his hands around hers.

'I thought so. They're absolutely frozen. Put these on.'

Geraldine let him slide them onto her hands and felt the warmth of him, as soon as they were on. He took off his scarf and draped it around her neck, then pulled up his coat collar to shield himself against the cold air.

'Thank you,' she said, the words catching as they came out. If she wasn't careful, she was going to end up crying.

He shrugged. 'That's all right. Proper Sir Galahad, I am.'

'You are. Sir Art, my knight in shining armour.'

'You've been spending too much time with Karen.' He laughed again. 'I'm enjoying this walk. It's fun.'

She pulled the scarf up around her chin and breathed in his scent. 'Me too.'

'We must do it again sometime. How about tomorrow, and Saturday?'

'You're on.'

## 20

## SUCH A HEAVY BURDEN

GERALDINE – 2019

Netta was back again. She and Arthur were speaking in low voices, downstairs. She'd been here every day since Saturday.

Geraldine wasn't sure what day it was today. Probably Friday. Yes, Friday. It was a foodbank day for Netta. Funny how much she liked that place. Geraldine would never in a million years have thought her daughter would be one for doing that sort of thing. Especially after Colin Grey got his hooks into her.

Geraldine never liked Colin. And it wasn't just because she preferred Netta's first university boyfriend, Doogie. Although Doogie was lovely. Arthur had really liked him too. They got on terrifically. Hardly surprising, since they both loved music so much. They'd be up in Arthur's music room for hours sometimes, listening to his records.

There was just something genuine about Doogie that you couldn't help warming to. That's what Ada had said about him when she got to know him, and she was right. What's more, you could tell he absolutely worshipped Netta. Well, they worshipped each other really. That much was plain to see. Unlike Colin, who always seemed too in love with himself to care about anyone else. To this day, Geraldine couldn't understand why Netta ended up dumping Doogie and marrying that shifty, selfish piece of dog muck.

Still, Colin was gone now. Sort of. Given that he was the father of her grandchildren, they couldn't get rid of him completely. He was still very much a part of Liza's life, unfortunately. Not Will's though. Will hadn't spoken to him for over a year now. Not since he found out that Colin had been fleecing Netta, and had a big row with him over it.

Geraldine missed Will, now that he was away at university. More than she'd expected to. It was strange how you got used to people just being there in the background. Until one day they weren't, and then… Still, it was nearly Christmas. He'd soon be back for the holidays. Not that it would make any difference, because she wouldn't see him. She'd already told Arthur to send Liza away twice this week. She kept telling Netta not to come back, but would she listen? No. That was Netta all over. She could be very bloody-minded when she wanted to, and not just when it came to her choice of men.

She surveyed the unappetising meal on her lap. Small chunks of dried up pork, lumpy mashed potato, and peas. Arthur appeared to have run the full gamut of his culinary skills and, unfortunately, it didn't extend very far. He'd also taken to cutting up her food for her now, and serving it with a fork and spoon, as if she were a small child. Or an imbecile. He must be under the assumption that she was so addled, she hadn't noticed he'd stopped giving her sharp knives. He obviously thought she was going to top herself. Well, there was no need to worry on that front: she didn't have the courage for it. The best she could hope for was to fade into oblivion. She dropped her fork and pushed the tray away. It was all too much effort.

Arthur pushed the bedroom door open.

'Look who's here to see you.'

He made it sound like the surprise visit of someone she hadn't seen for years, rather than yet another intrusion by someone who just wouldn't go away. He moved out of the doorway to let Netta in.

'Hello Mum.'

She looked tired. She was probably having trouble sleeping again. Most likely the worry. It affected her that way. It was one of the few things they had in common. That, and the ability to irritate each other.

Arthur picked up the tray and looked at the half-eaten meal with disappointment.

'You couldn't manage all of your dinner then, Gee?'

'Perhaps if you'd given me some proper cutlery, it might have helped,' she snapped.

'Point taken, love. Do you want a cuppa?'

'No thank you.' She really couldn't take any more dishwater today.

'Okay. I'll take Minnie out for a walk and leave you two to have a chat.'

Another chat? Geraldine sighed. He had no idea. Either that, or he was being deliberately dense. Now that she thought about it, he was probably talking in code again. Yes, that was it. 'Have a chat' would be their code for, 'keep an eye on her and make sure she doesn't do anything stupid while I get out of here, before she drives me as mad as she is'.

Netta sat on the chair that Arthur had brought up from the dining room. He'd been spending hours parked on it, talking to her about all sorts of nonsense. Sometimes she pretended to fall asleep, just so he'd go away.

'He means well,' said Netta as soon as the front door closed.

It was her way of telling Geraldine she was being spiteful. Geraldine didn't need telling. She already knew and, much as she wanted to, she couldn't stop.

'I'm sure you all mean well, but it's not really helping.'

'Then tell us what will help?'

She didn't like Netta's tone. There was a hint of annoyance in it that, in Geraldine's view, was unwarranted. After all, she hadn't asked her, or Arthur, to faff around her like a couple of missionaries. In Netta's case, she'd clearly told her to bugger off, but her request had fallen on deaf ears.

She tried again. 'What will help is if you leave me be.'

Netta pinched the top of her nose.

'I'm not going to do that unless you tell me what's wrong. This is my fault, so it's my responsibility to fix it.'

She just wasn't going to give up. If Geraldine had been her usual self, she'd have shrugged it off, but she was worn out. Maybe, if she shared her burden with someone again…? Oh but it was such a heavy burden to share. Could she do that to her daughter?

'Look, if this is to do with Len not being your real dad, no one cares about that sort of stuff these days.'

Netta took her hand and looked her straight in the eye. She was so like Ada in some ways. Not in her looks, but in her ways. Yes, in her ways she sometimes reminded Geraldine of Ada. And if Ada wasn't here anymore, then perhaps Netta could help rid her of this darkness, this ugliness.

'He was a brutal man. Brutal. Living with him was like living with the devil. My mum always said he was a different person before the war. Golden. He'd seen the worst of life out there, you see, so there were no barriers left for him. When some men went away to war, they came back altered. You can't put your finger on it, but you know they're not quite right. Then, one day it hits you, and you realise they're not normal. And you've become tainted by them, so you're not normal either. No matter how much you try, you can never be normal.'

Netta had her exasperated face on. 'Mum, you're not making sense. If something happened, you can tell me.'

Geraldine sighed. Her daughter was a very clever woman but, sometimes, she could be very stupid.

'You must promise me that you won't tell your dad, and you must keep that promise this time.'

'I promise. I won't tell him, if you don't want me to. Just tell me, please.'

'You won't like it.'

'I don't care.'

Netta was still gripping Geraldine's hand, looking right into her with those wonderful deep blue eyes. Geraldine's heart began to pound. It grew louder, filling her ears and pressing against the back of her eyes. Something was rising inside her, screaming to get out. She opened her mouth and let out a great, sorrowful wail.

## 21

## CINDERELLA AFTER THE BALL

GERALDINE – 1961

It was Sunday afternoon. Yesterday was Geraldine's birthday. She'd been keeping it quiet. Not intentionally. It was just that birthdays weren't really something they celebrated in her house. Especially birthdays this close to Christmas. But Ada had sprung a surprise birthday tea on her at the end of the day. There was even a cake, with candles to blow out, and presents. Ada gave her a little navy jumper with a Peter Pan collar. They made her try it on and everyone said it really suited her. Ruby gave her some Yardley eau de cologne and Karen gave her some Milk Tray chocolates. Arthur's present made her laugh. It was a bright red scarf, with matching gloves, and a beret.

'It's getting too cold to be sharing,' he'd joked. 'At least now, I'll be able to wear my scarf and gloves without feeling bad.'

Geraldine had been quite overwhelmed and embarrassed by it all. It was the nicest birthday she could remember having. Made even nicer when Arthur walked her home. She was so happy she didn't even feel the usual gloom when she said goodbye to him, but then she got in and found a card from Bree waiting for her. Bree had brought it round earlier. Geraldine was suddenly filled with longing for her old friend. She wanted to tell her all about the party, and Arthur. She really wanted to tell Bree about Arthur.

Last night, she'd somehow managed to stop herself from going straight round to Bree's and snuggling up on her bed to talk for hours and share secrets, like they used to. She convinced herself that she had a new life now that was too far removed from the one she'd had as a schoolgirl. Plus, she had a new friend. A new confidante, who might not be Bree but was becoming just as good a friend. She had Karen.

This afternoon she was at Karen's house. She'd been there three times now and had finally got past being in awe of everything. It wasn't Karen's family. They were very friendly. It was just that they had such a nice home and Karen's dad, Stan, was lovely. The loveliest man she'd ever met. It was a lot to take in.

Karen was teaching her some dance steps because, amazingly, Geraldine's dad had said she could go to a Christmas dance with the Wildes, as long as Karen's parents were there and saw her home. It had taken a lot of persuasion from her mum, but eventually he said yes. Geraldine didn't want to think about how much her mum had to belittle herself to get him to agree. That would have spoiled the excitement, and she was unbelievably excited. The only drawback was that Tina was going too.

They sat down on the bed for a break. Geraldine's eyes were drawn to four teddy bears sitting on a shelf opposite her. They looked as if they were smiling at her.

'That's Horace, Algernon, Oswald and Tedward, or Ted for short. He's the oldest and my favourite.' Karen pointed to them individually as she said their names. 'I know it's childish but I've had them since I was a baby, and they were from the people I love the most – Mum and Dad, and my nan and grandad.'

'I don't think it's childish. I think they're sweet. Like little protectors watching over you.'

'Yeah, exactly. They bring me love and luck. Have you got any?'

Geraldine shook her head. 'I don't think I ever had any, or if I did, they'd have been passed on to my little brothers.'

'That's a shame.'

She shrugged. 'We don't have much money.'

Karen nodded. 'That must be hard.'

Geraldine didn't answer. She didn't think Karen was expecting her to. She was just thinking out loud. It was one of the things she liked about Karen. She never pitied her, or looked down on her, and she didn't make a mountain out of a molehill about plain facts. The plain fact was that Geraldine's family was poor. Karen accepted this and didn't make Geraldine feel like less of a person because of it.

'You can hold them if you want.' Karen took the bears from the shelf and put them on Geraldine's lap.

Geraldine picked them up, one by one, and squeezed their soft bodies against her. Algernon was particularly squeezable. She held him close to her face. He smelt of lavender.

'I give them all a spray of scent every day to keep them smelling nice,' explained Karen.

Geraldine held Algernon's squishy body against her. 'He's so soft. Thank you.'

'Anytime. Hey, are you enjoying your walks home with Arthur?' She gave Geraldine a lopsided wink.

It was so funny, Geraldine couldn't help giggling. She tapped Karen's arm.

'Stop it. You know he loves Tina.'

Karen pulled a face. 'She'll be gone before Valentine's Day, believe me. I know Art too well. It's you he likes.'

'Do you think so?'

'I know so.'

'We'll see.'

Geraldine didn't like to think about it. It was best not to get your hopes up. Besides, it was a bit mean of her to be glad that Arthur might break up with Tina. It wasn't as if Tina had ever done anything against her. She probably didn't even know Geraldine existed.

On Thursday morning, as soon as they opened up, Ada announced that she was going shopping in town. It was the last Thursday before Christmas. Arthur and Karen had broken up from school, and Ruby had come in early. There were so many of them in there that they were practically falling over each other.

'Get your coat, Geraldine. You can come and help me. You three will manage for a few hours, won't you?' said Ada.

Ada was like a whirlwind, rushing around the shops and buying presents, lots of them – for Arthur, and her brothers' families, and for Ruby and her children. They stopped for coffee and a cake at a fancy café called Drucker's. Ada said she could have whatever she wanted. Geraldine chose a slice of creamy chocolate gateau and Ada had something called apple strudel.

'I want to buy you something for Christmas, love,' she said. 'Have you got a nice dress to wear to the dance on Saturday?'

'Not really,' said Geraldine.

The lack of something to wear had been worrying her. She had a little bit of money put by, but it felt wasteful to buy the sort of dress she'd only wear to an occasional dance. Particularly as she didn't know if she'd ever be allowed to go to another one. She had a couple of nice day dresses that she'd bought since starting work and had decided to wear the prettiest one, in the hope that she wouldn't look too out of place.

Ada put down her fork and wiped the corners of her mouth with a napkin.

'That's it then. I'll buy you one. You can have it as an early present.'

They found a red taffeta and chiffon dress in Wallis. It had a fitted bodice and a full skirt. It was so beautiful and grown-up that Geraldine couldn't help but feel pretty in it.

'Let's have a look then,' called Ada through the curtain.

She stepped outside. Ada looked her up and down.

'That's the one, sweetheart. You look lovely in it. A real heartbreaker.'

She didn't want to break anyone's heart. But if she could capture someone's, that would be wonderful. Especially if it belonged to Arthur.

At last it was Saturday night. She put on the dress, brushed her hair, and sprayed on her birthday perfume. She put her make-up in her bag. Karen said she'd help her put some on in the toilets at the dance, and she didn't want to put it on at home. Grunt was always going on about women who wore make-up. You'd think the way he carried on that a bit of mascara was a hanging offence. Unusually for a Saturday, he was still at home. Normally he'd have been in the pub by now.

Her mum was waiting for her in the living room. She clapped her hands together.

'Oh bab, you look absolutely beautiful. Doesn't she look beautiful, Len?'

Grunt kept his head in his paper.

'You know, I've never noticed before how much you look like your Auntie Frances. You're the image of her. Don't you think so, Len?' said her mum.

This time he raised his head. 'You look like a tart. Where did you get that dress from?'

'It was a Christmas present from Mrs Wilde,' said Geraldine.

She'd been feeling quite good about herself getting ready for the dance, but now he'd gone and ruined it. That was him all over, the nasty, vicious pig. She knew he was lying too. Ada would never have insisted on buying it for her if she looked like a tart in it. She was very particular about clothes.

'Waste of bloody money,' he snapped. 'What right has she got dressing you up like that? There's something wrong about that woman.'

He threw his paper on the floor and stood up abruptly. Geraldine and her mum instinctively took a step back. He moved to within a few inches of them. There was a smell of stale alcohol coming off him that made Geraldine's stomach turn.

'You make sure you get that lift back. You walk home on your own, dressed like that, men'll think you're on the game.'

He slammed the front door as he left.

'Take no notice,' said her mum. 'He doesn't mean it. He's probably a bit wound up with it being Christmas. The extra cost. And because you look so much like our Frannie. He had a soft spot for Fran, yer dad. He asked her out before me, you know? But she wasn't interested so he asked me, and we really fell for each other. He was proper cut up when she was killed.' She wiped her eyes and tutted. 'Look at me, silly fool.'

There was a knock at the door. It was Ada, dressed in an elegant turquoise dress. She looked like a film star.

'Merry Christmas, Mavis.'

The two women hugged each other like old friends. It took Geraldine by surprise, given that her mum always seemed to be running Ada down.

'Ada, you look lovely,' said her mum.

'Thanks. I brought some little presents. Nothing special. Just a few bits for the kids. This one's for you, Mave. Len doesn't need to know about it.'

She handed Geraldine's mum an envelope. Geraldine guessed it was probably money.

Her mum looked embarrassed but she took the envelope. 'Thanks, Ade. What do you think of our Geraldine, then? Doesn't she look like Frannie?'

Ada looked at Geraldine properly for the first time. There was faint smile on her lips and, if Geraldine wasn't mistaken, a tear in her eye. For a minute, she thought Ada was going to cry but she gathered herself and spoke: 'Yes she does. And like you too, Mave. But then, you and Fran were so alike, you could have been twins.'


Geraldine was disappointed to find that Arthur wasn't in the car. Although there wouldn't have been any room in there for him. She, Ada and Karen were in the back with Karen's mum in the front and her dad driving.

The first thing Karen did when they got inside, was to whisk Geraldine off to the ladies to apply the make-up. With her transformation complete, they went back out to join the rest of the Wildes. Geraldine scanned the room for Arthur. When she saw him dancing with Tina, her heart sank.

'Come on, let's dance.' Karen pulled her on to the dance floor and they began to follow the steps they'd been practising for the last few weeks.

'Hello Gee. You look great.'

Arthur had somehow sidled up to her without her noticing. He was wearing a continental suit with a white shirt and a slim silver tie, just like one she'd seen Billy Fury wearing in a magazine.

'Hello Art,' she shouted over the music. 'I didn't notice you there. I was concentrating on my dance moves.'

'Looks like you're getting the hang of it,' he said.

Tina appeared at his side.

'There you are Arthur.' She gave Geraldine a cursory glance. 'Honestly I can't turn my back on him for a minute. Let's go and get a drink, shall we?'

She took his hand and pulled him away.

'Okay. Gee, do you want a drink?' he called back to her.

'No, I'm all right for now thanks,' she said.

As soon as they were out of sight, Karen folded her arms and did her Tina impression.

'Honestly, I can't turn my back on him for a minute.'

'Don't be so cruel,' said Geraldine, trying not to laugh.

'She deserves it. I mean, it's obvious isn't it?'

'What is?'

Karen rolled her eyes. 'She's jealous of you, you dope.'

A good-looking boy who was twisting next to her leaned over and asked: 'Do you wanna dance?'

Karen nodded approval.

'Okay. Why not?'

She had to face it, Arthur was taken. So she might as well enjoy herself anyway. The boy said his name was Ritchie. She had a few dances with him until, realising she was being impolite, she excused herself to go back to Ada and the rest of the Wildes.

Ada was talking to a handsome, well-dressed man. He was looking at her like there was no one else in the room. She seemed to be enjoying his company too. He said something to her, and she threw her head back and laughed out loud. She had so much more life in her than Geraldine's mum. Maybe that's what living with Len Corcoran did to you. Knocked the life out of you. Literally. Geraldine would never marry someone like him. Never.

The evening finished much too quickly for Geraldine. She'd learned lots of new dances, danced with so many boys, and had a wonderful time. When they stepped outside, they found it was snowing. Tomorrow was Christmas Eve, so there was every possibility it would be a white Christmas. She should be happy and yet, on the way home in the car, Geraldine felt like Cinderella, after the ball. All of the fun and the wonder would soon be forgotten when she stepped through that door. She had three days off for the holidays and each one would seem like a year.

Her mum was still up when she got in.

'Did you have a good time?' she said.

'Yes, it was brilliant. I had a great time. Everyone in bed?'

'Your dad's not back yet. You'd best get up before he comes home.'

'Night Mum. I'll tell you all about it tomorrow,' said Geraldine, as she made for the stairs.

She'd only just put her foot on the bottom step, when Grunt opened the front door. He was steaming drunk. She tried to get out of his way, but he grabbed her arm and pulled her back into the living room.

'Still dressed like a tart. Get all the lads running after yer, did yer?'

'Come on now, Len, you know our Geraldine's not like that. She's a good girl,' said her mum.

'What would you know about that, you stupid cow? Never know when to keep yer mouth shut, do yer?'

He lashed out his hand. It met with her mum's face and sent her reeling backwards. Her mum steadied herself against a chair.

'Please, Len. Let her go to bed. We've a busy day tomorrow.'

'I said be quiet.'

His fist caught the side of her head and she went down. The only noise was the thud of her body when it hit the floor. She lay lifeless, eyes closed.

Geraldine ran over to her. She was breathing. Out cold, but still breathing.

Grunt stood over them. 'Leave her.'

'But she's unconscious.'

'Leave her, she'll come round in a bit. Make me a brew.'

Geraldine was paralysed by fear. Afraid to leave her mum. Afraid to disobey him.

'Get in the kitchen, now!'

He grabbed her by the hair and propelled her towards the door.

She somehow managed to stay on her feet and ran into the kitchen. For a second, she thought about escaping through the back door, but she could hear his footsteps in the hall. She filled the kettle and put it on the hob. Her hands were shaking. She couldn't keep them steady enough to strike the match to light the gas

His footsteps were in the room now. She turned and found him standing by the table, staring at her. He unbuckled his belt. Now she was in trouble. Now she was going to get it.

## 22

## CHIN UP

GERALDINE – 1961

It was morning. Geraldine lay in bed. Every part of her hurt. Had she slept? She didn't think so. Surely, she wouldn't have been able to sleep after last night? Surely, she would never be able to sleep again?

She could hear noises downstairs. Laughter. He must be out. There'd be no laughter if he was in. Everything sounded so normal that she began to question if it had really happened, if she *had* perhaps slept and it had been one of those nightmares that you wake up from, thinking it was real. But it had happened. The bruises were there to prove it. The dampness. The filth, planted inside her.

She looked over at the dress, crumpled and torn on the floor. She'd done that, not him, after he'd finally let her go to bed. Finally finished with her. She, in her tart's dress, barely able to walk; disgusted with herself: *Look what she'd done; look what she'd made him do. Filthy bitch. Filthy, dirty bitch.*

She'd dragged herself upstairs, unable to do anything other than stand in the middle of the room, holding her arms away from her soiled, revolting body. Then came the itching and the scratching, scratching,

scratching. Until parts of her felt as raw as her insides. She'd walked round and round the walls. Still it wouldn't go. She'd torn off the dress, repulsed by its foul smell of beer, sweat and spunk. It was a whore's dress. She was a whore. Nothing like Fran at all. That's what he'd said to her: 'Filthy, dirty whore. Filthy, dirty bitch'. It was her fault. Not his. 'Her and that bitch, Ada Wilde'.

She'd expected him to lay into her, but she was wrong. He pushed her onto the table, ripped off her knickers and did that unspeakable thing to her. He'd told her to shut up, as she lay whimpering on her back like a terrified animal while he shoved it inside her, over and over. Told her she deserved it because she was a filthy whore. Just like her mother.

So, it was morning now, and she would have to get up. She would have to get out of bed, go downstairs, and pretend that this was just a normal day, because she couldn't stand the thought of what he'd done, and because no one would believe her anyway. Besides, she needed to wash. She needed to get clean.

She picked up the dress and looked around for last night's underwear. Her knickers, the ones he'd torn off her, weren't there. She realised then that in her rush to get away, she hadn't picked them up. She shoved the dress into a drawer, out of sight, and went downstairs.

The bathroom was off the kitchen so she had no choice but to go down in her nightie. Her mum was in there, washing up. She had her back to Geraldine.

'Morning. You're early. I thought you'd want a lie in after all the excitement of last night.'

She meant the dance of course but that was a distant, unreal memory to Geraldine now.

Geraldine scoured the room for her knickers, but they were nowhere to be seen. Perhaps he'd picked them up. Unless … unless her mum had.

Her mum turned around. 'Are you all right?'

The whole of her right cheek was bruised and her right eye, black and swollen. Len Corcoran's Christmas present to his devoted wife.

All at once, Geraldine remembered her mum being knocked out cold on the living room floor.

'Are *you* all right?'

'Yes, of course I am,' said her mum.

'But last night.'

'It was nothing. Go and get washed. Go on. We've got a lot to do today.'


Geraldine sat in the bath, shivering. The hot water had run out and it was freezing. The insides of her private parts were stinging. The soap she'd used to try to banish all trace of him from there was too harsh. She had washed herself inside and out twice over, but still she felt dirty. No matter how times she washed, she would always feel dirty now.

Her mother was banging on the door, telling her to get a move on. For a moment in the kitchen, Geraldine had considered telling her, but now she was just angry with her. How could she pretend nothing had happened last night with a face like that? What was the use in telling her anything? She'd just make out like Geraldine had made the whole thing up, and then she would feel even more ashamed. For all she knew, her mum already knew what had happened. She could have found Geraldine's torn knickers.

She could have come to, and seen or heard everything. And, if she did, she was no better than that evil bastard.

Geraldine dragged herself out of the bathroom, back through the kitchen.

Her mum's hands dropped down to her hips. 'You've never had a cold bath? You silly sod, you'll catch your death. Put something warm on.'

'I'm all right,' said Geraldine, still walking.

'Bring your clothes down and get dressed in front of the fire, while it's quiet.'

Geraldine ignored her and trudged upstairs to sit, trembling, on the end of her bed.

She could have been sitting there for ten minutes or ten hours, she didn't know which, but the sudden opening of her bedroom door made her jump out of her skin. It was Ralph. She let herself breathe again.

'Ralph, you could have knocked. I might have been getting dressed.'

'Yeah, merry Christmas to you an' all. Mum said you've got to come down and help.'

She put on some clothes and did a couple of circuits around the walls to calm herself, before going back downstairs.

Her mum was rolling out pastry. The radio was on, and the sound of Christmas carols filled the room, just like any other Christmas Eve.

'About time. Everything okay? You feeling all right?'

'Yes, I'm fine.'

Her mum stopped rolling and squinted at her through her half-closed eye.

'You sure? You don't seem yourself this morning. I thought you'd be full of beans after the dance.'

The front letterbox rattled, saving her the need to answer, and a few minutes later they heard Phil teasing Tony and Ralph in the hallway.

Her mum called out to him: 'We're in the kitchen.'

Phil came in with an armful of presents.

'All right, Mum. All right, bab. Happy Christmas.'

He put the presents on the table and pulled out a twig of mistletoe from his coat pocket.

'Right, who's first?'

He gave them both a peck on the cheek. It was all Geraldine could do not to flinch.

'Old Grunt not here then?' he said.

'If you mean your dad, no. He's gone to get Ma.'

'So, am I allowed to ask if he's responsible for that?'

Phil pointed to their mum's swollen face. She was filling the rolled-out pastry with sausage meat, and didn't look up.

'It's nothing.'

'Nothing?'

'Don't make a fuss. Anyway, I didn't expect you to be gracing us with your presence today. I thought you were off to your girlfriend's posh house for Christmas.'

'I am, but not 'til later. I still wanted to see you. Most of you, anyway. Sounds like I timed it just right, if I've managed to miss the miserable old git.'

'You watch your mouth, young man. Show some respect,' said her mum.

'He don't deserve any. Does he, Gez?'

Phil winked at her. Geraldine suddenly needed to throw up. She ran into the bathroom.

'Oh, for goodness sake,' said her mum. 'I don't know

what's wrong with you today, Geraldine but if you don't pull yourself together, we won't be finished until midnight.'

Phil stayed long enough to see Janet and Trevor arrive with the turkey. Trev had a good job at the Austin factory in Longbridge, and had insisted on buying it as their contribution to Christmas dinner.

'Got a better offer, have you?' Janet asked Phil.

She waddled into the kitchen. She was so big, she made even walking a few steps look hard. Trevor followed her in, fussing after her. He took her coat while she plonked herself down on a chair.

'You're not kidding,' said Phil. 'Anything's better than having to spend a day with Grunt.'

Their mum scowled at him, but Jan and Trev found it funny.

'Yeah well, no offence, Mum, but we'd have gone to Trevor's mum if we could. But we can't risk it.' Janet stroked her belly. 'I'm sure this little sod's going to drop any minute. It's not you, Mum, honestly. You know I'd be here all the time, if it was just you.'

'Talking of which, I'm off before he gets back.' Phil held up his mistletoe and kissed his mum and sisters, then jokingly held it over Trevor's head.

'We can't stop long either,' said Trevor. 'You're our last stop. Jan's dead on her feet. She'll be out for the count when we get home and that's not a pretty sight, I can tell you. All that dribbling and snoring.'

Janet punched him playfully on the arm. He pretended to wince. Geraldine couldn't help wondering whether Grunt had done the same thing to Janet that he'd done to her. Surely not? Surely, if he had, Janet wouldn't be sitting here now, happy and content with a decent, loving husband?

'Hang on, I've got you a present, Phil,' said Geraldine.

She fetched it from her room and followed Phil out through the front door.

'Thanks Gez. You didn't need to. You okay?' he said.

No, she wasn't okay. She wanted to tell him why. He'd understand, wouldn't he? Didn't he get out of here as soon as he could? He lived in a tiny little bedsit with nothing more than a couple of gas rings for cooking on, but he still thought it was a million times better than living under the same roof as their so-called father. Phil would look after her. He'd make it all go away.

She opened her mouth but she couldn't say the words. How could she tell him what had happened to her? How could she tell anyone? It was all her fault. She was a filthy, dirty whore. If she told him, if she told anyone, that's what they'd think of her.

'What is it, Gez?'

'Nothing.'

He looked up the road.

'I've got to go now, or I'll be late. And the old man'll be back in a few minutes. I don't want to be around when he's here.'

Back in a few minutes? Of course he would be. She began to shake.

'You're shivering. Go back inside, it's cold out here.'

'Take me with you,' she whispered.

He screwed up his eyes. 'Don't be daft, Gez. I can't just turn up with you, without asking first, can I? It's not really that bad here, is it?'

She shook her head.

'Come and see me after Christmas. I'll take you to the

Kardomah for a nice coffee. I'll bring Cissy. I'd like you to meet her.' He gave her another kiss. 'Chin up,' and then he walked away.

Chin up? What sort of a useless comment was that? She could hear Janet and Trev larking about. They couldn't help her either. There was only one person who could make her feel better. She reached for her coat on the hook, in the hallway, and slipped back out, down the path, up the street and across three blocks until she got to Bree's house.

Bree's sister, Rita, opened the door to her.

'Hello stranger. Bree's upstairs, finishing off her homework. You'd better go up.'

Tentatively, Geraldine climbed the stairs and opened the door to Bree and Rita's bedroom. Bree jumped up in surprise.

'Gez! What is it? What's the matter?'

Geraldine shook her head. The tears were already falling. 'I can't … I can't…'

Bree took Geraldine in her arms. 'It's all right, don't worry. We don't have to speak.'

Geraldine rested her head on Bree's shoulder and sobbed.

## 23

# CHRISTMAS IS SAVED

### GERALDINE – 1961

Geraldine stayed at Bree's for a couple of hours. She didn't tell her what had happened last night, and Bree didn't push her for an explanation. Although, Geraldine could sense that Bree knew something really bad had happened.

At first, Geraldine did a lot of crying, but then they talked. She told Bree about Arthur and Bree told her about a boy that she fancied. It was just like old times. Except it wasn't really. Although Bree laughed along with her when she recounted funny stories about the shop, Geraldine was embarrassed that her world was limited to selling tins of Spam and corned beef. But it was worse when Bree talked about school. Geraldine hadn't realised just how much she'd missed it and how much she envied Bree. She knew then, if she didn't know already, the old times were just that. In a few years, Bree would go to university and would only ever think of her as poor Geraldine, the girl who never escaped. She couldn't stand that.

'Will you come round again?' said Bree, as she was leaving.

'I'll try,' she said, knowing full well that she wouldn't. 'Happy Christmas, Bree. And thank you.'

Bree hugged her. 'That's okay, we're friends, aren't we? Happy Christmas, Gez.'

Christmas was saved by two people. The first was Trevor. He seemed to have made it his mission to bring some fun and laughter into the Corcoran household over the two-day period. He brought a box full of drinks to keep the adults happy, and organised games, including a Subbuteo tournament – his and Janet's present to Tony. He even helped Ralph build a strange-looking Meccano car – their present to him.

It was Trevor who got them all playing charades while the boring religious stuff was on the telly, and it was Trevor who made Geraldine's mum sit down and have a rest while he, Janet and Geraldine put out the Christmas tea. Thanks to him, everyone had a good Christmas. Except for Geraldine. Although she did her best to put on a decent show of it, she couldn't enjoy it, which was a shame, since this was probably one of the better Corcoran Christmases.

Geraldine could tell she was closing in on herself, each day becoming more withdrawn, but there was nothing she could do to stop it. She'd become a bystander, watching from the side-lines. She was even watching herself. As if she were facing herself, examining very action and every expression.

She was watching Grunt too, waiting for a word, a look – something, anything – of remorse, guilt, or shame. She was also waiting for him to do it again. Maybe when Trevor and Janet went home for the night and the house grew quiet. But no. Nothing.

From the moment he came back on Christmas Eve, he behaved as if he nothing at all had happened. He was his usual self. Better than his usual self, in fact. He was on his best behaviour. That had nothing to do with what he'd done to her, or even because it was Christmas. It was down to the person he'd brought back with him. The second person to save Christmas.

Geraldine didn't much care for Ma Corcoran. She was a loud, coarse old woman who belched and farted whenever the need arose, which seemed to be quite often. But she did have one saving grace; whenever she was around, Grunt made an effort to behave like a normal human being. Ma spent Christmas with each of her six sons on a rota basis. This year was their turn which meant she arrived on Christmas Eve and plonked herself on the settee, fully expecting to be entertained and waited upon, until the day after Boxing Day.

There was a spare bed in the boys' room. It had been Phil's until he moved out earlier that year. For now, it was moved in with Geraldine, and Ma shared her room. For the period of Ma's stay, Geraldine was kept awake at night by the old woman's loud snores. Ordinarily this would have annoyed her but right now, she found it a comfort because she knew it kept him away. For those three days, Geraldine became Ma's shadow. Each night, she went to bed at exactly the same time as her and didn't leave the room until Ma did. Even if she needed the toilet. On Christmas night she was so desperate for a wee, it began to hurt. Even so, she couldn't bring herself to leave the room. Instead, she forced herself to use the bucket Ma insisted on having by the bedside, in case she was caught short in the night, which she usually was.

On Boxing Day night, it was more than her grandmother's snores that kept her awake. She lay fretting about what would happen the next night, and the one after that, when she'd be alone in here. For once, she was sorry to see the back of Ma Corcoran. Geraldine thought of pretending that she'd enjoyed Ma's company, and asking if she could go and stay with her for a while, to try to eke it out until she was old enough to leave and get a bedsit like Phil. But she knew it was impossible. The old woman had no time for anyone but her own sons. In fact, the only time she'd really spoken to Geraldine, over the whole three days, was to tell her she was too pretty for her own good and she needed to watch herself. As if she didn't already know that.

There was nowhere for Geraldine to go. She had no choice but to stay where she was. She was trapped.

## 24

## IT WAS STARTING

GERALDINE – 2019

Geraldine watched Netta pacing the room, like a restless animal on the prowl. Every now and then, she'd stop and look at Geraldine, as if she was going to say something, but then she picked up the pacing again. It was starting to become annoying.

'Will you please sit down, Netta?'

'Yes, sorry.'

She sat on the edge of the chair and started picking at the skin around her nails. She seemed to be incapable of sitting still. Geraldine couldn't blame her. It's not every day your mother tells you she'd been violated by her step-father. Still, she asked for it. She wanted to know. If she hadn't come round here with that bloody letter…

'I can't believe you've kept that secret for so long. It's no wonder…' Netta's voice trailed off and the words were left hanging in the air.

Geraldine gave it a minute for her to pick it back up again, but she didn't. Or couldn't. Geraldine wasn't sure which of the two it was.

Up until that moment, Geraldine had been shaking. It

was the nerves. She hadn't spoken about that night in detail for such a long time. Not since Ada took her in. It was a miracle that she was able to get through it with just the shakes. Except that she had slipped her hand under the covers, and done the thing a few times when she'd thought she couldn't go on. But she did go on. She told Netta everything about that dreadful Christmas of 1961 and, even though it left her raw, there was some comfort in sharing it with someone again.

But then Netta had done that pacing and said: 'It's no wonder'. The response hadn't been what Geraldine was hoping for. It was nothing like Ada's response. Of course it wasn't. Netta wasn't Ada. She was nothing like Ada at all and Geraldine had been a fool to think otherwise. The shaking had stopped. The nerves were gone, and in its place, she felt angry.

'What? It's no wonder I'm such a crackpot? Is that what you were going to say?'

'No, I was going to say it's no wonder you find life difficult sometimes.'

So that was it. It had taken Netta a while to find the right words but they'd come out, eventually, and now Geraldine knew. That was how her daughter saw her, as someone who found life difficult, but only sometimes. Apparently. Well, thank the lord for small mercies. At least she didn't find life difficult all of the time. Apparently.

'Difficult?'

'Yes. I know that sometimes things get too much for you and make you feel a bit … under the weather.'

Under the weather? Under the bloody weather? That was another of their code words, she supposed. Code for doolally, no doubt. Netta had her empathy face on today. It was rather irritating.

'I kept it secret it because I had to. I've learned to live with it. I never think about it. Or at least, I didn't until you brought me that letter.'

Netta looked as if she was about to cry.

'I'm so sorry.'

'What's done is done. Your dad will be back in a minute. You can go then.'

She shook her head. 'I'll stay.'

'I want you to go. But remember your promise, Netta. Your dad must not know. It would destroy him and everything we've been to each other.'

They heard Arthur and Minnie coming in.

'You won't tell him, will you?' said Geraldine.

'I give you my word,' said Netta.

'Good. I hope you keep it this time.'

Netta went back to picking away at her fingers, her bum firmly stuck to the seat. She looked like she was settling in for the duration. Geraldine attempted a kindly smile.

'Chin up, Nettie. Time for you to go.'

As soon as she said it, Geraldine was transported back to that Christmas Eve when Phil had said the same thing to her. He didn't help her then, and she doubted it was helping Netta now.

Geraldine sat alone in bed listening to Arthur and Netta downstairs, willing Netta not to break her promise. She really wanted to believe in her, but she'd believed in Ada once and look where that got her. All these years assuming she'd taken their secret to the grave, only to learn she'd left the evidence behind for someone to find. What was Ada thinking? She felt betrayed, and then she felt regret. Regret at telling Netta. What a selfish fool she'd been to share her burden like that. It was too much for poor Nettie to deal with. She'd expected too much of her. She should have been strong and kept it to herself. Now she'd tainted Netta too. How could she have been such a cruel, bad mother to do a thing like that to her child?

The door slammed shut. A minute later, Arthur was in the room.

'Netta seemed upset. Have you two had words again?'

So, she hadn't told him then? That was something to be grateful for, at least.

'Not exactly, but I don't want to see her again, Arthur. If she comes back, send her away.'

He looked shocked. 'Are you sure, Gee? You know that would devastate her, don't you?'

'She'll get over it.'

'No, love, she won't.'

He turned away from her and walked out the door.

Geraldine shoved her face into the pillow. Arthur was beginning to lose it with her now. It was starting. Soon he'd hate her, and so would Netta, and it was all her own fault. She switched off the bedside lamp, pulled up the quilt and curled into a ball.

She woke up in a sweat. She'd been dreaming of that night again, her red party dress stained, her body sullied. As usual, there was no air in the room. No air in her lungs.

She stumbled out of bed in the dark and felt for the wall. She followed it round, gathering speed, as if the faster she got round the sooner she'd feel safe. Her leg suddenly caught on something hard and she tumbled over it, crashing to the ground. It was the chair. Arthur must have moved it while she was asleep.

Geraldine heard him on the stairs. She had to get up and finish her walk, but there was no breath left in her. The air was gone and she was suffocating. He was on the landing. She couldn't get up. She was wheezing now. There was a terrible searing pain in her chest. She was going under. God help her. She was going under.

## 25

# CAUGHT OUT BY THE NEIGHBOURHOOD WATCH

NETTA – 2019

Netta couldn't go home. Not with this in her head. She messaged Liza, Kelly and Frank to let them know she'd be back late, then drove to the church where the Corcorans were buried. Her mum had never taken her there, either before or after Nanny Corcoran's death. She understood why now. She was astonished that her mum managed to go there every year, with the rest of the Corcoran clan, to put flowers on the graves.

It was hard to concentrate on the drive there. Images of her poor mum and what that man did to her kept flashing through Netta's head. Liza was only a year older than her mum had been at the time. If someone did that to her, she'd have wanted to kill them with her bare hands. Netta couldn't believe that Nanny Corcoran wouldn't have reacted in the same way, if she'd known. But then, as her mum had said, they were different times. And Nanny Corcoran had no will of her own. It had been battered out of her by the very same man.

Somehow, Granny Wilde had found out and kept it a

secret too. When she next saw her mum, she'd ask how that happened. The strangest thing of all was that her dad had no idea: that between them, her mum and Ada had managed to hide it from him. Before Netta had left him that evening, he'd begged her to tell him what it was that was wrong. It had taken every ounce of self-control she possessed not to do it. If anyone should know, it was him but how could she tell him when she knew it would kill her mum, if he found out? The secret had been passed on to her in good faith and it wasn't hers to share. All she could do was keep her promise and do her best to persuade her mum to seek help, and to tell him herself.

She found somewhere to park the car. She had a rough idea where the graves were. She'd come across them once, a long time ago, when she was a teenager. Back then, she and her friend Claire sometimes used the graveyard as a place to get drunk on cheap booze. They had other friends in the area, and it was quite far away from where they both lived. That made it a great place to hang out, without the fear of being caught. In those days they'd often meet other kids who were there for the same purpose, or the occasional wino looking for somewhere quiet to sleep. There were none here tonight. Other than that, it looked the same as it did back when she was a more regular visitor.

It was a cloudy night. Although there was a thin crescent of a moon, it was largely hidden. She used the torch on her phone to light the way. It had been raining earlier, and it gave the grass that freshly wet smell that always seems to bring out the slugs and snails. One of them crunched under her foot and made her feel even sicker than she already was. She adjusted the torchlight's direction downwards and walked around them, just as she did with the rows of graves.

Netta couldn't bring herself to walk over someone's final resting place. Except perhaps for one.

She stopped in front of the graves and shone the beam at the inscription on one of the headstones:

*'Beloved husband and father'.*

What on Earth made them write such out and out lies? Even without the knowledge of what he'd done to her mum, the whole family must have known he was a complete bastard. They certainly must have all hated him. How could they stand here every year and not feel like hypocrites?

To the right was her grandmother's grave:

*'Mavis Corcoran.*
*Devoted wife and much loved mother'.*

There were matching pots of flowers on both graves, still reasonably fresh. Winter bulbs were beginning to shoot through the ground.

Netta crouched down in front of Len Corcoran's grave. If there were any positives to come out of this awful affair, it was finding out that he wasn't really her grandfather. The moon had escaped the clouds and was giving off a dim light. Enough for her to switch off the torch.

She imagined the kind of life her mum could have had, if this monster hadn't done that awful thing to her. Her parents would still have married. Netta was sure of that. But, if her mum hadn't been scarred by what happened to her, how much happier she'd have been. Her moods, her ups and downs, finally all made sense to Netta.

She cast her eyes over the tidy grave. He didn't deserve a resting place like this. He didn't deserve to rest. She grabbed the pot of flowers and sent it crashing against the gravestone.

'Bastard. Evil bastard.'

She tore the flowers apart, shoved her fingers into the

wet earth and scratched away at it, following the shoots until she reached the bulbs.

'She was just a child, you pervert. You filthy, disgusting pervert.'

She tugged the bulbs out and stamped on them, until they were crushed. The hurt she felt on her mum's behalf – the sheer, raw anger – surged through and exploded from her mouth in a wild, guttural roar. She fell to the ground, beating at it with her fists, screaming and crying like a feral thing – half animal, half human.

'I think you should know I'm calling the police.'

A shaky, well-spoken voice called out from the darkness and made Netta start. There was a figure, in the shadows. She screwed up her eyes to help her focus. The figure helpfully took a step forward so that she could see the shape of a small, elderly man, brandishing a mobile phone.

'I have you on film.'

Netta ran her hand across her face to wipe away the tears and the snot.

'I'm going. There's no need to call the police. I don't normally do this kind of thing. Believe me, I have a good reason.'

'There's never a good reason to desecrate a grave.'

'Sometimes there are special cases.'

Before the old man could say any more, she ran across the graves that she'd so respectfully avoided earlier, and out of the gate. Still running, she fumbled in her pockets for her keys and pressed the fob. As soon as she got into the car, she locked the doors and tried to push the fob into the ignition but she couldn't keep her hand still. She steadied it with the other hand and managed to start the car up, and drive away.

. . .

She took the circuitous route home: she didn't want to be tailed. Netta was aware how ridiculous that sounded. She was hardly a fugitive on the run, but the last thing she needed right now was to be branded a criminal.

The curtains were still open in the living room when she got home. Netta could see Kelly and Liza in there, with Liza's friend, Jade. She parked up outside Frank's house, so that they wouldn't spot her. She wasn't ready to face them yet. She crept up Frank's path and rang the bell.

He opened the door and was immediately taken aback by the sight of her.

'Jesus, what happened?'

'Oh Frank, it's awful. Just awful.'

As soon as he brought her indoors, she began to shiver. He swaddled her in a duvet and gave her a hot drink.

'I'll run you a bath. You're freezing.'

Worn out, she pulled the duvet up closer and let him take care of her.

It was only when she got into the bathroom and noticed herself in the mirror that she saw what a mess she was. Her clothes, hands and face were caked in mud. She cleaned off the worst on her hands and face, and scrubbed her nails before stepping into the bath and sinking down into the inviting warmth of the water.

Frank came in and sat on the floor.

'Good job on the mud, but the hair needs a bit more work. I think you may actually have some earth-dwelling wildlife settling in there.'

He picked out some debris, then washed her hair. It felt like an act of love. His way of telling her that he cared for her. It was lovely but at that moment, it was enough to bring the tears. He kissed her clean head.

'Do you want to talk about it?'

'I can't. I want to but I made a promise, and this time, I must keep it.'

## 26

## FRANK PICKS UP THE BATON

NETTA – 2019

Of course, Netta told Frank everything. She hadn't meant to but she needed to tell him about the incident in the graveyard, in case the police came after her. Naturally, he asked why she'd been driven to do it. In fact, he'd already half-guessed by then. She tried to skirt around the reason but, in the end, it all came tumbling out. Frank, in his usual way, listened without judgement, soothed her distress, and told her it would all work out in the end. She wanted to believe him, but she wasn't sure she could.

She woke up early that morning in his bed. Because she hadn't been able to face anyone but him last night, he'd popped round and told the girls she was staying over at his. When they asked why she hadn't come herself, he told them she was feeling a bit under the weather. The irony of that phrase wasn't lost on her. Much as she hated to admit it, there were some things she and her mum had in common.

Frank was still asleep. It would have been nice to stay in bed with him and feel the security of having him next to her but she had a market to go to. Christmas was only a couple of weeks away and they had markets every Saturday and Sunday, until then. Will was coming home today and, at some point over the weekend, they had a Christmas tree to buy. On top of that, she'd go to see her mum again and try to sort some of this mess out.

She crept downstairs to make some tea. Her phone rang while the kettle was boiling. It was her dad. She was immediately filled with apprehension.

'Dad, what is it?'

'Your mum had a bit of an episode last night. I had to get the doctor in.'

'An episode? Is she okay?'

'Yes, she's fine now, if you can call it fine. The doctor said it was a panic attack. The thing is, Netta, she doesn't want you to come round anymore. I'm sure it's just temporary until she gets better, but she wants to be left alone. She doesn't want to see the kids either. I'm sorry, sweetheart, but she really isn't herself at the moment.'

'This is all my fault. I shouldn't have shown her that letter.'

'There's nothing we can do about that now. I just wish she'd talk to me. If she'd only tell me, I'm sure I could help her work though whatever it is that's wrong. I feel like I'm losing her, but I don't know what I'm losing her to.'

He sounded at his wits' end. She hated seeing him like this and maybe he was right. Maybe he was the only one that could help her mum get better. She was tempted to tell him everything, but she knew that she had to keep her promise. For now, at least.

'Did the doctor say anything else?'

'She talked about seeing a therapist or counsellor. Your mum won't tell her what's wrong, either. She's left a prescription for some tablets to calm her nerves. I've got to get them this morning but I'm scared to leave her, the state she's in.'

'I'll get them for you. I'll come over as soon as the shops open.'

'I don't think that's wise, love. She already thinks you and I are conspiring against her. It's best you stay completely away.'

'Tell him, I'll come,' said Frank.

He was standing in the doorway. The noise must have woken him.

'Frank will come. Is that all right?'

'I think so. Don't get yourself in a state over this, sweetheart. She'll pull through. She always does. We'll get to the bottom of it, one way or another.'

Before they opened up the stall, Netta told Neil and Kelly that her mum had taken a turn for the worse. Neil asked lots of questions. She answered them as honestly as she could, without giving too much away. In the end, she just had to tell him that she couldn't say any more. Kelly didn't say much. It wasn't like her to take things so quietly but it wasn't as if she was that close to Netta's mum, so Netta decided not to let it bother her. She had other, more pressing priorities. Later, when Will was back, she'd have to sit him and Liza down and tell them their grandmother didn't want to see them. That was not going to be an easy conversation.

Frank turned up at the stall, halfway through the morning.

'Did you go inside? Did you see her?' said Netta.

'No, I didn't go inside but I saw her through the window. She was sitting in an armchair in the living room. I was longer than I thought because I did some shopping for them and took Minnie for a run.'

'Would it help if I went round to see her?' said Neil.

'I don't know, you'll have to ask Arthur,' said Frank.

Netta took Frank to one side. 'You didn't say anything to Dad, did you.'

'No, don't worry. But he looks absolutely done in himself. I said I'd pop round after work on Monday to get them some more shopping, and give Minnie another run.'


Will was already there when Netta and Kelly got home. Liza was making a fuss of him and, for once, her friend Jade was nowhere to be seen. She nearly always stayed over on Saturday nights.

'No Jade?' said Netta.

'She's gone to a show with her mum. She did invite me but I wanted to be here on Will's first night back.'

Poor Liza. Things weren't great for her at the moment. She was worried about her nan, and she'd been missing her big brother terribly.

Kelly was grinning from ear to ear. She was as fond of Will as Liza was. 'We should celebrate you being back. Get a takeaway or something.'

'Takeaway sounds good,' said Will. His phone beeped. A message. 'It's Belle. She's back home too.'

'Cool. Is she coming over?' said Liza.

'Not tonight. She's going out with her family. We'll see each other tomorrow.'

Kelly's face lit up. 'Takeaway then?'

'Takeaway it is,' said Netta. 'But first I need to talk to you all about Nan. She's not very well at the moment.'

'She's having a mental health issue,' said Liza, with all

the confidence of an expert. 'I'm really quite concerned.'

'Shit. I didn't realise. Why didn't anyone tell me?' said Will.

'It all happened rather quickly and we kind of hoped it was something she'd get over in a couple of days, but I'm afraid she's been getting worse,' said Netta.

'She'll be all right though, won't she?' he said.

'I hope so, but for the time being she just needs peace and quiet. She doesn't want to see any of her family until she's feeling better.'

Liza's expression changed. A few minutes ago, she'd been all self-assured and matter-of-fact, and now she looked like anxious and unsure. 'How long's that going to be?'

'I don't know. The doctor's mentioned a therapist, but I'm not sure how Nan will feel about that. I think it might take a while. She and Grandad probably won't be here for Christmas.'

Liza's face fell further. Tears were forming. This, it seems, was the last straw.

'I knew something was up when Grandad said she was too ill to see me. She's never been like that before. Never. Oh God, she hasn't tried to kill herself, has she?'

Netta put her arms around Liza. 'No, nothing like that. I know it's awful but we have to be patient and try to carry on as normal. Nan would hate it if she thought this was upsetting you. Tomorrow afternoon we'll go and get the tree, and we'll play Grandad's favourite Christmas tunes while we put the decorations up. We'll film it and send it to them, so they can still be a part of our Christmas.'

Liza wiped her eyes. 'It won't be the same though, will it?'

Will rubbed Liza's arm. 'No it won't, but we totally have to do it, Lize. For Nan and Grandad's sake.'

## 27

# OPERATION GERALDINE

### KELLY – 2019

The sitting room in the care home looked proper Christmassy. Kelly's nan said they'd had some kind of dance there earlier. That probably explained why half of the residents were fast asleep in their chairs. Her nan was just about walking with a stick now, but one of the carers said she'd had a good go at the waltz with Alec, an old Scottish bloke who kept shouting at everyone as if they were as deaf as he was.

Kelly gestured in Alec's direction. 'He your new boyfriend then?'

'Don't be so cheeky.' Her nan winked. 'We're just good friends. Anyway, what about you? You got another boyfriend yet?'

'Nah. Not interested. Too much like hard work.'

'They're not all like that last one, you know. What was his name?'

'Craig.'

'Don't know what made you go with him. Nice girl like you. Your mum wouldn't have been happy.'

'Yeah, all right, Nan. You've made you're point. Anyway,

gotta go. I've got another appointment. Before you ask, it's not with a fella.'

'Well I hope it's with somebody nice.'

'Sort of. I'll see you at the weekend, yeah?'

She kissed her nan and walked over to Alec.

'Nan wants some company.'

Alec screwed his face up and put his hand to his ear. 'Eh?'

Kelly raised her voice to shouting level: 'I said, Gladys is missing you. She wants company.'

'Oh right you are. That's me away then.'

She helped him up and watched him hobble over to the chair she'd just left. Her nan rolled her eyes at her and wagged her finger. Kelly smirked and stuck her thumb up. She'd been really pissed off with her dad and Carol for persuading her nan to move here, but she had to admit that her nan was really happy. Kelly hadn't seen her this lively in years.

The care home was like a sauna and as soon she stepped outside, the cold hit her. It was mid-afternoon. Normally she'd be busy making jam at this time of day, but she'd taken the day off to do some Christmas shopping in town, before coming to Kings Heath. She had a bit of money of her own these days now that the business was doing okay. Not loads, but enough. Especially as Netta wouldn't take any rent off her. She'd tried to give her some but Netta refused. She was a good friend. And good friends deserved paying back. Since Netta wouldn't take anything from her, Kelly was going to have to find some other way to express her gratitude. Yesterday she came up with the perfect solution. She was going to save Geraldine.

From what Netta had said on Saturday, it sounded as if Geraldine had finally gone off the rails. Poor old Geraldine. She could be a bit snappy sometimes, but Kelly liked her. It was a shame for Liza as well. She was a nice kid really. In her own little world most of the time – Lizaville, Will called it – but she was all right. They'd been getting on pretty good since Will went to university. Kelly supposed they both needed something to fill the gap he'd left behind.

She reached the garden gate. Arthur was in the front window looking a bit surprised. No going back now that he'd seen her then? Kelly waved at him with her free hand. In the other she had a paper carrier bag with three fancy cakes inside. They were the most expensive cakes she'd bought in her life. In fact, until a couple of hours ago, she didn't know it was possible to spend so much money on a shitting cake. But what did she know? Nothing apparently.

Arthur opened the door, still looking as if he was in a state of shock.

'Kelly?'

'All right, Art? Got the day off and I was bored. So I thought I'd come over and see ya, as it's been a while.'

'You'd better come in.'

He had dark circles under his eyes and he looked like he could do with a good sleep and a haircut. It wasn't like him at all. Usually he was so neat and twinkly.

Minnie was pleased to see her, anyway. She bounced about, wagged her tail, and sniffed at Kelly's legs. She could probably smell Maud and Betty on her. She was probably really missing them.

'Wait in the kitchen a minute, would you? I'll just let Geraldine know you're here,' said Arthur.

'You don't need to announce me,' she said.

'It's better if I do.'

Kelly could hear mumblings in the living room. After about five minutes, Arthur came back into the kitchen.

'You can come in now. I'm afraid she's not herself though, so tread carefully.'

Geraldine was sitting in an armchair, stuffed with cushions. It looked as though they were swallowing her. She'd lost weight. Her clothes were loose. Looser than usual that is. That was something else Kelly had noticed about Geraldine. She didn't really make the most of herself. Even though she was really old, she was a good-looking woman. If she bought some better clothes, did something with her hair and put some make-up on, she'd look tons younger.

'All right, Geraldine?'

There was no answer.

'So, I'm not gonna ask how you are because I already know you're not great at the moment.'

Kelly could have sworn Arthur winced. Bad start. She sat down on the settee.

'Sorry, that was a bit stupid. I mean, I know you're not well. Netta said –'

'Netta said what?' said Geraldine.

'Netta said you weren't feeling good, and you didn't want to see anyone in the family.'

'So why are you here, then?'

'Because … well, I don't know. Because I thought that maybe you might like to see someone who was like family, but not blood. I brought cakes.' She held up her bag. 'Posh cakes. Really expensive cakes. Go down great with a nice coffee.'

'We only have instant,' said Arthur.

'Nice cup of instant then. Or tea.'

Arthur took the cakes. 'I'll put the kettle on. Could you manage a cake, love?'

Geraldine shoulders moved a tiny fraction. From the look of her she could have eaten all three cakes and they wouldn't have touched the sides.

It was so quiet in the room that the sound of the kettle boiling in the kitchen was almost deafening. Arthur came back in.

'I've just realised we're out of milk. Sorry. Taken my eye off the ball a bit. Gee, would you be okay if I nipped to the shop while Kelly's here? You don't mind do you, Kelly? I'll give Minnie a quick run as well. I'll be twenty minutes, tops.'

Poor sod, he looked like he was desperate to get out for a breather.

'Fine with me,' said Kelly.

She looked at Geraldine who just about managed a slight twitch of the head. This was going to be hard work.


Kelly stood in the window watching Arthur and Minnie disappear up the road. She looked around the room. It was tidy but, with the exception of a few cards, there wasn't one Christmas decoration up. That was a bit sad because she knew for a fact that Arthur always made a big deal of Christmas. She went back to the settee.

Geraldine was doing the hand thing again. One, two, three, four, stroke. One, two, three, four, stroke.

'I used to do that sort of thing when my mum was ill. Went a bit OCD. Had to have counselling for it.'

Geraldine looked confused.

'What sort of thing?'

Kelly picked up a cushion and began to do the hand thing herself. 'One, two, three, four.'

Geraldine glared at her. Kelly carried on. In for a penny, as her nan would say.

'With me it was blinking and foot tapping. It's a way of coping with something you can't face. That's what the counsellor said. It was my mum dying that set it off.'

Geraldine scowled at her for a few minutes then, out of the blue, she said: 'I used to have to walk around a room, following the walls with my hands. I couldn't take my hands of the walls until I got to the end.'

'Yeah, I can see how that might work. I suppose it made you feel safe, having the walls around you.'

'Yes, that's it. Over time, I've managed to contain it and make it a bit more…'

'Underground? I'm not sure anyone else has noticed. I just pick up on stuff like that. You can get counselling for it, you know. They'll help you.'

'How do they help you? What do they do?'

'Talk mostly. About why you need to do it.'

'Oh no, I couldn't do that.'

'That bad is it?'

'Mind your own business.'

'Please yourself, but you ain't gonna get any better wasting away in your armchair.'

'I will please myself, thank you very much, and if you don't like it you can hop it.'

Kelly did her best not to look too amused. That was more like the Geraldine she knew.

'Can't do that, Gee. I told Art I'd look after you.'

Geraldine sniffed. 'Don't call me Gee. Only Arthur calls me Gee.'

'Okey dokey. So do you wanna talk about it then? The reason why you do the hand thing.'

'No I do not. Why are you here?'

Kelly was about to say the same thing about being bored but that wasn't going to work with Geraldine, and neither was trying to be all nice. Nice people don't get anywhere. She'd been through enough well-meaning social workers when she was a kid to know that much. Still, she couldn't be too hard. Geraldine was ill and she needed delicate handling.

'Because your family's in bits worrying about you, and I care about them. And believe it or not Geraldine, I care about you as well. You can be a snotty, miserable old cow sometimes but I actually like you. Don't ask me why, because sometimes you treat me like shit, but I do.'

She stopped there. It hadn't come out quite as she'd wanted, and now Geraldine looked like she might start crying at any minute. She might just have made things worse. Fuck.

She saw Arthur and Minnie bouncing down the path. Minutes later he was inside.

'Coffee's on the way.'

Minnie lumbered in and slapped her front paws on Geraldine's lap. They were muddy but Geraldine didn't seem to care. She even smiled when Minnie licked her face.

'It's a lovely day out,' said Arthur while he was bringing in the coffee and cakes.

He looked like the walk had done him good. He had some colour in his cheeks.

'These are nice cakes, Kelly. I hope you haven't gone to too much expense?'

'Completely blown the budget, Art, to be honest. But you're worth it. You pick first, Geraldine.'

Geraldine picked the smallest cake but she ate it all, which was good.

When they finished, Kelly helped Arthur clear away the plates and cups.

'When you putting up your tree, Art?'

'I don't think we're in the mood for Christmas this year,' he said.

'Don't be daft. Everyone loves Christmas, don't they Geraldine?'

Geraldine didn't answer. Kelly wasn't going to let that put her off.

'I'll help you.'

Arthur looked over at Geraldine who only blinked back at him, or possibly she did a tiny little smile. It was difficult to tell.

'Okay,' he said. 'Give me a hand to bring it all down, would you?'

It took a couple of hours to get everything up. They really did have a lot of Christmas tat. Arthur put some music on. It was the same music Netta had made them listen to on Sunday when they'd done the Christmas decorations in their house. Arthur said it was Phil Spector, or something like that. It was pretty good actually. Made you feel really Christmassy. The mood must have been catching because when she looked over at Geraldine, she was actually properly smiling and she didn't look quite so lost in those cushions.

'It looks great in here, doesn't it, Gee?' said Arthur, when they were finished.

'Yes, it does,' said Geraldine, her voice sounding like a little mousey squeak.

Kelly folded her arms.

'Yeah, it's pretty full on Christmas now. I'd better get going. Net'll be starting dinner.'

Arthur walked her out to the front door.

'Thanks for coming, Kelly. It's made a real difference to Gee. I haven't seen her this bright in ages. Do you think you'd be able to come again before Christmas? I could really do with getting out for an hour.'

'Yeah, sure. I'll see if I can leave early on Thursday. I'll check tomorrow and message you.'

Kelly walked back to the bus stop on the High Street, feeling quite pleased with herself. She'd done a good thing. She felt like a good person for a change. Although how Arthur could tell it had made a difference to Geraldine she had no idea. But he'd know better than anyone, so she'd take it.

She decided not to tell Netta and the others yet: she didn't want to get their hopes up. Also, they might be a bit pissed off with her for poking her nose in. She couldn't have that. Bad enough if Net was a bit off about it, but if Will was, she'd be gutted.

She'd have to think of a way of wangling a couple of hours off on Thursday without letting on where she was going. Perhaps if she let Neil in on her secret project. Operation Geraldine. He'd understand. Yeah, that was it. She'd get Neil onside.

## 28

## GERALDINE OPENS UP

KELLY – 2019

Neil was great about it. Mind you, Neil was great about everything. He was so bloody perfect he could be really annoying sometimes, but that was probably because Kelly was a bit of a mardy cow. Give it long enough and pretty much everyone and anyone got it in the neck from her, at some point. Everyone except Will, that is. It was impossible for her to be pissed off with Will, even though he insisted on dragging Belle around with him. Belle though. She was definitely very bloody annoying. It was quite easy to be permanently pissed off with her.

'If you say you're going to do something with your nan, I'll back you up and say we can manage without you,' said Neil.

'Something like what?' said Kelly.

'I don't know, use your imagination. Say you're taking her somewhere or something. Right let's get this batch in the jars.'

Netta came back from dropping off the latest delivery just as they were sealing the lids on the last few jars of Christmas marmalade.

'Good timing. I was just saying to Kelly, we'd be able to manage tomorrow if she took another couple of hours off to be with her nan. Chris can come and help us with the deliveries, now he's on holiday.' Neil was looking all innocent, like butter wouldn't melt and all that.

'Oh! Yes, I suppose we could,' said Netta. 'Doing anything nice?'

'Er.' Kelly could feel herself freezing up. Neil hadn't given her time to think of something; hadn't given her any warning.

'Big reunion, isn't it Kel? Her dad's taking her brothers over there.'

Honestly, he looked like he was really, really telling the truth. If Kelly didn't know any better, she would have believed him herself. Except she did know better. Her dad was still on her blacklist. Maybe it was more of a dark grey list right now, but she wasn't ready to forgive and forget just yet. Shame in a way, because they'd been getting on sort of okay until Nan had the stroke, and he turned back into the same weak twat he'd been after Mum died. Yeah, shame. But, you know, that's what you get for believing people can change.

She did her best to match Neil's honest face. 'Yeah, that's right. Nan wants us to kiss and make up.'

'Definitely then. You should absolutely go. Talking of which, I'll just try Dad to see if I can get an update on Mum.'

Netta went into the other room and closed the door.

'Fucking hell, Neil!' Kelly whispered.

'What?'

'Did you have to make it about my dad? Fuck's sake.'

'Well it was the first thing I could think of. Anyway, you

weren't exactly quick on the mark there yourself. What was it you came up with? Oh yeah, that was it – er.'

She grabbed a tea towel and whipped it across his chest.

'Up yours, smart-arse. You took me by surprise, didn't yer? Anyway, you're a pretty good liar for a goody-goody.'

'Why thank you. It's my secret weapon. I'm so angelic, nobody would ever believe I wasn't telling the truth. Just to be clear though, I wouldn't normally condone lying but this is for a good cause.'

'That's all right then. Wouldn't like to think your halo had slipped.'

'Mind you, it wouldn't be such a bad thing for your nan if you did kiss and make up with your dad and Carol.'

'Fuck off, Neil.'

'Just saying.'

'Well don't.'


If she didn't feel bad enough already about lying, the guilt got ramped up to danger point when Netta said she hoped it went well, as Kelly was leaving on Thursday. It sounded as if Netta really wanted her to patch things up with her dad. Maybe, in time, she would. But there was always that part of Kelly that told her there was no point, because he'd only let her down again. Just like he always did. When the going got tough, her dad crapped himself. Besides, if she made up with him, she'd have to be nice to Carol and that just wasn't going to happen.

Kelly knew Carol wasn't a bad person. Her brothers liked her. But they were too young to remember their mum properly. Kelly remembered. She remembered having to do everything because her dad lost it completely, when her mum died. She remembered Carol coming in and making herself at home as well. Truth be told, she might have been able to make a go of it with Carol, if she hadn't used the mug. The mug was the last straw.

She turned into Arthur and Geraldine's front garden. Arthur was looking out for her and had the door open just as she reached it.

Geraldine was in the same chair, sinking into the same cushions. She'd changed her clothes but they were still too loose on her.

Kelly handed a box of Neil's mince pies over to Arthur. He'd given them to her when Netta wasn't about.

'Neil sent these. He said you liked them last year. He sends his love as well. Especially to you, Geraldine.'

'That's very kind of him,' said Arthur. 'Did you tell anyone else you were coming?'

'No, just Neil. I needed his help to get away. You go out and do your stuff, Art. I'll get the kettle on.'

It took Arthur another ten minutes of fussing before he finally left. Minnie whimpered after him. She took a lot of persuading to come away from the window and lie down.

Kelly ran her fingers through Minnie's rough coat and scratched her belly the way their pup, Betty, liked it.

'She's a bit of a diva this one.'

'I suppose so,' said Geraldine. 'What you said the other day about me treating you like...'

'Shit?'

'I don't like that word, but yes. I've been thinking about it. It's not true.'

'Yeah, right.'

'Is that supposed to be sarcastic?'

'You're doing it again.'

'I am not. Look, it's true that you often irritate me and if I've been rude to you, then I'm sorry.'

Kelly sighed. 'Gez, I'm not here to have a go at you. You've got enough going on. I didn't mean to say it the other day, it just came out. But, since you mention it, yes, you are sometimes rude to me. That's okay, though, because I do it to other people. It's a, what's it called? A defence mechanism. You and me are the same in that respect.'

'I know you're not here to have a go at me. You're here to babysit me, because my husband is frightened to leave me alone.'

Geraldine stroked the cushion. She was doing the hand thing again. She caught Kelly looking at her. 'Yes, I know. I can get counselling for it.'

'I'll come with you if you want, being as I've got experience. Or Netta could, if you prefer. She'd be here in a shot, if you let her.'

Geraldine slammed her fist on the cushion.

'No, not Netta. I can't face her. I shouldn't have told her, but she wouldn't let it rest. She brought that bloody letter here and stirred everything up, and then she kept asking me over and over. I had to give in, just to make her go away.'

The letter. Lettergate. Her and Liza had joked about it, but Arthur had looked really upset when they got home that day. Arthur never got upset, so it must have been something pretty bad.

'Okay, so you told Netta what? Something secret? You can tell me, Gez. I can take it.'

'All these years I kept it to myself and then, by chance, it all comes to an end.'

'What comes to an end?'

'The secret. My life. When Arthur finds out … Well, he'll know, and it'll be over.'

Fuck. This was beginning to sound like an episode from EastEnders. Kelly was way out of her depth here, but something told her she had to press on. Geraldine badly needed to open up and get something off her chest, and Kelly was absolutely certain, it should be to her.

'You sure about that? I mean Arthur, he'd stand by you, whatever. That's obvious.'

'You think so? How would you feel if the person you've spent your life with had a dirty secret that they'd hidden away from you for the whole of your married life? You don't understand how that would hurt a person. You're too young.'

'You're right, I am young and I don't understand a lot of things. But I understand hurt. I understand that, on all kinds of levels. More than you think. And I don't know about how Arthur would feel if you told him, but I can tell you're carrying too much hurt. And I can tell that it's spreading. To Arthur and Netta, your grandkids and everyone else that loves you.'

'I know, but I can't do anything about it,' said Geraldine.

'Yes you can. You can talk about it. You can own it.'

'Own it? What on earth are you talking about?'

'It means you can beat it, instead of letting it beat you.'

'Beat it?'

'Yeah. Take control of it. Fight it. Beat it. You can do it, Gez. If you let people help you.'

'Can I? I would like that very much, but I'm too far down.'

Geraldine made a sound like a whimpering dog. It disturbed Minnie. She jumped up and put her front paws and head on Geraldine's lap and began to whimper herself. That dog really loved Geraldine.

Kelly grabbed a nearby box of tissues and knelt down on the floor next to Geraldine. 'No you're not. Come on. Blow your nose. Take a deep breath, and tell me.'

Geraldine took a huge breath, then another, and another.

'When I was sixteen, my step-father did a terrible thing to me. He … he ra…'

She put her hand over her mouth. She couldn't say the word, but Kelly had a pretty good idea what the word was.

'He what? Raped you? Did he rape you? Is that what you're trying to say?'

Geraldine nodded.

Kelly blew out a low whistle.

'Fuck. That's really shit, Gez. What happened? Did the dirty bastard get locked up?'

'Nothing happened. Besides me, only two people knew. Three if you count him. Ada, Arthur's mum, and a friend of hers who was a doctor. I made Ada promise not to tell anyone. She persuaded the doctor to keep quiet about it too.'

'You didn't even tell your mum?'

Geraldine shook her head.

'Why not?'

'Because her life was bad enough, and because I thought I was as much to blame as him for what happened. Because I couldn't stand the shame, and I couldn't bear the thought of Arthur finding out and turning away from me.'

'Well, for a start, how can you be to blame? You were sixteen. Just a kid. The man was obviously a perv and a paedo. For another, I have to say Gez, I think you've got it wrong about Arthur.'

'Things were different back then, Kelly. Men looked at women differently. They expected them to be more respectable.'

'Yeah, I get that. But Arthur, though? Never in a million

years can I see him turning his back on you. Think about it Gez.'

'I can't risk it. My life would be nothing without Arthur.' Geraldine starting crying again.

'Okay, okay. Let's take this one step at a time,' said Kelly. 'Let's forget about Arthur for now and concentrate on you. You've got to get better, Geraldine. If you don't, that bastard will have won. Promise me you'll think seriously about the counselling. I'll come too. I'll hold your hand, and I'll be with you every step of the way. You and me together, Gez. We're gonna beat it.'

## 29
## THREE DECISIONS AND A NEW FRIEND
### GERALDINE – 2019

Geraldine was finally beginning to believe what everyone had told her about Kelly. She was a lot smarter than she looked. Not in the conventional sense, like Liza and Will. She might not know the sort of stuff they teach you at school but she was clever, that one. Very clever. She watched people. She noticed things. She worked out what was going on inside.

It had taken ages to stop the crying. The tears had been endless. If someone was to ask her what had happened, she wouldn't have been able to say. But Kelly's words unlocked something and, once it started, it was close to impossible to stop it. Who would have thought a foul-mouthed slip of a girl would be the one Geraldine was waiting for? Certainly not her. She wasn't even sure she liked Kelly Payne that much. For all her strong points, and there weren't many, she was still a cocky little madam. And yet she had stirred something up in Geraldine. Something rebellious? Yes. For once in her life, Geraldine felt rebellious. She was sick of the fear and ugliness that had overshadowed her entire life. She did not want to be cowed any longer. Kelly was right. She had to beat it because, if she didn't, that bastard would have won. She couldn't have that.

She just about got herself back together by the time Arthur returned. He'd brought some fish and chips back with him for dinner, and Kelly took that as her cue to leave.

'Give me a bell anytime, Gez. Yeah?'

She put a hand up to her face. Presumably that was to indicate Geraldine should call her. It was highly unlikely that she was going to call Kelly, but she appreciated the offer.

'You and Kelly seemed to be getting on,' said Arthur.

They were eating their dinner on trays. Normally she couldn't abide eating on a tray in the living room, especially when it was fish and chips. It took so long for the smell to go. But she'd let her standards slip somewhat lately.

'I wouldn't call it getting on, but she's not as bad as I thought. I wish she wouldn't swear all the time, though.'

'I know what you mean but her heart's in the right place. She's certainly perked you up, I'm happy to say.'

The corners of his mouth turned up very slightly. He was trying to stop himself from smiling but, she suspected, he wasn't trying that hard. It was infectious and she could feel her own lips twitching in the same upwards direction. It made Arthur grin all the more.

'What's that? Is it a smile I see?'

'Not quite,' she said.

'Fancy one of Neil's famous mince pies with cream for pudding?'

'That would be nice.'

The mince pie was as good as she remembered from last

year. Neil was such a good cook. She'd have to ask him for the recipe. Oh! It suddenly occurred to her that, for the first time since this dreadful business began, she'd thought of doing something in the future. Something normal, and positive. Fancy that! She noticed Arthur was watching her from the settee with a look of mild delight.

'What's that look for?'

'It's just nice to see you smiling.'

'Was I smiling?' she said.

'Yes. Second time today. Shocking isn't it?'

'You know what you are, Arthur Wilde? You're a tease.'

'That's me.' He patted the cushion next to him. 'Why don't you come and sit over here? I've missed our cuddles.'

'No Arthur, I've hardly showered lately. I'm all dirty and sweaty.'

'You always smell sweet to me, my lovely. Anyway, I stink of fish and chips. Come on. I've got something to show you.'

'Well don't say I didn't warn you.'

She pulled herself up, suddenly feeling quite light-headed. Arthur caught her before she fell back and helped her over to the settee. The feeling of weakness came as a shock. It was the lack of eating and exercise that had done it. That, and maybe those tablets the doctor had given her. They were very like ones she'd been given years ago, after the other thing happened. They made her permanently sleepy and spaced out.

Arthur sat next to her and began to mess with his phone.

'Netta sent this last weekend. I wanted to wait until you were feeling better to show you.'

He started a video rolling and put his arm around her. 'Frosty the Snowman' began to play. It was the Ronettes, one of Arthur's favourites.

For as long as they'd been married, Christmas had always been a big event in their house. It was all Arthur really. From her point of view, Christmas should have been spoiled by so many ugly memories, but he seemed to have made it his mission to turn it into the most magical time. The result was that for most of their married life, she'd stopped equating the season of goodwill with the monstrousness that should have blighted it. Arthur had saved Christmas for her, even if he didn't know it.

The film was of Netta, Liza, Will and Kelly putting up their Christmas decorations. The dogs were misbehaving and getting into all sorts of silliness, and everyone was joking around. At the end, they all looked into the camera and said: 'Happy Christmas.' Just before it finished completely, Liza and Will came on: 'Get well soon, Nan. We miss you.' They blew her a kiss and the film ended.

A tear trickled down Geraldine's cheek. Arthur wiped it away.

'Do you want to see it again?'

She nodded: it was too hard to speak. They'd planned to spend Christmas at Netta's, but all this had made it impossible. It wasn't right.

They watched the film five times.

'That's made me feel quite Christmassy,' said Arthur. 'It's a pity you can't drink with those tablets, or I'd suggest a small sherry.'

'You have one, love. You deserve it. Give it a couple of days and I'll join you. I've decided I'm not going to take them anymore.'

'Are you sure about the tablets, Gee? The doctor seemed to think they were important to help you with your nerves.'

She straightened herself up.

'I don't need them now. I've got something else to

help me.'

She hadn't realised, until she'd said it, that she was going to stop taking the tablets but with that decision came another, and another. For her family's sake, as much as her own, she was not going to spend any more Christmases like this. She would ask Arthur for Kelly's number and tomorrow she would call her.

Arthur looked a bit taken aback. 'Really Gee? What's that then?'

'A friend. She's going to help me beat this. She's going to come to counselling with me.'

'I see, and this friend is…?'

'Kelly.'

## 30

# A SLIVER OF HOPE

### NETTA – 2019

Netta was sitting in the little breakfast room off the kitchen. She loved this room. In summer it seemed to be permanently sunny and even in winter it was bright and cheery. She'd spent a lot of time in here since moving into this house.

Was it really less than two years? Sometimes it felt as if she'd been here for much longer: so much had happened. Mostly those things were good, but this last one was definitely not, and she was still reeling from her own stupidity because there was no one else to blame for it but herself.

But there was a tiny sliver of hope. Just when she thought there was no end in sight. Her dad had messaged to say how much they'd both enjoyed the film she'd sent. Both. He definitely said they'd both enjoyed it. Netta checked the message three times, to be sure. Perhaps it was an indication that her mum was coming out of the black hole that she was responsible for. Perhaps.

Frank's dog, Fred, ambled through the interconnecting gate into her garden. Betty and Maud, who until then had been asleep next to the French windows, stirred. At least,

Maud stirred. Betty shot up and scraped at the window. Netta let her out and held the door open for Frank, who'd been a few steps behind Fred.

Frank gave her a kiss and went through to the kitchen to make a coffee with the machine she'd bought for him, a few months ago. He had one at home but maintained that this one was better, despite using the exact same coffee. Netta couldn't tell the difference. She was no coffee expert.

He brought in two mugs.

'How are you holding up?'

'Not too bad. Dad messaged me to say they enjoyed that little film we put together. That's heartening. I thought we could do some more over Christmas.'

'Good idea. I have some other news to make you feel better. I'm happy to report that your episode of graveyard vandalism will not be taken any further. You're not going to have your collar felt anytime soon.'

'What? How do you know?'

'I went to the church and had a discreet chat with the vicar. The old fella with the camera phone was doing his neighbourhood watch duty. Apparently, they get a lot of kids hanging around there drinking. He didn't actually film you. He just said it to scare you off. From what the vicar said, the poor wee man was probably more frightened of you than you were of him.'

'Probably. I must have looked quite demented. You didn't let on it was me, did you?'

'No. I said it was a relative who'd received some distressing news about Mr Corcoran. The vicar seemed happy to leave it at that. Particularly when I left a donation to the church fund. I took a look at the grave. They've tidied it up. You'd never know.'

Netta wasn't sure she wanted it tidied up but it wasn't for her to say. She wouldn't be going back there again.

'Thank you. I have to admit, I've been dreading a knock on the door from the boys and girls in blue. Kids still hang around there you said? Funny. Some things don't change.'

The landline rang. Very few people rang on the landline. Those that did were either selling something, or her parents. She rushed to the hall to answer it and was pleased to find it was her dad.

'Good news. Your mum's agreed to see a therapist.'

'That's great, Dad. You managed to persuade her, then?'

'Not me exactly. Minnie, no! Come away. Sorry love, Minnie's digging up the crocuses. She's bored, bless her. Not going out for many walks, what with one thing and another.'

'Where are you?'

'In the garden. I didn't want your mum to know I was phoning you. Oh, too late. She's at the kitchen window. I'm just going to… Oh hello, love. Should you be out here in this cold, without your coat on?'

From somewhere in the background came her mum's voice: 'Well you are. What are you up to, Arthur? Who're you on the phone to?'

'Just Netta, love. That's all.'

'And you couldn't ring her from inside on the normal phone? You had to come out here, behind my back? What have you been talking about?'

'Nothing really. Just giving her an update.'

Even from the other end of the line, Netta could tell her dad was on the back foot. It was very nearly like the old, pre-Lettergate days.

'An update? On me I suppose? Give me the phone,' said her mum. There was a long pause, punctuated by birdsong at the other end of the line. 'I said give it to me, Arthur.'

The birdsong was replaced by a rustling and then: 'Hello Netta.'

'Hello Mum. You sound a bit better.'

'More with it you mean? Yes, thank you Arthur. You can go inside now, while I talk to Netta. Can you shut the door behind you please, love?'

Netta heard the door close.

'I meant you sound a bit more like your old self,' she said.

'Huh, not sure if that's really a good indication of me being better, but I suppose it is better than sitting around like a zombie.'

'So, you're not feeling any better, then?'

'About the things I told you? No, not really. But a friend gave me some very good advice recently, and it made me realise it was about time I did something to change that. It's not fair on your dad, or you and the kids.'

'Mum, it's not about what's fair on us. It's about you. You're the one that matters.'

'If you say so, Netta. But knowing that I'm dragging you all down with me gives me a reason to buck up. I've decided I'm going to beat this.'

There was a firmness in her mum's voice that took Netta by surprise.

'Right. Okay. That's good. Dad said you're going to see a therapist. That's really great. Is he going with you?'

'No. He still doesn't know what it's all about and, you know your dad. He won't ask.'

'Do you want me to come with you?'

'No thanks, love. Someone else is coming with me. Someone with experience of this sort of thing. For the first one, anyway. You don't mind, do you? Only, I think I'd rather do it this way.'

'No. Whatever's best for you.'

'Good. Now, Netta, I don't want you and the kids mithering over me. You've spent enough time doing that. I want you to enjoy your Christmas. Your dad and me will be fine here, on our own.'

'Okay, Mum. Maybe we could come over and see you? The kids are really missing you.'

'No, I don't think so. I'm missing them too, but I'm not ready. I'm sorry. Tell them I'm sorry. I'm going to go now. Happy Christmas.'

The line went dead before Netta had a chance to pass on her own good wishes. She lingered in the hall for a few moments replaying the conversation in her head. Her dad was right. It was good news. Hopeful news. And yet, there was something that her mum had said…

'Was that your mum?' Frank called to her from the breakfast room.

Netta went back in to join him.

'Yes. She sounded like her old self again. She's going to see a therapist.'

'Great. That's fantastic news.'

'Yeah.'

'You look a bit perplexed.'

'I am a bit. It was just something Mum said that sounded really strange. She said she was going to beat it.'

'And that's strange, how?'

'It was so positive. So determined. So unlike Mum. She's got someone to go there with. She said they had experience of counselling. Or was it therapy?'

Netta was trying to remember her mum's exact words. It still wasn't quite hanging together.

'Do you know who?' said Frank.

'No. Maybe it's some kind of volunteer. Can you get volunteers for things like that?'

'Probably. It wouldn't perhaps be a friend?'

'I doubt it. Mum doesn't really have any friends.'

And then Netta realised the other reason why it had all sounded so weird. Her mum had said she'd been talking to a friend. Who the hell was that then?

## 31

# ANGELICA AND THE WONDERFUL SMILE

GERALDINE – 2020

'Kelly's messaged to say she's ten minutes away,' said Arthur. 'Do you want a bit of time to yourself before she gets here?'

'Yes please,' said Geraldine.

Her nerves were running riot at the moment and she really needed to steady them. As soon as Arthur was gone, Geraldine put her hand on the wall and walked slowly around the bedroom. It made her feel a little better.

When she'd decided on this course of action, she'd been all pumped up with bravado. The day after her decision, she'd marched into the doctor and told her, no more tablets. She wanted counselling. In the privacy of the doctor's surgery, Geraldine had even been brave enough to hint at why she needed it. As it turned out, the doctor said that what she probably wanted was therapy. If someone was to ask Geraldine what the difference was, she wouldn't have been able to tell them. Nonetheless, she'd agreed there and then.

The trouble with bravery is that it rarely lasts that long if you're not a truly brave person. So, by the time they'd got through Christmas, Geraldine's was beginning to waver. If she hadn't already told Arthur and Kelly, and Arthur hadn't told Netta, then she may very well have changed her mind. She may have just tried to soldier on, in the hope that the ugliness would fade sufficiently and return to where it came from – the darkest depths of her mind.

The only problem was that said ugliness was taking its time to loosen its grip. In fact, it was absolutely refusing to go anywhere. Geraldine was still getting the nightmares and the chest pains and, without the doctor's pills, she was left in a state of permanent agitation. What's more, she continued to have very little appetite and was wasting away to nothing. She'd always been slim, but any extra pounds she'd put on with old age had disappeared. Now, she was all skin and bone. Something had to be done. She knew it, but she was avoiding it.

Thank goodness for Kelly who once again saved her from herself by pointing out that the longer Geraldine let this go on, the more Len Corcoran was winning. Kelly was right. Geraldine was only letting herself down by not going to see a therapist. What's more, she was also letting everyone else down, because the more she dragged this out, the harder it was for her family.

So, with the new year only a few weeks gone, Geraldine made a resolution. No matter how afraid she was, for once in her life, she would be bold. She would take control and go to a therapist.

The doctor had said it was possible to arrange for one on the NHS, but she and Arthur decided against it. It wasn't that they were snobbish about these things at all. It was more a question of practicality. Practicality and guilt, if she was honest. On the practical side, now that she'd committed to therapy, she wanted to go there straight away without having to wait for the institutional wheels to turn. The quicker the better, before she got cold feet again.

The guilt side of it was a bit more complicated. There were bound to be people with much worse problems than her. The worry that she was taking a valuable place away from someone who needed it more, was just another thing to add to Geraldine's anxiety. Besides, they could afford it. They had savings. Arthur had a decent pension, and Ada had left them a lot of money when she died. She felt sure Ada would have approved of her dipping into it to get herself well. It was, after all, what Ada had always wanted.

The doctor provided a list of therapists and websites to look at, and Arthur diligently threw himself into finding the right one. When his search was finished, he presented Geraldine with a shortlist to choose from. She picked a lady called Angelica Roy. Angelica's website said she had over twenty years' experience, so she sounded like she knew what she was doing. But it was her photo that made Geraldine's mind up. Angelica had a nice face. A kind face. Geraldine reminded herself of that now, as she did a few last minute rounds of the thing with her hand for good measure.

The doorbell rang. It was Kelly. Geraldine glanced at herself in the mirror. She was looking even more hideous than she normally did. She really had let herself go. She hoped Angelica wouldn't be put off by her appearance and consoled herself with the thought that Angelica, with her twenty years' experience behind her, had probably seen a lot worse than her.

Kelly was waiting for her in the living room, with Arthur.

'All right, Gez?'

'Yes. Let's go,' said Geraldine, sounding a lot more decisive than she actually felt.

Arthur jangled his keys. 'Right then, ladies. Your carriage awaits.'

They could see Minnie's head at the window as they got into the car. Her expression could only be described as mournful. It was quite comical really.

'She don't like being left behind, does she?' said Kelly.

'I suppose not, but I won't be long,' said Arthur.

He switched the engine on and 'For Your Love' by the Yardbirds blasted through the speakers. He was obviously going through his *Sounds of the Sixties* CD collection. Very loudly. He turned it down.

'Sorry. I get a bit carried away when I'm driving on my own.'

Geraldine imagined him driving along with the sound turned up loud, bobbing his head along in time with the music. Just as he had done the first time they heard this song. He might look a bit ancient but when it came to music, age had not vanquished Arthur. And when it came to love, age had not vanquished her either. Her feelings for him were as strong as they always had been and they would never weaken. Even if he turned away from her, she would never stop loving Arthur Wilde.

'Good song. Is it like, really old?' said Kelly from the back seat.

Arthur laughed. 'Yes, really old. Gee and I used to dance to this when we were about your age. We used to go out to clubs and coffee bars all the time to listen to music like this.'

'Couple of ravers, were ya?' said Kelly.

'Yes, we flipping well were,' said Geraldine. 'We still are.'

Kelly laughed. 'So long as you're home in bed by nine, is it?'

Geraldine pretended to be outraged.

'That sounds about right,' said Arthur.

He began to sing along to the music and Geraldine joined in. She was still anxious, but it didn't hurt to have a laugh and a joke. If anything, it made her feel marginally calmer.

Arthur dropped them outside Angelica Roy's office. It was actually a big house in Edgbaston, with a side entrance for patients. Or was it clients? Geraldine didn't know the correct terminology.

'Are you sure you don't want me to stay?' he said.

'No, you go back home. I'll call you after,' said Geraldine

In truth, it would have been better for him if she'd let him stay because, by the time he got home, it would be nearly time to come back again. But there was every chance that she'd be a complete mess when she came out, and she didn't want him to see her like that.

The side entrance door was locked but there was a sign instructing them to ring the bell.

'S'pose that's so people can't just wander in off the streets,' said Kelly.

Geraldine didn't answer. Her chest pains had returned and she felt quite sick.

Kelly took her hand. 'It's all right, Gez. I'm here. I'll look after you.'

Suddenly the door was opened by a plump woman with greying hair. She wasn't Angelica Roy. This woman was white and probably in her sixties. If the photo on the website was correct, Angelica was black and at least ten years younger.

'Hello,' said the woman.

Whoever she was, she was quite friendly. All the same, Geraldine was still having trouble speaking.

'Yeah, hello,' said Kelly. 'This is Geraldine Wilde. She has an appointment with Angelica Roy.'

'Ah yes. Welcome, Geraldine. Please come in. Angelica's expecting you.'

The woman showed them into a waiting room. It was quite modern with stylish, but comfortable-looking, sofas and armchairs.

'I'm Carmel, by the way. Angelica's assistant. Can I get you something to drink?'

Kelly said she'd have a coffee but Geraldine couldn't even contemplate taking a drink. She shook her head and gripped Kelly's hand. They sat next to each other on one of the sofas.

Kelly whispered in her ear: 'Do you want me to come in with you?'

At that moment, another door opened and they both looked up at it. A middle-aged woman walked towards them. This was Angelica Roy, Geraldine recognised her from the website photo. As she got closer, Angelica's lips parted into the most wonderful smile and, despite her jitters, Geraldine found herself smiling back. She let go of Kelly's hand.

'I think I'll be all right on my own.'

## 32

# ON THE RIGHT TRACK

GERALDINE – 2020

'Our time's up for today,' said Angelica.

'Already? I feel like I've just got going.'

Geraldine blew her nose and looked at the number of used tissues in the bin. Goodness, she had got through a lot.

'You've done very well, Geraldine.'

Angelica treated Geraldine to another of her smiles. Geraldine doubted she'd ever get tired of those smiles. They were like little rewards.

It was the end of her second week. Last week, they'd talked more generally about Geraldine's life and her feelings. It was quite a nice chat really. There were a few moments that were a bit upsetting but, by the time they'd finished, she'd been as high as a kite with excitement and full of certainty that she was going to get better. She was fizzing so much, she and Kelly had to go for a walk and stop off at a café before calling Arthur to pick them up, and all she could talk about, on the way home, was what a lovely woman her therapist was.

This week, Angelica wanted to talk about Geraldine's childhood. Geraldine told her about being upset by the three little pigs story. It upset her all over again. Talking about the beatings doled out to her mother had really set the waterworks off. The funny thing though, was that, despite all the tears, Geraldine felt a bit better for having talked about it. She would have liked to have carried on, but Angelica said you shouldn't rush these things. You had to do it in stages.

Angelica opened the door to let Geraldine out into the waiting room.

'Until next week then. Make sure you practise those breathing exercises, won't you.'

'I will. I'll be an expert by next week,' said Geraldine.

Kelly was waiting for her.

'How'd it go?'

'Very good. I got through an awful lot of tissues, mind you. Shall we go back to that café? I'll show you my breathing exercises. They're supposed to help when you get stressed.'


The next seven days really dragged. Geraldine practised the breathing exercises diligently. Most of the time, she didn't actually need to do them but they gave her a bit of purpose in the long wait for her next consultation. It was only once or twice, when thinking about the previous session, that she really needed to call upon them.

In fact, she'd been thinking about that session all week and had hardly got properly upset at all. Angelica had asked her to remember what it felt like to be that child, lying in bed and being forced to listen to what was going on downstairs. Oh, that had been distressing. So very distressing. But Geraldine did it, and she'd been doing it every day since then.

Yesterday, while she was thinking about that time, Geraldine realised something. She'd only ever seen those beatings from her point of view. She'd never really thought about her mother. It was true that she'd been constantly afraid her mum might die, but that was because she didn't want her mum to be taken away from her. She'd been a child, of course, and children were naturally self-centred. It was nothing to be ashamed of. But later. When she'd grown up a bit. When she was an adult. She still only saw her own side of it. She never considered what it must have been like for her mum.

She felt rather ashamed of that now. It was the first thing she'd told Angelica when she got into the consulting room, ten minutes ago. Angelica told her there was no need to feel shame. It was a perfectly normal response. It was normal? Perhaps that meant she was normal too. Geraldine was feeling better already.

While she was still basking in the glory of being a normal person, Angelica asked Geraldine to talk about the night Len Corcoran had done that appalling thing to her.

'I think I'm going to find that rather challenging,' she said.

'I know, but shall we try?'

Geraldine nodded. She'd been expecting Angelica to ask her, sooner or later. She'd even been going over it all in her head, to prepare herself, but that was different to saying it out loud. The last time she'd spoken about that night, step by dreadful step, had been when she told Netta, and look how that had affected her.

'Take your time. Take a breather when you need to,' said Angelica.

Geraldine opened her mouth. She was going to do it. She needed to.

. . .

Of course, the difference between Netta and Angelica was that Angelica was a professional. She knew how to draw things out of Geraldine without completely destroying her. Geraldine had finished that session absolutely exhausted, but optimistic that she was on the mend. She knew that she'd spend the next week reliving that night over and over, but that was okay. It would be difficult, but she could do it.

This week, Geraldine started doing the cooking again, which was something of a relief. It gave her something else to think about, and she'd just about had all she could take of Arthur's cooking.

She went to the supermarket with Arthur, for the first time in ages. It was surprisingly tiring. When they got home, she lay down on the sofa for a nap.

When she woke up, Arthur made her one of his dreadfully weak teas.

'You were out for the count. Must have been the extra exercise,' he said.

'I didn't realise how unfit I've become. I don't seem to have a problem walking from Angelica's office to the café. It must be the adrenalin that keeps me going. Or the promise of coffee and cake.'

'You just need building up again. That's all. Perhaps you'll be able to eat a bit more now you're doing the cooking again.' He gave her a little cheeky grin.

Oh dear. Had he guessed that she wasn't exactly enamoured with his culinary efforts? She didn't want to hurt his feelings, after all he'd done for her. Geraldine kissed him on the cheek.

'Thank you, my darling. You've done so much for me lately and I really appreciate it. It's just that me doing the cooking again... Well, it helps. It feels like I'm doing something normal again. Do you see?'

Arthur put his arm around her. 'Of course I do. I'm all for a bit of normality.'

So was she. Not that she was there yet, but at least she was on the right track.

## 33

# THE ALMOST BREAKTHROUGH

GERALDINE – 2020

'So, shall we carry on where we left off last week?'

Angelica smiled. She had a lovely smile. Warm and inviting. The sort that made you want to trust her. Geraldine had seen that from the first time they met. As soon as Angelica walked into the waiting room and smiled at her, she knew she'd made the right choice. That's what she told Kelly when she came out of her first consultation, giddy as a schoolgirl with a crush.

Of course, she hadn't realised then that she was being eased into it. Lulled into a false sense of security before the trapdoor shut and she was stuck there in the spotlight, being subjected to some very personal questions. More personal than any that had gone before.

It had only been five weeks but Angelica said she'd come really far. She could almost say the r-word now, without faltering, and she'd talked through her feelings about it. Laid herself bare before this woman. Surely, that was enough? Surely, Geraldine was on the way to beating it?

But no. Apparently, there was more to come. Apparently, the lovely, smiley Angelica seemed to think it was necessary to talk about the events leading up her telling Ada. She'd started with all of that nonsense last week but Geraldine had refused to go there, so they'd ended up talking about Bree. But now Angelica was at it again.

'In one of our previous sessions you mentioned that you moved in with Ada. How did that come about?'

Geraldine's eyes flitted about the room. She couldn't look at Angelica.

'Does it matter?'

'I think so.'

'Well I don't.'

'Why is that?'

For goodness sake. All this woman ever did was ask questions. There was no end to them.

'Ada took me in and I was saved. I'd rather not say any more than that.'

'Can you try?'

Another bloody question. Geraldine clenched her jaw.

'No, I don't think so.'

'We will have to talk about it at some point, Geraldine.'

No, they wouldn't. Some things were too private to share. Even with your therapist.

'I'm sorry. No.'

Geraldine stood up and left the room.

Kelly scrambled up from the sofa, the magazine on her lap tumbling to the floor, as Geraldine shot through the waiting room.

'Gez, what the fuck?'

The lock on the side door wouldn't work for her. Geraldine was all fingers and thumbs. Kelly reached around her and opened it up. She was still talking but Geraldine could no longer hear her.

Once outside, Geraldine flung herself against the brick wall and walked from one end to the other.

'I can't do it. I won't.'

She was walking faster now. Back and forth. Back and forth. Kelly caught her in her arms. Geraldine tried to resist, to carry on walking, but Kelly wouldn't let her go.

'I've got you, Gez. I'll take care of you. You'll be okay.'

A sharp pain shot across Geraldine's chest. She was choking.

Suddenly, Angelica appeared from behind Kelly.

'Geraldine, remember your breathing exercises. Come on, do them with me. In out, in out. And again. Slowly. That's it.'

They led her back into the consulting room, sat her down on a sofa and gave her a glass of water. Her breath was flowing normally now. Angelica was telling her she was nearly there, nearly at the breakthrough point. It didn't feel much like that to Geraldine. It felt more like Angelica was trying to kill her. If this was almost a breakthrough, she wasn't sure she'd survive the real thing.

Angelica knelt down in front of her.

'I understand this is painful for you but the only way to get better is to let it out.'

Geraldine sobbed. 'But it hurts. It hurts so much. You have no idea.'

'Tell us then, Gez,' said Kelly. 'I'll stay with you if you want me too. We're going to beat this together. Right?'

Geraldine clung to Kelly. Her chest and lungs felt like they were being ripped open, and so did her heart.

## 34

# IT STARTS WITH SPAM

GERALDINE – 1961

At last Christmas was over and Geraldine was back at work, with Ada and Ruby. Arthur was around too but she couldn't face him, now that she was tainted. She was sure he'd be able to see how disgusting she was. How dirty and ugly.

But if he did, he was doing a good job of not showing it. He seemed pleased to see her. As if there was nothing different about her at all.

'Gee, come and see what I had for Christmas.'

He grabbed her arm, seeming not to notice her jump. Even Arthur's touch felt wrong. How could that be?

'I can't. I have to work,' she said.

'Mum won't mind. It's all right for five minutes isn't it, Mum?' he said.

'Just five minutes,' said Ada. 'Oh, and Arthur, in the kitchen. It wouldn't be proper in your bedroom.'

Arthur brought his new prized possession down from his bedroom and placed it on the kitchen table. It was a smart red box with a white lid. A record player of his own.

'I can play LPs, as well as singles. What do you think?'

He reminded Geraldine of her little brothers cooing over the presents Trevor and Janet had bought them. So much nicer than the paltry bits and pieces their mum had been able to afford. She ran her hands over the casing, her fingers lingering on the shiny nameplate on the front. 'Dansette.' She whispered it softly to signify its importance.

'Isn't it a beauty?' he said, his clear, ice-blue eyes full of wonder and excitement.

Yes it was a beauty, but not half so beautiful as him. He switched his gaze to her and grinned. The room lit up. It may have been cold and miserable outside; there may have been snow on the ground, but it was summer in the kitchen. In Geraldine's head, the sun was shining and the birds were singing, and she was happy, warm, and safe. In spite of the terrible thing that had happened to her, or maybe because of it, she wanted to stay with him in this room, forever. Just him and her. She wanted it so much she felt queasy. She was sick with love for him.

'Oh Arthur, it's smashing. I can't imagine a nicer present,' she said.

'I know. Good old Mum. I'll play you something on it at lunchtime, if you like?'

'Yes, that would be nice. I'd better get back downstairs.'

'Yes, sorry. I get a bit carried away sometimes. By the way, this is for you. I didn't have time to give it to you before Christmas.' He gave her a thin package wrapped in Christmas paper. 'I hope you like it.'

She tore the paper off. It was a record. 'I'd Never Find Another You' by Billy Fury. She remembered that she'd told him how much she liked it just before Christmas. It was so unexpected, and so touching that she wanted to cry.

'That's one of my favourites. Thank you. But we don't have a record player at home.'

'You can play it here, on this, if you want to. Sorry Gee, have I upset you?'

So she had cried all after all. She wiped her damp face with her sleeve.

'No, it's just … nothing. It's lovely Arthur. So thoughtful. Maybe your mum will let us play it later. I have to get back to work now.'

She locked herself in the downstairs toilet and made herself presentable. When she joined the others in the shop, she could see them casting sideways glances at her. Perhaps only other women could see when a girl had been sullied.

'Honestly Rube, he's like a kid in a sweetshop with that thing. You'd think I'd got him the crown jewels,' said Ada. 'Did you have anything nice for Christmas, Geraldine?'

'Yes, I had a cardigan my mum knitted for me, a bracelet from my brother, Phil, and a new handbag from my sister. And Arthur's just given me a present. A record.'

'Has he?' said Ruby. 'Sounds like you had some nice things. All I got was a tin of talc from Woollies and a box of Cadbury's Continental. So, you had a good Christmas then?'

'Yes. Very good, thanks.'

She bit her lip and wondered if they could tell she was lying.

She'd been doing all right until Mrs Price came in. She always got a bit flustered when she had to serve her but today, Mrs Price was even worse than usual, and Geraldine was so busy concentrating on not breaking down that she wasn't listening properly.

'I said Spam not corned beef,' said Mrs Price. 'Bloody cloth-ears. That's the trouble with you kids. Head in the clouds. No respect and no sense.'

Tears began to sting Geraldine's eyes. 'I'm sorry.'

'Oh, now what's the matter. For goodness sake girl, grow up. Whatever happened to the stiff upper lip? You'd have been no good in the Blitz.'

Geraldine's lungs felt like they were being wrung through a mangle. She was suffocating. She had to get rid of Mrs Price and get out into the fresh air. She turned, too quickly, to grab a tin of Spam and crashed into a display of cut-price Christmas stock, showering herself and the old woman with marked down chocolates and crackers.

'Well!' said Mrs Price.

The noise brought Ada and Ruby from the back of the shop. Geraldine rushed past them, out through the back kitchen and into the small yard. She tore around the yard walls, sucking the air in so fast that it scratched at her throat. She pressed her body against the last wall, hoping its coldness would cool her down. She mustn't break down. She must not. Break. Down. She saw Ada coming towards her.

'I'm sorry, I'm sorry. I'm so sorry,' she cried.

Ada put her arm around her. 'Hush now, it's all right. Ruby's sorted the silly old cow out. Don't worry. What is it Geraldine? What's the matter? Something's not right with you, is it?'

Geraldine couldn't look at her. 'It's nothing, I'm just a bit under the weather.'

'You don't seem like the sort of girl to get upset just because she's feeling a bit poorly. Has something happened? Is it Janet?'

Geraldine shook her head. From the corner of her eye she saw Ada gesturing for someone to go away. Ruby perhaps? She hoped it wasn't Arthur. Please don't let it be Arthur. He mustn't see her like this.

'Is everything all right with your mum then, your brothers?' said Ada.

'They're all fine. I'm sorry. I'm just being silly.'

How could she tell her? It might get back to her mum and, if she didn't know already, she'd find out that her daughter was a slut. And what if Ada told Arthur? She couldn't bear it if he thought that about her too.

'It's just my monthlies. I'm still not used to the pains.'

Ada looked as if she didn't believe her.

'If you say so, love. If you change your mind, you know you can talk to me, don't you? About anything. Anytime. I won't say anything to anyone else about it, if you don't want me to.'

She lifted Geraldine's chin up. 'Anything, Geraldine.'

## 35

## AN ALL TOO BRIEF RESPITE

GERALDINE – 1962

The new year had come and gone, without celebration, and the atmosphere in the Corcorans' house was back to its usual joyless gloom. With Ma Corcoran gone, Grunt went back to ignoring everyone. He may as well have not been there. Except that he was there, ruining the lives of each and every one of them in some way. Especially hers.

Geraldine did all she could to stay out of his way. At the same time, she dared not be alone anywhere in the house, in case he came to look for her. At night, she pushed her chest of drawers in front of the bedroom door, but still froze every time she heard his footsteps on the stairs. She thought of going to see Bree again, to hear about what was going on at school and to feel the comfort of being on safe old ground, but she remembered her last visit and talked herself out of it. It would be a mistake: they were too far apart now.

An escape came two weeks after Christmas. Trevor was put on the night shift and Janet asked her to stay over, in case anything happened. Geraldine jumped at the chance and hardly ever went home, even finding an excuse to stay over at the weekend when Trev wasn't working. They didn't seem to mind. For a short while at least, Geraldine was able to relax.

She'd been so tired that, at first, she slept straight through the night. It was only a couple of days later that the nightmares caught up with her. In one, she was back there, with him leaning over her, his foul odour seeping into her with every breath and every push. In another, she saw herself scrubbing at her skin to make the smell of him go away. But it wouldn't budge. She scrubbed harder. So hard that she began to bleed thick, black blood. It was pouring out of her. One minute, it was up to her knees and the next, to her neck. She always woke up just before she drowned in it. If the only dream she had was the one where he was the wolf on the other side of the door, rattling it and calling to her to let him in, she counted herself lucky. Even though she still woke up from those with no air in her lungs and no voice with which to scream, it was a good night, because she didn't have to relive the feel of him on top of her and inside of her.

Whichever nightmare it was, she followed the same pattern when she woke up. She sat up and took huge, deep breaths until she was able to stand. Then, it was necessary to do her walk around the bedroom that would soon be the baby's room. After that, she went to the window and looked out onto the long, narrow garden below. There was never anything out there but she had to be sure. She had to know he wasn't down there, watching and waiting.

It was her second Saturday at Jan and Trev's. She was making her way back there after a day at work. They'd had a lot of snow in the last few weeks and it was still frozen solid on some roads. On the busier roads, like the High

Street, it was slippery and slushy. Either way was treacherous and it took all of Geraldine's concentration to stay upright.

Although she was still having the nightmares, things were settling down a bit. Geraldine was able to get through the day without falling to pieces, even when she had to serve Mrs Price. Ada and Ruby had stopped asking if she was all right all the time. She guessed that probably meant that they thought she was back to her old self.

She'd been getting on well with Arthur too. He was back to only helping out on Saturdays now, but he'd pop in after school to say hello. That morning, he'd gone on a school trip to somewhere out in the country. She didn't envy him in this weather but he seemed to be looking forward to it. He'd be away for a whole week, and she was already pining for him.

She trudged along the road in the old wellies Ada had lent to her, because her winter shoes were useless in this weather. The wellies were too big and Geraldine's feet slopped around in them. At least they kept them warm and dry. Especially if she wore two pairs of socks.

In spite of the let-down of Arthur's trip, Geraldine was feeling mildly positive. Earlier, she'd made up her mind to offer to stay longer, and help out until after the baby was born and Janet was back on her feet. She'd have to get Trevor to ask Grunt. Geraldine couldn't ask him. She couldn't even look at him. But if Trevor asked, Grunt might say yes. She would make the offer this weekend.

When she got to the house, Trev answered the door to her. He was panic-stricken.

'I think she's having it. Stay with her while I go and call the midwife.'

He pushed past Geraldine and ran up the road to the

phone box. She watched him go down twice, on the icy road, before Janet's cry brought her to her senses.

Still in her coat and oversized boots she went into the living room. Janet was on her knees on the floor.

'Bloody hell, that hurt. Help me up, Gez.'

Geraldine got her up onto the settee.

'When Trev gets back, will you get Mum for me?'

Trevor was back in no time. His trousers were soaked from the falls.

'Midwife's on her way. What shall I do now, Jan?'

'Help me upstairs. Oh God, oh God. Where's Mum? I want Mum.' She was nearly screeching now.

'I'll go and get her,' said Geraldine.

She ran the half mile between the two houses. Her feet slid around unsteadily in the boots and she almost lost them once or twice. It was freezing cold but, by the time she reached home, she was sweating.

Her mum had the door open before she got to it. She must have seen her coming.

'What's the matter? Is it Jan?'

Geraldine could hardly catch her breath. 'It's happening. She wants you.'

'Has someone called the midwife?'

'Trev.'

Her mum's face was the picture of control. 'How often are the contractions coming? The pains, Geraldine. How often is she getting them?'

'I don't … I don't know. Ten minutes, I think. Maybe a bit longer.'

'Right. I'll get my things together. Go and knock Brian's door and see if he can give me a lift. Hurry up now. Tell him it's urgent, or I wouldn't have bothered him.'

She ran over to Brian's – one of the few people on their street with a car – and banged on his door. Brian answered.

She was till out of breath. 'It's our Jan. She's having the baby. Mum needs a lift.'

Brian pulled his braces up over his jumper and shouted to the back of the house. 'Gotta give Mavis a lift. Urgent. Their Jan's havin' the babby.'

Her mum came out of their house with her coat on, her handbag and a bulging shopping bag.

'There's no one at home. The boys are out playing and your dad's at the pub. You'll have to stay in and let them know what's happening. Make sure the boys get to bed on time and wait up for your dad. You know he likes a cup of tea and something to eat when he gets in.'

She climbed into Brian's car and left Geraldine alone.

She'd walked around the walls of her bedroom and the living room, but the fear and dread wouldn't go away. Geraldine hated this place. For as long as she could remember, she'd hated it. But now the loathing was more physical. She ached all over. Her belly was contracting, pulling itself in, tighter and tighter.

She pressed her ear against the living room wall. If she quietened down her breathing, she could hear next door's telly and their kids running up and down the hall. There were other people nearby, leading perfectly normal lives. She traced the walls, from corner to corner, again. When she reached the final one, she sat on the floor, her arms wrapped around her knees. All she could do now was wait.

The sudden light from the hall, through the open door,

made her blink.

Tony flicked on the switch in the living room.

'What you doing sitting in the dark? Where's Mum?'

She shaded her eyes. 'Jan's baby's coming. Mum's gone round to help.'

'What's wrong with putting the lights on then? Thought no one was in ... or something...' He called out to Ralph. 'It's all right. Gez is in 'ere. Nothing to worry about. Mum's gone to Jan's. She's having the baby.'

Ralph strolled in and threw himself on the settee. 'Thought something bad had happened. Anything to eat, Gez?'

She pulled herself up. 'How should I know. I haven't been here, have I?'

'Do us a jam piece then.'

'Do it yourself, lazy sod. I'm not your slave.'

Ralph shrugged. 'Our mum'd do us one.'

'Yeah, well I'm not her, am I. Make one yourself, or starve.'

Ralph tutted and stomped out to the kitchen.

'Make us one an' all Ralphie,' shouted Tony.

He was fiddling with the dials on the telly, trying to get a decent picture. Ralph was moaning about having to do everything, or something like that. Neither of them could hear him properly, over the fuzzy sound. A few minutes later, he came back with two folded slices of bread and jam and gave one to Tony.

With her brothers for company, there was at least some distraction. She ignored her mum's orders and let them stay up as long as they wanted. If they were still up when she returned, they could always pretend they were too excited about the baby to sleep. But as the hour grew later, it dawned on her that her mum wasn't coming back. When the boys eventually took themselves off to bed, she had to acknowledge the inevitable. She was going to have to face the Grunt on her own.

About an hour after the boys had gone up, Geraldine heard him stumbling through the front door, into the hall. The rattle of the living room door made her jump up from the settee. She could hear him on the other side, muttering to himself, cursing. Just like her dream. She held her breath as it opened.

He staggered in and looked at her, as if she were nothing. 'Where's Mavis?'

'She's at Jan's. The baby's coming.'

He looked confused, like he was trying to remember who Jan was. Then, he fell into his chair.

Geraldine had never seen him so drunk. Usually, he could at least stand. With any luck, he'd be too drunk to stay awake. Still, she had to get out of the room. She had to pretend everything was normal, and follow her mum's instructions.

'Shall I get you a cup of tea, or something to eat?'

He moved his head. She couldn't tell whether it was a yes or a no. He slurred out something that sounded like: 'Tea.'

'I'll put the kettle on.'

The memory of the last time she'd done that for him, flashed through Geraldine's head. She began to tremble. The only way to the door was to walk past his chair. She veered as far away from him as she could, but he caught her arm and pulled her back.

'Don't go.' It was almost soft and pleading.

She'd never heard him speak like that. Perhaps, he was

ashamed of what he'd done to her. Perhaps, he was going to say sorry. He pulled her towards him and she fell awkwardly onto his lap. She knew then she was wrong. He wasn't sorry at all. He forced his lips onto hers. She tried to get away, but he wouldn't let her. He pulled her closer and murmured something in her ear. He was too drunk. She couldn't make out what he was saying. She hardly wanted to know. He said it again, just one word. Had she heard it right? Yes, she was sure she had.

He held her in his grip, pushed her onto the floor and kneeled over her. The full horror of what he was about to do took possession of her. This time, she wouldn't lie back and let it happen. She couldn't. She tried to wriggle away, to fight him off but, even drunk, he was too strong for her.

'Please don't hurt me again. Please,' she begged.

He moved his hand up her legs, his fingers clawing at her knickers. He was on top of her now.

She punched him and tried to kick out. 'No Dad, don't.'

He stopped and stared at her, as if seeing her for the first time. He lurched backwards and scrambled up, into the chair. With his head in his hands, he let out a great sorrowful sigh. His shoulders began to shake. Was he crying?

Geraldine hauled herself up and pulled up her knickers. As soon as she stood, she felt faint and almost went back down. Somehow, she willed herself not to.

He was properly sobbing now. He didn't seem to notice her creeping around him, into the hallway, and out the front door.

The freezing air nearly knocked her for six, but she didn't stop. She kept on walking, through the front gate and past the houses, until she'd gathered enough strength to run, blindly, yet with a single purpose in mind. To get away.

## 36

# A DASH TO SAFETY

GERALDINE – 1962

Twice in one day she'd been running until her lungs were bursting. The first time, she'd been running towards something, in anticipation of a happy event. Now, Geraldine was running away. She didn't know where to. She didn't care. It was enough to be clear of him. Her legs were jelly and her knees cut to shreds. She wasn't sure how many times she'd slipped over. She knew her feet were wet and frozen, but she'd lost all feeling in them. She kept on going, until she found herself outside the shop, banging on the side door.

A window opened above, but that alone was not enough to stop her hammering.

'Who's there?' It was Ada's voice. 'Geraldine? Is that you?'

'Let me in. I have to get in,' she screamed.

'Hold on, I'm coming down.'

At last the sound of footsteps descending the stairs; the unbolting of locks; the door opening. Then Ada was there, in her dressing gown.

Geraldine fell into Ada's arms, shrieking, hysterical,

wretched and bloody. 'Close the door. Close it. Don't let him get me.'

'What's happened? Is someone after you?'

'Don't let him get me. Help me. Please help me.'

She folded and fell to the floor, howling and sobbing at Ada's feet.

It took some time for Ada to get her upstairs. It was as if the very act of getting to the shop had taken everything out of Geraldine, and she had nothing left to give. She collapsed on every step. Ada was nearly carrying her into the living room. She lay Geraldine down on the settee.

Geraldine became aware of sharp pains in her hands and feet. Particularly her feet. She looked down at them. Ada was looking at them too. She hadn't realised that she was still wearing her slippers. They were torn. The sole was hanging off one of them. Her dress was wet and dirty with mud, and something else. Blood. There was blood all over her.

Ada was talking. It sounded soothing but the ringing in Geraldine's ears blocked out the words. All she could take in, was the gentle tone of Ada's voice, tender and reassuring. Geraldine was so tired and cold. She just wanted to sleep and never wake up. She closed her eyes.

When she opened them again, the grey daylight was doing its best to lighten the room. She tried to lift herself up, but the weight of something was holding her down. She was covered in a mound of blankets. She heard footsteps getting closer and turned her head towards them. It was Ada.

'Morning sweetheart. I've brought you a cup of tea. Do

you think you can sit up? Let's take a few blankets off, shall we? You were so cold last night I couldn't get you warmed up. Your feet were blue.'

As soon as she sat up, Geraldine felt the pains returning in her hands and feet, her head, and knees. Everywhere. Worst of all was her belly. It felt like she'd been punched in the gut. Then, something inside her began to rise, winding its way up through her windpipe and crawling over the roof of her mouth.

Ada sensed it and held out a bowl for her to be sick in.

'Shouldn't think you'd have anything left by now. That's the third time.'

The third time? Geraldine couldn't remember. Everything was a blank after she'd closed her eyes last night. 'I … I'm sorry, Ada. The mess.'

'Not really, love. I already had a bowl with me when it happened the first time. I was trying to clean up your cuts. So I caught it in time. Try this tea now. See if you can keep it down.'

She obediently sipped the tea. The heat of it burnt her throat, but it was sweet and strong and tasted like the best she'd ever had.

Ada sat at the other end of the settee.

'Geraldine, I don't want you to be frightened, but I need to tell you that you've been bleeding down below. Quite a bit. I know it's rather personal but I've put you a sanitary towel on and I managed to put some old bath towels underneath you to help soak it up.'

Geraldine lifted the blankets. Underneath her was a growing circle of red, seeping across the towels. She buried her face in her hands.

'I shouldn't have come here. Look what I've done now.'

'No, sweetheart, don't cry. It's nothing to worry about.

Let's try to get you to the bathroom. You can take that dirty dress off and put on a clean nightie. I've asked a doctor to come over. He'll be here soon. He's a very nice man. An old friend of mine. No need to be frightened. When he's gone, you and I can have a talk.'

Geraldine rose unsteadily. Together they walked to the bathroom. The blood from her privates was running down her legs and dripping onto the floor. She looked down in horror, then relief when she saw that Ada had already rolled the rugs away.

'It's just a bit of blood. It'll wash off,' said Ada.

When they got to the bathroom she dropped down on the toilet. The blood was sticking to the inside of the basin. It was thicker now, like fat, slimy slugs, and was the colour of Trevor's Christmas port.

'Are you normally this heavy?' asked Ada.

Geraldine shook her head. Unlike Bree, the curse had never really bothered her much, before now. Sometimes, she hardly bled at all.

There was a knock at the downstairs door.

'That'll be Charles, my doctor friend,' said Ada. 'Stay there. Don't try to get off. I'll be right back.'

Ada returned a few minutes later.

'The doctor's here. I'm afraid he's going to have to take a look at your insides, to make sure there's nothing wrong with you, down there. Do you understand what I mean, Geraldine?'

Geraldine shook her head. 'I can't Ada. I couldn't stand it.'

'I know, my love, but we have to make sure you're all right. He's very kind and gentle, I promise. I'll stay with you the whole time.'

She didn't have the strength, or confidence, to argue.

Ada helped her put on a fresh sanitary towel and pulled down her dress. She found it hard to stand up straight, the pains in her stomach were so bad. She was bent double, like an old woman.

A rubber sheet was laid out over Ada's bed. A man was standing by it. He was smiling and frowning at the same time. It was the same man who'd been with Ada, at the dance.

'Hello Geraldine. I'm Doctor Samuels. Charles. Can you sit down on the edge of the bed? I'll take a look at these cuts and bruises first.'

He checked her head and eyes, and asked how many fingers he was holding up. Then he wiped something over the right side of her brow and under her eye. It stung.

'Nothing too bad there, as far as I can see. There's some grit which I can get out. You'll have quite a shiner for a while, but no permanent damage. Do you remember what happened to you?'

'I was running and I fell over. Lots of times,' she said.

'That would explain the hands and knees.' He turned her hands over. 'And the knuckles? Was that the fall too?'

'I don't remember.'

'I think it might have been when she was banging the door to come in,' said Ada.

'I see. Now, Geraldine, I need to examine you to see why you're bleeding quite so much. Could you to lie down on the bed? I promise I'll be as quick as possible. Please tell me if anything hurts.'

Geraldine began to cry. Ada held her hand.

'Hush now, sweetheart. I'm here with you. I'm not going anywhere. Charles is the best doctor in Birmingham. He only wants to help you.'

The doctor smiled again but his eyes were still serious. 'Maybe not the best, but I've had no complaints so far.'

Geraldine flinched when he touched her tummy, every now and then pressing down and asking if it hurt. When he put something cold inside her, she tried to think about something else. She fixed her mind on the record that Arthur gave her for Christmas, singing the song in her head. Arthur. Thank goodness he wasn't here to witness this.

'Do you have a boyfriend, Geraldine?' the doctor asked.

'No.'

'I'm sorry to ask you this, my dear, but have you ever had sexual relations with a boy. Even if he wasn't your boyfriend?'

She pressed her lips together and shook her head. He wasn't a boy. She wasn't lying to the doctor really.

'You do know what I mean by that term, don't you, Geraldine?' he said.

She nodded, pinching her mouth tighter.

The doctor and Ada were both watching her. They probably didn't believe her.

'Well then, has someone done something to you that you didn't want them to? Have they … forced themselves on you, Geraldine? If it's a secret, it's okay to tell me, my dear. I'm like a priest, you know? I won't tell anyone if you don't want me to.'

Ada gave squeezed her hand. 'Do you want to tell us what's been happening to you, sweetheart?'

Her face crumpled. 'Yes.'


When the doctor had gone and it was just the two of them there, Ada helped her into the bath. A slick of red slid out from between Geraldine's legs, turning the bath water pink. It was revolting, but the hot water was soothing. Ada handed her some soap to wash herself down below, while she washed Geraldine's back. She gave Geraldine some fresh knickers and a nightie, and helped her back to the settee, wrapping her up in the warm blankets, with a hot water bottle for the pain. She threw more coal on the fire. Its flames lit the room, giving it a relaxing red glow. Geraldine lay watching it flickering while Ada busied herself in the kitchen.

Ada brought in a tray of tea and sandwiches. Geraldine couldn't remember when she'd last eaten. Probably a couple of biscuits in yesterday afternoon's tea break. She bit into it. Cheese and onion. It was so good.

'Got your appetite back then?' said Ada.

She realised she'd been gobbling it down. 'Sorry. I was hungry.'

'That's all right. Good to see you eating something. Here, have another one.'

Ada watched Geraldine eating, picking at one of the sandwiches herself.

'I've sent word to your mum, to let her know where you are.'

Geraldine stopped chewing.

Ada carried on: 'Stan, Karen's dad, went round this morning and told her for me. I expect she's been worried about you. I told him to say you'd had some kind of accident and that I was looking after you. That's all. Obviously, I didn't know the full story at that point. Geraldine, do you understand what's happened to you?'

'Yes. He ruined me. Forced himself on me. That's what the doctor called it, wasn't it?'

'Yes, love, it is, but do you know what happened to you last night and this morning?'

'He tried again, but he was too drunk.'

'You poor, poor love. Do you understand what's wrong with you now? Why you're bleeding?'

'I fell over, and I'm having my monthlies … my period.'

'Not your period exactly. I'm afraid you had a baby inside you and you lost it. You've had what's called a miscarriage.'

A baby? No, that wasn't possible. Janet was having the baby, not her. She couldn't be. She didn't have a husband. She wasn't old enough.

'You know, what your dad did to you is against the law? If you report it to the police –'

'No. I couldn't. Please don't make me do that.'

'Of course I wouldn't, but don't you want to tell your mum?'

Geraldine shook her head.

'What about Janet then? Will he have tried it with her?'

'No. It's only me. I'm the only one that looks like her.'

'Like who?'

'Frannie.'

'Frannie? You mean Frances?'

'It's all my fault, Ada. If I hadn't made myself look like her. He'd never have done it to me. I'm to blame. I'm the whore. You can't tell my mum. You can't tell anyone. Ever.'

## 37

## MAVIS PAYS A VISIT

GERALDINE – 1962

Geraldine spent most of that week in Ada's bed while Ada slept upstairs, in Arthur's room. If she hadn't been so racked with exhaustion, she'd have felt more guilty about it. The bleeding down below had stopped. Doctor Samuels said there was more blood than he would have expected, but he didn't think there was anything wrong. When she was stronger she'd have to have a proper check-up. Geraldine didn't want to think about that right now. All she wanted to do was sleep, while it was safe to do so. The doctor said rest would help her recovery and it did seem to be working. The pains in her tummy were getting milder and the cuts on her knees were clearing up, but her hands and feet were swollen and sore. The doctor told her they'd get better in time.

Ada and Doctor Samuels had been all for going to the police, but she begged them not to. It was only when Geraldine said she wouldn't be able to live with herself if it all got out that Ada said she would keep it to herself. After some persuasion on Ada's part, the doctor agreed too. It wasn't that Geraldine had made up her mind to kill herself, but she hadn't ruled it out yet. It all depended on what happened next. Arthur would soon be home. She really wanted to see him, but she was afraid he'd find out about the disgusting things she'd done and never want to see her again. She asked Ada, over and over again, not to tell anyone. Especially Arthur. Ada gave her word. For a few days that gave Geraldine some peace of mind but, as his return drew nearer, one question began to dog her. Where would she go when Ada needed her bed back?

The anxiety was beginning to take over her and, once again, Geraldine couldn't sleep. Sometimes, when the panic seized her, she'd have to get out of bed and walk around the walls.

Once, Ada came in, right when she was in the middle of it, and she had to confess that she was scared to death of going home.

'I know, sweetheart. I know. Don't worry, I'm going to do everything in my power to make sure that doesn't happen,' she said.

Ada must have told the doctor, because he gave Geraldine something to help calm her nerves. After that, she could hardly stay awake.


Geraldine woke up from one of her sleeps. It was Friday afternoon, the day before Arthur was due to return. She'd been dreaming about him coming home, like a soldier in the war. She was waiting for him at the station and, when he got off the train, they ran into each other's arms. It was all very romantic. Nothing at all like reality.

She was still groggy but she heard voices in the kitchen. One of them was Ada's. The bedside clock said it was one o'clock – dinnertime. The other voice was probably Ruby, and yet, it didn't sound like her. It sounded like – she listened hard – it sounded like her mum.

Geraldine got out of bed and crept into the hallway to hear better. Yes, it was definitely her mum.

'And this doctor friend of yours said she's all right now?'

'Yes. She'll be back on her feet soon, but she doesn't want to go home. I'm sorry Mave, but the doctor thinks it's for the best if she stays here.'

'Did she say why she doesn't want to come home?'

'Well … it's Len.'

Geraldine held her breath. Ada promised. She promised.

'What about Len? Has she said anything? Something must have happened. All I know is I get back from Janet's and he's lying drunk on the living room floor. The next morning I get up and find she's disappeared. He won't say a word about it. I've tried asking him, and all I got was a slap. Do you know what's going on? Because I'm sure I don't.'

'I think she's frightened of him, Mave.'

By now, Geraldine was standing in the kitchen doorway.

Ada saw her. 'Hello Geraldine, look who's come to see you. I've told your mum all about your accident on Saturday night. Luckily no broken bones. The doctor thinks the car must've just clipped her, Mave. You two go in the living room, it's warmer in there. I'll bring the tea in.'

Geraldine relaxed a little. Ada hadn't given her secret away. Alarm gave way to relief

Her mum sat awkwardly on the big, comfortable settee. It was obvious she felt out of place.

'How are you feeling?'

'All right. Better,' said Geraldine.

'I should think so. You must have looked a right state

when you turned up on Ada's doorstep, if those bruises are anything to go by. What were you doing out at that time of night, Geraldine? Why weren't you in bed?'

Geraldine couldn't look at her. She didn't want to lie, but she didn't want to tell her the truth either.

'Was it your dad? Did he have a go at you? Is that it?'

Geraldine shrugged.

'Well, something must have upset you,' said her mum.

'I don't want to talk about it.'

'Well that's all right then, isn't it? I mean, there I was, dog-tired after being up half the night with our Janet. Not a clue where you'd gone off to. Only to have Stan bloody Parsons knocking on my door and telling me you'd been wandering the streets at night, and had some kind of accident. Tell me this much at least, will you? If you were upset, why did you come here? Why didn't you come round to Janet's? Why didn't you come to me?'

Her mum glared at her. She was furious, but she was also hurt. Geraldine could see it in her eyes.

At that moment, Ada came in with tea and cake.

'Sorry, it's shop-bought. I've never been any good at baking. Do you still make that fruit cake your mum used to make, Mave? That was lovely cake.'

Geraldine's mum softened a little. 'Sometimes. I'll make you one next time I come. Geraldine likes it. She'll miss it if she's coming to live here.'

'Am I?' asked Geraldine. 'For good, you mean?'

'If you want to,' said Ada. 'Arthur will help us get the box room shipshape when he gets back tomorrow. You can move in there.'

Her mum straightened herself up, her attention fixed on the fire. Her mouth was pinching and pulling. She was upset and it was taking all of her control not to show it. Geraldine wasn't sure if that was for her benefit, or Ada's.

'I don't know what your dad'll say, mind you. If he says no, then you'll have to come home.'

'Sorry Mavis. If Geraldine wants to stay, she's staying. If Len says no, tell him to come to me. I'll sort him out,' said Ada.

Her mum sniffed. 'Well if you manage it, let me in on the secret, will you? I've been trying for years and look what good it's done me.'

She nibbled on her cake as if she was only eating it to be polite, and she wanted them to know it. In the end, she put the plate down and cast her eyes over the paintings on the walls.

'You've got it nice here, Ade. You've got lovely taste. It's no wonder she prefers it to her own home.'

'You know that's not the reason,' said Ada softly. 'She'll always love her mum. You know that, don't you?'

Her mum was fighting back the tears now. Ada had said that to be kind, but it was probably the worst thing she could have said. She picked up the teacup handle with her thumb and forefinger and looked at it like it was lost treasure.

'Proper china.' She took a sip. 'He wasn't always like this. He was golden when we were courting. Tell her, Ada. You remember how lovely he was when we first got married? When he came back, he was different. The war. It did that to some men. It changed them.'

Ada stood up. 'I've got to go and open up the shop. Geraldine, I've left you something for your lunch in the kitchen. I'll ask Stan to come over at the weekend to pick her things up, Mave. Come and see her whenever you want to.'

'I would if I had any time to myself. It's cost me an arm and a leg to get here today,' said her mum.

'Well, you'll always be welcome. Stay as long as you like and help yourself to tea and cake. I'll see you in a bit,' said Ada.

Her mum waited until she knew Ada had reached the shop before she started: 'Just in case you were wondering, Janet had a boy. Ian. Thank you for asking.'

'Sorry, I…'

'Forgot? Wasn't interested?'

She picked up her half-eaten cake, examined it closely and let it fall back onto the plate, a look of disgust on her face.

'This is what you've left me for, is it? Shop-bought cake and lunch. Dinner not good enough for you? What does she call your tea, eh?'

'Dinner,' said Geraldine.

'Typical.'


Geraldine ate her lunch alone in the kitchen, after her mum left. She was trying to make sense of her mum. Before she'd come to work for Ada, she'd thought her mum was the nicest and most selfless person she knew. Lately though, she'd seen another side to her. There was a bitter spitefulness about her and it always seemed to be directed towards Ada. Geraldine didn't like it at all.

When it came to her feelings for her mum, Geraldine had always been so certain about where she stood. Love wasn't a word that was banded about in their house but, until recently, there'd been no doubt in her mind that her mother loved her. Now she wasn't so sure. Because, if her mum really did love her, why hadn't she wanted to know more about the reason Geraldine had run away? And why had she not protected her better in the first place? She could only conclude that her mum didn't love her at all. Not in the way proper mums did. Well, so be it. If her mum didn't love her, then she didn't deserve Geraldine's love in return. There was someone else who was making a better job of mothering her. Ada.

Geraldine washed up and prepared some vegetables for dinner. If she was going to be staying here, she wanted to make sure Ada didn't regret it. She was going to do all she could to be useful. She got washed and found her clothes. Thankfully, the stains had washed out. Ada must have done that. By the time she'd had a quick tidy in the living room, she was tired again and sat down for a rest. Before she knew it, her eyes were closing and she was asleep.


Ada woke her up for dinner. It was steamed haddock.

'Thanks for getting the veg ready for me. I've been rushed off my feet downstairs, so it was a nice surprise. Did you do that sort of thing for your mum?'

'Yes. I'm sorry I haven't been working this week, Ada. It must have been really hard for you when Ruby wasn't here. I'll come back tomorrow,' said Geraldine.

'Don't you worry about me. I can cope and Ruby's done some extra hours. It's helped her to make up for her Christmas spend. Karen will be here tomorrow, so we'll manage. Doctor Samuels will be back on Monday. If he gives you the all-clear, we'll have a think about you coming back to work. Everything go okay with your mum, did it?'

'Not exactly.'

'She'll come round. Her pride's a bit hurt, and she's got a lot on her plate.'

'Old Grunt, you mean?'

'What?'

'It's what Phil calls him. Old Grunt.'

Ada laughed. 'I can see why. Mind you, if I had to pick a name for him, it would be a lot worse than that.'

'Same here. Ada, can I ask you something? I think you might be the only person I'd believe.'

Ada frowned. 'Go on then.'

'Phil says he's not really our dad. It's true isn't it? I mean he wouldn't really have done that to me, if he was my dad. Would he?'

Ada put down her knife and fork.

'Yes, it's true. It would have been impossible for him to be either yours or Phil's dad. He disappeared off the face of the Earth just after your aunt Fran was killed. That was before he was captured, by the way. Just stopped contacting your mum after she wrote and told him about Fran. He didn't come back until after you were born. Fran died in September 1942.'

'And what mum said, about him being golden before the war. Was it true?'

'I wouldn't have said so, no. But your mum was mad for him. Maybe she saw a different side to him. She was right about one thing, though. He was much worse when he came back.'

'Do you know who my dad was?'

'There was a Canadian fella your mum was sweet on. I think it was him. You mustn't think badly of her. The thing is, everyone thought Len was dead, including her. She did try to find out what happened to him, but even the Government didn't know. The Japanese weren't like the Germans. They didn't notify the War Office when they took prisoners. When your mum found out he was alive and on his way back, she didn't know what to do. I don't know why she chose him over the Canadian. I'm sure the Canadian would have stood by her. I mean, it's not as if Len was ever that nice to her, as far as I could see. Perhaps she thought she should stay and look after him after all he'd been through. I expect she's had plenty of time to regret it since. Geraldine, when you came here last week in that state, you said something about Janet not being like Fran. What made you say that?'

'In that state'. Geraldine replayed the words in her head. She didn't like to think about that night but it seemed important to Ada and she owed her that much.

'When he tried to do it to me, that night, he said Fran's name. I think he thought I was her.'

Ada put her hand to her mouth. 'Dear God.'


The next morning, Karen came in to see her.

'I've got you a present. I hope you don't think it's too soppy. I know how much you liked Algernon and I thought you could probably do with someone to keep you company.'

She gave Geraldine a bag from Greys, one of the big department stores in town. Inside was a cuddly teddy, very like Algernon.

'It's never too late to have your own bear, is it?'

Geraldine squeezed the bear and sniffed him. 'He smells of lavender.'

Karen grinned. 'I wanted to give you the full experience. Do you like him?'

'I adore him. I'll have to think of a name for him.'

'Hmm. How about Arthur? He looks like an Arthur to me.'

Geraldine laughed. 'We've already got an Arthur.'

'Arthur Two, then.'

Karen dipped her finger in a glass of water by the side of the bed and pressed it onto the bear's head.

'I hereby name thee, Arthur Two. God bless you, and all who sail in you.'

## 38

# GRUNT BREAKS THROUGH

GERALDINE – 1962

Grunt's letters started coming not long after Geraldine's mother had been round to see her. The first ones were addressed directly to Geraldine but she recognised the writing on the envelope and put them straight in the fire. Then Ada started getting them. Geraldine didn't ask Ada what she did with them.

It was nearly closing time. Geraldine was thinking about the weekend. She was going to the pictures on Friday night. On Saturday evening, she, Arthur and Karen were going to a coffee bar to see a new group that was playing there. She had the day off on Monday and was going to use it to go shopping. There was a nice dress she'd seen in the window of C&A that she couldn't wait to try on.

Ada interrupted her thoughts, calling to her from the back kitchen.

'Can you lock up, Geraldine?'

Still thinking about the dress, Geraldine turned the lock on the shop door and flipped the sign over to 'Closed', then went to pull down the blinds. The traffic had died down now, and the road was quieter, or else she wouldn't have noticed the man standing in a shop doorway, on the other side of the street. It was him. She was sure of it. It was definitely him, and he was watching her. She jumped back and gasped.

'What is it?' said Ada.

'He's over there.'

Geraldine pointed at the doorway but, when she looked again, he was gone.

'Who? Len? Was it him? You're sure?'

'I ... I think so.'

'Wait here.' Ada unlocked the door and went outside to look up and down the street. 'If it was him, he's gone now. If you see him again, tell me straight away.'


A week had passed. She was beginning to think she'd overreacted and that it hadn't been him at all. Ada seemed to be making sure Geraldine wasn't on her own in the shop but, other than that, things were back to normal. Arthur was out and she and Ada were clearing everything down before they closed. Geraldine was sweeping the floor behind the back counter.

Ada checked her watch. 'Right, that's it. I'll lock up.'

The doorbell tinkled. Someone must have made it just in time. Geraldine looked up from her sweeping. To her horror, she saw Ada falling backwards as the full force of the door hit her. Behind it was Len Corcoran, his fists balled and his face full of fury.

He slammed the door shut. Within a few paces, he was close enough for her to smell him. Swarf, oil, and beer. He was still wearing his work clothes. He must have stopped at the pub on the way home. He leaned over the counter to grab her arm. She instinctively drew back before he could get hold of her.

Ada scrambled up. 'Get away from her.'

He ignored Ada and kept his eyes fixed on Geraldine. 'You're coming home. Move!'

He lunged for her again but this time Ada pushed her way in front of him.

'Geraldine, go upstairs and lock yourself in. Wait by the phone. If I don't come up in five minutes, I want you to call our Stan. Tell him to come straight over with the rest of my brothers.'

'Stay there,' roared the Grunt.

Geraldine wanted to run but she couldn't make her legs work.

'Off you go now, there's a good girl,' said Ada. On the face of it she appeared calm but there was a tremor in her voice that gave her away.

The fear of staying overcame everything else and Geraldine backed away. She ran up the stairs but she was afraid for Ada. Instead of locking herself inside the flat, she waited by its open door and made herself listen to what was going on.

She could hear Ada, her voice more composed now, strong and determined: 'I'm giving you the chance to go home, Len, before my brothers have to come over and give you the kicking you deserve.'

'I'm going nowhere without my daughter. She belongs at home with her family, not with a pervert like you.'

'It's a bit late to be calling her your daughter isn't it? We both know she's not, and we both know what you did to her. So don't you dare speak to me about perversion.'

'Don't know what the fuck you're going on about.'

'You know exactly what I'm going on about.'

'It's lies,' he said. 'She's just making it up. She needs to come home so we can sort this out.'

'Sort it out?' said Ada. 'Make sure she hasn't told anyone else, you mean. You forget, I was Frannie's friend. I know you, Len Corcoran. I know everything about you. I know what you're capable of. You're an evil bastard, and you're not getting anywhere near that girl ever again. Now get out while you still can, with both your legs intact.'

There was silence then Geraldine heard the doorbell go. She heard bolts shutting and then Ada calling to her: 'It's all right, Geraldine. He's gone.'

Ada came up to her. She was shaking, and so was Geraldine.

'I don't think he'll be back. You're safe.'

Ada went over to her drinks cabinet, poured herself a small whisky and knocked it back. Geraldine had never seen her do anything like that before.

'Arthur will be home soon. I'll get on with the dinner,' she said. 'Do you need something to calm your nerves?'

Geraldine shook her head. 'No, I'll just go to my room for a bit until…'

Ada nodded. There was no need to say more.


Geraldine closed the door to her bedroom and walked around the walls. With each new wall she repeated the mantra: 'He's gone. I'm safe.'

Arthur Two was propped up against her pillow. She lay on the bed and held him tight, squeezing his soft body and breathing in his lavender scent.

'He's gone. I'm safe,' she said again. 'He's gone. I'm safe.'

Eventually, she heard Arthur come in. Ada was chatting to him as if nothing had happened. She got up and tidied her clothes, checked in the mirror for stray tears and went out to join them.

## 39

# KELLY HANDLES THE AFTERMATH

KELLY – 2020

Kelly put the cup down in front of Geraldine.

'One cappuccino.'

It was actually Geraldine's third cappuccino since they'd arrived nearly two hours ago. Although, in fairness, the first one had gone cold before Geraldine had been able to finish it.

'I've ordered us both a cake as well. The guy's bringing it over in a minute.'

Geraldine nodded. She still looked a bit shell-shocked.

'How're you doing, Gez?'

'Erm, I'm not sure really. I feel a bit lightheaded,' said Geraldine.

'That might be the coffee though,' said Kelly.

'Hah, you could be right. I have had rather a lot, haven't I?'

'Here we go, ladies.'

The guy stood over them. Without the counter to cover him, Kelly could see that he was dressed kind of retro. He looked like someone off the covers of Arthur's old vinyls.

'Right then,' he said. 'I have one chocolate brownie and one tiramisu.'

Kelly took the brownie. 'That last one's for you, Gez.'

'Oh dear, more coffee,' said Geraldine.

'Is it? Sorry. He said it was guaranteed to put a smile on your face.'

'House speciality,' said retro guy. 'People come from far and wide for this little taste of heaven.'

'I see. Well then, I'd better try it.'

Geraldine took a tiny forkful. She was still eating like it was hard work. She raised an eyebrow and loaded up her fork again. This time, when the food went in, a faint smile flickered across her face.

'Mmm. That really is a little taste of heaven.'

Retro guy looked happy. 'Told you.' He turned to Kelly. 'Would you like a sample, on the house?'

'Nah, you're all right mate. I'll stick with my brownie.'

'She's got very plain taste. Not very adventurous,' said Geraldine.

Retro guy tutted and went back to the counter.

Kelly grinned. 'Oi missus.'

'I know, I know. Pot, kettle, black.' She made a noise that was very nearly a laugh. Maybe the coffee was getting to her.

Kelly took a mouthful of the brownie. 'You did good today. Angelica seemed really pleased.'

'She did, didn't she? Thank you. I couldn't have done it if you hadn't been there.'

Kelly shrugged. 'That's okay. We're friends, aren't we?'

'Someone else said that to me, a long time ago. I went to her for comfort when no one else could give it to me. Then, I dropped her like a stone straight after. I kidded myself we'd grown apart but, really, it was because she reminded me of what I could have had, and I didn't want reminding.'

'You were in a bad place. It's understandable.'

She sighed. 'Perhaps. I can't help feeling that I used her though. Sorry to unload all this stuff on you.'

'Like I said, we're friends.'

Geraldine reached across the table and took Kelly's hand. 'We are, aren't we?'


Arthur dropped Kelly off up the road from Netta's. Ordinarily she'd have stayed in Kings Heath and popped in to see her nan, but she didn't have the energy today. She wouldn't have said it to Geraldine, but the afternoon had been pretty traumatic for her as well. Gez running out of the building like some batshit crazy woman and being impossible to calm down was bad enough. But then, the story she told was almost too much. Gez had been shaking so much, it had taken a couple of attempts to get the story out. It was so fucking awful, Kelly didn't know how she'd managed to stop herself from crying. And she didn't cry easily.

Kelly opened the front door and the smell of curry hit her. Netta and Frank were in the kitchen, chatting. Netta was stirring a pot of something on the hob.

'Good timing. We've done a curry for dinner. I was just about to put it out. We've made it mild, just the way you like it.'

Kelly took a seat. She didn't particularly fancy socialising right now, but they looked like they really wanted her to sit with them.

'How did it go with your nan today?' asked Frank.

'Yeah, okay. Usual.' She hated lying to them but what else could she do?

'Everything all right? said Netta.

'Yeah, fine. Sorry. I'm a bit knackered.'

Her body ached all over. Especially her chest. It was because she caught hold of Geraldine when she'd been running up and down the wall. It had sent Gez into fight or flight mode. Since she couldn't choose flight, she fought. Tomorrow, Kelly would have the bruises to prove it. Tonight, she just felt sore. She ate her food at breakneck speed, and finished it before they were halfway through theirs.

'I might go up and have an early night.'

'Are you sure you're okay. You're not feeling ill or anything?' said Netta.

'Nah, just tired.'

Netta was worried about her. It was nice. But how could she tell her the real reason? Netta was probably the only other person that knew what had happened to Geraldine and it would have been a help to talk to her about it, but it wouldn't be right. Kelly had brought this on herself by interfering. She'd just have to keep her mouth shut until the time was right. Besides, she knew that in a few days' time when she'd processed it, she'd bounce back again. Whereas Geraldine had been stuck with it for most of her life, and if she was going to help Geraldine see this through, she needed to be strong.

## 40

# LOST IN THE JUKEBOX

GERALDINE – 2020

Angelica put a fresh box of tissues on the table. Geraldine took a handful and blew her nose.

'You should get shares in Kleenex. I expect you get through a ton of them.'

'You could be right. I'll have to look into it.' Angelica's lips parted into one of her lovely smiles and Geraldine basked in its warmth.

After that day of the 'almost breakthrough' it had taken a couple of sessions for her to trust that smile again, but the trust had come back. She understood now that Angelica's persistence had been necessary to dislodge something that had been stuck since 1962.

'Do you want to carry on?' said Angelica.

'I'll try.'

'We were talking about the time your mum came to visit you at Ada's. About your feelings.'

'Yes. Ada wasn't wrong about much but she *was* wrong when she said I'd always love my mum. Before the ... before the rape, my mum meant everything to me. I really loved her and I was terrified of losing her. Terrified that I'd get up one morning and find her dead on the floor. But the day after he did that to me, when I came downstairs and she was acting like nothing had happened, despite having this enormous black eye, I couldn't get rid of this feeling that she knew what he'd done to me. That's what started it. And the missing pants, of course. I never found out where they went to, but I half-suspected that she found them and disposed of them.'

Angelica sat almost completely still while Geraldine did the hand thing. It was okay to do it here, in the open, without worrying about anyone thinking she was odd. Angelica had said it was perfectly normal to do it. Nothing to hide.

Feeling better, Geraldine rested her hands on her knees and carried on: 'What finally did it, was when she came to visit me at Ada's that time. It was like I saw her for the first time. You know when people say the scales fell from their eyes? It really was like that. She was so spiteful and two-faced about Ada. Like it was wrong for Ada to better herself. It was just so small-minded.'

She looked down at her lap and realised she'd been twisting her skirt around into a knot.

'Take your time, Geraldine,' said Angelica.

'Like I said, she didn't want to know. About why I'd run away, I mean. She was more angry that I'd gone to Ada and not her. She asked me why I'd left in the night like that but the way she asked it, she really didn't want to hear the answer. It was as if she was frightened of it.'

'Why do you think that was?'

'I think I was right in the first place. I think she already knew. She knew, and she couldn't face it.'

'And how did that make you feel at the time?'

'Unloved. Unlovable. Angry. I think I've been angry with her ever since.'

'And now? How do you feel about it now?'

'Still angry. And disappointed. Very disappointed.'

Kelly was in the waiting room when Geraldine came out. These days they only met up afterwards. Geraldine no longer needed her to come for the whole thing, but she did enjoy their little chats afterwards. A debrief was what Kelly called it. A while ago Geraldine had changed her therapy sessions to Tuesday afternoons, so that Kelly could come straight from the foodbank to meet her for the debrief, before taking the bus home.

Kelly looked up from her magazine and grinned. She was really quite pretty when she smiled.

'All right, Gez? Usual place?'

'Of course.'

The café was half-empty so they managed to find a table quite easily. It was done out like a 1960s coffee bar. It was very authentic, except for the coffee and cake which were miles better than any on offer in the sixties. They even had a jukebox playing the old tunes that she and Arthur loved. She and Kelly had been coming here since they found it after that first session with Angelica. They'd got to know Sonny, the owner, quite well – or retro guy, as Kelly insisted on calling him. When Geraldine walked through the door that first time, 'All or Nothing' by the Small Faces was on; the coffee machine was hissing in the background, and she was immediately transported back in time. She could have easily been back at the Stage Door, or El Sombrero. She'd wasted a lot of her spare time in those two, along with Arthur and Karen, after she moved into Ada's. Happy days.

'How did it go then?' said Kelly. 'How many boxes of tissues did you get through?' It was a standing joke between them.

'Only half of one today.'

'Result. Wanna talk about any of it?'

Geraldine took a sip of her cappuccino.

'Do you know what? I don't think I do. I'm worn out with talking about it. How are Netta and the kids doing?'

'All right. They're still worried about you. Arthur calls Net with an update every now and then. Did you know that?'

'I guessed it. He and Netta have always been very close. You don't think she's said anything to him do you?'

'Nah, but I think she's finding it hard not being able to talk about it. And not seeing you and Arthur. Her and Liza are pretty cut up about that. Will's worried about you as well. We keep in touch.'

'Do you? I suppose the two of you have always got on well.'

'Yeah. We're good mates.'

Kelly's cheeks went pink. It was easy to spot on her because she was normally so pale, and it was quite unusual to see her embarrassed. In fact, the only time she ever showed any hint of it was when she talked about Will. It reminded Geraldine of the days before she and Arthur got together, when she would look at him and Tina in envy. Poor Kelly. Unrequited love was a hard thing to bear.

'How's your nan getting on?'

'Yeah, she's tip top. Says she should have done it earlier. She's walking a bit better, and dancing. She won't admit it, but she's got a bit of a romance going on with this old fella, Alec. Talking of which, I said I'd go over there. You ready to go?'

'No. You go. I'm going to have another coffee. I might see if Arthur wants to come over. He'd like it in here. It's just like the coffee bars we used to go to when we were courting.'

Kelly pulled a soppy, most un-Kelly face. 'That's kind of sweet. Shall I get you another coffee before I go?'

'No, I'll get it.'

Kelly raised her eyebrows. 'This is a first, you going to the counter yourself. You'll be getting the bus on your own next.'

Geraldine got up and made for the counter. 'Go on, Miss Sarky Pants. I'll manage.'

She returned to her seat feeling quite pleased with herself. She couldn't remember the last time she'd sat in a café on her own. Let alone, order a drink by herself. It was probably before Ada died. Everything got so much more difficult after that.

She checked her phone. Neil had messaged her again. They were corresponding regularly now. Just little messages, a couple of times a week, about this and that. The latest was about a meditation class. Angelica had suggested it because she'd been doing so well with the breathing exercises. She couldn't, in a month of Sundays, imagine herself meditating and that's what she said to Angelica.

As usual, Angelica was not one to give up easily.

'If Ada was alive today, do you think it would be something she might try?'

Geraldine had already told her Ada was very cultured and always up for new things, so she only had herself to blame for Angelica bringing Ada into the equation. Ada was fast becoming a benchmark for things Geraldine should consider.

'Probably. I'll give it some thought,' she'd said.

'If you decide to go, I can recommend a good class. Perhaps your friend could go with you.'

'Kelly? No. That one couldn't sit still to save her life.'

'Your daughter then?'

'No. I'm not ready to see her again. I'll ask my friend Neil. He's very spiritual. He probably already does it.'

It was only after she'd messaged Neil that Geraldine realised she'd been unwittingly talked into it. She was very good at her job that Angelica.

She noticed she'd had a reply from Arthur. He was on his way. Although she'd been meaning to invite him along for a while now, she hadn't said much about the café to him so far. Mainly because she rather liked the way being here made her feel, and she was reluctant to spoil it. In here, she was different. Not young and carefree exactly, but no longer old and afraid. And confident. She felt confident. Although that could be because she'd just come out of her therapy session. Whatever it was, it was doing her the power of good and she didn't want to lose it. On the other hand, she really wanted to show Arthur this place. She couldn't wait to see his face when he walked in. Not only would he be surprised to see her on her own, sipping a cappuccino, but he couldn't fail to be whisked back to the days of their youth, just as she was.

Fontella Bass, 'Rescue Me' was playing on the jukebox. The coffee machine bubbled and hissed its reminder that it was still there. Geraldine closed her eyes, the taste of fresh coffee on her tongue, and lost herself in her memories.

## 41

# ARTHUR'S FIRST CONFESSION

GERALDINE – 1962

Geraldine's mum hadn't been to see her since the first week of her recovery. Most likely it was because Grunt had forbidden it, but Geraldine couldn't help questioning if it was because she couldn't look her in the eye.

Phil came to see her now and then, and she was able to fill him in on the details about who their real father might be. He was impressed with Ada's home, and said he'd like to have somewhere like this when he and Cissy got married. He only asked once what had happened that night. Geraldine told him she didn't want to talk about it and he didn't ask again.

Janet came to see her once, with her new baby, Ian. They took him for a walk around Kings Heath Park. Jan tried to persuade her to visit their mum. She got quite huffy when Geraldine refused, but made no attempt to find out why. It was a bit strange really. Geraldine was sure she'd have asked, if the boot had been on the other foot. Because she didn't want to talk about it herself, Geraldine pushed it to the back of her mind. But every now and then, a thought popped up in her head. A niggle. Why didn't they want to know more?

She'd been living at Ada's for four months now. At first she'd been scared to go out on her own, but she was just as frightened of being alone in the flat. That was probably why Ada asked if she'd like to accompany her on Wednesday afternoons. Ada was the only person Geraldine felt one hundred percent safe with, so she'd jumped at the chance. Wednesday afternoons were Ada's cultural afternoons. Sometimes, they'd go to one of the museums in town. Sometimes, they'd go to a music recital, the theatre, or a poetry reading. Often, they'd be joined by Ada's friends who were a mixture of ages and quite a lively bunch. It opened up a whole new world to Geraldine.

As her confidence grew, Geraldine started going out with Karen and her friends. They were too young for the pubs and clubs, but they went to a dance occasionally. Most of the time they went to coffee bars. They were great places to hang out. There was usually a jukebox that played all the latest hits. Sometimes, they even had groups playing in them. Her favourite coffee bars were the Stage Door, and El Sombrero.

Occasionally, she'd bump into Phil with his mates or his girlfriend, Cissy. Arthur would often come along too. Usually with Tina. Once, she even saw Bree at the Stage Door with some of the other girls from school. They said hello to each other, but it felt awkward and Geraldine spent the evening avoiding them. It seemed like she was a few years ahead of them now that she was living with Ada.

Thanks to Ada, she was doing the kind of things she always expected she'd be doing with Bree when they got to university. She was starting to become the kind of person she would have wanted to be, if circumstances had been different. Except, of course, that she was working in a shop. Not furthering her education. Aside from that minor detail, Geraldine had never felt so free. Ada wouldn't take any money for her keep, so she had more than she'd ever had in her life. She bought new clothes, make-up, and records that Arthur let her play on his record player. She even had her hair cut at a proper hairdresser.

On the whole, things were getting better. She was still having nightmares. Still waking up some nights unable to breathe. But a walk around her bedroom helped to calm her down. She knew that the ugliness Grunt had forced inside her would always be there, but she was finding ways to mask it, as long as she had Ada to protect her. She would have liked to be sure she'd always have Arthur too, but he had Tina and they seemed very keen on each other, despite Karen's insistence that it was Geraldine he was sweet on.

It was a Friday evening. Ada was at the theatre with Doctor Samuels, so there was just Geraldine and Arthur listening and dancing to the records on his Dansette. She'd never known anyone who loved music quite so much as him. It was hard to keep up with all the singers and groups that he followed.

'I've just bought this one, Gee. I think you'll like it,' he said.

It was the latest one by Ray Charles, 'I Can't Stop Loving You.' They both liked Ray Charles.

When it finished he put it on again. 'You know, that's how I feel about you, Gee.'

'What do you mean?' She wasn't sure she'd heard him properly.

'What it says on the label. I can't stop loving you.'

She blushed. 'Stop messing about.'

'I'm not messing about. I mean it, Gee.'

'But what about Tina?'

He ran his finger along the seam of his jeans.

'We're not together anymore.'

'She broke it off?'

'No, I did. It was no use me carrying on with her when all I can think about is you. I didn't tell her that much. I didn't want to hurt her feelings. I think she guessed though. Gee, do you think you might feel the same about me some day?'

Arthur loved her. He actually loved her. She could hardly believe it.

'I already do,' she said.

He grinned. 'Oh boy. You've made my day. You've made my year. Does that mean you'll be my girl, then?'

'Just you try and stop me.'

He touched her hand with the tips of his fingers.

'Don't worry, I won't. Can I kiss you? I've been wanting to do it for so long.'

Something fluttered inside her. She felt sick with joy. 'Yes.'

He moved closer. His fringe fell over his pale blue eyes and, at that moment, she knew there would never be a time when she didn't love Arthur Wilde.

## 42

# NEIL AND KELLY SPILL THE BEANS

NETTA – 2020

'The therapist is definitely helping,' said Netta's dad. 'Yesterday your mum invited me to meet her in a coffee bar. Nice place it was. Just like the old coffee bars we used to go to when we were courting.'

'A coffee bar?'

He was calling Netta while walking Minnie. A truck must have gone past, making it hard to hear him but Netta was sure that's what he said.

'Yes. She's been going there with her friend, after her sessions with Angelica.'

'Angelica?'

'The therapist. Lovely woman, by all accounts. Anyway, this week, your mum decided not to leave with her friend. She messaged me instead and asked if I'd like to meet her there. As you can imagine, I was a bit worried about her being there on her own but when I got there, I found her with her a cup of coffee in her hands, her eyes closed and big smile on her face. And do you know what she said to me?'

'No Dad, what?'

'She said, "I was just thinking about the first time you kissed me." I wasn't expecting that, I can tell you.' He sounded full of beans.

'That sounds great. She's still going with her friend, then?'

'No, she meets her afterwards. I know your mum being alone in a café doesn't sound like much, but it really is. I haven't told you before because I didn't want to worry you, but she's lost a lot of confidence in the last few years. She's been going downhill since your gran died really.'

'I didn't realise. I wish you'd confided in me, Dad. I might have been able to help.'

'All water under the bridge now, Nettie. Your mum's improving. I can feel it. I'd better go, I'm almost home. Oh, by the way, are you being careful? They reckon that Coronavirus is over here now.'

'I know. We're trying to be. Just as well you two are hardly going anywhere at the moment. Give my love to Mum.'

Netta hung up, a tiny bit happier for the news that her mum was on the mend. Her dad called once a week and he always finished on a positive note, no matter how small. Netta wondered if he did this to convince himself, as much as her, that things were improving. Although this latest news really did sound promising. Perhaps the therapist really was helping.

She hadn't spoken to her mum since before Christmas when she'd told her she was going to try therapy. She'd tried calling her, but she either didn't answer or refused to speak to her. She didn't even reply to Netta's messages. Before the letter, her mum sent messages throughout the day, thanks to

Neil who'd introduced her to WhatsApp. If Netta was honest, she'd found it to be a bit of a pain. What she wouldn't give now to get them. Even one a week would make her happy.

So, her mum had been on a downward slide since Granny Wilde's death? If only her dad had told her before, but that was her dad all over. Much as she adored him, Netta found his habit of keeping bad things to himself a little bit annoying. It was like he had this mad need to shield them from anything unpleasant. It was almost a compulsion.

Not that she could blame him for her own lack of attentiveness. She should have noticed. It was true she'd had a lot going on in her life, but what kind of a daughter was she not to see what was happening? A bad one, as it turned out. She loved her mum with all her heart but she had to admit that she also found her tedious on occasions. It came from a lifetime of having to tread softly around her moods. After the first fifteen years or so, they became a sort of background noise. Netta was conscious of them being there, but took very little account of them. If only she'd kept her eyes and ears open, she might have seen her mum properly. She might not have shown her that letter.

Netta scrolled through the messages on her phone, back to one her dad had sent at Christmas. It was a selfie. Her mum and dad with put-on smiles on their faces, both holding a glass of something to the camera. It was meant to cheer the family up, to let them know they were all right really – no need to worry – but every time she looked at it, she wanted to cry. They looked old and tired. Especially her mum. There seemed to be hardly anything left of her. That's what Netta had done to her. To the both of them. Even in Netta's darkest days, they'd always been there for her. But one day they wouldn't be. She was suddenly overcome with a deep sadness. God, she missed them.

Neil walked into the office-cum-rest room, where Netta was supposed to be making tea.

'Kelly's just finishing off, then she'll be in for lunch. Kettle on, is it?'

Netta looked up distractedly. 'Er no, sorry. I've just been on the phone with Dad. He thinks Mum's therapist is helping.'

'Great. I'll make the sandwiches.'

'Okay. I'm just going to send Mum a message.'

She tapped out a few words in the hope that this might be the one her mum answered:

*'Hi Mum. Dad tells me you're doing well. Do you think you'd be up to a visit from me tonight?'*

Just as she'd finished making the tea her phone beeped. It was her mum. At last, a response:

*'Sorry love, I'm going to a meditation class with Neil. Give it a while longer and I might be ready to see you again.'*

A meditation class with Neil? For fuck's sake! She could have taken her to one of those if she'd said. She could have done all sorts of things for her, if she'd only asked. And another thing. Why hadn't Neil told her he was seeing her mother? Was he this friend who was accompanying her to the therapist? It was the kind of thing he'd offer to do. But to not tell her? She threw her phone down on the table. It was loud enough to make Neil look up from his sandwich making.

'Everything all right?'

'Not really. Mum tells me she's going to a meditation class. With you.'

'Ah.'

'I mean, don't get me wrong, I'm glad she's going there with you. I'm just a bit surprised you didn't tell me.'

Neil had the guiltiest expression she'd ever seen on him. It made Netta feel quite bad for having a go.

'Sorry. We weren't sure how you'd take it, and we didn't know whether Geraldine wanted you to know. But, if she's told you, then she obviously doesn't mind.'

'Quite.'

Netta took an angry sip of tea and hurriedly swallowed it down to get to her next point, because she'd just processed what he'd said. The tea was hot and burnt her throat so she had to swallow several times before she was able to speak.

'Hang on. We? You said *we* didn't know whether Geraldine wanted you to know.' Then she remembered her dad's words. He'd referred to the friend as her. It wasn't Neil at all. 'Who else is in on this with you?'

Kelly opened the door, just as Netta thought Neil was about to throw himself at her feet and ask for forgiveness. Instead he flashed Kelly a look that spoke a thousand words.

Kelly stopped in her tracks. 'What?'

'It's you, isn't it?' said Netta. 'You're the friend who's been going with Mum to the therapist. That's why you've been leaving the foodbank early on Tuesdays.'

Kelly sat down at the table. 'Fuck it. Yes, it's me. I talked her into doing the therapy. I've been going with her every week.'

'But she said she was going with someone who had experience of counselling,' said Netta.

'Yeah, well I have,' said Kelly. 'When my mum died, I had mental health problems. The doctor got me into counselling and it helped a lot. So I told Gez she should try it because it might help her. She asked me to go with her. I used to wait for her while she did the session. Then we'd go for a coffee and cake, and talk about stuff. Now she's okay going on her own and I just meet her afterwards, for the coffee and cake bit. She talks about her stuff and I talk about mine. I dunno why, but it just makes us both feel better. Clearer, I suppose.'

Netta turned to Neil. 'And you?'

Neil put his hands up, as if she were about to shoot him.

'She just messaged me about meditation class. We'd exchanged a few messages before. That's all. Her therapist suggested it, apparently. Tonight's the first time.'

It had been a strange day, all in all. After the revelation that her two closest friends had been secretly supporting her mum, the afternoon had been a little strained. Not that Netta held a grudge or anything. It was just that she didn't want Neil to feel guiltier than he already looked. So she decided not to talk about it. The problem was, not talking about it made everything else seem a bit false. So yes, the afternoon had been a tricky one.

Unlike Neil, Kelly didn't seem to have been visited by the guilt monster. Aside from electing not to mention Netta's mum at all for the rest of the day, she carried on being her usual self, which was probably just as well, since she had nothing to be guilty about. If anything, Kelly deserved a medal. All the same, even though Netta loved Kelly, she couldn't imagine her mum seeing her as a friend. She wasn't even sure her mum liked Kelly.

Netta had so many questions she wanted to ask. How had Kelly become her mum's closest ally? How had she got her mum to listen to her and, most pressing, had her mum told Kelly what Len Corcoran did to her? From what Neil said, it was doubtful that her mum had shared her trauma with him but, unlikely as it might seem, it was possible she'd told Kelly. Netta decided the drive home was the perfect time to find out.

They hadn't got far when Kelly gave her the opportunity to ask.

'Net, I'm sorry I didn't tell you about Geraldine. I wanted to but I thought you might be mad at me, and Gez wasn't keen.'

'It's okay. I understand. Sorry if I went off on one,' said Netta.

'You're all right. I don't blame you. I'd be a bit pissed off about it as well.'

'Has Mum told you what happened?'

'Yeah. Bad enough to be raped. But her own stepdad? He must have been some twisted fuck. Is it just you and me that knows, do you think?'

'I er, I told Frank. No one else though.'

'That figures,' said Kelly.

'I wish she'd let me see her.'

'Give her a bit more time. She feels like she's failed you. I know, I know. I've told her that's stupid, but it's what she thinks. I'll talk to her again.'

They drove on listening to the sound of the radio, each seeming to be lost in their own thoughts, until they turned into their road. Netta brought the car to a stop outside the house, but she was in no rush to get out. She had something to say first.

'Thank you, Kelly. You might just have saved my mum.'

Kelly's face lit up. 'That was always my plan, Net. It's my way of saying thank you for saving me. You took me on when no one else wanted to know. If it wasn't for you I'd probably still be bumming around with that shit, Craig. Or sleeping on someone's sofa. I did it for you but, to be honest, I'm doing it for Gez now. We're pretty tight now, the pair of us. I hope you don't mind.'

'Not at all,' said Netta. 'I'm glad Mum's finally found a friend.'

## 43

# NETTA IS KNOCKED SIDEWAYS

NETTA – 2020

Liza was at her dad's house and Frank was working late. There was a lot of speculation that the country might go into lockdown because of this virus, and the college where Frank worked part-time was holding a meeting about what to do if that happened. So it was just Netta and Kelly for dinner. It gave Netta the chance to talk freely.

'How is Mum, really?'

'She's doing okay. I know she doesn't look it, but she's strong,' said Kelly.

Strong? That wasn't a word Netta would have used to describe her mum. Perhaps, like beauty, strength was in the eye of the beholder.

'And this therapist. Angelica, was it? Is she good, do you think?'

'Yeah. I mean, she's nice. She comes across all soft and understanding, but she's dead firm. She's really pushed Gez sometimes. Like, this one time she wanted Gez to talk about why she went to live with Ada. Gez had a complete meltdown, and she was hyperventilating like crazy. It would have been so easy to leave it for the next session, but Angelica got her through it. She got Gez to talk about it.'

'About the rape?'

'No, she'd already done that. The other thing.'

'The other thing?'

Kelly was watching her. She was probably trying to read her, to see if she knew what this mysterious 'other thing' was. Netta stared her out. Sooner or later, one of them was going to have to give. It turned out to be Kelly.

'You don't know, do you?'

'I think I probably don't,' said Netta.

Kelly put her head in her hands. 'Shit.'

'Please tell me.'

Kelly sighed. 'If I do, Geraldine mustn't know.'

'She won't.'

'Okay then. She ran away to Ada because her step-dad tried it on again, although he was too drunk to do anything.'

There was a long pause. Netta waited. She was sure there was more to come.

'She had a miscarriage when she got to Ada's. Turned out she'd been pregnant from the first time.'

The words hit Netta like a punch in the gut. She felt winded. Unable to speak. Unable even to react.

'Net, are you okay?'

'Yes, of course.'

'It's just that you're shaking.'

Netta looked down at her hands and then she began to feel her body quivering. Kelly was right. She was actually shaking.

'I think I need…'

Kelly took a half-empty bottle of wine from the fridge

and poured her a glass. Netta took a large gulp and let it wash down.

'I was going to say, I think I need a bit of time to let it sink in, but this helps. Thank you.'

Long after Kelly had gone to bed, Netta sat in the breakfast room with Maud and Betty, thinking about this latest revelation. She knew that her mum had had other pregnancies and miscarried, although she didn't know how many. The other thing she didn't know, until earlier, was that one of them had been as a result of what Len Corcoran did. And there she was, thinking she knew everything she needed to know about the horrors of her mum's early life. Just when she thought it was safe to start feeling a bit positive, Netta had been knocked sideways again.

She recalled telling her parents about her own miscarriage, last year. Just like her mum, she had carried that secret with her for a long time. A secret Netta thought only she and Colin knew. But when Colin's new partner, Arianne, had smugly informed her that she'd known for years, it had been the impetus that Netta needed to tell her family and friends. No wonder her mum had been so understanding when she told them.

Netta had been thirty-six when she miscarried. More than twice the age her mum had been that first time. She couldn't even imagine what must it have been like to deal with all of that when you were only sixteen. It had been hard enough at thirty-six. From the sound of it, her mum was still deeply traumatised by it. Who wouldn't be?

Netta's face was wet. She'd been crying silently so that she didn't alert Kelly, but the dogs had noticed and were leaning against her legs. If she'd been crying for herself, perhaps she'd have found some comfort in their warm bodies pressed up close, but she wasn't. She was crying for her poor, poor mother. For all the things she'd had to overcome, and for those she had yet to face.

## 44

# ARTHUR TWO MAKES A RETURN APPEARANCE

GERALDINE – 2020

Arthur was out doing the shopping. He reckoned Geraldine would find it too stressful, what with all the rules about keeping your distance and the queueing. They were only letting so many into the supermarkets at a time, apparently. So it was best for only one person in the family to go. Geraldine had to laugh when he got back last week and declared it was like wartime Britain out there.

'How would you know? You weren't even alive then,' she'd scoffed.

'Take my word for it, Gee, it is. You should see the empty shelves. They're having to ration some things. One chap had four family-size packs of toilet rolls and he was really put out when they made him take three back. I wouldn't mind but he was about our age. He'll probably be dead before he opens the last pack.'

It wasn't like him to have a rant. Although, by other people's standards, it wasn't what you'd call a rant. But Arthur was so mild mannered that this was the nearest he came to anger. It was getting to him all of this – her breakdown, this pandemic, the deaths, the endless worry. It was definitely getting to him.

She tried to make it easier for him but Geraldine knew that top of his worry list was her. He was afraid she was going to plummet into despair any day now that her ties with the outside world were limited. He was wrong of course: Neil and Kelly were calling her every couple of days and Netta had set up a family and friends WhatsApp group so, even if she didn't contribute, she could see all the funny messages going back and forth. What's more, unlike a lot of people, lockdown rather suited Geraldine. Its rules were like walls. So long as you stayed within them, you were safe.

The biggest misunderstanding on Arthur's part was to assume that she missed the outside world. She didn't particularly. The truth was that her ties with it had always been limited and, even though Netta had brought her new friends into Geraldine's life in the last year or so, the ties had been diminishing for a while. Geraldine could see that now. Thanks to Angelica, a lot of things were becoming clearer.

She was still seeing Angelica. In fact she'd be seeing her in a few hours. For most of lockdown, they'd used Skype on Arthur's old computer, but it didn't really work for Geraldine. She missed having Angelica in the room with her, and the computer kept crashing so Arthur had to be on hand to put things right, which meant she didn't feel safe enough to talk openly. Recently, Angelica had taken pity on her and had let her go back to face-to-face consultations. She'd set up a 'Covid secure' space in her garden. It wasn't quite the same as being in the consulting room, but the garden was big enough to allow them some privacy. Between them, they made it work.

Geraldine was on a stepladder in Netta's old bedroom, trying to ease a small box from the top of the wardrobe. She should have waited for Arthur to do it – he was taller and stronger than her. But this was a private thing, between her and Angelica. She just about managed to get the box down without falling off the ladder. The effort made her realise again just how unfit she was. It was a good thing she'd started making the most of the allowed hour of exercise. She and Arthur used it to take Minnie for a long walk.

Minnie was with her now, stretched out on the carpet, but not asleep. She might have looked relaxed but she was watching Geraldine intently, following her every move. She did that a lot. It was as if she was on constant alert, ready to spring up and reassure Geraldine whenever she got upset. Before Minnie came into her life, Geraldine had no idea just how sensitive dogs were to human emotions. Sometimes it felt as though she and Minnie were directly connected to each other. Funny that. Kelly would probably say she'd turned into a crazy old lady – if she was having one of her more polite days. Perhaps Geraldine was. Perhaps that was why she chose a dog with separation issues, and an obnoxious girl with a foul mouth to be her guardian angels. Quite an unlikely pair but then not all guardian angels have wings and halos, do they? Sometimes they come in the most unlikely packages.

Geraldine sat on the floor next to Minnie and stroked the top of the dog's head.

'This is my good memories collection, Min. That's why it's not very big.'

She made herself laugh with that little joke, but Minnie didn't get it at all. She dropped her head onto her paws and whined. Maybe she just thought a collection that size was nothing to laugh at.

Geraldine opened the box. It was an accumulation of all the things that had mattered to her in the past. She hadn't opened it for a few years. Even then, the last few times were just to put something in. It had been lot longer since she actually took something out and looked at it.

She did that now. She picked up the box's contents, one by one, and really looked at them. There were Valentine's cards from Arthur, including the first one. She read it for the first time in years:

*'To my girl, Gee.*
*You're the best.*
*All my love,*
*Art xxx'*

She kissed it, then went through the rest of them. Eighteen in all. Arthur still sent her Valentine's cards but she'd stopped keeping them a long time ago. Probably about the same time she stopped calling him Art.

She went through Netta's things. A lock of her baby hair, the hospital name bands, a tin containing her baby teeth, and the clothes they'd brought her home from the hospital in. Her darling daughter. Daft as a brush sometimes, but she loved her so much. She hoped she was all right. Arthur said they'd had to scale the business right down because they were only able to sell through the shops they had contracts with, if they were open. In the meantime, they'd opened up the foodbank for an extra day and were doing door to door deliveries to the vulnerable. Geraldine still had difficulty sometimes believing that this Netta was the same downtrodden person who had been married to Colin Grey. She was so very proud of her. If only she could face her again and tell her that.

She found what she was looking for, wrapped up in a plastic bag. She put her hand inside and squeezed his soft, squishy body. Arthur Two. It was good to see him again, after all this time. Also in the bag was a glass bottle. She pulled it out, sprayed its contents over Arthur Two and breathed in. Lavender.

'Got to get the full experience,' she said to Minnie, who sniffed the air and sneezed.

Geraldine examined Arthur Two, her first and only teddy bear. He didn't look too bad considering his age. She thought about the day Karen gave him to her. Karen had been on her mind a lot lately. Karen and Bree.

She put Arthur Two to one side. She had to get a move on if she wanted to finish before Arthur One got home. There was one final bag that she needed. It was at the bottom of the box. She'd lied to Minnie. It was not only a good memories collection. Her fingers hovered over it, daring herself to open it, but she couldn't. Not yet.

'So, this is Arthur Two,' said Angelica. 'You must be quite attached to him if you've kept him for so long.'

'Yes, I suppose so,' said Geraldine. 'He was a great comfort, just after the rape.' She was able to say it these days without hesitating.

'And later?'

'Yes, and later too. He helped me to get over my need to walk around the walls when I got the jitters. I transferred it to him, you see. That's how I started with the hand thing. I did it to him.' She demonstrated the strokes and taps on Arthur Two's tummy. 'I had to wean myself off him when I got married. I couldn't have Arthur thinking I was mad. Sorry, I know we don't use that term now, but you know what I mean.'

Angelica gave her one of her smiles. 'Is that when you started doing it secretly on other things?'

'Yes. I thought I had it pretty well hidden, but Kelly saw

through me. I don't know if anyone else did. Perhaps one day, I'll ask them.'

'Can you tell me about the times when you felt you needed him most?'

Geraldine's heart began to pound and the butterflies in her stomach were at it again.

'Oh dear, Angelica. You do ask me to do the hardest things.'

'Would it help if you held Arthur Two? You can do the hand thing if you want.'

There seemed to be no end to Angelica's patience. Geraldine picked up Arthur Two and stroked his fur, then tapped out the usual rhythm. The bear's happy face seemed to be willing her to open up and peel away another layer of fear. She breathed in his lavender scent. She could do this.

## 45

# THE GHOST OF LEN CORCORAN

### GERALDINE – 1967

Geraldine was on her way home. She'd just been to town to get the last things for the baby. Only seven weeks to go. Arthur had a wall planner up in the kitchen to count off the weeks and days. It had been there since the doctor said they'd passed the danger zone. It looked like this one was going to survive. Not that you'd know, the way Arthur behaved. She could hardly cough without him getting into a tizzy. She'd been the same too really. Lately, though, she was beginning to feel more positive. This one was a fighter. She could feel it. This was going to be the one.

They'd been married nearly three years. Arthur had proposed to her on their way home from a Rolling Stones concert at the Odeon, in town. It had been a month before her eighteenth birthday. He told her later, he'd been planning to ask on her birthday, but he'd been so pumped up after the concert that he couldn't stop himself. They were married the following year.

For the first year, they carried on living over Ada's shop. Ada bought a double bed, and Geraldine moved into

Arthur's room. Arthur got a good job with the Civil Service, and she continued working in the shop.

Two years ago they bought their house. Not having to pay Ada any rent had given them a chance to save, but the deposit would still have been a stretch, if Ada hadn't helped out. The house was cheaper than most because it was a bit run down. Arthur called it a fixer-upper. He enjoyed fixing things up. They'd done some work on it already. It was good to have something to focus on. Something to take them out of themselves. Especially after they lost their first baby.

Geraldine got off the bus. It was a sunny day. The birds were singing and the trees that lined their street were full of blossom. On the journey home, she'd thought about getting off the bus early to see Ada and Ruby, but she couldn't be sure Ada would be there. Now that she had two shops and had learned to drive, Ada was always flitting back and forth between them. It would have been nice to see Ruby, but Geraldine was too tired. She needed a bit more energy to cope with Ruby on her own. All that conversation was exhausting. Everything was exhausting at the moment. She'd have a lie down before putting the hoover round.

She walked up the garden path, her mind on the steak she was going to cook for dinner. She rooted around in her bag for the keys. Where were they?

'Geraldine.'

She froze. Geraldine hadn't seen him in five years, except in her nightmares, but she knew that voice. She would never forget that voice. She searched the bag frantically and seized upon the keys as soon as she saw them.

Before she could put the right one in the lock, Len Corcoran had his hand on her shoulder and pulled her round. She had no choice but to face him. The sight of him was a shock. His skin was yellow and so too were his eyes.

She remembered him as a big man, but he looked smaller. Diminished somehow. He was like the ghost of the man that used to be Len Corcoran, but she was still afraid of him.

'Geraldine, I–'

'No!' she screamed. 'Get away from me.'

If it hadn't been for the baby Geraldine would have crumbled, but she had to fight. She had to keep him away from her child. She shoved him with all the strength she could muster and was surprised at how easily he fell.

She rammed the key into the lock and turned it, pushing it open against her weight and crashing onto her knees in the hall. Her legs hurt. Her stomach twisted and turned. She wanted to collapse, but she could not give way to it. She had to think of the baby. She saw him picking himself up off the ground. Still on her knees, Geraldine lunged for the door. With all her might, she slammed it shut.

Within seconds, he was on the other side of it. She could hear his raspy breathing. 'I want to talk you, that's all. I'm not going to hurt you.'

Not going to hurt her? If she wasn't so terrified she'd have laughed in his face. He'd already hurt her enough to last a lifetime. He did that terrible thing to her. He made her unable to carry a child. It was his fault she'd lost the other baby. Not that wretched thing that slid out of her after he'd violated her, but a proper baby that was loved and wanted.

He banged on the door. 'Let me in.'

For a moment, the tale of the three little pigs flashed through her mind and she was that small girl in infant class again. The big bad wolf was back and he was coming to get her.

She pulled herself up off the floor and ran upstairs to the baby's room. Arthur Two was sitting on a shelf. She grabbed him and curled herself up into a ball in the corner.

Len Corcoran was shouting through the letterbox: 'I just want to speak to you.'

Geraldine put her hands over her ears and screwed her eyes shut. If only he would go away.

Arthur found her, still in the corner, when he got home from work. Geraldine wouldn't tell him what had happened. All she said was that she needed Ada. He helped her into the car and drove straight round to the shop.

They put her to bed in their old bedroom. Arthur stayed with her for a while, then went back home to collect some things. Arthur Two was sitting on the pillow. She'd refused to let go of him until she was safe with Ada. She clung to the bear now and prayed that Len Corcoran had not tainted their unborn baby; that his mere presence hadn't been enough to kill it. If she lost this one, she didn't know what she'd do.

When Arthur came back it was late. He'd probably needed some time alone to calm down. He climbed into bed and wrapped himself around her.

'You'll be okay, Gee, and so will the baby. I'll take care of you both. It's going to be all right.'

Geraldine fell asleep in his arms. She hoped he was right.

When she woke up the next morning, Arthur had already gone to work. Ada was in the kitchen making breakfast.

'What happened yesterday?' said Ada. 'Was it Len?'

'He came to see me. He said he wanted to talk to me. I

was frightened. The baby. I can't go back there now. He might come again.'

'Okay, love. Stay here for now. I'll sort it out.'

The next day was Wednesday. In the afternoon, Ada went out as she always did, but was back within a few hours.

'I've been to see your mum. Len told her he wanted to make things right with you. I don't think she knows what he did to you. She thinks he just hit you too hard.'

'So she gave him my address, then?'

'Yes.'

The anger rose in Geraldine. How could her mum do that when she knew how much she feared him? They'd been getting on a lot better since she'd moved out of Ada's. Her mum had been coming round to the house and helping her to make things nice. She'd knitted some things for the baby. Yet, all this time, she'd been getting ready to betray her. Well, that was it. No more. From now on Geraldine would keep that woman at arm's length.

'Len's dying, love. Cirrhosis. Liver disease. They don't think he'll last much longer. I think she thought she was doing the right thing.'

'She wouldn't know the right thing if it hit her in the face. Dying, you said?'

'Yes. Not long, your mum said.'

'Good.'

## 46

# THE END OF LEN CORCORAN

GERALDINE – 1967

It was a wet June afternoon. Baby Wilde was an hour old. Geraldine was sitting up in bed, in the Sorrento Maternity Hospital, waiting for Arthur to greet his daughter. She'd refused to go back home after Grunt's visit, so she and Arthur were still living at Ada's. They'd already settled on a name for the baby. At Ada's suggestion, they'd chosen something new that had no ties with either of their families.

Arthur came into the ward, his head going this way and that as he scanned the beds for his new family. In one hand he had a bunch of flowers and in the other, a box of chocolates. She noticed the flowers weren't roses. Very wise. Roses were for remembrance, not new life. For them anyway. He gave her a big kiss, but his attention was on the baby sleeping in the cot next to her.

'Say hello to your daughter,' she said.

His eyes glistened. 'Oh my gosh, I'm a dad.'

Annette Sophia Wilde yawned, opened her eyes and stretched out a hand above her head.

Arthur touched it with his little finger. 'Hello beautiful.'

'Do you want to hold her?' said Geraldine.

'Can I?'

'Of course you can, you silly sausage.'

She picked the baby up and put her in his arms.

'I can't believe she's here, safe and sound,' he said. 'My darling little Nettie. When you grow up, you're going to be as gorgeous as your mum.'

Geraldine studied her brand new daughter. With her mass of dark brown hair and deep blue eyes, it looked like she hadn't inherited Arthur's looks. That was a shame: she would rather Nettie didn't look anything like her. Still, the nurse said babies can change quite a lot in the first year, so there was still a chance. She kissed little Nettie's tiny foot.

'And if you're very lucky, you'll meet someone as lovely as your dad.'

Geraldine had been out of hospital for two weeks. So far, Phil and his wife, Cissy, were the only members of her family to have come round to see the baby. Phil told her that Grunt was in hospital, and it was only a matter of time. He didn't seem too upset about it. Geraldine wondered if that was why her mum hadn't visited yet. It was possible, but Geraldine couldn't help thinking there was more to it than that. Maybe it was because of everything that had gone before, or because her mum was still jealous of Ada. Whatever it was, her lack of interest in her new grandchild was disappointing. There seemed to be no end to the disappointment Geraldine felt when it came to her mother.

The phone rang while she was in the middle of feeding Nettie. She heard Ada telling the person on the other end of the line to hold on. A minute later she popped her head around the door.

'It's Janet, asking to speak to you.'

Although she hadn't visited, Janet had been calling regularly and it was mostly to moan at her for not showing her face at the hospital. Geraldine shook her head. She couldn't be bothered to listen to one of Jan's lectures today. Ada went back to the call and explained that she couldn't come to the phone. It went quiet, and then Ada was back.

'Len's dead.'

Little Nettie sucked contentedly at Geraldine's breast. Geraldine stroked the baby's head and smiled.

'About time.'

She hadn't intended to come to the funeral. In fact she'd been set against it, but Ada talked her into it.

'Do it for your mum's sake,' she'd said.

And so Geraldine was here, at the back of the church, flanked by Arthur and Ada, watching the farce unfold.

It was a small group of mourners. No friends, she noted. Just family. Her own and his brothers and mother. She no longer thought of them as her uncles and grandmother.

Her own mum was at the front, sobbing and wailing. Geraldine couldn't understand that. If she'd been his wife, she'd have been dancing a jig and singing Hallelujah at the top of her voice. Not her mum. She was putting on a big show of being the bereaved wife.

Geraldine didn't recognise the man that the vicar was talking about. There was no mention of the drunk, the wife-beater, the monster. She had no idea who this quiet family man was that had replaced him, but she had a good idea who'd fed the vicar that particular bag of lies. Her mum never could face the truth. Geraldine didn't think she'd ever be able to forgive her for that.

The service finished, and the front row began to file out.

Ma Corcoran was the first to pass her. When she reached Geraldine's bench, she glanced her way, but didn't acknowledge her. Her mum came next, supported by Phil. She was too busy making a meal of it to notice Geraldine. Trevor led a tearful Janet out, then Tony followed with his new wife, Eileen. Geraldine had only met Eileen a couple of times, but she was a bit too sneering for her liking. At least Ralph had met someone nice. His girlfriend, Sheila, was rather quiet but that probably suited Ralph. He nodded as they walked past, his eyes wide and glazed over. He was all grown up now, but he still seemed like a lost little boy to Geraldine.

The mourners congregated around the open grave and Len Corcoran's coffin was lowered in. It set her mother off again. She was so distraught, Geraldine thought she might actually throw herself in the grave and beg to be buried alive with him. It was all rather distasteful and pathetic really. And Janet wasn't much better. Geraldine knew she should be feeling some sympathy for them, but she didn't have any. They'd sided with the devil, as far as she was concerned, and they didn't deserve it.

As the mourners moved away, Janet and Trev held onto her mum and helped her to the funeral car. Phil hung back and came over to her. He was alone. There was no sign of Cissy.

'What the bloody hell was all that about, eh? All a bit sugar-coated, wasn't it? Didn't think you'd be here,' he said.

'I'm only here for Mum, and to make sure he's really dead.'

He lit up a fag. 'Yeah, me too. Perhaps she'll have a bit of a life now.'

Geraldine looked at her mother, weeping on Trev's shoulder. 'I wouldn't hold your breath. Cissy couldn't come then?'

'I expect she could, but we've separated.'

'Oh Phil, I'm sorry.'

'You're all right, bab. It's been on the cards for a while. Divorce should be coming through soon. Adultery.'

'Cissy? Surely not? She always seemed to be devoted to you.'

He smirked. 'Not her, you dopey sod. Me. I'm with someone else now. Yvonne. We're getting married when the divorce comes through. Her dad's got his own business. He wants me to join it. I'm going up in the world, Gez.'

Poor Cissy. Bad enough to be cast off like last year's fashions, but how awful must it be to find your husband has a replacement waiting in the wings? Not even waiting, from the sounds of it. Already at it. There was something quite callous about her brother sometimes. He may not have been physically cruel, but there was a hardness about him that surfaced every now and then. A hardness that could only have come from living in the shadow of Len Corcoran.

The next day, she and Arthur moved back home. It was a beautiful summer's day. Arthur sat in the garden and rocked Nettie to sleep in her pram while Geraldine was upstairs, unpacking their things. From the open window, she could hear him singing to the little one. He appeared to be going through the track listing of *The Most of the Animals* album, in no particular order, and was currently half-way through 'The House of the Rising Sun'. She laughed to herself. If that was his idea of a lullaby, she dreaded to think how that poor child was going to turn out.

Arthur Two was in Nettie's cot. She'd been thinking of passing him on to her but, after the funeral, she'd had a change of heart. He belonged to a sad little girl called

Geraldine Corcoran and she didn't want her daughter to have any association with that person. Besides, Karen had already bought Nettie her first teddy. Maybe it was time to retire him. She gave him a kiss.

'Bye, Arthur Two. I think I can manage without you now.'

She wrapped him in a plastic bag, and put him away in a drawer.

# 47

# TURNING A CORNER AND THROWING CAUTION TO THE WIND

GERALDINE – 2020

'Would you like to show me what's in the other bag?' said Angelica.

Geraldine didn't reply straight away. She was thinking about it.

'We can do it another time, if you're not ready.'

'No, I think I'm ready. I just need a minute to…'

The last time she'd opened that bag was in 2015, after Ada had died. There were things in there that were painful to see. Things that left her anxious and fearful.

Kelly's words were ringing in her ears: 'You and me together, we're gonna beat it.' Geraldine wished Kelly was here to back her up. She wished Ada was here. They would both have wanted her to open it. She had to do it. For them, but most of all, for herself. She opened the bag and took out its contents – a letter from Ada that the solicitor had given to her after the reading of the will, three cards, and a square of red material.

'What shall we start with?' said Angelica.

'The cards.'

Geraldine took them out of their envelopes and showed

them to Angelica. Written inside each one was a year. In one of them, there was a name. Paul. In all of them, there was a single pressed rose.

'We planted a rose bush for each of them. These are the first flowers. It was our way of managing the grief. The thing is no one expects you to grieve for half a baby, do they? It's not like it's a proper one is it? That's what they all seemed to think anyway. No one talked about it. Or if they did, it was always unhelpful things about nature getting rid of something that wasn't quite right, or having plenty of time to try again. They didn't do counselling in those days. You just had to get on with it. I suppose you know that, being in the profession? So that's what we did. Even we stopped talking about it after a while.'

'Why was that?'

'I suppose neither of us wanted to upset the other. Arthur spends a lot of time with those rose bushes though. They must be the most well-looked-after plants in the city.'

'Tell me about Paul,' said Angelica.

'That would have been his name. We were going to call him after our favourite Beatle. He came after Netta. I lost the others too early, but I carried him long enough for them to know he would have been a boy. We tried one more time after him. After that, Arthur convinced me to stop. He was worried about what it was doing to me and so were the doctors. I was more worried about what it was doing to him. He wanted a bigger family, you see. He'd have loved two or three children. He tried to hide it but, every time it happened, he was devastated.'

'And what about you, Geraldine? How did you feel?'

'I suppose I felt like it was destined to be.'

Angelica sat quietly. The tears were blurring Geraldine's vision but she knew she was waiting for her to continue.

'I suppose I thought that Len Corcoran had planted this ugly seed in me, and it was killing off my babies.'

'Do you still think that?'

Geraldine blew her nose and noticed the tissue box was getting low again.

'No. I don't know why I had trouble carrying a child, but I know now that it had nothing to do with that man's devil seed. We were just unlucky, Arthur and me. But not entirely unlucky. We had Netta. Have Netta. She's a little bit bonkers sometimes. Come to think of it, she'd probably benefit from a few sessions with you, but I wouldn't change her for anything.'

Angelica's face cracked and she let out a little laugh. 'She sounds great. My kind of person. Do you want to carry on?'

Geraldine picked up the square of material and rubbed it between her fingers.

'It was a beautiful dress. My first proper one. After we were married, Arthur told me when he saw me in it, his heart exploded. I told him it probably wasn't his heart. I never really saw it back then but, actually, I did look lovely in it. Karen used to say I looked like Jean Shrimpton. I don't suppose you remember her. You're too young. When Ada's brother fetched my things after I ran away, he brought it with him, but I couldn't wear it again. After Len Corcoran died, I cut this square out and threw the rest of the dress away.'

Angelica's expression was back to a blank slate. 'Why did you keep the square?'

'To remind myself of what he did to me. No, not that. It's not as if I was ever going to forget that, was it? I think … I know, what it was. It was to remind myself that I was dirty. Ugly. It was to punish myself.'

'And how do you feel about that now?'

'That I've spent too long punishing myself for something I didn't do.'

Angelica's practice was a thirty minute walk from Edgbaston Reservoir. Instead of calling Arthur to pick her up, Geraldine turned towards it. She wanted to see the Tower Ballroom, a dancehall that stood near its entrance. She'd been to it many a time with Arthur and Karen, when they were younger. It was derelict now. Such a pity. Still, the reservoir was nice, with the sun glinting on the water and the city in the distance. There was a path leading all the way round. It was an ideal place to walk when you wanted to think, providing you kept a safe distance from the other walkers. She and Arthur had already had their allotted hour's exercise for that day, but what the hell. It was about time she threw some caution to the wind.

Geraldine set off along the path, side-stepping the other people as they came towards her. Lots of them greeted her with a 'thank you' or 'hello'. Some ignored her but she couldn't care less. There was a lightness about her that made her feel almost dizzy. She always felt this way after talking to Angelica but, today, she was positively elated.

It was the realisation that she'd been punishing herself all these years that did it. Her lightbulb moment, she supposed. Or perhaps it was coming to the decision that she'd punished herself enough. Then again, it could have been the ceremonial binning of the last remaining square of that dress. Whatever it was, it had done the trick.

She stopped at an empty bench and, even though she wasn't sure it was allowed, she sat down on it. For the first time in a long, long time she was happy. Geraldine wanted to call Arthur straight away and tell him the good news but she had some more thinking to do yet.

Angelica hadn't left it at the point of her realisation that she was sick of punishing herself. There'd been a lot of discussion after that. She'd even got Geraldine to read the letter from Ada. Then, just when Geraldine thought she was on the home straight, Angelica asked about Karen.

'What happened to her?'

'She moved to France about twenty years ago. Her second husband was French, you see. We keep in touch. Arthur and I went over there a couple of times in the early years.'

'When was the last time you saw her?'

'About ten years ago. Ada's health began to fade after that, and I couldn't leave her.'

'And after Ada died?'

'After that, I didn't want to go anywhere.'

Before Kelly and Neil, Geraldine had only ever had three proper friends in her life, not counting Arthur. Bree, Karen, and Ada. Karen eased the pain of losing Bree but, unlike with Bree, they stayed friends through thick and thin. Karen made her feel normal and they were in each other's pockets right up until she moved to France. Thinking about it now, Geraldine could see that Karen's leaving was the start of a gradual decline that only worsened when Ada became ill and died.

'And after Ada died?' What did happen after Ada died? Ada was gone and everything was too hard without her. She'd failed Ada. That's what happened. Just like she'd failed Netta.

Her phone rang. It was Arthur.

'Hello Art,' she said.

'Art? That's a blast from the past. Was that the sound of

geese? Where are you?'

'Edgbaston Reservoir. I fancied a walk. It's really nice here. You'd never believe it was so close to town. Why don't you come and join me for a walk. Bring Minnie. To hell with the regulations.'

Arthur laughed. 'That's my girl.'

'Yes, I am, and I always will be.'

'Well I'm glad to hear it. I'll be there in twenty minutes. Shall I meet you by the Tower?'

'Yes but just to warn you, it's a bit past its prime. Then again, aren't we all?'


While she waited for Arthur, she called Kelly to give her an update.

'How many boxes of tissues today?' said Kelly.

'Don't ask.'

'That doesn't sound good.'

'No, it was good. It was very good. I've turned a corner, according to Angelica.'

'Brilliant. Listen, me and Liza are thinking of giving you a wave-by later, if you're up for it?'

'A what?'

'A wave-by. We'll walk past a couple of times and give you a wave. I've been doing it with my nan. It's good,' said Kelly.

A wave-by. Whatever next?

'Okay, why not.'

'And you're okay with Liza coming? She really wants to see you.'

'Yes. I'd love to see her,' said Geraldine.

'Cool. I'll message you in a couple of hours when we're close.'

'Okay. No earlier though. Arthur and I are being naughty and having our second walk of the day.'

'Shit. Sounds like you really are turning a corner.'

Geraldine said goodbye and went to find Arthur. He was surveying the derelict building that used to be the Tower when she reached him.

'It's quite a mess, isn't it?' he said. 'Pretty sad really.'

She slipped her arm into his. 'Let's take a walk around the water.'

They strolled along the path with Minnie at their side, excitedly exploring this new place.

'I was talking to Angelica about our lost babies today,' she said.

'Oh yes.'

Was it her imagination or did she feel him stiffen?

'Do you still think about them, Arthur?'

'Yes, but not as much as I used to. I suppose having Liza and Will helped. What about you?'

'Yes, I do. For a long time I tried not to think about them because it upset me, but I think I'm all right about it now. And I know what you mean about Liza and Will. And Kelly too, in a way. We've finally got that big family.'

'Yes, I suppose so.' Arthur relaxed. She must have said the right thing.

'Would you mind if we talked about the babies sometimes? Not all the time. Just occasionally, when we both feel like it?' she said.

'Not at all. I'd like that.'

'Good. By the way, Angelica thinks I've turned a corner today.'

He put his arm around her and gave her a gentle squeeze.

'Sounds like we both have.'

## 48

# SOMETHING TO CELEBRATE

NETTA – 2020

Netta sat in the car, outside the house that used to be hers. She used to dread coming here, even before she moved out. Nowadays it didn't bother her too much. Not that she needed to come too often. In normal times, Liza generally made the transition between the two homes on her own. She'd spend most of the week here, with Colin, and would head over to Netta's for the weekend on a Thursday or Friday, after school. Things had been gradually changing since lockdown though. Liza had been spending more and more time at Netta's, and she always seemed to be finding an excuse not to go back to Colin's.

Netta had let it go unmentioned. Liza was upset enough about being unable to see or speak to her nan, and she didn't want to make things worse. Then, a few days ago, Colin had called her to ask what was wrong with Liza. Of course, being Colin, he'd made it sound like it was all Netta's fault. No doubt the woman he lived with, the idiotic Arianne, had been feeding him some ridiculous drivel to stir things up. She'd been tempted to tell him to piss off and speak to his daughter about it himself, but then she remembered that wasn't how they were supposed to behave now. For Liza's sake, they were being civilised.

At the first opportunity after that call, she'd sat Liza down to ask her, as sensitively as possible, why she'd stopped going to her other home.

'Obviously, I'm absolutely fine with you being here, darling. I love having you here. It's just that your dad's called me to ask if there's anything wrong.'

'Couldn't ask me himself, then? Typical,' said Liza.

'I thought it might be better if it came from me. Is there something you want to talk to me about?'

'Not really but since you ask, they're driving me up the wall. Honestly, Mum, you wouldn't believe the fuss Arianne makes every time I get back from here. I have to shower the minute I get in the door, and put every last stitch of clothing straight in the wash. She even makes me put my trainers in a tray of disinfectant. They're bloody ruined! And, she makes me stay two metres away from her, all the time.'

'Oh dear. She must be terribly worried about it. Poor Arianne.' It had been hard for Netta not to smirk at that point.

'You'd think so, wouldn't you? She says she's got asthma, but she never uses an inhaler and she spends all the time sunbathing in the garden. Also, when she's not doing that, she's sneaking off to see her sister, even though it's not allowed. And Dad does nothing. If I say anything, he stands up for her. It's no wonder Will won't speak to him. It's really not worth the hassle.'

'Would you like me to speak to your dad? Maybe if I explain–'

'To be honest, Mum, I prefer it here. It's more like a family. If it's okay with you, I'd rather just live here full-time, at least until after lockdown.'

So that was it, settled. They told Colin that Liza had decided it was best for Arianne's health if she stayed away. She and Liza had agreed that the little white lie would save any awkwardness, in case Liza decided to go back to the old arrangement after lockdown. Now, here she was, outside Colin's house, about to pick up Liza's school books and other important things. Liza had emailed him with a list.

Netta wondered what kind of reception she was going to get. Colin had accepted the story about Arianne's health quite easily. A little too easily, in Netta's mind, for someone who always made such a big deal about his relationship with his kids. Maybe Arianne was more than enough for him to handle and he just wanted a quiet life these days.

Netta knew only three things about Arianne. The first was that she had a penchant for squeezing herself into an undersized Clash T-shirt which happened to be a copy of the one Netta used to wear, before she married Colin. The second was that she appeared to be jealous of Netta to an extent that was positively infantile. The third was that Colin had been seeing Arianne long before he threw Netta out. Netta had worked that last one out on her own. It hadn't been hard to do. Particularly as Arianne had practically told her that herself when she let on how long she'd known about Netta's miscarriage.

Colin appeared in the bay window. Within seconds, Arianne was there too. She had some kind of bright green bandeau thing stretched across her ample bosom. Perhaps she'd decided to take a short break from sunbathing, so that she could give Netta a withering glare through the safety of the double glazing. On the bright side, she wasn't wearing the Clash T-shirt. Netta supposed she had to be grateful for small mercies. Time to get out of the car and face the music.

Colin left Arianne in the window and had the door open as soon as Netta stepped onto the drive. He stretched his hand out to indicate she should stop walking. He was wearing a pair of those thin plastic disposable gloves.

'Hi. If you stay there, I'll put everything in a safe space.'

Netta stopped and waited for him to carry a couple of boxes and a suitcase out to a point, halfway between them. Just inside the door, in the hall, she noticed what looked like a big Tupperware box filled with liquid. The trainer dip, presumably. So Liza hadn't been exaggerating then.

Instead of stepping back, Colin hovered over the suitcase and boxes.

'How's Will getting on? I've tried messaging him, but he's still not speaking to me.'

'He seems to be doing okay. He's a bit fed up being stuck in halls, but we're keeping in touch with him all the time.'

'Good. It's worrying isn't it, all this? I wish he'd message me to let me know…'

He did look worried. For the first time in ages, she felt sorry for him. Perhaps she'd mention it to Will.

'I'd better take the stuff. If you could back off?'

'What? Oh yes.'

He moved sideways, rather than back up towards the house. She picked up the first box.

He hunched his shoulders up to meet his ears.

'Sorry, I'd help but, you know.'

'Best not.'

She noticed that Arianne had repositioned herself in the window. Most likely to keep her eye on him and make sure he didn't contravene her safety regulations. Colin's eyes followed Netta's and, for a few seconds, they both watched Arianne watching them.

'And Liza? Is she okay?' he said.

'Yes, she's fine. Missing her friend. Missing Will.'

'Not missing me though?'

Netta shrugged. She didn't know what to say. His expression changed into a sneer.

'Is she still upset about Geraldine? I hear she's finally cracked.'

Netta snatched up the second box and threw it in the boot, then grabbed the suitcase. He took a few steps towards her. This time it was her turn to put her hand up.

'Stop right there, Colin. Can't have you contaminating me.'

She jumped in the car and drove off. The bastard. The nasty, fucking bastard. And to think she'd felt sorry for him.

She was still seething by the time she got home, but then she noticed a message had come from her dad:

*'Therapist says your mum's turned a corner. Been for a lovely walk. On our way home now. The girls are going to give us a wave-by soon, whatever that is.'*

Ah, the wave-by. The girls? Perhaps Liza was going too. Hopefully that wasn't going to freak her mum out.

She let out a long, loud sigh. Colin Grey was a nasty arse of a man. He didn't deserve any help from her to reconnect with his kids. She'd had to do it on her own. Let him. He wasn't worth the effort, or the anger. Her mum had turned a corner. Now that was something to celebrate.

## 49

## THE WAVE-BY CONCEPT

KELLY – 2020

They'd got pretty tight now, Kelly and Liza. That's what happens when you're stuck in the same house with nowhere to go. Not that Liza was supposed to be here all the time, but Arianne was doing Liza's head in. So she fed them some excuse about it being better if she stayed at Netta's, what with Arianne being vulnerable with asthma and everything.

Frank and Netta had set up a kind of hybrid household across both houses, and the four of them moved between the two buildings, just as they always did. Probably more than they always did, seeing as there wasn't really much place else to go.

Will was still in York. Stuck in his halls and doing all of his lectures online. It was driving him mental. He was thinking about coming home as soon as he could, and not going back until things were normal again. Whenever that was. He and Kelly were messaging and speaking to each other, pretty much every day. Something good to come out of Coronavirus, at least.

Netta was worried about him, and Frank was worried about Robyn. That was what parents did though. Worrying about their kids was built into their DNA. Proper parents anyway. Kelly doubted her own dad would be wasting too much of his time fretting over her.

Will and Robyn both meant a lot to Kelly, but she wasn't worried about either of them. They were young. It was the old ones that bothered her. Her nan's boyfriend, Alec, died. People in the care home seemed to be dropping like flies. Much as she tried to hide it, Kelly was terrified that her nan was going to be next.

Netta's car pulled up outside. She'd been doing another foodbank delivery and had picked up some of Liza's stuff from her dad's. Sometimes, Kelly helped her with the deliveries. Not today though. She and Liza had stayed home to help Frank pick the ripe fruit in the garden.

When they'd first started making jam, they'd got the fruit from the two gardens. They still used it to supplement their other supplies. Normally Arthur would have led a fruit-picking party with their friends and family. For obvious reasons, this year it was just them, and Kelly was only just beginning to realise a) how much fruit was in the garden and b) how much like hard work it was to harvest it. Fucking Covid.

Liza took one of the boxes out of Netta's car.

'That's us done for today. Nothing left to pick. Plus, me and Kelly are going out for a bike ride. Guess where we're going, Mum.'

'Er, the park?' said Netta.

'Nan and Grandad's. We're going to do a wave-by.'

'Oh right.'

Netta had a silly grin on her face. Kelly guessed she was just humouring Liza and that she already knew. Arthur had probably told her.

'You do know what a wave-by is, don't you,' said Liza.

'I am aware of the concept. Are they okay about you doing it?' said Netta,

'Yeah, yeah. Kelly's sorted it with Nan. She's fine with it. Kelly, tell her what Nan said about the corner.'

'Angelica reckons Gez has turned a corner,' said Kelly, guessing this wasn't the first time Netta had received the news. 'Gez called me after her session. She sounded … chirpy.'

Netta scrunched her forehead up. 'Chirpy?'

'Yeah. Chirpy.' Kelly knew it was a crap description but she couldn't think of a better way to say it.

'Wow.'

'Yeah, I know. Great isn't it,' said Liza. 'We were thinking, if this wave-by goes well, we might be able to get you in on it too.'

'That would be good,' said Netta. 'Really good.'


They cycled to Kings Heath. Kelly was using Robyn's old bike. Frank had fixed it up for her so that she could get around without having to use the bus. He'd had to lower everything because Rob was tall – like, model tall. It was weird cycling along the roads that were normally full of traffic and people. There was no noise. It was like someone had switched on a giant mute button. Except for the birds. You could really hear them. It was bizarre how everyone was crazy about listening to the birds, all of a sudden. Even her.

It took longer than expected to get to Geraldine and Arthur's because Liza insisted on stopping off at her friend Jade's house to do a wave-by that ended up being an illegal garden chat. Kelly was pissed off with her at first, but it didn't last long. Her heart melted when the girls were so happy to see each other, they started crying. Kelly couldn't imagine what it was like to have a friend you were that close to at that age. She'd already left school well before she was seventeen, and no one really wanted to know her there anyway. Netta was her first proper friend and that wasn't the same, because Net was a lot older and was as much like a mum, as a friend.

Eventually they reached the street. They dropped their bikes in the front garden and tapped on the door. Arthur and Gez came to the window.

'Let's do a Royal wave,' said Liza.

They walked slowly past the house, nodding their heads and doing little in-synch waves. Geraldine and Arthur beamed at them from the other side of the glass. On the way back, Kelly and Liza added a stupid walk. They went back and forth about ten times until Liza got overexcited, ran into the front garden, and started doing star jumps.

Arthur opened the window a bit. He was laughing so much that tears were rolling down his cheeks. 'You pair of silly sods. You've made our day.'

Liza blew them a kiss. 'We miss you and we love you both so much.'

'We miss you and we love you too,' said Geraldine. She looked at Kelly. 'Both of you.'

'Yeah,' said Kelly. Sometimes she wished she could be like Liza and just tell people how she felt. It didn't come that easily to her.

'Mum sends her love,' said Liza.

'Give her ours,' said Arthur.

'Grandad, close the window so we can get nearer.'

Arthur closed it. Liza stepped up to the window and placed her hands on the glass.

'Come on, Kelly. You do it too. Cross one arm underneath mine.'

Kelly slipped one arm under Liza's and put her hands flat against the window so that Geraldine and Arthur could put a hand on each of theirs, on the other side.

'Keep safe,' said Liza.

'Yeah, keep safe,' said Kelly and, once again, she thought of her nan.

On the way back they stopped off at the care home for another wave-by. Liza got Kelly's nan and the other residents laughing with her star jumps. She even threw in a few cartwheels across the grass, and made Kelly do the same. Lined up at the conservatory windows, the old folks were lapping it up.

'They looked sad,' said Liza as they walked back to their bikes. 'They must be really lonely. And scared. I guess they're probably scared, as well.'

'Yeah, I guess so.'

'You must be scared too. For your nan.'

'Yeah, I am,' said Kelly.

Liza hugged her. It was enough to start Kelly crying. Stupid, fucking useless tears. What good did they do?

Liza held her tighter. 'It's okay. I understand. I'm the same.'

'Yeah?'

'Yeah. Kelly. About Nan. Something really bad happened to her, didn't it?'

Kelly nodded.

'I know she doesn't want you to tell me but will you? I won't let on to anyone, I just need to know,' said Liza.

Kelly sat down on the lawn, by the side of the car park. 'You won't like it.'

Liza flopped down next to her. 'I'm prepared for that. I've been building myself up to it.'

Kelly picked at the grass. She'd promised Geraldine, but she understood how Liza felt. If it was her nan, she'd want to know, even if it killed her to hear it.

'She was raped when she was sixteen.'

Liza's head moved up and down, slowly. 'I thought it might be something like that.'

'It was her dad that did it. Len Corcoran. Not that he was her proper dad. He was her stepdad.'

'Fuck. I wasn't expecting that. Poor Nan. No wonder she's been in such a mess.'

'Yeah. She's kept it secret from everyone for years. That letter that your mum found, it triggered it all off again.'

'That must have been really hard to keep to herself. I suppose that's why she does that thing with her hand when she gets stressed.'

'Oh, you noticed that, did you?'

'Of course. You picked up on it too then?'

'Yeah. Not sure who else has though.'

'Grandad has, I think. I've seen the way he looks at her when she's doing it. Like he's trying to pretend it's not happening, and everything's perfectly normal.'

'I expect you're right. He doesn't know about the rape though.'

'Then we won't tell him. Nan will tell him when she's ready. I'm sure of it.'

## 50

## YOU'LL BE OKAY

KELLY – 2020

Netta was on deliveries again so Kelly was cycling back from the foodbank. She was really getting into this cycling thing. She was actually getting leg muscles. which she was quite pleased about because her legs were normally like two sticks. Not even long ones either. Two short sticks with knobbly bits where her knees were. She'd have to show her nan and Gez her new legs, see what they thought of them.

On her way home, she was stopping off to do some more wave-bys. She'd been doing them a lot lately. Sometimes with Liza, and sometimes on her own. Gez and Arthur seemed to like them. They said it perked them up. If you asked Kelly, they looked pretty damn perky anyway. The lockdown didn't seem to have hit them too hard at all. On the phone the other day, Gez said it was like it had given them a chance to rediscover each other, all over again. It was a really beautiful thing to say. Pretty kind of amazing, actually. Imagine being with someone for nearly sixty years and still being that loved-up. The longest she'd stuck it out with anyone was eighteen months with Craig, and she'd absolutely hated the fucker by the time she walked away.

The care home was going to be her first stop. She was feeling a bit anxious about her nan. Nan had been fine when Kelly saw her a few days ago but, when she'd called the care home yesterday morning, they said she was asleep in her room which wasn't like her at all. Nan never had a lie-in.

Kelly had tried calling again but the phone was always engaged. She guessed it was all the other relatives, wanting to speak to their nans and grandads. So today, she'd made up her mind to do another wave-by, to cheer Nan and her friends up. Afterwards, she'd treat Arthur and Geraldine to one too. Even if they didn't need it as much.

Her phone went, just as she was passing through Moseley village. She ignored it and carried on. When it rang again for a second time, she was at the top end of Kings Heath. She stopped and looked to see who it was. It was a mobile number. She didn't recognise it, but answered anyway: sometimes the care assistants at the home let the residents use their phones to speak to their loved ones.

'Kelly, it's Carol.'

The voice itself was enough to irritate her. 'What d'ya want?'

'Kelly, I'm sorry, I've got bad news. It's your nan. She's passed away.'

Kelly let her bike drop to the floor. It had to be a mistake. 'But I only saw her three days ago. She waved to me. She was laughing. I was making her laugh.'

'It's the virus. It takes them suddenly. They said she'd been under the weather for a few days, then came down bad with it yesterday. I'm so sorry. Your dad's at the home now. They won't let him in, but he drove over there anyway.'

Kelly hung up before Carol could say any more. It wasn't true, it couldn't be. Her nan was getting better. She was walking better and everything. Kelly had to get over there and see for herself. She got back on the bike and pedalled, as hard as she could. Her lungs were on fire and her legs were cramping up, but she ignored them.

She came to a crashing stop outside the home and pressed on the buzzer.

A voice answered from within. 'Hello.'

Kelly was panting so much she couldn't speak.

The voice said again: 'Hello.'

'My nan. Gladys Payne.'

'Gladys, Gladys Payne?'

'Yeah. Someone told me she was dead.'

'Who is this, please?'

'Kelly. Kelly Payne. Her granddaughter.'

'Kelly, yes. I'm afraid we can't let you in, Kelly. But if you wait there, someone will come out to you. Can you stand away from the door, please?'

Kelly backed away. Minutes later, a woman came out. She was covered in, what looked like, a big plastic bag and she was wearing a mask. This was all too fucking surreal.

'Kelly, I'm so sorry. Your nan's health deteriorated quite quickly and we didn't have time to get her to a hospital. I'm afraid she passed away at two-twenty this afternoon. I know this must be very difficult for you, but I thought you'd want to know, she wasn't alone. Katya held her hand and your dad was talking to her on the phone, on loudspeaker, in the final minutes.'

Kelly covered her mouth to stop herself screaming. Of course it was true, why shouldn't it be? All of her nan's friends were dead. Why wouldn't she be too? Her nan wasn't exactly superhuman. Just a frail old lady. Why was she so surprised? Hadn't she been expecting it for weeks now? As soon as they told her yesterday that Nan was in bed, Kelly knew, she just knew, it had got her too. Fucking Covid. Fucking, bastard Covid.

'I really am very sorry,' said the woman. 'I think your dad's over there.'

Her dad was sitting in his car, the top half of him bent over the steering wheel. Even before she got there, Kelly knew he'd be crying. He was the same when her mum died, moping about and bursting into tears all the time. No self-control. No use to anyone.

Kelly knocked the window and startled him. His face was all red and blotchy, and full of snot. Fucking useless. He wound the window down. He didn't even bother getting out of the shitting car.

'She's gone, Kel. Mum's gone.'

'Yeah, I know.'

'I can't believe it.'

'No? Well believe, Dad. Because you put in her in there. It's your fault she's dead.'

'What? Look I know you're upset, but that's a really bad thing to say. Your nan wanted to go there. She was having a great time until—'

'Until she caught the Covid and pegged it.'

'Don't say that.'

'Oh sorry, did I hurt your feelings?'

Her dad's face buckled and there they were again, the fucking waterworks. Just like before. Only this time, she wasn't a twelve-year-old martyr trying to keep her little brothers from going into care.

'Poor you. Poor, fucking you. You weak, selfish bastard.'

She held onto the roof and kicked at the door. Through

the open window, her dad tried to push her away but she clung on and kicked, again and again.

He opened the door and it forced her backwards. Kelly fell onto the ground. He got out and stood over her.

'You're upset. I understand.'

'No you don't. You haven't got a fucking clue.'

He made her sick. She couldn't be near him. She had to get away, before she did something she really regretted. She scrambled up and went to get her bike.

The residents were in the conservatory, watching. Just a few days ago, her nan had stood in the same room while she and Liza had acted like idiots to make her laugh.

An old lady held up a big piece of paper with a heart painted on it. Underneath the heart, in capital letters, she'd written:

*'YOU'LL BE OKAY.'*

It broke Kelly's heart all over again. The paper was a bit dog-eared. It probably wasn't the first time the old lady had stood at that window with it. Kelly waved limply at the old people and wondered how many of them would still be there when this pandemic was over.

Her dad was inspecting the damage to his car as she cycled past. She didn't look at him. She didn't speak to him. She wanted to shout and scream and beat the shit out of him, but there was no fight left in her. Oh Jesus. Oh fuck. Her nan was dead.

## 51

# ARTHUR TWO SAVES THE DAY

GERALDINE – 2020

Geraldine heard the front gate bang. Arthur had only just gone out to the supermarket and the car was nowhere to be seen, so it couldn't be him. She went to the window to check, and there was Kelly, standing on the path, sobbing.

Geraldine opened the window. 'What's happened?'

'My nan's dead.'

'Oh my poor love.' She was all at sixes and sevens. She wanted to bring Kelly into the house and hold her, but it wasn't possible. 'Come round to the back garden. I'll unlock the gate.'

Geraldine grabbed a box of tissues and went through to the back, with Minnie at her side. She put the tissues on the garden table, arranged the chairs a safe distance apart, and unlocked the gate.

Kelly wheeled the bike in and let it drop down on the patio. She looked as if she'd had all the stuffing knocked out of her. Minnie was excited to see her, but Kelly hardly acknowledged the dog.

'I wish I could give you a hug,' said Geraldine.

'Best not. It might kill you. I couldn't take it if you went as well.' Kelly put her head in her hands. 'I didn't even get to say goodbye to her. A woman at the home said my dad was talking to Nan on the phone right up until the end. Carol was probably there with him. They didn't even think to let me know. Bastards.'

'That sounds awful. It must have been horrible for your dad too, not being able to be with his mum.'

Kelly blew her nose. 'I expect he would have only made things worse, if he had been. Katya was with her. One of the care assistants. She held her hand. Nan liked Katya. I wish it had been me though. After my mum died, Nan was the closest I had to a mum. Until Netta came along.'

Kelly reached for another tissue. Geraldine was beginning to feel like Angelica. She decided to follow Angelica's example and let Kelly carry on talking, when she was ready.

'Were you the same when your nan died?' Kelly said, after a few minutes.

'No. My mum's parents were killed in the war so I never knew them, and I hated the other one. Not that she was my real nan.'

'Your mum then?'

'Not exactly. Things were never the same after the rape. Rightly or wrongly, I blamed her as much as him. Ada though – Arthur's mum – I'm only just getting over losing her. But that's because I needed her, much too much. You're a clever and independent young woman with your own mind. You'll get over it, in time, and then you'll be able to remember your nan fondly.'

Kelly sniffed. 'I don't know. I just want her back. I just want to give her a sloppy kiss and tell her I'll take care of her. But I can't. I can't because she's dead and gone, and she's never coming back.'

She pulled her knees up to her chest and sobbed. It set

Minnie off whimpering. It was distress all round and, for once, Geraldine was the only one that wasn't in a state. There had to be something she could do, other than physically reaching out to comfort her.

Geraldine squirmed in her seat, watching her newest friend in despair. Then, it came to her. 'Wait there.'

Geraldine hurried through the house, and up the stairs. Within a matter of minutes, she was back down with the only thing she could think of that might help. She put the plastic bag down on the table and returned to her chair.

'I know what you need right now is the biggest cuddle I can give, and I wish I could give it. But this is a good substitute.'

Kelly let her knees fall down. 'What is it?'

'Open it and see.'

She peered into the bag and shot Geraldine a confused look. 'It's a teddy bear.'

'I know. Take him out and cuddle him.'

Kelly was now looking at her as if she was off her rocker.

'Go on. I promise you it'll help.'

With what seemed like some reluctance on Kelly's part, she took the bear out and held him to her. Gingerly at first and then, so tight, it looked as though she might burst his stitching. For a moment or two, Geraldine was a little concerned. He was an old bear, and she wasn't sure he could sustain that sort of pressure.

'This is Arthur Two,' she said.

'Arthur Two?' One corner of Kelly's mouth turned up slightly. She sniffed back her tears. 'Is that because Arthur gave him to you?'

'No. A very good friend gave him to me, a long time ago. She was Arthur's cousin actually. She was always ribbing Arthur. The name was a bit of a joke, but we liked it.'

This time Kelly's mouth formed into a grin that if, she didn't know better, Geraldine would have described as shy.

'Wow! You had a friend?'

'Cheeky madam. Yes I did. Her name's Karen. She lives in France now. I'm going to go and see her when all of this is over.'

Geraldine sat back in the chair, with a certain amount of astonishment. Where on earth had that come from? She'd really surprised herself there. But now that she thought about it, why not?

'He smells of lavender,' said Kelly.

'Yes. I've been giving him a spray every now and then, recently. It's a smell that reminds me of Karen.' Geraldine nearly added 'and happier times' but now was not the time to be maudlin.

'My nan always smelled of Yardley English Rose. She loved the stuff.'

'I've got some rose perfume upstairs. Not Yardley's, but close enough. You can have it to spray it on Arthur Two, when you take him home.'

'You want me to take him home with me?'

'Only if you want to. As a young girl going through my own personal trauma, I found him very comforting.'

Geraldine changed her tack, realising she'd accidentally fallen into Angelica mode. 'You can borrow him for as long as you like. You can keep the perfume, though. I've never much cared for it.'

Janet had given her the perfume two years ago, when she and Arthur went to stay with her and Trev for Christmas. Geraldine wore it while she was there, to please Jan, then put it away in a drawer, the minute they got home.

Roses reminded her of the babies. Perhaps now that she was on the mend and could look at the rose bushes in the garden without mourning her lost children, she might one day think of their perfume differently. Not yet though. She'd spent too long thinking about loss. It was time she stepped away from the sadness, and focused on the goodness in her life.

'Thanks. That'd be good,' said Kelly, sounding like a small child herself.

For all her bluff and bluster, Kelly was so small and delicate, she always looked like a puff of wind would blow her away. Especially today. Poor kid. To have gone through so much death, and still only twenty.

'I'll make us a nice cup of tea. They say that's always good for shock,' said Geraldine.

While the kettle was boiling, Geraldine sent a message to Arthur and Netta to let them know what had happened. Netta replied to ask if she could come over. Geraldine hadn't bargained for that. It had been months since she'd seen her daughter in the flesh. According to Angelica, it was one of the final barriers for her to get through. She knew that but she hadn't expected it to be today. Her fingers hovered over the phone. No. She'd leave it for now. Wait and see how things pan out with Kelly. She went upstairs to retrieve the perfume from its hiding place.

Kelly was still squeezing the life out of Arthur Two when Geraldine returned to the garden. Good. He was obviously helping her too.

'There's a slice of cake there for you as well. I've taken all the necessary precautions to keep us both safe, and I'll put my rubber gloves on before I touch your cup and plate. I don't want you worrying about killing me off.'

Kelly gave her another of those shy little smiles. 'Cheers Gez. Liza's lucky to have you for a nan. She's always telling me how great you are.'

Geraldine's heart lurched. What a lovely thing that was to say.

'Well, if you'd met her other grandmother you'd know there's not much competition in those stakes. She's a right old battleaxe, and such a snob. Look, love, I know there's no one that will replace your nan but, if ever you want a stand-in who occasionally treats you like shit, you know where to find me.'

Kelly gave her a proper smirk this time. 'You just said shit.'

'Yes, well, I'm branching out. Trying to expand my vocabulary and my outlook. I'm quite enjoying it.'

'You're all right you know?' said Kelly. 'And you haven't treated me like shit for ages.'

'I should hope not, seeing as I wouldn't be here today without you. Seriously though, sweetheart, I know it's probably not the right time to say this but, if you do ever need a stand-in nan, I'd be happy to do it.' She paused to think carefully about her next words. 'In fact, I'd be honoured. Oh look. Now I've made you cry again. I'm sorry, my darling.'

Kelly wiped her eyes. 'Nah, it's okay Gez. It's not bad crying, it's good crying. I don't get too many compliments like that. I think I'd like you as my stand-in nan. I think my real nan would like it too.'

Geraldine flicked a tear away from her cheek and tutted. 'Now I'm doing it. Honestly, what a pair we are. Listen, is there anyone else you want to speak to? Your dad, or another relative?'

Kelly shook her head. 'I don't want to see that useless fucker. Carol's welcome to him.'

'I understand, love. He's let you down, and you hate him right now. I know how that feels. I felt the same about my mum and I never forgave her. Lately though, I wish I had. Lately, I've started to realise that there can be extenuating circumstances that you don't necessarily pick up on. My mum had been ground down by Len Corcoran, and she just didn't have the capacity to take any more. Maybe that's the same with your dad. It must be very hard losing your life partner. If Arthur went before me, I don't think I'd want to live. But your dad had no choice, he had you and your brothers to look after.'

'I see where you're going with this Gez, but there's a big hole in your theory. My dad didn't look after us. He left it to me and my nan to do it.'

Geraldine sighed. Yes, she was definitely clever, that one.

'I didn't say he was good at it, did I? And I'm not saying you have to forgive him. I'm just saying you might want to consider everything before you set a pattern for your life.'

'Okay. I'll think about it. There is someone I want to speak to, though. Netta. She's probably home by now. I'll go.'

Netta. Of course she needed to speak to her. Netta would be able to hold her and do all the things a mum could do, when your mum was long dead.

'I've already messaged her. I'll give her a call and tell her to come over,' said Geraldine.

'Are you sure? I mean … you know … you're not seeing her. I don't want to make you have to see her.'

Geraldine put her hand to her mouth and blew Kelly a kiss.

'Bless you. I want to see her, nearly as much as you do.'

. . .

It had been a quick call. No time for niceties. Just a few facts about what had happened with Kelly. Now they were waiting for Netta to arrive.

'She's here,' said Arthur.

He'd got home just after she called Netta. Geraldine could have easily gone inside and let him deal with everything, but she was determined to stay.

Netta came through the back gate, as instructed. Kelly threw herself into her arms and began to cry all over again. Seeing Netta soothe her was quite touching. Geraldine noticed Arthur's eyes were wet too. He was such a big softie.

'Let's get you home,' said Netta, leading Kelly out of the gate.

'Oh wait,' said Kelly. 'I forgot something.' She pulled away and grabbed the bag containing Arthur Two and the rose perfume. 'I'll take good care of him. I'll bring him back.'

'Keep him as long as you like,' said Geraldine. 'As long as you need him.'

She followed them out to the car, at a safe distance. Kelly got inside.

Netta lingered by the driver's door. 'It's good to see you, Mum.'

'It's good to see you too. When we're allowed to, we must sit down and talk,' said Geraldine.

'I'd like that,' said Netta. She opened the car door.

Geraldine watched as Netta got in the car and switched on the engine. She was suddenly filled with an urgency to say something that, absolutely, needed to be said: 'Nettie. The letter. You did the right thing.'

## 52

# DOING THE RIGHT THING

NETTA – 2020

'You did the right thing.' Those were the sweetest words Netta had heard for a good while. For the first time since she'd given her mum that letter, she felt good about herself. Not exactly vindicated. That was a step too far. Because if she'd known then, the effect it was going to have on her mum, she might not have done it.

'How did it feel, seeing Geraldine again?' said Kelly.

'Good. A relief. Although, I wish it could have been for happier reasons.'

'Yeah, me too.' Kelly was in the passenger seat, clinging on to that old bear Netta's mum had given her.

Netta flicked the indicator and turned into their road. 'Is the bear helping?'

'A bit, yeah.'

'I don't think I've seen him before. He looks quite old, though.'

'He is. Gez said a friend gave him to her after the rape.'

'A friend?'

'Yeah. Can't remember the name. I wasn't really taking

it all in. You'll never guess what his name is though, Net. Arthur Two.'

Netta stopped the car outside their house and looked at the bear. 'Arthur Two? I suppose there is something about that passive smile that's reminiscent of Dad.'

Liza ran down the path and took Kelly in her arms.

'Oh Kel, I'm so, so sorry. I've got Will on Skype in the study. Do you want to talk to him?'

Kelly nodded and let Liza lead her back inside. They'd be in there for hours now, probably. Perhaps that was what Kelly needed right now.


Netta stuck her head around the study door. Will's face was on the screen, listening to Kelly offloading. She would have liked to crash the call and speak to him as well, but that would have been selfishness on her part. Kelly needed her time with him now, and maybe Liza did as well. She'd probably been unsettled by all this too. Sometimes you had to accept that they needed their own space and get out of their hair.

'I'm going to pop over to Frank's. I'll be back soon but, if you need me, just come over.'

Frank was preparing online lessons for tomorrow. He seemed to spend more time working now, than when he was physically going into college every day.

'I'm not stopping. I just thought I'd let you know we're back,' she said.

'How is she?'

'Not sure. I think Mum saw the worst of it. She's calm for now. I've left her with Liza. They're talking to Will, on Skype.'

'And your mum, did you see her?'

Netta smiled. 'Yes. She seemed better. Still looking a bit thin and bedraggled but, I dunno, something's changed in her. I couldn't tell you what, but it feels like a good change. We didn't really talk, but she said one thing to me. She said I'd done the right thing with the letter.'

Frank stood up to face her and put his arms on her shoulders. He smiled. There were no words needed.

She smiled back and then, from nowhere, a lump appeared in her throat. 'I think she might have forgiven me.'

Netta was in the study sitting at the laptop. The girls and Frank were in the living room watching TV. She'd logged on to check the rota for tomorrow. They were delivering food parcels in the morning, and making jam and chutney in the afternoon. Neil had set up a website for them to sell direct, and they'd started advertising on social media. They'd had some orders already. She didn't know if the business would survive this pandemic, but they were doing everything in their power to keep it going.

She mailed her friends who didn't live in Birmingham, to make sure they were okay. First, Claire in Brighton who reported that she was just about staying sane, in spite of being shut up twenty-four hours a day with three kids – including one very stroppy teenager – and one husband, who was missing work and sport. As if that wasn't bad enough, Claire had nothing else to do, seeing as her shop wasn't an essential service. She said she was looking forward to the two of them meeting up at some point in the future, and getting absolutely shitfaced. Netta sent Claire a quick reply to say that was definitely a plan they should stick to. Even if they had to bring their own wine and sit two metres apart.

Next, she mailed Doogie. As usual, he was completely cool about everything. Very little had changed for him but then, he did live in one of the more remote parts of Scotland. Even on a good day, he probably saw no more than two people anyway.

Netta shut the laptop and went to join her family. In the living room, all three dogs were sprawled out on the floor in front of the fireplace. Frank was pretending to be interested in whatever rubbish it was that Liza and Kelly were watching.

'All done?' he said.

'Yes. Shall I make us all a drink?'

He jumped up. 'No, no. I'll do it.' Clearly it had been the excuse he'd been waiting for to extricate himself.

Liza and Kelly sat next to each other on the sofa. Liza was concentrating on the programme. Kelly was looking in the TV's direction, but her eyes had that glazed over appearance that told Netta she wasn't really watching it. Her mind was elsewhere and Netta knew where it was.

'Scoot up,' she said.

Kelly and Liza parted enough for her to slide in between them. She slipped her arms around her girls, and kissed each one on the top of their heads. The girls snuggled up closer and, for the second time that day, she felt good about herself.

## 53

## KELLY TRIES A SLICE OF HUMBLE PIE

KELLY – 2020

Kelly had only been to two funerals in her life. This one was probably the worst. That was most likely because she'd pretty much blanked out the first one which was her mum's, and also because there were a lot more people there than today's. Being more crowded had somehow made it easier to get through that service without making a tit of herself. Mind you, she was only twelve then, so maybe behaving like a tit hadn't really been on her radar. Only ten people were allowed at this funeral, and they were so far away from each other that it looked like there was no one who cared enough to celebrate her nan's life. The crematorium should have been full. It should have been creaking at the seams with family and friends, grieving for Gladys Payne. Kelly couldn't stop crying. Not just because she didn't want her nan to be dead, but also because this turnout was so pitiful. Her nan deserved better.

Her dad was on the front bench and she was at the very back. Because the place was so empty it was impossible not to see him hunched over, his shoulders moving up and down with each sob. Kelly looked over to her uncles and aunts, each with a bench to themselves. They were all doing the same, and so was she. For once, she couldn't single her old man out for being weak, because they were all as bad as each other.

The curtains closed around the coffin and the music started up. Before long, her nan would be reduced to a pile of ash. It was so unfair.

A memory of her mum's service popped into her head. The curtains wrapping around her coffin. Kelly thought they sang a hymn, but she couldn't be sure. What she did remember though, was her dad reaching down and holding her hand. He'd kept hold of it all the way through the rest of the service. They'd walked out of the crem, still holding hands, to the sound of 'I Will Survive'. Her mum always did have a weird sense of humour. Kelly remembered her dad laughing and crying at the same time. 'That's what you get for letting Cait plan her own funeral,' he'd said to someone. Kelly couldn't remember who.

When they got outside, he'd said to her: 'We're gonna get through this together,' and she'd believed him. She really did think that everything was going to be okay, because her dad was there and he was going to make everything all right again. How stupid had *she* been?

She'd been thinking about what Geraldine had said, about her being sorry that she'd never forgiven her mum for the stuff that happened to her. She got what Gez meant about seeing things from the other person's point of view, but it wasn't easy.

Her nan's service ended. Kelly got up and walked out. The others followed in an awkward, isolated trickle. They stood outside, in a circle, at a safe distance from each other. No one spoke.

One of her uncles eventually broke the silence. 'Not quite the send-off I'd have liked for Mum.'

'She'd have wanted a party and a knees-up,' said her dad.

They all laughed, sad laughs.

He carried on. 'She did love a good party.'

They laughed again, and one by one, started to talk about Nan and her famous parties, all of which were before Kelly's time. She was the only grandchild there, and she had nothing to contribute.

Her dad caught her eye and jerked his head to indicate they should break off. She sighed. This was where he was going to have a pop at her for kicking his car in.

'How are you holding up?' he said.

'All right,' she mumbled.

'Good. I'm sorry about the day she died. I'm not very good around death.'

'That's a fucking understatement,' she said, but she surprised herself with how fondly it came out.

He shook his head. 'All right, I'm shit at it. When your mum went, I know I was a terrible dad. She's helped me to see that.'

He pointed to a car that was just pulling in. It was his. Carol was in the driver's seat and Kelly's half-sister, Emily, was in the back.

'Anyway, I just wanted to say I'm sorry,' he said.

'Okay.'

They stood next to each other without saying anything else. They seemed uncomfortable in each other's company. Or was that just her?

'Pity we couldn't have had more people here,' he said, without looking at her.

'Yeah.'

Kelly focused on the rest of the family, still standing in a circle outside the chapel, and thought about Geraldine. If Geraldine could find forgiveness in her heart, after what she'd been through, then maybe it was time for her to stop hating her dad, just a little bit.

She cleared her throat. 'Cheers for letting me come today.'

He shoved his hands in his pockets. 'That was Carol's doing, not mine. She persuaded the others that you should come, being as you were the one that saw the most of Nan.'

'Right.' Fuck. Kelly felt sick. If Carol was on her side, where did that leave her? Bollocks. She was going to have to show some gratitude. She was going to have to speak to Carol. 'I'll just go and say hello … to Emily.'

***

Carol got out of the car and stood in front of the driver's door, not quite covering the massive dent that Kelly had made in it on the day her nan died. She was wearing a long black cardigan over her jeans and it was fluttering in the chilly breeze. She wrapped it around her, and folded her arms to keep it in place.

'Hello, Kelly. How was it?'

Kelly waved to Emily, who was playing with a toy in her car seat. 'Awful.'

'I can imagine. How about you, are you okay?'

'Yeah, I'm being looked after. Thanks, by the way. For getting the others to let me come.'

'No problem. You deserve it. Half of them never even visited her once. It was mainly you and your dad.'

'Yeah, well thanks and er, sorry for being such a cow.'

'That's okay. I didn't take it personally. It can't have been easy for you. Especially when I turned up.'

Kelly grimaced. 'No it wasn't but, well…'

'I know. It really is okay, Kelly.'

Kelly swallowed hard. It wasn't okay. It really wasn't. Carol was being nice to her. Carol had only ever been nice to her and, in return, all she'd done was treat her badly. She deserved some kind of explanation: 'It was the mug that did it,' she blurted out, like a complete dick.

'The mug? Sorry, I'm not with you.'

'Whenever you came to the house, you used to make yourself a coffee. You used her mug.'

Carol was still looking puzzled.

'The one with the C on it. C for Caitlin,' said Kelly.

Carol put her hand to her mouth. 'Oh God. Kelly, I'm so sorry. How stupid of me not to realise it was your mum's mug. I think I must have seen the C and thought Carol. Oh, I feel terrible. It's no wonder you hated me.'

'You weren't to know. Maybe me or Dad should have told you.'

'No, don't make excuses for me. I should have guessed. I'm really, really sorry.'

Inside the car, Emily began to kick up a fuss.

Carol tutted. 'Look, we've got to go now. I've left the other kids home alone. It'll be a madhouse by the time we get back. Do you think we could start again, you and me?'

'Maybe. We'll see.'

Carol looked knackered. She was probably having to do all the home schooling herself and keep everyone in order, including Kelly's dad.

'Your brothers have been asking after you. They miss you.'

'Yeah?' said Kelly.

'Yeah. So do your dad and me. When we're allowed to be together again, it would be nice if you came over.

Emily could do with another sister. Too many boys in this family.'

Kelly looked at her little sister, trying to free herself from the car seat. She was only two and kind of comical. It might be nice to spend more time with her.

'I'll think about it.'

Her dad came over and kissed Carol on the cheek. For once Kelly didn't turn away in disgust.

'We've got to go. They're throwing us out. How are you getting home, Kel?'

'I've got a lift.'

He nodded. 'Okay. Take care of yourself, girl. Be careful. I wouldn't want anything happening to you. And call us, yeah?'

'Yeah.'


Kelly waited until they'd driven off before messaging Netta to pick her up. Netta sent one back to say she was on her way. She found a bench to wait on and rang Geraldine's mobile. Geraldine answered straight away. Normally she spent ages trying to find it before answering, just before it cut over to answerphone. She must have been waiting for her to ring.

'Hello, sweetheart. I was hoping you'd call.'

'Hello stand-in nan. How's it going?'

'All fine here. What about you? How is it going with you?'

'Well, the funeral was a bit shit. We weren't even allowed to sing which would have mightily pissed Nan off, if she'd been looking down on us. I know for a fact that she wanted 'All Things Bright and Beautiful'. And obviously, there's no wake. I was the only grandchild there. Turns out my bastard aunties and uncles didn't want me to come, and Carol had to stand up for me and make sure I got an invite.'

'Carol? *The* Carol?'

'Yeah. Quite! So now I've had to eat humble pie and say thank you to her, and sorry for my previous behaviour.'

'How dreadful. Humble pie, eh? How did it taste?'

She could tell Geraldine was having a good old titter down the other end of the line.

'Not as bad as I thought it would, actually. When this shitty pandemic is over, I might try another slice, and go over to visit her and my dad.'

## 54

# THE UNBELIEVABLE WAVE-BY TREND

KELLY – 2020

'So, let me get this straight,' said Will. 'You basically cycle over to your nan's old care home, act like clowns for a bit, then cycle off. Is that it?'

'Yeah,' said Kelly. 'The old folks like it. It cheers them up.'

'We like it too, don't we Kel?' said Liza.

'Yeah. It's nice.'

'Yeah, nice,' said Liza. 'In fact, I've started it off as a thing at school. There's a group of us now that go to different care homes to do a wave-by. It's really trending.'

'A wave-by?' Will looked like he was having trouble understanding them.

'Yeah, a wave-by,' said Kelly. 'Fucking hell, Will, I thought you were supposed to be intelligent. Is it really that difficult to grasp? We go there. We wave at them. We do a few star jumps and cartwheels, and other stupid things. Then, we leave. The old people think it's funny. It cheers them up. End of. Got it?'

'Yeah. I got it the first time. I just couldn't imagine you

doing something like that, that's all. I mean Liza, yes, but not you.'

'What's that supposed to mean?' said Kelly.

'Nothing. It's just that you don't let yourself go very often,' he said.

'He's got a point,' said Liza.

'Yeah? Well I'm letting myself go now.' Kelly grabbed her bike. 'So are you coming, or what?'

Will picked up his bike. 'Of course I'm coming. I'm looking forward to seeing you letting yourself go.'

Kelly threw him a warning glare and his face cracked.

'I mean, do you actually know how to do a cartwheel?'

She put her foot on the pedal and shouted back at him: 'Just you watch me.'

He overtook her, the show-off. He didn't even know where he was going. They were approaching the turn-off point and she considered taking it, without ringing her bell. It might be funny to let him carry on sailing down the main road, not realising they'd left him behind. That'd show him. Wanker.

Liza caught up with her. 'I was just thinking about turning off without telling him, just to see how far he got before he realised we were gone.'

Kelly laughed. 'I was thinking the same thing.'

'Hmm. Could we do that to Will, do you think?' Liza put a finger to her lips. They both giggled.

Kelly rang her bell. 'Oi wanker, we turn off here.'

They watched him turn around and cycle back to them.

'We did think about leaving you to bike off into the distance, but we're too nice,' said Kelly.

'Just be grateful we love you so much,' said Liza.

'Sorry,' he said. 'I have no idea what came over me. I'll try to be less macho in future.'

Kelly leaned over and pinched his arm and he squealed like a little girl.

'Macho, my arse,' she said, then set off along the back roads before he could do the same to her.

Kelly was in her element. Not just because Will was home, although that did play a big part in it. Her and Liza were like best mates now, like proper sisters even. Things had been bad for Kelly for a long time. Not like Geraldine's kind of bad, but still bad. From the time Carol first came into their lives, until very recently, she felt like she didn't belong anywhere. But when no one else wanted her, Netta had let her in. That had been the start of it, but it was deciding to save Geraldine that finally brought her the thing she'd been craving. Something close to a real family. Maybe, at some point in the future, her actual family might feel like a real one. She'd have to wait and see. There was a long way to go yet.

She turned into the care home car park. Her heart still broke, just a little bit, every time she came here but she made herself come, even so. Nan would have wanted it. There were times when the loss of her hit Kelly like a hard rock. When that happened, that bear of Geraldine's got some serious cuddling. All in the privacy of her bedroom, obviously. She didn't want people thinking she'd gone soft.

After the funeral she'd phoned the home to say sorry for her meltdown, the last time she'd been there. It felt like they were owed an apology. The manager told her not to worry, because they'd seen a lot worse lately. She said the residents always enjoyed their antics and it was a shame they'd stopped coming. That's what she'd called them – antics. When Kelly told Liza and Netta afterwards, Liza said they should keep going until they weren't needed anymore. It was August now and they were still coming.

. . .

They left their bikes in the car park and went to the conservatory.

'Just follow our lead,' Liza told Will.

They ran along the length of the conservatory, waving and whooping at the pensioners sitting inside. Will looked a bit embarrassed, but he did it anyway. The care assistants brought the people in wheelchairs closer to the windows. There was an old guy with a walking frame who was practically running to get a better view. Before long, there wasn't a space left on the other side of the glass.

'Let's do the funny walk,' said Liza and, as soon as they did, the pensioners cheered. Those old people loved the funny walk.

'Star jumps,' said Kelly.

They jumped up and down like crazy. Some of the oldies were even sticking their hands up in the air with them. Kelly scanned their smiling faces. She was looking for one in particular. Willing her to be there. Then she saw her. The old lady who'd held up that drawing of a heart, the day her nan died. Kelly checked for her every time she came. She was there. She was still alive. Still holding up her heart. Kelly blew her a kiss.

Liza ran from one end of the conservatory to the other, blowing kisses to them all. The old people did the same back.

'Let's cartwheel,' she said. She dropped onto her hands and did one, two, three elegant cartwheels, landing on her feet like an Olympic gymnast.

Kelly did the same. Less like a gymnast, and more like an elephant. She turned to Will. 'Your go.'

He made one attempt and clattered to the ground.

Without stopping he forward rolled over and over. Kelly and Liza rolled after him, and they all ended up in one single heap on the grass. They were laughing so much their sides hurt.

The people in the conservatory were banging on the glass and clapping. They stood up and took a bow.

Will was grinning from ear to ear. 'That was just unbelievable.'

'I know,' she said.

## 55

# GERALDINE CHOOSES FREEDOM

GERALDINE – 2020

Geraldine turned the corner into her street. What a glorious August afternoon it was. The gardens were in full bloom, and the birds were twittering and chirping all around her. There was more traffic on the roads now, but not so much as to drown them out. She'd just spent a couple of hours with Liza, Kelly and Will in the local pub's beer garden. The girls had taken Will to his first wave-by, and he was absolutely fizzing with enthusiasm for it. It was a wonderful thing they were doing. She was full of pride for them.

It had been such a lovely afternoon, and so exciting to do something normal again after lockdown. Normal? She rolled her eyes in a 'hark at me' sort of way. It had never been normal for her to take herself off to a pub on her own. Even if it was to meet her nearest and dearest. But there was a new normal now. The experts were saying that all the time on the telly these days. She agreed to a point. What they meant was that the public had to get used to a more restricted life, but they'd never met Geraldine. They couldn't know just how restricted her life had become since she lost Ada. For her, the new normal was a liberation.

In the near distance, she could see Arthur getting out of the car, outside their house. He hadn't seen her. Geraldine stopped to watch him. She remembered that first time she saw him in the doorway of Ada's kitchen; the leanness of his body; the clearness of his eyes. The beauty of him. He was so very beautiful that the sight of him had made her blush. Of course, when she got to know him better, she realised he was just as beautiful on the inside and that was the part that really mattered. He was an old man now. His sandy hair was almost white. His startling ice-blue eyes, a little less clear. But he was still the same boy that dazzled the fifteen-year-old Geraldine Corcoran. He was still her Art.

The terrible fear of losing him had blighted her for almost as long as she'd known him. In some ways, it had paralysed her nearly as much as the rape itself. If she really wanted to be free, she had to tell him. He deserved to know, and she deserved freedom. Whatever the consequences.

Arthur let Minnie out from her travelling cage and took a box of something from the boot. Probably some veg from Clyde's allotment. That's where he'd been today. Geraldine was glad he was going back there again. He'd been cooped up at home for too long. They both had.

Minnie saw her and raced up the street to greet her. She was such a sweet darling. It was hard not to feel anything but joy when she was around. Geraldine grabbed the lead, before Minnie trailed it across an unsavoury looking pile on the grass verge, and gave the dog a big hug.

'What were you doing there?' said Arthur when she reached him.

His face had caught the sun and his freckles were coming out. He was wearing a T-shirt and shorts, and she noted that his arms and legs were still quite muscular.

'I was watching you. I'd forgotten what a dreamboat you were.'

He raised an eyebrow. 'Were?'

She kissed his lips. 'Are. Let's go inside.'

She unlocked the door and let him go in first. He went into the kitchen, put the box down and put some fresh water in Minnie's bowl. Then he filled up the kettle and switched it on.

'Did you get on all right at the pub, with the kids?'

'Yes. I got there first, so I ordered myself a drink on the app thingy with my phone.'

'Really? I'm impressed. And the kids, how were they?'

'They were great. I had a really good time.'

She moved closer to him. He smelt of earth and sweat. The kettle clicked. She kissed him on the lips again.

He put his arms around her and kissed her, softly. 'I'm all dirty and smelly.'

She looked into those pale blue eyes of his. It might be the last time he allowed her to come near him. She should make it count. She brushed her cheek against his.

'I don't care.'


Geraldine slipped on her dressing gown while Arthur took a shower. She'd never done that before – started it off. She'd always waited for him to make the first move. Maybe it was another one to add to the new normal list. It all depended on how he reacted to her confession. No, she mustn't call it that. Angelica had told her that word implied she'd done something wrong, when the reality was that she was the victim. Angelica was right, of course. Except that Geraldine still felt guilty for keeping it a secret from Arthur for all those years.

She went out onto the landing. She could hear him singing 'Wild Thing' over the splashing water. The door to his music room was ajar. It was the spare bedroom really. When they decided to stop trying for another baby, it had been her suggestion to use it for his record collection. There were CDs as well now, but he always preferred the records.

Geraldine went inside and looked around the walls, filled with music from across the decades. From the 1950s to this year. He'd never stopped buying them. Never stopped being excited by new and old music. Somewhere in here, he had his own collection of punk albums. Although, he never let on to Netta. She was too young when they were a thing and, by the time she and Claire discovered them, she was at that age when she would have been horrified to think her parents had been there and done it, before her.

It was like a record of their life, this room. Their shared history. Arthur still kept his old Dansette in here. Almost every one of these singles and albums had been bought either with her, or for her. She could see that Billy Fury single that was his first Christmas present to her. Next to it was the Righteous Brothers' 'Unchained Melody'. What a song. He'd given her that one for their first wedding anniversary.

The music room was Arthur's special place. He lost himself in it when things were bad. It was the music really, rather than the room itself. It was the music that was at the very heart of his existence. That and his family. He'd always been so sure of his family. Of her. How would he feel when she told him it was all a sham?

She shut her eyes and relived the last wonderful hour. Her husband had made love to her. He'd told her she was gorgeous and sexy, and the only woman he could ever love. She could still smell his earthy scent on her.

'Please.' she whispered, 'Please, don't let it be the last time.'

'What did you say, love?' Arthur was in the doorway, his cheeks pink and fresh from the shower.

'Nothing,' she said. 'Just thinking out loud.'

He swept her up and gave her a passionate kiss. 'That was the best. I can't tell you how good it is to have my Gee back with me.'

Geraldine looked into his eyes. Every inch of her was screaming: 'Don't spoil it' and it took all of her resolve to fight it. She'd rehearsed this with Angelica, so many times. She had to tell him. She just had to. If she didn't, she would never be free of Len Corcoran.

'Arthur, would you sit down? There's something I need to tell you.'

She sat next to him on the bed. 'I never told you the real reason why I came to live with you and Ada, all those years ago. I couldn't, at the time. I couldn't bring myself to, but I have to tell you now. Even if you hate me for it.'

'It's all right, Gee. You don't have to say anything.'

'No. I do, Arthur. I do. The night of that Christmas dance. You remember, I wore that red dress Ada bought me? Afterwards, that same night, Len Corcoran raped me. The night I came running to yours, he tried again, but he was too drunk. I didn't know, until after Ada called Doctor Samuels, that I'd been pregnant and had a miscarriage. You were away at the time. It was all done and dusted by the time you got back.'

He sat next to her, motionless. Oh God, oh God. She'd done it now. She'd ruined everything. She watched him cast his eyes around the shelves, his life's passion. She'd destroyed it all.

He cleared his throat. 'I know, love. It's all right. You

don't have to tell me any more than you want to. It's all right.'

'You know?'

He reached over for her hand. 'Yes.'

'But I thought we'd…' She stopped. She was going to say she thought they'd managed to keep it from him, but Ada must have told him. There was no other way he would have known. Unless it was Netta? No, she swore she wouldn't tell him, and so did Kelly. It was Ada. It had to be. 'How long?'

'That day Len came to the shop. He ran into me on the way out.'

'He told you?'

'No. We didn't speak. Mum told me. She had no choice. I forced it out of her.'

'I don't understand. How could you have known all this time, and not said anything?'

'Mum said you wanted to keep it a secret and, I didn't think you wanted to talk about it. I suppose, I hoped you'd put it behind you. I thought, if I dragged it back up, it would just upset you. I should have known it wasn't that simple.'

'But Arthur, if you knew then, why did you ask me to be your girl? Why did you marry me?'

He looked at her as if she'd asked the most stupid question in the history of stupid questions.

'Surely that's obvious, Gee? I loved you, and I still do.' He moved close enough to hold her in his arms. 'Sometimes Geraldine Wilde, you can be a bit of a nit.'

*She* could be a nit? Well really. 'I can't believe you knew. All this time I've been so afraid that you'd find out and be repulsed by me.'

'Repulsed? What must you think of me? Repulsed by

him, yes. But never you. It wasn't your fault. He was the one to blame. What he did to you was horrible, just horrible, but it didn't make you a bad person. My heart belonged to you the first time you looked at me with those big blue eyes. There was never anyone else. Nothing that bastard could do to you would ever change that.'

'Oh Arthur.'

She couldn't get any further. Her mind was desperately racing back to those early days, searching for clues that Arthur knew – an accidental comment, a sly look, a change in his attitude – but there was nothing. He'd just accepted what Ada had told him and said nothing. All this time, waiting patiently for her to open up to him. He was such a decent, gentle man. How could she have ever doubted him?

## 56

# ARTHUR'S SECOND CONFESSION

ARTHUR – 1962

Three weeks ago, everything Arthur Wilde held dear had been smashed to pieces. His beliefs, his hopes, his entire outlook. All gone. And all because he happened to be on his way home, minding his own business, when Len Corcoran stumbled into him. Literally, stumbled into him. The man was unsteady on his feet. Not drunk exactly. A few drinks shy but, by the smell of him, he'd already had a few. Dutch courage, no doubt. A lot of men needed a dose of that before facing his mother.

Drink aside, what really did for Corcoran was the fact that he'd been looking over his shoulder and trying to walk very quickly. Always a bad move when you've had a few. The result was that he lurched from one side of the street to the other. Arthur was like a goalkeeper waiting for a penalty, unsure which way to swerve. He thought he'd judged it well, but then Corcoran suddenly changed direction and they collided. Corcoran wasn't a big man, but he was solid. Solid enough to knock Arthur back a few feet. The bump made

Corcoran stop abruptly and spin round, to check what the obstruction was. He squinted at Arthur, hacked up a cough, and went on his way.

Arthur watched him go. He must have been to the shop. His mum had refused to say why Gee was living with them now, and he was too glad to have her there to make a big deal of it. But this much he did know, Gee's parents weren't happy about it. He knew a lad whose younger brother hung around with Gee's little brothers. Through him, he'd found out a lot about the Corcorans and what a bastard their dad was. But he still couldn't find out why Gee had suddenly left home, and what had happened to make her afraid of her own shadow, half the time. No one seemed to know that but, more than likely, it had something to do with Len Corcoran. So, if he was turning up at the shop, half-cut, it could only mean one thing. He was there to cause trouble. Arthur ran.

He was so agitated, he took the stairs two at a time, calling out: 'Mum, Gee, are you up there?'

Gee was nowhere to be seen, but his mum was laying the kitchen table for dinner.

'Hello, love. Just in time. You look a bit flustered. Is everything all right?'

'Yes, I er … yes. Is everything all right here?'

'Yes, why wouldn't it be?'

His mum's expression was completely blank. It immediately gave the game away. Her expression was never blank and, if he wasn't mistaken, he could smell whisky on her. As a rule, she didn't drink whisky, and never at this time of day.

Gee came down from her room. There was something not quite right about her either. He could tell from the redness of her eyes that she'd been crying, but it was more than that. Something, or rather someone, had scared her and he knew who that someone was.

'How was the Sombrero?' Gee asked, without actually looking at him.

'Good. Some of the guys were talking about this new band they'd seen up in Liverpool. They reckon they're terrific.'

'Great,' she said, without much enthusiasm. Something was definitely wrong.

Over dinner they just talked about their usual day in the shop. No one mentioned Corcoran's visit, but he had to have been there. Arthur was absolutely certain of it. What he couldn't work out, was why they were acting as if nothing had happened.

He had to wait until the next day before he could get his mum alone.

'Gee's dad ran into me last night, outside. He was here wasn't he?'

'What makes you think that?' his mum said.

'Why else would he be just up the road from our shop?'

'Could be any number of reasons.'

'Mum! He was in the shop, wasn't he? I'm not stupid. I could tell something was off, as soon as I came in last night.'

'All right, yes. He came in, but I got rid of him. I don't think he'll be coming back.'

'Why? What's going on?'

'I don't want to lie to you, Arthur. So I'm just going to say, I can't tell you. It's best you leave it at that.'

'I can't. I need to know.'

'Why? Why do you need to know?'

'Because whatever it is, it's frightening Gee, and I need to stop it.'

'It's not something you can do anything about, Arthur. Some things are best left alone. Don't mention it to Geraldine. You'll only upset her.'

But Arthur couldn't leave it alone. Over the next week he pushed and pushed, until his mum eventually gave in and told him everything.

'So, now you know,' she said. 'I've broken my promise to Geraldine. She'd be devastated if she knew I'd told you. You mustn't let on.'

For the only time in his life, he'd been angry with his mother. How could she spoil his happiness like that? How could she say those things about Gee?

But, the more he thought about it, the more it all made sense. Then, he became really angry with Len Corcoran. He wanted to kill him. Arthur spent nights tracking Corcoran. Watching, and waiting for his chance. Now, here he was. Standing in the shadows, waiting opposite Len Corcoran's favourite pub.

At closing time, a familiar shape shuffled out of the bar and crossed the road in his direction. Corcoran was alone, naturally. Arthur had seen enough of him in the last couple of weeks to know he had few friends. Probably none at all.

As Corcoran got closer, Arthur stepped out onto the empty street. Corcoran stopped and looked him up and down. Arthur stood under the street lamp and Corcoran flashed a look of recognition. He curled his lips and came in closer so that Arthur's nostrils were swamped by the smell of stale beer.

'Fuck do you want? She send ya, did she? Piss off home to yer mother's tit, nancy boy.'

He spat thick yellow phlegm in Arthur's direction. Arthur instinctively jumped back and it narrowly missed his shoe. Corcoran grunted and walked away.

Arthur stood rigid for a moment, stupefied. Not by Corcoran's behaviour but, by the hate he felt for the man. Hate he never thought himself capable of. Snapping out of it, he ran after him and called out his name.

As Corcoran turned, Arthur hit him as many times as it took to see the perverted bastard fold and curl up on the ground. He didn't want to think about poor Gee cowering beneath this foul pig, as he did that unspeakable thing to her, but Arthur made himself, as he kicked out at Corcoran's gut. Was it three, four or five times? He wasn't counting. All he knew was, he wanted to kill this excuse for a man more than anything in the world. He would have done so too, if the realisation hadn't hit him that he'd become no better than Len Corcoran. Much as he wanted to beat him to a pulp, this was not right.

Arthur pulled himself back and stopped before it was too late. He was out of breath. Sweat was trickling into his eyes.

'You ever come near Geraldine or my mother again, I will kill you, you evil, fucking bastard. Do you understand me?'

He could hear a noise coming from Corcoran that sounded like sobbing. Then, he realised it was laughter. Len Corcoran was laughing.

Corcoran rolled himself over. 'Fuck me, lad, I didn't know you had it in yer. Yer more of a man than I thought you were.'

Incensed, Arthur grabbed the man's throat and

squeezed hard until the laughing stopped, and Corcoran was choking.

'I'm more of a man than you, you disgusting animal. My mother's more of a man than you. I could kill you now, and not feel an ounce of regret, but you're not worth me wasting my life on. I'll tell you again, for the last time. Stay away from Geraldine and stay away from my mother.'

Arthur walked a few steps, then something else occurred to him. 'And if I ever hear of you beating your wife or kids again, I'll come after you and I will make you regret it.'

As he walked away, Corcoran called after him: 'Come on then, kill me. You'd be doing me a favour, son.'

It sounded as if he was pleading. As if he actually wanted to die. Arthur wouldn't give him the satisfaction.

'I heard someone beat up Len Corcoran last night,' said his mother, as she bathed his raw knuckles. 'It wasn't you was it, Arthur?'

'Don't be daft, Mum. You know I don't do things like that.'

'He's in a bad way, apparently. Broke a couple of ribs.'

'Got what he deserves then.'

'Came off your bike, you said?'

'Yes.'

She dabbed his hands with disinfected cotton wool. 'Yes, I expect you did.'

'About Gee, Mum. I love her. I want to marry her one day, if she'll have me.'

She carried on treating his wounds without looking up. 'In that case, you need to understand, she may never get over what happened to her. You could have some hard times ahead of you.'

'It doesn't matter. You telling me about what happened, only made me realise the depth of my feelings for her. I'll always love her and take care of her. No matter what.'

His mum put down the cotton wool. 'You're a fine young man, Arthur Wilde. I couldn't have asked for a better son.'

## 57

# ARTHUR'S ABSOLUTELY FINAL CONFESSIONS

ARTHUR – 2020

Gee was staring at him as if she hardly knew him. It had been easy enough for Arthur to tell her that he knew everything. He'd wanted to do it for years, but his mother's presence had stopped him. She'd always been adamant that Gee must not know she'd broken her promise of silence. It was odd really. Odd that a woman as strong as his mum could be so worried that Gee would think badly of her. But then, they'd always had a special bond, Gee and Mum.

He'd only realised, after Mum died, just how much Gee had depended on her and, although he was then free to tell Gee he knew what Len Corcoran had done, it was not an ideal time. So Arthur said nothing and instead, watched that bewitching girl he'd loved, from their first meeting, slide further and further away. So, yes, it had been easy to tell her that he'd always known. Easy because he'd been waiting for an opportunity to show her his love knew no bounds. Although, to say he'd left it a little late in the day, was an understatement.

Less straightforward a choice, was telling her about that night in 1962 when his base instincts overtook him. But he'd decided enough was enough. There had been too many dark spaces for them to retreat to. It was time to let in the light.

'It seems I'm not the only one who's been hiding the truth,' Gee said, eventually.

'It seems not. I'm sorry. Mum didn't want you to know. She felt she'd let you down.'

Gee was swallowing furiously. Trying to keep the emotions under control, he supposed.

'Poor Ada. I shouldn't have made her promise.'

'No, no. Don't blame yourself. Don't ever blame yourself, my darling.'

She swallowed again. 'This is just like being at Angelica's. Talk about cry me a river. You know, it's amazing how much snot can come out of one person. It never ceases to surprise me. And I have to say, Arthur Wilde, all these years I thought you wouldn't hurt a fly. And now I find out, you're quite an animal when roused.'

'Yes, I'm not proud of it, but there have been times in my life when my temper's got the better of me.'

He didn't say that what he saw in himself that night, as he beat a man senseless, had frightened him and stayed with him for the rest of his life. He didn't say that if he hadn't pulled back at the last minute, he could very well have murdered Len Corcoran. He didn't say any of those things because, for his own good, some things had to remain in the shadows.

'I think he got what was coming to him, and I think you actually are my hero, Sir Art. Do you remember that Christmas when I worked late in the shop, and you used to walk me home? That one time when those two boys bumped into us outside the pub. I was worried sick they'd beat you up. You told me then you could look after yourself. I should have believed you, shouldn't I?'

He smiled. 'That was a long time ago. Fancy you remembering that.'

'Yes, well, I've had to do a lot of recalling lately. So tell me, when were the other times that your temper got the better of you?'

Oh dear. He'd been hoping she wasn't going to ask that. 'You don't miss a trick, do you?'

'I try not to, Arthur. I'm only going to ask you once, but I'd really like to know. It's about time we were completely honest with each other.'

He couldn't argue with that. 'Okay. Well, there was that time when you were pregnant with Netta, when Len came to the house. I knew, as soon as I saw you in that state that it had to have been him. Do you remember I left you at Mum's, and went back home to collect some things? I did pick them up, but I actually went to find him. I was all set to … well, I wanted to kill him. I went to the pub he always used to go to but he wasn't there. I tried all sorts of places, but I couldn't find him. So I went back to you.

'The next morning, I called in sick and went to the Corcorans' house. I was so angry, Gee. I really thought you were going to lose the baby again. I waited outside for him to set off for work, but he didn't come out. So, I banged on the door and your mum opened up. I nearly knocked her flying when I stormed in. Given all the things he'd done to her, I was definitely out of order. Anyway, I found him sitting in front of the fire with a blanket wrapped around him. It was obvious I had no need to kill him, because he'd already done a good job of doing himself in. He looked like a man waiting for death to claim him. Your mum was screaming at me to get out, and I just shouted something at them about staying away from you and the baby, and left.'

'I see. That explains a lot. I thought Mum was rather reticent to come and see her new grandchild. Is that it? Anything else you want to tell me?'

'I suppose I should tell you about the incident with Colin.'

'Colin? You mean, Netta's waste of space sneaky, sly ex-husband, Colin?'

'Yes, the very same.'

Gee folded her arms under her chest. 'This should be good.'

'I know you've never liked him, and you've always thought I was too easy-going with him. Perhaps I was. I tried not to interfere. Even though I could see how much he was dragging her down. But when he threw Netta out of her own home and turned the kids against her, that was the last straw. I'm afraid I went over there, under cover of darkness, and slashed his tyres.'

Gee's face was a mixture of shock and amusement.

'Oh Art, I wish you'd told me what you were up to at the time. I'd have come over and given you a hand.'

After she stopped laughing, Gee gave him a big kiss. 'That really is the funniest thing I've heard in ages.'

## 58

## TIME FOR NEW THINGS

GERALDINE – 2020

Geraldine was sitting in Phil's garden. It was Fenella's garden really. It was her house, not his. Like the house, the garden was very big. Just as well, because Geraldine hadn't wanted the neighbours to overhear what they'd been talking about.

Of all the Corcorans, she'd chosen to tell Phil first. He could be a selfish sod sometimes but she was closer to him than the others. Perhaps that was because she and Phil weren't really Corcorans. What was it he used to say when they were kids? Him and her against the rest of them. That was a bit unfair really but then, Phil always did have a habit of putting himself first. If he'd looked beyond his own problems, he'd have seen that Tony and Ralph were just as hard done by. It was probably only Janet who got off reasonably lightly. No wonder she was so keen to keep up with that ridiculous annual pilgrimage to the graves.

Phil came back out of the house with a jug of something alcoholic. The drink had been his idea. He said he needed one after what she'd told him. He didn't want to drink alone, so she'd agreed. But as he got nearer, Geraldine could tell he'd already started without her. He poured her a glassful, and flopped down onto one of the garden chairs. It was just the two of them. Geraldine wanted to do this without Arthur. He'd gone for a stroll around Southwold. They'd left Minnie back in Birmingham, with Netta.

Phil demolished his drink as if it were a glass of fizzy pop and topped himself up again. The jug was going down fast. Geraldine made no comment. She'd learned a few things from Angelica and knew it was best to give people the space to process new things.

'I wish you'd told me back then,' he said. 'If I'd known, I might have been able to do something.'

'I tried once but I found it too difficult to speak about it. He made me believe it was my fault. I thought you'd all think I was a prostitute, or something.'

Geraldine took a sip of her drink. It wasn't bad actually. Definitely up there with the Strawberry Splits.

Phil was staring at his glass. He seemed to be struggling.

'Fucking hell, Gez. I would never have thought that about you.'

'Thanks, Phil. That means a lot to me. But you must remember what it was like back then? Any girl who had sex before marriage was seen as a tart. Imagine what people would have said about me, if they knew. They wouldn't have seen me as an innocent victim, would they?'

'I suppose not, but I would've. You don't think he did the same to Jan, do you?'

'No, I don't think so. She was his real daughter, after all. Anyway, I think it had something to do with Mum's sister, Fran. He came to the shop for me once. Ada stood up to him and said something that made him go away. Something about Fran. I think Ada knew that he'd done the same with Fran, or at least tried to, but I never asked her. I wish I had.'

'Christ. And I thought I had it bad.'

'You did. He was always picking on you. Always knocking you about. It's no wonder you left home as soon as you could.'

'I couldn't wait to get away from there. Didn't give anyone else a minute's thought. I should have realised. I really was a self-centred little prick.'

'You were just a kid, trying to make the best of things. That's all.'

'And you're sure he didn't do the same to Jan?'

'Fairly sure, but I'll ask her when I tell her.'

She and Arthur were playing it Covid-safe and staying in a holiday flat that belonged to one of Fenella's friends. That night they went out for a romantic candlelit dinner, just the two of them. Geraldine wanted to give Phil time to talk it all over with Fenella.

After dinner, they strolled around the pretty Southwold streets. Then they went back to the flat and made love.

'I could get used to this,' said Arthur.

They were sitting in fluffy bathrobes on the balcony, watching the sun go down and drinking a bottle of chilled white wine.

'Yes, we should do it more often,' she said. 'Arthur, I'd like to go to see Karen when we're able to. I'm sure Netta wouldn't mind having Minnie. What do you think?'

'I think that's a splendid idea. While we're on the subject of doing new things, I'd like to do a bit of cooking every now and then, if you don't mind. I actually quite enjoyed it when I had to do it.'

Arthur cooking again? Oh dear. She was less fussy about who did what job now, but she remembered those rather unappetising dishes he brought to her when she was too ill to do it herself. Still, she was all for change these days. Perhaps a compromise was in order.

'How about if we did it together to start with? I've got some new recipes from Neil we could try.'

He refilled her glass. 'I'd like that.'

---

The next day, they met Phil and Fenella for lunch. Phil was quiet, but Fenella made up for it. She asked lots of questions about Angelica and the therapy. For a while, it seemed as if they were talking about nothing else, until Arthur changed the subject to France. Fenella loved France.

'Where are you going to?' she asked.

'Nice,' said Arthur. 'That's where my cousin lives.'

'I adore Nice,' said Fenella. 'Oh, the Promenade des Anglais. And everyone's so stylish. What will you wear, Geraldine?'

'Just the usual, I suppose,' said Geraldine. 'I don't bother too much about clothes.'

Fenella looked quite appalled.

'Well you should. You're still a very attractive woman. Isn't she, Arthur?'

Arthur smirked, no doubt remembering what they'd got up to last night in Fenella's friend's bathtub. 'Yes she is.'

'There you go then,' said Fenella. 'You must let me help you choose some new clothes. After lunch, I'm going to take you to my shop. You men can amuse yourselves, can't you? I'm going to make a new woman of you, Geraldine. You wait and see.'

---

As soon as they were away from Arthur and Phil, Fenella

confessed that, while she was all for helping Geraldine find a new image, she did have another reason for getting her alone.

'It's Phil. I think he could do with some therapy too. I know he didn't have to go through the same trauma as you did, Geraldine, but he's definitely carrying a lot of baggage. I'm certain that's what makes him drink so much. I've tried to talk to him about it, but you know what men of his generation are like. They think it's weak to admit they have a problem. I need your help to convince him it's not.'

Now that Fenella mentioned it, he did seem to be drinking a lot.

'I'll do my best.'

'Thank you. I'd be so grateful. Right then. Let's get you kitted out. And then, we're going to call on my friend, Veronica. She's a hairdresser. We need to get that hair sorted.'

## 59

# MORE SECRETS COME TO LIGHT

GERALDINE – 2020

Geraldine rang Tony before the others. Tony said Phil had already called him, so he knew what it was about. But he still wanted to talk to her, face-to-face, and so did Ralph.

Janet had called Tony too, after speaking to Phil herself. Apparently, she'd been less keen to speak to Geraldine, but Tony had managed to talk her into it. He suggested they all meet in Sutton Park. The park was on the north side of the city, near to his house. It was a vast place with plenty of space to find somewhere quiet.

Arthur and Geraldine pulled into the car park. Minnie, spotting the potential for fun, began to whine.

'Looks like Minnie's going to enjoy herself here,' said Arthur.

Tony was already waiting for them.

'You found it all right then?' he said. 'All the different entrances and car parks can be confusing, if you're not a regular.'

'No, all good,' said Arthur. 'I'll leave you to it, Gee. Let me know when you're heading back. If I don't hear from you, I'll come back anyway in two hours.'

'He's worried about the phone signal. Big open place like this,' Geraldine explained. She was waffling, but it was hard making small talk when they both knew what they really needed to talk about.

'Eileen didn't come with you, then?' she said.

Tony shook his head and looked away, across the expansive parkland. 'She doesn't like to think about that sort of thing. It upsets her.'

Lucky Eileen, to have the luxury of not having to think about 'that sort of thing'. A fleeting rush of bile emerged in the pit of Geraldine's stomach, but she ignored it. She was not that person anymore. Bitterness no longer ruled her. She'd turned a corner, towards a new and bright future. She was the lucky one. Not Eileen.

Ralph pulled up. He had Sheila with him. He looked so ill that Geraldine asked if he should be out.

'I'm fine,' he said. 'Just … ye know. Here's Jan and Trev's car.'

Janet got out of the car. Her face was like thunder. Trev took a bag and two folding chairs from the boot, and scuttled along behind her.

'Hello there. Long time, no see. Haven't been here in years,' said Trev.

It would seem Geraldine wasn't the only one who felt the need to waffle. Janet had no such concern. She was more intent on saying absolutely nothing at all, which was most unlike her.

They followed Tony's lead to a clearing that was free of other people. Geraldine wondered if there would ever be a time again when private conversations could be held indoors.

Trev unfolded the chairs for him and Janet, then proceeded to put a blanket down in the middle of their encampment and lay some snacks out on top of it. He seemed to have decided that, rather than waste the day completely, they were going to make a picnic out of it. Or perhaps that was Jan's doing.

The rest of them looked on, rather incredulously. It was quite funny really. Geraldine got busy opening out a rug to distract herself from laughing. Tony sighed and put one down too, followed by Ralph and Sheila who sat closely together on theirs.

Tony cleared his throat. 'So, as you know, Phil called me, and I've filled everyone in. We thought it was best to hear it from you though, Gez. If you want to talk about it, that is.'

'Yes, I do. I have to.'

Geraldine went through it all again, noting the discomfort on their faces. It wasn't an easy story to listen to. It wasn't an easy story to tell.

When she finished, Geraldine looked around their little group. Janet had her arms tightly folded and was staring straight ahead of her. Her brothers were looking at the ground, and so was Trev. Only Sheila was looking at her. Mousey Sheila, who always seemed frightened of her own shadow, was the only one who could meet her eye.

Finally, Tony looked up. 'No wonder you always act so funny when we go to the graves.'

'Yes, it has been a real struggle for me to go there,' said Geraldine.

Janet shook her head. 'I'm sorry. I'm finding this very hard to believe. Don't get me wrong, I know what Dad was like, but–'

'No Jan, you don't know what he was like. Not really. If you did, you wouldn't be suggesting I was lying,' said Geraldine.

'Hang on a minute, I didn't say you were lying. I was just trying to say, I couldn't believe he'd do that to his own daughter. He never touched me.'

Well at least that was cleared up then. At least that was one difficult subject that Geraldine didn't need to broach.

'Well he did. And if all you're worried about is whether or not he could do it to his own daughter, then don't bother worrying, because I wasn't his daughter. Phil and me had a different dad.'

Janet shot back in her seat. She looked as if she'd been slapped in the face.

'Of course he was your dad. What the hell are you suggesting about Mum?'

Trevor put his hand up. 'Jan, stop. You know full well, Len wasn't their dad. Mum told us.'

He turned to Geraldine. 'My mum let it slip ages ago. For what it's worth, I believe you. Mum always said there was something strange about him. There were rumours when they were younger. They all knew each other's business in that neighbourhood.'

'What do you mean, rumours?' said Janet, sounding even more agitated.

Trevor shrugged. 'She didn't say, but she didn't seem surprised when I told her Gez had run away.'

'Yeah, Phil told me and Ralph about your dad, ages ago,' said Tony.

Janet glared at Tony who seemed to have found his courage, at last, and glared back. It was Sheila who broke their concentration.

'Ralph has something to say.'

They all turned to Ralph.

'Tell them, Ralph,' said Sheila.

'Tell us what?' said Geraldine.

Sheila held Ralph's hand. 'It's for Ralph to say. Come on, love. You'll feel better for it.'

Ralph looked at Sheila. She smiled at him and held his hand. He rubbed his eyes and turned to Geraldine.

'I was awake. That night he did that you. You know I hardly ever slept. I heard him shouting. I heard you crying and begging. The names he called you. I heard it all. I thought he was giving you a belting. I was desperate to go to the toilet but too scared to go down, in case I was next. I waited 'til it all went quiet. When I got to the kitchen, the back door was wide open. I thought maybe someone had gone out to the toilet, but it was empty. So I had a wee and went back inside. That's when I saw something on the floor. It was a pair of pants, Gez. I didn't know they were yours then, but I do now. They were torn. I picked them up and went to close the back door, but then the old man appeared. He must have been out there in the dark, watching me. I nearly crapped myself. I couldn't move. He just walked past me and went up to bed.'

Poor Ralph. Geraldine thought of that little boy who used to wet the bed because he was too frightened to go downstairs. She thought about Phil and Janet, back then, not really wanting to know why she'd run away. She thought about Trev, who knew there was something wrong with Len Corcoran, but couldn't bring himself to do anything about it. It would have been easy for her to lay some blame on them, but that wasn't fair. They were just kids. It wasn't their fault.

'Oh Ralph, that must have been awful for you,' she said.

'It was worse for you. The thing is, Gez, I thought the

pants were Mum's. I didn't want her to feel bad about leaving them lying around. She was always so particular about everything being spotless.'

'Yes, she was. You did the best thing by picking them up. I always wondered what happened to them. Did you throw them away?'

'That's what I'm trying to tell you. Like I said, I thought they were Mum's. The next day, I put them in her underwear drawer.'

There was little left to say after Ralph's revelation. Even Janet couldn't argue with that. They sat in silence for a while, until a big Labrador ran through them and tried to eat Trev's picnic. Chasing it off broke the ice, and they even managed to eat a sausage roll or two.

Arthur messaged to say he was back at the car, and they decided it was time they all went.

When they got to the car park, Janet began to march off.

Geraldine called after her: 'Oh Jan, before you go. Have you got Rita Sweeney's phone number? I'd like to get in touch with her sister, Bree.'

'I thought you didn't remember her,' snapped Janet.

'Well I lied, didn't I? Have you got a problem with that?'

Janet huffed. 'I'll send it to you.'

'Thank you. I'll wait to hear from you, then.'

Janet got in her car without replying.

'Don't worry about Jan. It's just come as a shock. She'll get over it. I'll make sure she sends that number to you,' said Trevor.

Geraldine considered suggesting therapy, but she couldn't be sure that Jan wouldn't tell her to stick her therapy where the sun don't shine.

'I'd appreciate it. I treated Bree badly when we were girls. It's time to clear my conscience.'

'I'm sorry, Gez. I should have done more at the time to protect you. All of you,' said Trevor.

'Why? You didn't know.'

'No, but I could see what he did to your mum. I could see you were all terrorised by him.'

Poor Trev. He looked as if he had the weight of the world on his shoulders.

'Trev, that Christmas, after it happened. You and Jan came to ours. Do you remember? That was the best Christmas we had in that house, thanks to you. You made us all feel like a normal family for once. You were lovely. You were always lovely.'

## 60

## A MOMENTOUS DAY

GERALDINE – 2020

Geraldine sat in the garden with Minnie at her feet. It was nearly time for her to go to Angelica's office and she was gathering her thoughts, in readiness. It was a little routine she'd fallen into over the summer months. Strange to think that it wouldn't be needed soon.

Today was going to be quite a momentous one. All being well, it would be the last time Geraldine would be visiting Angelica. There were a few loose ends to tie up before that was going to be an absolute definite, and they'd be discussing those today. But Geraldine was confident she could manage them on her own. The thought of her being confident about anything, made her smile. She'd come a long way.

There was another reason that this was going to be a big day. She was meeting Netta after today's session with Angelica. It would be the first time they'd be in the same space since the day Kelly's nan died. Geraldine was quite excited about it.

She hadn't meant to leave it so long. At first she couldn't face Netta. But the reasons for that had been silly, and were no longer important. For a long time, Geraldine couldn't even speak to her. But Netta had kept faith with her. She'd sent those funny videos at Christmas that had cheered Geraldine and Arthur up. She'd sent regular messages as well. To let Geraldine know that, even though things were difficult, she was still there, waiting for a time when they'd be together again. Geraldine had to admit, Netta had been persistent. Bloody obstinate really. It was one of the many things she loved about her daughter.

When Geraldine had felt ready to see Netta again, she'd fully intended to arrange a date. But something had stopped her. Mentally, she'd been well on the way to recovery, but she'd wanted to wait until her physical transformation was complete. She wanted to wow Netta. Vanity was not something Geraldine had bothered with before, but she had to admit, she was a touch vain these days. Thanks to Fenella.

She and Fenella had become very friendly recently. Geraldine had been helping her to get Phil back on the straight and narrow with his drinking, and Fenella was calling her every few days with the latest news. In return, she'd become Geraldine's self-appointed style guru. She was making a pretty good job of it too.

Arthur came out of the kitchen, into the garden. 'Someone on the phone for you. An old friend.'

'Karen?'

'Bree.'

Geraldine felt a flash of heat run right through her. It was only a week ago that she'd called Rita Sweeney. Rita had been a bit sniffy about her pretending not to remember Bree, but said she'd pass the message on, when she next spoke to her sister. She didn't offer Bree's contact details, and Geraldine didn't want to press her. It had been a long time, after all. It was best to leave the ball in Bree's court.

But, to Geraldine's surprise, Rita must have been true to her word and, to her even greater surprise, Bree was on the phone. Now!

'Oh my goodness.' Geraldine shot up. She was all over the place.

Arthur held out his hand. 'She's waiting, Gee.'

He helped her into the hall. She could barely pick the phone up, she was shaking that much.

'Is that Geraldine?' said a voice on the other end of the line.

It didn't sound like Bree at all. Not the Bree Geraldine remembered, anyway.

'Yes, it's me,' she said. 'Is that you, Bree?'

'Hello Gez. Yes it's me. How wonderful to hear from you, after all these years. I'm so pleased you got in touch.'

Geraldine laughed. She was welling up. Oh bother. She'd have to do her make-up again.

'Oh Bree. Is it really you? I have so much to tell you.'

'I bet you have. We've got a lot of time to catch up on. I'll be in Birmingham in a couple of weeks. Shall we meet up?'

'Yes, let's. I'd like that.'

'Me too,' said Bree. 'I've never forgotten you, Gez. You've always been in my thoughts.'

'And you've been in mine too. Sort of. It's complicated.'


Arthur dropped Geraldine off outside Angelica's office. She watched him drive off and stayed in the car park for a few minutes, mulling the last hour over.

She and Bree had talked non-stop. It was only when Arthur tapped at his wrist that she realised she'd have to go to her appointment. They'd made plans for another call, and to see each other when Bree came to visit Rita, the week after next.

Was it possible that she might get her old friend back, or was that too fanciful a hope? It had been a long time ago. They'd both had a whole lifetime of experiences that neither had shared with the other. There was a chance they'd changed too much to rekindle that dear friendship she'd once felt unworthy of. But, if Geraldine had learned one thing this year, it was this. It was worth the try.

## 61

# THE LONG-AWAITED REUNION

NETTA – 2020

Netta was oddly nervous. She was waiting for her mum to finish her final therapy session with the famous Angelica. Their meeting place, a 1960s-style coffee bar, was her mum's suggestion. Kelly said that was where she and her mum normally went for a debrief. Before the pandemic that was. Since then, they'd managed with a telephone chat. Although, now that the rules had relaxed a bit, the kids were seeing her mum once or twice a week. Neil was also seeing her mum every week. In fact, the only person that didn't seem to have regular access to her mother was Netta. She'd thought, when Kelly's nan died, her mum was going to ask to see her within a matter of days, but that hadn't been the case. They'd had a couple of heart-to-heart phone calls, recently. But it wasn't until last week that her mum finally suggested they meet up.

The café door opened and she glanced up. Two stylishly dressed women breezed in, chatting to each other. She looked away and checked her phone. She was just wondering whether to get another coffee, or wait for her mum to get here, when the sound of her mum's voice startled her.

'Here she is. Angelica, this is my daughter, Netta. Netta, this is Angelica.'

Netta shot up. The two women she'd hardly paid any attention to, were her mum and the therapist.

The tall, elegant Angelica gave her the most fantastic smile. 'Pleased to meet you, Netta. I've heard so much about you.'

Netta resisted the urge to say that she hoped it was all good. Particularly, as there was a chance the answer might come back as an embarrassing silence. Instead she said: 'And you too, Angelica. Are you joining us?'

'Oh no. I just popped in to grab a sandwich and a coffee. Geraldine wanted to introduce you.'

'I'm going to get a cappuccino, love. Do you want another one?' said her mum.

She whisked off a navy trench coat to reveal a Breton top and black straight-leg jeans. Netta noticed her mum's long grey hair had been cut into a proper style, and she was wearing lipstick. She looked like an elderly Jean Shrimpton. Although thinking about it, Jean Shrimpton *was* elderly now. She looked astonishing. Quite fabulous.

'I can get them,' said Netta, still reeling from the shock of new Mum.

'No, no. I'll get them. Americano, is it?'

Netta muttered something in the affirmative and sat down, somewhat dazed. This confident, self-assured woman who was chatting and smiling – yes smiling – with her chic clothes and shiny hair, was surely not her mother? Her mum came back with the coffees and she had to admit that yes, it was her mother.

'Sonny's just sorting us out some tiramisu,' she said. 'I

thought you might like some. They make their own here. It's delicious.'

Sonny turned out to be a middle-aged mod, with a Paul Weller haircut and a pair of fancy shoes.

'Here you go ladies,' he said in broad Brummie. 'When are you bringing Art in again, Gee?'

'The weekend, I expect. He's champing at the bit now he knows you're open again,' said her mum.

'Brilliant, I've got some new tunes I'd be interested to hear his opinion on.'

'I'll tell him to call you and let you know for definite,' said her mum.

'Art?' said Netta, as soon as Sonny was back behind the counter.

'He's just picked up on your dad's nickname.'

Her dad had a nickname? Who knew? Her mum turned around to face her. That's when Netta saw that she was also wearing foundation and eye make-up. Art and Gee? Her mum looking like she'd just come from a photo shoot for Saga, or something? Who were these people, and what had they done with her parents?

Her mum raised her eyebrows, as if to say: 'What?'

'You look amazing, Mum,' Netta said, in response to the implied question.

'Do I? You like my new image, then? It's all Fenella's doing. She keeps finding new things for me to wear. Her friend tidied up the hair. She's a hairdresser. I hadn't had it cut in over a year before then. It had got quite long, but your dad likes it long. So she just gave me a fringe and a trim, and I'm using this fancy shampoo to make it shiny and silvery.'

'It looks lovely. So, you and Fenella are friends now?'

'Sort of. She's a bit over the top but we get on well.

We've been talking a lot lately. We're trying to get Phil to have therapy. I think he's coming round to it. We're getting there.'

Well, well. Mum and Fenella. That was another turn up for the books.

'And the make-up. I love the make-up.'

'Fenella again. And the girls. Well, Liza mostly. Kelly hasn't got much of a clue, to be honest with you. I think she's actually learned a thing or two herself.'

'Talking of Kelly, she asked me to bring Arthur Two back, in case you were missing him. I bought her one of her own this week. She's called him Arthur Three.'

Her mum laughed out loud. 'Goodness, we're going to have a whole family of Arthurs, at this rate. There was no rush to get Arthur Two back, though.'

'She was worried that she might do him some damage. We thought he must be very precious to you.'

'Yes, he is. He was my first and only teddy. Did she tell you it was your Auntie Karen that gave him to me?'

'She couldn't remember who it was.'

'I don't suppose there was much sinking in on that day. Karen gave him to me not long after I went to live at Ada's. Not that she knew what had happened to me. She thought I'd been run over by a car. That little bear was a lifeline for me back then. Did you tell Liza and Will?'

Netta nodded.

'Thanks, sweetheart. I would have told them myself, but I thought it might be better coming from you. How did they take it?'

'They were upset for you but, otherwise, they were okay. To be honest, I think they already knew.'

'Kelly, probably. Is she all right, do you think? I mean

she seems it when she comes to see me, but you know her better than anyone.'

'Yes, she's doing just fine. She seems to be getting on better with her dad and Carol. We talk a lot about her nan and her mum too. I think the pain of losing her mum has resurfaced with her nan dying. Luckily she's got a couple of stand-ins to help her get by. She told me what you'd said about being her stand-in nan. That was such a nice thing to do.'

Her mum sipped on her cappuccino. 'It was the least I could do. Kelly brought me back to life. You both did.'

Netta pulled a face. 'Maybe not me, Mum. I probably only made things worse for you.'

'For a while, yes, but what is it they say? Sometimes things have to get worse before they get better. I'm glad you found the letter. I really am. There's something else I need to tell you about, but not here. Finish off your coffee and cake and we'll go for a walk.'

They took a walk around Edgbaston Reservoir. Her mum told her all about the miscarriages she'd had – four in all, including the one from Len Corcoran. Netta didn't let on that she already knew about it. She was getting better at keeping things to herself these days. Although she'd never be able to match the scale her parents appeared to have operated on. Fancy her dad knowing all this time? She remembered the day she'd shown him the letter. His reaction made sense now. When he said, 'What have you done?' it wasn't really a question. He already knew exactly what she'd done, and was probably imagining the darkness she'd unleashed.

On the second lap, her mum pointed out the old Tower

Ballroom. She told Netta all about the dances she'd gone to with her dad, back when they were sweethearts. Then she got onto the coffee bars and clubs, and the bands they'd seen. She talked about the first time she saw Netta's dad, and how utterly transfixed she'd been by his beauty. All this openness was new, and it was rather strange hearing her dad described in that way. It took Netta back to the first time she saw Doogie, her first love. Although things had ended up differently for her and Doogie.

The really rather marvellous thing was that her mum still felt exactly the same about her dad, and it was plain to see that he did too.

'You know, you and Dad were made for each other. It's like destiny. Bloody hell, I've gone a bit Barbara Cartland there. Sorry about that.'

Her mum chuckled. It was lovely. Like they were two mates having a reunion, after a long spell away from each other.

'I know what you mean. We're very lucky. And, with everything that's happened recently, it feels like we've fallen in love all over again. We can't keep our hands off each other.'

An image of her mum and dad in the heights of passion suddenly flashed across Netta's brain. Ugh. Now that was definitely a step too far. On balance, maybe the two mates thing had its disadvantages.

Her mum gave her a lopsided grin. 'Sorry, sweetheart. I know you're a bit squeamish about me and your dad enjoying marital relations, but he's a full-blooded man and I still fancy him to bits. It doesn't dry up just because you're past your prime, you know. I hope you and Frank are—'

'Me and Frank are just fine, thanks Mum. Although, from the sounds of it, we're not getting it as much as you two are. I'm going to have to have words with him and tell him it's time to crank up his libido. Not that it's a competition or anything.'

They stopped in the middle of the path and faced each other. Her mum's eyes twinkled, her shoulders twitched, and a bubble of laughter escaped from her lips. Before she knew it, Netta was doing the same. They laughed so much they were in tears. Their sides hurt and they were in a state of near collapse, but they kept on laughing.

They found a bench to sit on and looked out across the water and beyond, to the cityscape behind it.

'Do you think you're over it then?' said Netta.

'I'm at peace with it. I just have one more thing to do and then, yes, I think I finally will be over it.'

A drop of water splashed onto Netta's nose. A minute later, there were several. Two minutes later, it was a shower.

'Did you bring a brolly?' said her mum.

'Afraid not.'

Her mum shuffled around in her new stylish bag and pulled out two umbrellas. 'Lucky for you, my darling, I checked the weather forecast this morning.'

The rain came down properly. They sat under their brollies, still getting ever-so-slightly wet.

'You don't want to go then? You're all right staying here?' said Netta.

'I'm not in a hurry, unless you are. Besides, who'd want to be cooped up inside on a beautiful day like this?'

They caught each other's eye and burst into laughter again.

Up in the sky, the sun shook off a rain cloud, and Netta could have sworn she saw a rainbow shining high over Birmingham.

## 62

## WE DID IT

GERALDINE – 2020

Arthur popped his head around the bedroom door. 'All set, Gee?'

Geraldine checked her appearance in the mirror and was pleased with what she saw.

'I think so.'

He came up behind her and kissed the nape of her neck. 'Sure you wouldn't rather do something else?'

She giggled. 'Down tiger. Time for that later.'

Once again, Minnie looked less than impressed as they shut the front door. They couldn't help but find her comical expression funny.

Arthur switched the car engine on, and the CD came to life. The Beatles, 'And I Love Her'. It was the first dance at their wedding reception. In those days, they didn't have big dos like they have now. Just a room above the pub and back home, or off on honeymoon, if you were lucky. They hadn't wanted a big flashy wedding anyway. It wasn't their style.

Geraldine's mum had been upset about them banning

Len. She'd threatened not to come, but Jan and Trev talked her into it. Even then, she sat through the whole thing with a sour face. It would have been better if she'd stayed away.

Geraldine and Arthur went to Cornwall for their honeymoon but they spent their wedding night at home, in Ada's flat. Ada stayed at Stan's house.

Before they went to bed, Arthur played this tune again on the Dansette and they danced up close. Then, they made love. It was the first time she and Arthur had done it and he was so careful not to hurt her. Afterwards, he asked her if it was okay, and promised it would get better the more they got used to it. He was a virgin too, he said. They'd learn together. They had plenty of time.

From the driver's seat, Arthur caught her eye and she knew he was thinking about that night too.

'I think we learned pretty well. Don't you?'

He winked and he was back again – that cheeky young boy standing in Ada's kitchen doorway, watching her blush.

She leaned over and kissed him. 'I think we did.'

'You know, when all this started, when things were at their worst, all I wanted was my old Geraldine back. I'd have given anything to have that tetchy little woman shouting at me for stepping out of line. Well, I didn't get her back. I got something better. I got that gorgeous, amazing, strong girl that captured my heart when we were kids. Lucky me.'

She kissed him again. 'No more treading on eggshells, Arthur. I promise. And yes, I am strong aren't I?'

'Don't forget gorgeous and amazing. Welcome back, Gee.'

. . .

They stopped in almost the exact same spot they parked in last year.

'Are you sure you don't want me to come in with you?' said Arthur.

'Absolutely sure. You stay here and plan your new allotment.'

'Ah yes, about that. You definitely don't mind me signing up for one?'

'Definitely. I might even come along occasionally to give you a hand. Not too often, though. I don't want to cramp your style. Now, get your pen and paper out and start planning, Percy Thrower.'

'Okay. I'll be right here if you need me.'

Geraldine stepped out of the car. It was almost winter the last time they'd been here and she'd been frozen to the bone. It was September now and, thankfully, much warmer. She took a few slow, deep breaths and walked through the entrance, along the path, to the matching headstones. Her breathing was steady and she had no need to do the hand thing. She rarely did these days.

There were some dead flowers in the pot on her mum's grave. She replaced them with the roses they'd cut from the garden. It seemed appropriate to bring some from the bushes they'd planted for their lost babies. It was Geraldine's way of sharing something precious. To show that she no longer blamed her.

Geraldine thought about Ralph lying in bed, having to listen to those dreadful things. Just a baby and too afraid to step outside the bedroom. She thought about the last thing he'd said to her in the park, before they'd goodbye: 'The day that man died was the best day of my life. Nothing has ever topped it. Not my wedding day. Not even when my kids were born.'

Poor, poor little Ralphie. She had, of course, recommended therapy to him. She was going to have to start charging commission at this rate.

She ran her finger along the top of her mother's headstone. What had she thought when she found Geraldine's torn pants in her drawer, and who did she think put them there? Did she guess what had happened that night? Had she known anyway? Geraldine would never know the answers, but she understood, it no longer mattered.

'I forgive you, Mum.'

She took a single rose out of her mother's pot and put it in the one on Len's grave.

'This is for that poor innocent child you planted in me,' she said. 'For a long time I hated it as much as I hated you, but that was wrong of me. It was a victim too. I wish I could forgive you, but I can't. I know terrible things must have happened to you in that POW camp. I'm sure you loved Fran, and not Mum. It must have been awful when she died, and when you found out Mum had been with someone else, but it was no excuse for what you did to me; to Mum, and to all of us. She was always saying you were golden before the war, but I think she was kidding herself. I think there was always something wrong with you. So no, I can't forgive you, but I've stopped hating you. In fact, I feel sorry for you.'

For a minute, she thought she was going to faint. Everything seemed to be shifting around her. As if it were realigning with the new her.

She found somewhere to sit down and waited for it to stop, using the time to reflect on all that had happened since her last visit. The letter from Len that Ada, for one reason or another, had hidden away had been catastrophic. And yet, nothing but good had come from it. She'd been saved.

More than saved. She'd been given a chance to live properly, without fear.

Arthur had thrown the letter away ages ago but there was another one that she wanted to read again. It was the one Ada had left for her, to be read after her death. The one Angelica had asked her to read out.

Geraldine took it out of her bag. It would have been nice to have read it next to Ada's grave but Ada, being Ada, had stipulated a cremation, because she didn't want people 'mooning about over her' after she'd gone. What she'd failed to grasp was that people wanted to moon about over her, and the very fact that they had nowhere to do the mooning only made it worse.

Geraldine opened the letter. In the absence of anything else, this quiet corner of the graveyard would have to do:

*'My dearest Geraldine,*

*Do you remember the first time we met? You were standing outside the shop, soaked to the skin.*

*I never told you why I hesitated before letting you in. When I lifted the blind and saw you there, I thought you were my old friend Frannie, come back to me. You were the image of her and later, when I got to know you better, I realised that you were so like her in other ways too.*

*From that very first day, I felt such a need to protect you.*

*Geraldine, my darling, you have always been the perfect daughter. My Arthur couldn't have chosen a better soulmate. As we have aged together, I have also come to think of you as my dearest friend. We've shared so much together since that first meeting, and I have never stopped trying to protect you. But I'm tired now. It's time for me to rest.*

*My biggest regret is that I couldn't save you from the darkness you sometimes fall into. When I'm gone, you must not sink deeper into despair. You have survived something you should never have had to survive. You must continue to be strong. Please, my sweet girl, for my sake, promise me you will beat this.*

*Yours, with love,*
*Ada.'*

It was ironic really. Ada had spent her life trying to save Geraldine but it was only after her death that she managed to do it, with a little help from two unlikely candidates – Ada's bull-in-a-china-shop granddaughter, and a foul-mouthed slip of a girl who never even knew her. Netta had started it, but it had been Kelly's words that brought Geraldine to her senses. When Kelly had said they would beat it together, Geraldine knew that she'd found someone to help her fulfil Ada's dying wish.

She tutted at the absence of a gravestone to talk to, but then she realised she didn't need one. Ada was with her, and she always would be. So, she addressed the air:

'We did it, Ada. We beat it.'

## A WORD FROM THE AUTHOR.

Please consider leaving a review.

Your reviews are important. They help me to reach more readers and they help other readers to decide whether this book is for them.

**You can leave a review at your local Amazon store .**

To find out more about other stories written by Hazel Ward read on…

# BEING NETTA WILDE

**A lonely woman. A single decision. A second chance at happiness.**

Ever wished you could be who you used to be? Meet Netta...

Netta Wilde was all the things Annette Grey isn't. Netta Wilde was fun and just a little bit rebellious. She had friends who loved her. Friends she would love to the end of time.

Annette Grey is an empty, broken woman who hardly knows her own children. Of course, it's her own fault. She's a bad mother. An unnatural mother. At least, that's what her ex-husband tells her.

The one thing she is good at … the one thing that stops her from falling … is her job.

When the unthinkable happens, Annette makes a decision that sets her on a journey of self-discovery and reinvention. Along the way, her life is filled with friends, family, dogs, and jam. Lots of jam. Suddenly anything seems possible. Even being Netta Wilde again. But, is she brave enough to take that final step when the secrets she keeps locked inside are never too far away?

★★★★★ 'One of my books of the year'
★★★★★ 'A riveting book that I didn't want to finish.'
★★★★★ 'Loved the skilful characterisation throughout, loved Netta's journey, loved the writing style and love that there are others in the series to look forward to.'

# FINDING EDITH PINSENT

## Two women. Two Timelines. One heart-wrenching story.

Netta Wilde's house is heaving with the late Edith Pinsent's memories. Now that Netta's life is on the up, it's time to deal with them. Before she knows it, she's on a journey of discovery that begins with a wide-eyed young WAAF in wartime and ends with an eccentric old spinster, alone with her memories.

But the path to the truth is not easy. There are missing diaries to contend with, hidden clues to uncover and revelations that turn everything on its head. Revelations that make Netta question if her own life really is sorted.

Delving deeper into Edie's story, Netta finds a need to revisit her own past and put things right. Now she has two challenges on her hands. One to face the two people who once meant everything to her; the other to find the real reason behind Edie's plan. Neither seem to be going the way she'd expected. As the two challenges intertwine, Netta realises that Edie had a purpose for her that she must fulfil. Bit by bit, the house yields a lifetime of secrets and the real Edie begins to emerge. But will it be the Edie everyone thought they knew?

★★★★★ 'Outstanding!! Wow. Just wow.'
★★★★★ 'A rollercoaster ride and feelgood heart-warming experience'
★★★★★ 'Edie is so realistic, you will fall in love with her'

# BEING DOOGIE CHAMBERS

**A free novella, exclusive to members of Hazel Ward's Readers' Club.**

**A sometimes funny, sometimes moving tale of identity and human relationships. Part coming of age, part modern day love story.**

Doogie Chambers is in love with Netta Wilde.

No one knows him … no one gets him …like she does.

He thinks she's Debbie Harry crossed with Siouxsie Sioux. She thinks he's Heathcliff.

If it was just the two of them, everything would be fine. The trouble is, being with her unlocks the stuff he usually tries not to think about. Stuff like his need to belong. Stuff that makes him do stupid things that can only end badly.

When the inevitable happens, Doogie assumes he'll never see her again. Then, sixteen years later, she's back in Manchester. Still Netta, but different. Married with kids and a whole heap of emotional baggage.

If he had any sense, he'd stay well away. But when it comes to Netta Wilde, common sense doesn't apply.

## EDUCATING KELLY PAYNE

Kelly Payne has a new story to tell.

Keep an eye on her Amazon page for more details.

You can pre-order it now - out no later than 1st July 2023.

## KEEP IN TOUCH

Be the first to know about Hazel's latest news and the general goings on in her life. You can follow her in all the usual places or join her Readers' Club and get regular monthly newsletters, a free novella and the occasional free story.

https://hazelwardauthor.com

Printed in Great Britain
by Amazon